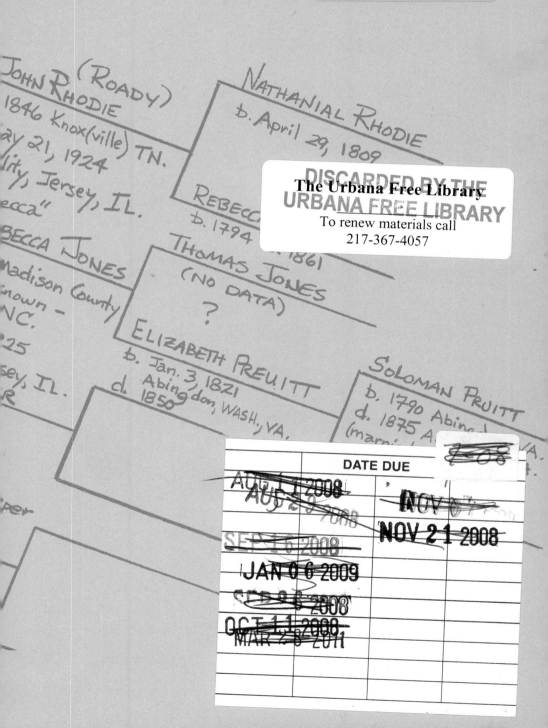

(ROADY)
JOHN RHODIE
1846 Knox(ville) TN.
ay 21, 1924
lity, Jersey, IL.
ecca"

BECCA JONES
madison County,
nown -
NC.
25
sey, IL.
R

per

NATHANIAL RHODIE
b. April 29, 1809

REBECC
b. 1794   1861

THOMAS JONES
(NO DATA)
?

ELIZABETH PREUITT
b. Jan. 3, 1821
Abingdon, WASH., VA,
d. 1850

SOLOMAN PRUITT
b. 1790 Abing
d. 1875 A
(marri

THE BAMBINO SECRET

DEDICATION

Lauren Leigh, Nicholas James Anderson,
& Chauncey Benjamin

SPECIAL THANKS & ACKNOWLEDGMENTS

John Hough, Jr., mentor and one of America's finest fiction writers; Indian Hill Writers Group – Martha's Vineyard; Lisa Pelto of *Concierge Marketing Inc.*, for marketing, the bail out, and her publishing knowledge and attention to detail; Stuart Lundgren, *Turnpost Creative Group* – Omaha, for the cover design; Langdon Elsbree – Claremont, for the motivation; Duncan Murrell, North Carolina, for his candor; Diane Dunaway and the San Diego State University Writers' Conference; Florence Maxwell; Beth Ann Ina, Lincoln, NE, for copyediting; Renae Morehead – *Red Bicycle Editorial Services* – Lincoln, NE, proofing; Michelle "Shelly" Johnson – Omaha, NE, for Spanish assistance and proofing; Deb Turner, Lincoln, NE, for technical advice; the Negro Leagues Baseball Museum, Kansas City; Dale & Dad for my appreciation of the game.

Special thanks and credit to authors Leigh Montville, *The Big Bam, The Life and Times of Babe Ruth*, and publisher Doubleday, as well as Robert W. Creamer, *Babe, the Legend Comes to Life*, and publisher Simon & Schuster; and many other books used for historical fact, as well as numerous websites and newspaper articles.

Finally, numerous enslavement and ancestry records were searched in numerous county and state archives, including many in North Carolina – especially Rockingham and Madison Counties, Virginia, Maryland, and Tennessee, including the University of North Carolina, the University of Tennessee, Rutgers University, the University of South Carolina, and the University of Virginia, and Ancestry.com. Special thanks to the local Historical Society in Abingdon, VA.

THE BAMBINO SECRET

A Novel of Love, Murder, and Scandal

J. ANDERSON CROSS

Elkhorn Publishing, Inc.
Elkhorn, NE

ELKHORN PUBLISHING, INC.
P.O. Box 818
Elkhorn, NE 68022
402-315-9600

Visit our website at *www.thebambinosecret.com*

Library of Congress Cataloging-in-Publication Data on file with the Publisher

ISBN10: 0-9795176-0-5
ISBN13: 978-0-9795176-0-0
Library of Congress Control Number: 2007938805

First Edition, September 2008

Printed in the United States of America

9 8 7 6 5 4 3 2 1

MUCH OF WHAT
FOLLOWS IS TRUE ...

PROLOGUE

1847

Leeza was just another slave uprooting tobacco seedlings from a plant bed and moving them to the field. Some slaves dug the seedlings from a central bed, transported them in a horse-drawn wagon, and laid them neatly in rows across the field. A second crew, usually the stronger ones, followed with four- or five-foot-long pointed sticks or "pegs" and bore down into the ground to form holes for the seedlings.

A third group, usually women, children, and older Negroes, followed behind and dropped the seedlings into the holes and patted soil around them to keep them upright. That was her job.

She was fifteen. She wore a soiled lightweight shirt because of the heat, and because she didn't have but one other top. The bright morning sun had given way to clouds from a fast-moving storm and a steady drizzle soaked her blouse so that it clung to her dark skin.

The overseer was unshaven and wore a tall gray hat with a wide brim that shielded his eyes from the steady rainfall. His dirty white canvas slicker hung to the top of his knee-high boots, and they sank in dark gooey earth. He looped a six-foot-long leather-woven whip in his hand.

Forty slaves labored through the steady light rain, but the overseer kept his eyes fixed on the young girl. He bit his lower lip and sighed. She heard him, felt his gaze, and turned.

"What's your name?" he asked.

"Leeza, suh."

"What kind of name is that?"

"It be showt for 'lizabet, suh." She stopped planting. Her hands were muddy. She wiped her brow with her forearm.

"Keep on," he said, and she bent back over. "Know who I am?"

"Yessuh, Mr. Herman."

"If I call for you, you come. Understand?"

She packed dirt at the base of an eight-inch tobacco plant. A portly woman, three times her size and age, performed the same task and looked over her shoulder at Leeza, then at the overseer.

———

The plants had grown two feet high by mid-July and had to be topped. Leeza Preuitt was one of a handful of slaves meticulously ripping off the tops of tobacco leaves so the plants would retain nutrients and grow stronger. She and other slaves suckered the new, smaller shoots from the stalks to keep the plants healthy.

The wrath of the sun bore down on the sweating slaves. Most wore wide-brimmed straw hats and long-sleeved shirts to protect their arms and backs. Leeza plucked cutworms and hornworms from tobacco chutes with her fingers and tossed them in the dry dirt near guinea fowl. The plump birds strutted at her feet, snatching up worms.

"Leeza, come see me in the root cellar," Mr. Herman said. The root cellar was beneath the master's house. She looked at him, then bent over a tobacco plant and continued cutting back its leaves. "Leeza, you hear me?"

"Yessuh, but I'z busy here."

"Do what I say. Come on, now." He turned and walked from furrows in the middle of the sun-scorched field up a dusty trail that led through long brown grass. When he reached the edge of the field, he turned. She lagged behind with her chin low against her chest. She looked up but tried to avoid eye contact. Her eyes welled up.

Herman turned and walked. The path grew shady as he neared the two-story white house. It had a redbrick foundation and stood in a grove of oak trees. A wide stairway ascended to a double-door entry, and a covered veranda surrounded the main floor.

Leeza slowed down and looked past her overseer into a catacomblike cellar under the house. Herman turned. She stopped. He grabbed her forearm and pulled her inside. The earthen floor cooled her bare feet. A moist, spoiled odor came from barrels of fruit, grain, and gunnysacks of coffee beans stacked six high and two deep. Herman squeezed tighter and pulled her against him. She twisted her head away.

"Don't fight me, Leeza."

"Whut yuh gonna do?"

"Phew," he said. He covered his nose with the back of his arm. "You need a bath." He grabbed a wooden bucket full of apples and emptied them into one of the barrels, then handed it to her. "Go wash yourself."

"It ain't my day, suh."

"I don't care," Herman said. "Go to the well and get that stench off. Scrub yourself. Go ahead, now; do what I say."

"But I don' wanna." A tear trickled down her cheek.

"God damn it. Go on." He pushed her into the sunlight, then followed her. They came to a waist-high rock wall circling a well. He yanked on a rope several times and clutched a bucket then doused her with icy water. She stood drenched and folded her arms over her breasts. He repeated the dousing several more times.

"Follow me," he said, and he started away. She remained motionless. He turned back. "Come on, I said." He wrapped his hand around her arm and pulled her back under the house and into the cellar. The ceiling was low, only six or seven feet high, depending upon the slant of the floor. Herman was over six feet tall. He ducked and swung Leeza against the bags of coffee beans.

"Please, suh. I wants to go back."

"This *is* part of your job—from now on." He reached around her waist with one arm and down her blouse with his other hand. She flailed her arms and struggled. He cupped one of her breasts. Tears flowed down her cheek. "Unbutton your blouse, so I don't have to rip it off. Others *don't* have to know. It's up to you."

———

She walked back to the field alone. She stopped on a knoll and looked over the tobacco field. She brushed her dress and hung her head. Her eyes were red, but she lifted her head and walked down a slope to the field with a cold trancelike stare.

The other slaves stopped their work. A tear ran from the eye of the heavyset woman. She walked to Leeza and hugged her. "Are you all right, baby?"

"I hate 'im, Mama," Leeza said.

"I gonna talk to 'im."

"No, Mama. He sell ya down da river. "

Within minutes, they were suckering tobacco again. A half hour passed, and Mr. Herman strolled to the edge of the field and stopped. He rolled a piece of grass over his tongue and placed his hands on his hips.

CHAPTER ONE

2001

The phone call came from a nonprofit organization. That meant pro bono services might be requested, so the receptionist passed it to an associate attorney.

"I need to talk to a lawyer," a scratchy voice said.

"Who's calling?" asked Darwin.

"Do I have to say?"

"The receptionist said you're calling from a museum."

"The Negro Leagues Baseball Museum."

"What's your position?"

The old man paused. Darwin swiveled in his chair and gazed out his fourteenth-story window. The view wasn't that great, but as the new guy in the firm, he considered himself lucky to have a window at all. Besides, if he moved close enough and looked to the side, he could just barely see the Missouri River and the old Kansas City Municipal Airport.

"Outfield, mostly," the caller said.

"I mean your job. What do you do there?"

More silence. "Ain't got one. I'm just callin' from here."

"What can my firm do for you, sir?"

"I'd rather talk in person. Alone," the old man said.

"You can come to my office," Darwin said. "Do you understand I'll have to charge you a fee?"

"I got money." He hesitated. "How much?"

"Three hundred dollars an hour."

"Do we have to talk a whole hour?" the old man asked.

"Most clients talk longer."

"What I say can't be told to nobody else. Not yet, anyway."

"I can keep a secret," Darwin said.

—•—

That afternoon, Darwin sat at his desk mulling over a legal brief he'd drafted for his boss, Bob Flynn. He was still trying to make a good impression at the firm and felt he couldn't afford to make a mistake. He turned a page, reading each line to be sure everything was perfect—no misspellings, no grammatical errors, no extraneous words. With his other hand, he stirred creamer into his coffee. The intercom buzzed.

"Darwin, your two o'clock appointment is here."

"It's only 1:15," he said.

"They're here."

"More than one?" He started clearing his desk.

"The Griffins."

He stacked his papers into a single pile and used his forearm to sweep pens, highlighters, and Post-it notes into his top drawer. In his rush, he knocked over his coffee, and it spread across his desktop. A brown puddle leaked toward the edge. He darted out of his office and down the hall to the kitchenette. When he rounded the corner, he brushed against the receptionist carrying a pot of coffee.

"What's the hurry?" she asked.

"I spilled."

She reached onto a counter, grabbed a roll of paper towels, and handed it to him. He raced back down the hallway and caught the spill, then reached for his suit coat, threw it on, and rushed toward the lobby, stopping briefly at the kitchenette again.

"Thanks, Jody."

"Slow down," she said. "Nobody's going to want to tell you their problems if *you're* rattled." She reached over and straightened the knot on his tie.

"It's my first client," he said.

"I know, honey." She was in her midforties and seemed to enjoy the role of office mom. "You're going to do just fine."

"Yes, ma'am." He turned and walked away with extra long strides.

"Don't call me ma'am," she said. "It makes me sound old."

He looked over his shoulder, grinned, and entered the lobby. It had a marble floor and leather sofas and chairs. A young woman in her midtwenties sat reading *Black Enterprise* magazine. Her skin was the color of the coffee with cream he'd just spilled. She wore cutoff Levi's shorts and a gray sweatshirt with a frayed neckline that draped at an angle and below one bare shoulder.

An elderly black man paced beside her. His pants were pulled high above his hips. They hung loose even though his belt was cinched tight and its end was tucked halfway around his waist. His glasses were thick and his shoulders were hunched as he leaned over an old baseball bat he used for a cane.

"Mr. Griffin?" Darwin smiled and reached out to shake his hand, but the old man peered over the rim of his glasses, looking him up and down before extending his wrinkled, gnarled fingers.

"*You're* Darwin?" the old man asked. His shake was limp and his hand quivered. "With a name like that, I was expecting a black lawyer." He shrugged. "This is my niece, Camille."

She stood and nodded but didn't look Darwin in the eye. They followed him down the hallway, and he ushered them inside his office. He couldn't help checking out Camille's smooth legs and tight shorts. As they sat in front of his desk, she glanced back and caught him staring.

Darwin blushed as he sat behind his desk and, in his embarrassment, leaned back too far in his swivel chair. His feet came off the floor, his stomach dropped, and his eyebrows rose. He lurched forward and grabbed the edge of the desk. Camille grinned and looked away.

"They called him 'Nigger Lips,'" the old man said. His dark face was creased and blotched with aging spots.

"Who are you talking about?" Darwin asked.

"The Babe," the old man said.

"Babe Ruth," his niece explained.

"The Sultan of Swat," Darwin said. "The Great Bambino." Darwin loved sports, though he'd been a frustrated participant. At age twelve, he'd struck out more than any other player on his Optimist Club Little League team—two years running. After that, the closest he'd come to an athletic field was when he painted his face and skinny torso blue and ran up and down the stadium track between the high school football team's bench and the grandstand, waving the school banner after touchdowns. And he was probably most remembered for tripping in front of eighteen hundred rabid fans and skidding face-first into a row of cheerleaders.

There was, however, one area where he'd outperformed his more athletic classmates. He'd scored higher on standardized tests—and looked like he would, with his thin face and round tortoiseshell, horn-rimmed glasses.

At thirteen, he'd been taller than his only two buddies—Lumpy Tvrdick and Dex (short for Dexter, which was short for Poindexter) Okamodo—but he hadn't grown since then and still wore the same style of glasses. Now, at twenty-six, he was the youngest attorney at the offices of McIntosh, Hartwood & Flynn.

"The Babe wasn't famous back then," the old man said.

"But I can't imagine he'd let anybody talk to him like that."

"He was loud and laughed more than not. And strong as a bull, but no bully." The old man edged forward in his chair and overlapped his palms on the knob of his Louisville Slugger. The bat had a rubber tip on its wide end, and its grain had darkened with age.

Darwin leaned forward and looked over the edge of his desk, examining the faded autographs covering its barrel, but the old man tugged it back against his chest.

Camille sat back with her legs crossed, her elbows resting on the arms of her chair. She stared out the window.

"You're here about Babe Ruth?" Darwin asked. His eyes drifted from the old man to Camille. She turned and folded her arms.

"I'm just his chauffeur. I've heard these stories before."

"I'm telling the truth, damn it," the old man said.

"Babe Ruth was a friend of yours?"

"I met him when I was jus' eight. I was shining shoes outside the old ballpark in Providence. The Babe, he comes down from the Sox to help the Clamdiggers for the las' two weeks of the season. He gave me a quarter when everybody else gave me a dime. The Babe had a heart big as the sky."

Darwin pushed his glasses up his nose. "So we *are* talking about Babe Ruth."

"Me and the Babe gets to talking,' and I says, 'Why ya let them jackasses call ya "Nigger Lips?"' He jus' laughs and says, 'Aw, they don't mean nothin' bad by it.'"

"You've heard *this* story too, Ms. Griffin?"

She turned and her voice was low and clear. "They don't change. They're either true or he's told them so many times, he believes them himself."

"I remember it like yesterday," the old man said.

"How's the rest of your memory?" Darwin asked.

"Hell, I can tell ya what the Babe said in '15 but can't remember what I ate for breakfast this morning."

"You too?" Darwin realized he was the only one smiling and stopped. "I'm still not sure what you want me to do for you, Mr. Griffin."

"Call me Choo-choo," the old man said. "That's what they called me in the Negro League."

"You *played* in it?"

"Sure did. Right here in KC, with Buck O'Neil, Josh Gibson, Buck Leonard—he mighta been the best—Satchel Paige, and even Jackie Robinson, my las' couple years. He called me 'Choo-choo.' Said I sound like a train when I come 'round third base."

Darwin looked at his watch.

"'27 was the next time I saw him in the flesh. Yes sir, twelve years after I shined his shoes. It was late October, one a those Injun summer days."

"The '27 Yankees might have been the best team in history," Darwin said.

Camille crossed a leg over her knee and flopped her foot up and down repeatedly.

"Back then," the old man said, "after the season was over, white ballplayers barnstormed to make ends meet. They rode trains across the country, stoppin' and playin' wherever they could make a buck. By and by, they comes to Omaha to play a exhibition game."

"I thought you played in Kansas City," Darwin said.

"Yep. I was playin' for the Monarchs by then. But we never played on the day of the Lord. No sir." He paused. "'Cept that day, anyway. We'd been itchin' to play the Yankees because they was the world champs. The Babe, Larrupin' Lou, and a buncha Yankees was on that team. We thought we was better. So we told 'em we would come up from KC and play 'em if they could find a field. And they did."

"You're not going to tell me you beat the '27 Yankees."

"Jus' listen, damn it," the old man said.

"Was anybody watching?"

"Yes sir. Two kids in the bleachers—for the las' couple innings, anyway. And my sister and her friend. They comed up with us."

"Nobody watched baseball on Sundays?"

"Not on the day of the Lord. Not back then. No TVs either. Anyway, we come two hundred miles to play 'em."

Camille examined her fingernails.

"Anybody call him 'Nigger Lips' in '27?" Darwin asked.

"No sir. Not me anyway. I got too much respect for that. But we was ahead of 'em in the las' inning. Then up steps the Babe."

Darwin put an elbow on his desk and rested his chin on his fist.

"He wallops one into the next county; we lose. And the Babe, he jus' laughs and trots 'round the bases like he coulda done it anytime he wants."

Darwin grinned, and the old man straightened up.

"You a Yankee fan?"

"Not at all." Darwin tapped a pencil on his desk. "But I don't want to bill you any more than I have to. Can you get to the point?"

"After the game, we all sits down under a tree and drinks some beer. Falstaff, I think it was. And I tells the Babe I shined his shoes one time in Providence. We gets to yappin' and the Babe says to me he might be part darky like me. And I laughs. But the Babe, he ain't laughin'."

"If he was black, somebody would have known about it before now."

"They knowed," the old man said. "It was a secret."

"Even if it was, what's it got to do with you?"

"Not me."

Camille finally said something. "Uncle Griff, nobody cares anymore."

The old man leaned forward against his bat and stood up. "*You* gotta believe me, honey. You more than anybody." His sad eyes seemed to beg her for understanding. Then he looked at Darwin, but Darwin didn't say anything, and the old man turned and headed for the door.

"Wait," Darwin said.

"Nobody believes me because I'm old. Anyway, I ain't got the money for more time." He pulled the door open and Camille stood up.

"Uncle Griff, wait."

CHAPTER TWO

1902

Pius Schamberger had grown weaker after his wife's death. Maybe it was the loneliness. Maybe it was the fact that he had to do more for himself. Or it could have been the stress of running his own business. His son-in-law, George, tended bar less than a mile away, but he rarely visited him there. So when he did, George knew there was a reason. The old man pulled up a stool.

"I've already lost my wife," Pius said. "I don't want to lose my daughter."

"What the hell do you mean by that?"

"You're killing her, George. She can't keep it up."

"You want me to give up the bar?" George asked.

"It's the kid. He's too much."

"I know he's kind of wild."

"He's a nightmare," Pius said, "and she's too weak."

"It'll be better when school starts again," George said.

Pius shook his head. "*If* he goes to school. He's truant more than he isn't. He's a hooligan; he runs the back alleys, smokes, and chews tobacco. He's the first little kid I've seen drunk. Kate tells me he robs whiskey from behind the counter."

"I'll take care of it," George said.

"You haven't yet. The only thing that's kept him out of jail is his age. Police know him by name. Most people think a kid that age is cute. They hate *him*."

"This is your grandson you're talking about."

"He is not," Pius snapped. "You knocked up Kate's best friend and then unloaded the baby on Kate. Everybody knows it."

George stared at the counter, then rolled up his wet towel and slammed it into a washbasin. "Is that what Kate told you?"

"Don't blame her. I'm trying to help you save your marriage."

"It's not that bad," George said.

"Don't be stubborn. She's lost three babies. She's exhausted. She'll have a nervous breakdown if you don't do something." Pius took a deep breath. "And this neighborhood is horrible. I don't know what you were thinking. It isn't good for Kate or your daughter. I've asked her to bring the baby and come live with me."

"What am I supposed to do?" George's eyes welled up.

Pius handed him a card. "Look up this guy."

———

It was one of those still summer days, hot and humid even early in the morning. By noon, George's white shirt was drenched with perspiration from the heavy harbor air. He walked down Conway Street with his hands in his front pockets and stared at the sidewalk.

At Lombard, he jumped aboard a trolley and gave the conductor a nickel. He rode four miles and stepped off before it came to a full stop at the end of the line. A stark, five-story tan brick building loomed on a hill and stretched across the horizon. A six-foot-high fence and a white double-gate entrance made the place look like a penitentiary. St. Mary's Industrial School for Boys was a reform school run by the Xaverian Catholic laymen.

"I'm Brother Matthias," the tall, pear-shaped man said. He wore a full-length black robe. "We've got eight hundred boys at St. Mary's, and most of them have had their share of troubles. I'm sure your boy will learn discipline and restraint."

"I don't have a lot of money."

"It'll cost you fourteen dollars each month."

"Will he be allowed to come home and visit?"

"After the first month," Brother Matthias said.

"He's only eight," George said.

"We can take him in tomorrow."

"I'll think about it," George said, "and see if I can come up with the money."

———•———

The trolley ride seemed shorter with his son at his side. The boy sat in knickers with a bag on his lap and tears in his eyes. His shirt was buttoned tight, and he stuck his forefinger down the collar and pulled it away from his thick neck.

"Why do I have to go?"

"Just until the new baby comes," his dad said.

"How long will that be?"

"Probably a month."

"I'll miss the guys."

"You'll meet new friends."

"Will you and mom come and visit?"

"Sure," big George said. He patted his son on the knee.

———•———

A brother in a long black robe bellowed daily announcements from a platform at the head of the dining hall. The walls were bare brick and the sound echoed. A boy across from George turned to listen, and George slid the kid's food tray to his side of the table and dug into the mashed potatoes. Then he stuffed a slice of beef in his mouth and chomped down. His cheeks bulged when Brother Matthias' hand came down hard on his shoulder. To others, George might have seemed like a heavy load, but Brother Matthias lifted him off his seat, into the air, and spun him around and onto the floor facing him, all in one quick motion.

"Go to your room and wait for me," Brother Matthias said. George slumped out of the dining hall while other boys heckled him. In George's room, the towering brother expressed himself clearly. "You will follow *all* rules. You will have *no* special privileges. You are on probation. If you bend or break any rule or do anything even questionable, you will be placed in lockdown, in your room for ten days, except when you are in class or working."

"That ain't fair."

"*You* do not decide what is fair. I do, and you will not steal other boys' food."

"We don't get enough," George said.

"You will give your Sunday dessert to Tommy, and you will apologize."

"No I won't."

"Now you will give him your next two Sunday desserts, and you'll stay in your room after school the next three nights. Anything more you want to say?"

"Can't you give a kid a break?"

"Learn to *earn* your breaks, George. You will follow rules and respect others while you live here. Any questions?"

"I'd rather you beat me than take my dessert."

1909

George found the note stuck on his dormitory door and took his time getting there. He stopped to talk with a friend. He offered to help a custodian take out trash, then entered a classroom and volunteered to erase the chalkboards. He stopped and gazed over a secretary's shoulder at the mahogany door that led to Brother Matthias' office.

The willowy secretary had gray hair tied up in a bun. She wore reading glasses that were looped around the back of her neck with a thin silver chain.

"George, right?" she asked.

"Yes, ma'am. Brother Matthias wants to see me."

"Have a seat." The secretary spun in her chair and rubbed a half-dollar-sized rubber eraser back and forth on a piece of paper inserted in her Remington typewriter. She bent forward and blew, then used the bristle end of the eraser to brush off the residue. Then she stood up and walked into the office.

She came out and said, "Brother Matthias will see you now."

Packed bookshelves stretched up his walls and a green-shaded lamp sat on his desk. Brother Matthias leaned back in his chair and wove his fingers together over his chest. The room was dim, and a black metal fan spun and made a rhythmic hum behind him. A ray of sunlight from his only window flickered off the rotating blades.

"Have a seat, George," Brother Matthias said.

"Am I in trouble again?"

"What do you think?"

"Probably," George said.

"How old are you now? Fourteen?"

"Almost. What are you mad about?"

"Your father's coming to get you this afternoon. If you behave, you may get to live at home."

"*This* is my home."

CHAPTER THREE

Thick, low clouds snaked down and curled around the tall buildings that helped form the Kansas City skyline. It was the first break from rain in two days. Darwin drank his morning coffee and scanned the *Star*. The Royals had played in Cleveland the night before and lost their sixth straight. *What's new,* he thought.

He'd anticipated a golf match that afternoon with Bob Flynn, his mentor and boss, but all morning long the rain had beat like a drumroll against the windowpanes of his office, and the forecast wasn't good. That meant he'd have time to catch up on the paperwork Flynn had asked him to finish. Then his phone rang.

"My uncle—he's dead."

"Ms. Griffin?" Darwin paused.

"I don't know what happened." She sobbed. "It's not right."

"Are *you* okay?"

"They say it's from asphyxiation. He was in the garage."

"Suicide?"

"That's what *they* say, but they're wrong and they won't listen. I need a lawyer. Can you come over?"

"I guess," he said. "Sure."

The drive took less than ten minutes. The clouds had opened up and the street glistened from sunlight shining on the wet pavement. He pulled up across from a gathering of neighbors in front of the house on Prospect Avenue. The police were there and red and blue strobe lights spun and flashed. She sat alone on the top step of the stoop in front of the 1930s brick bungalow. Darwin worked his way through a bunch of bystanders. Their heads turned to the side and their voices hummed.

"What happened?" one lady asked. She was winded, as if she'd run down the street to find out.

"Damn police," one male voice said.

"It's gotta be the old man," another woman said. "Poor old guy. Was it Old Man Griffin?"

Darwin stopped at the bottom of a concrete flight of stairs. He looked up at Camille while a neighbor gawked at him as if it were all his fault.

"What you want?" a heavy-set black woman said to him. "Who are you?"

Camille stood up, and he rushed up to meet her. Her eyes were red.

"It wasn't a heart attack," she said, "and it wasn't suicide either."

She looked vulnerable. He reached for her hand and squeezed it. They turned and walked up onto the covered porch.

"They won't listen to me," she said. He let go.

"How do you know?" A couple of uniformed police officers walked from behind the house and moved along the driveway toward a coroner's van. "It *looks* like they're investigating."

"Not the right things." She glared and put her hands on her hips.

"Have they taken him away, Ms. Griffin?"

"Call me Cammie," she said. "He's in the garage." She led Darwin to the back of the house. A single-car garage sat twenty feet to the rear and side of the home. White paint on its doors had blistered and was worn off in spots. One of two vertical doors was propped open with a large rock. A cop with his thumbs tucked in his belt stood next to the back of a maroon Toyota Camry. A hose was duct-taped to the tailpipe and rigged into the car's back window. The ugly gray tape had been wrapped in a sloppy manner. There were wrinkles and large gaps where it had been stretched eight to ten inches, not sticking to anything.

"His body was gray and bloated," Cammie said.

"*Sounds* like suicide."

"No, damn it. It wasn't."

Several police officers walked in and out of the house. Two men wearing white medical jackets and plastic gloves stood next to the Toyota, one on each side. The car doors were open and one of the men leaned inside the driver's side, over the corpse. A rectangular black metal box sat open on the garage floor next to the car. It had flasks and other lab items in it. The other man watched from the passenger side of the car, then lowered his head and bent inside too.

Darwin and Cammie moved closer, and one of the uniformed police officers moved from the side and put a hand up.

"Excuse me," he said. "This site is secured." They stepped back, turned, and walked toward the front yard. Two men in business suits stood under the shade of a giant maple tree at the end of the driveway. One in a brown business suit picked his teeth with a toothpick.

"How do you know they think it was suicide?" Darwin asked Cammie.

"They said he was old and probably despondent. When I told them they were wrong, they tried to patronize me. I hate that. They patted me on the back and told me they were sorry. Assholes."

Darwin walked closer to the men in suits. "Gentlemen, I assume you're the police."

"That's right," the one with a toothpick said.

"This is Ms. Griffin, the dead man's niece. She lives here."

"We talked to her. Who are you?"

"The deceased man's attorney, Darwin Barney."

"Was your client despondent, Mr. Barney?"

"I saw him yesterday. He seemed fine. His niece here seems to think you're not listening to her."

She cut in. "There are things I didn't realize at first. I couldn't think right."

"Sorry, ma'am. If you have anything to offer, we'll certainly listen," the same officer said, "but your uncle was pretty old."

"Can we go inside?" she asked. Cammie led the officers into the house. Darwin followed. She moved toward her uncle's bedroom, but an officer blocked her path again.

"Excuse me," he said. "We're not done here."

"Check that bat by the bed," she said, pointing at it.

"He wasn't bludgeoned, ma'am," the lead detective said.

"My uncle never went anywhere without it. It was his cane."

"It's a bat."

"See the rubber tip on the end? He wouldn't go to the garage without it."

"That's right," Darwin said. "He used it as a cane."

"People do unusual things when they're despondent," the detective said.

"But he wasn't," Cammie said. "And he sure as hell wasn't suicidal."

"Anything else, ma'am?"

"He was behind the wheel. He hasn't driven in years."

"How *else* would he have started the car?" the detective asked.

"He didn't," she said.

"I'm not saying you're wrong, ma'am. It's my job to ask questions."

"*If* he intended to commit suicide, he would have put some thought to it. Nobody just gets out of bed and suddenly says, 'I'm going to commit suicide.' They think about it and plan. He took an extra set of car keys off the key rack, walked outside without his cane, opened the heavy garage doors—by himself, mind you—closed those same heavy doors, got in the driver's side, and started the car."

"Would he have been able to do all that?" Darwin asked.

"When I found him in the car, he didn't have his glasses on," Cammie said. "He always wore them. He couldn't see without them. Every night, he got up in the middle of the night to use the bathroom. But not without his glasses. And not without his bat."

"You *saw* him in the middle of the night, every time he went to the bathroom?"

"Not every time. But when I did, he wore his glasses. And I never saw him without his cane. He could hardly see and barely could walk. He was ninety-seven, for God's sake."

"His billfold is still on the dresser," the detective said. "We haven't been able to establish a motive for homicide. Elderly people get lonely. They start aching—physically and mentally—and just want to end it."

"What are you, a psychiatrist?"

"No, ma'am. I'm sorry. And we're still investigating."

"Don't patronize me," she said. "And quit saying he was despondent."

CHAPTER FOUR

Brother Matthias was the only person at St. Mary's Industrial School for Boys that was bigger than George, and he was much bigger. He rarely smiled, and he wasn't this time either. He sat at his desk with his arms folded and a curious, narrow-eyed expression. Brother Albin sat in the corner, less than ten feet away. Clear leaded glass in the window made the dim office seem like a church sanctuary. George walked in reverently, dressed in knickers and a wool jacket. He held his hat in his hands.

"Welcome back," Brother Matthias said.

"I'm glad to be back. Can I have my same room?"

The brothers looked at each other and grinned. "We want to talk to you about baseball," Brother Matthias said. "Brother Albin seems to think you're ready to play with the bigger kids."

"On the high school team?"

"Can you handle it?"

"They make fun of me," George said. "They call me 'nigger lips.'"

"Brother Albin, see what you can do about that," Brother Matthias said.

Brother Albin nodded. "They're trying to be funny, and it's easier to pick on a younger kid."

"I'll smack 'em," George said. "I swear."

"That's not the answer," Brother Matthias said. "Let Brother Albin handle it. If somebody insults you, tell him."

"I'm not going to be a snitch."

"You're older now, George. Act like it. Earn the older boys' respect."

"They'll respect a sock in the mouth."

"Then you'll be disciplined and taken off the team."

He shrugged. "Yes, sir."

"What'd you do this time?" Brother Matthias asked. "Why are you back?"

"My mom's pregnant again," George said. "She hates me."

"You stole liquor again, didn't you?"

"It's not stealing; it's my dad's bar."

"Stealing from your dad? That's even worse. Anyway, you're too young to drink. If it's the last thing I do, I'll teach you to respect authority."

1913

At the end of practice, George started back toward the dormitory with the rest of his team, but he walked alone, behind the other players. He perspired, and his wool baseball pants were grimy. His cap was tilted back, and he was still breathing hard. A firm, strong hand came over his shoulder from behind. He turned.

"Hey, what's up?" George's voice was deeper now. He was seventeen, lean, and more than six feet tall. Though he was only a few inches shorter, he was almost eye-to-eye with Brother Matthias.

"You're awfully smooth out there, George. And fast for a big guy." George smiled. "I need to talk to you. Have a seat." As always, Brother Matthias wore a black cassock that fell to the top of his shoes. Brass buttons formed a straight line down the center of the gown. He and George sat on the bottom row of some wooden bleachers.

"Am I in trouble?"

"Not at all. When was the last time you saw your mother?"

"I went home for a couple days three or four months ago."

Brother Matthias placed his hand on George's knee. "I've got bad news, son. She died." George stared at the ground. Brother Matthias put his arm around his shoulders.

"How did it happen?" George asked.

"She died at the tuberculosis hospital. They said it was due to exhaustion, but your dad told me she had lung disease too."

"What about my sister? Who's taking care of her?"

"Your dad, I presume," Brother Matthias said.

"Why didn't *he* come and tell me?"

"I suppose he's busy running the business and taking care of your sister."

"Can I go to the funeral?" George asked.

"They already had it, son."

"Oh," was all George said. He got up and walked away slowly. He rested a baseball bat on his shoulder and strapped his glove over the knob.

———

George had just finished batting practice. He tossed his bat on the ground, took off his hat, and wiped his brow. Coach Albin walked up beside him.

"Did you know the Xaverian Brothers have a college?" Coach Albin asked.

"St. Joseph?"

"I've scheduled a game against them."

"Great." George said. "I want to bury those snobs."

"I just hope we can hold our own against them. They've got a star player named Morrisette, and he'll pitch against us to be sure they don't get embarrassed by a high school team."

"I've heard about him," George said.

"The Orioles want him to sign a professional contract."

"We can beat him."

"Jack Dunn will be there," Albin said, "the Orioles' owner. I'd like him to see *you* play."

George grinned. "Maybe he'll sign me too."

"Brother Matthias thinks it might be a mistake, playing the college team. I told him you can hold your own against the older kids."

After the game against St. Joseph was over, Coach Albin gathered the St. Mary's team in the outfield behind second base. Some players took a knee; those in back stood. He reviewed the game while a stocky man walked onto the field a hundred feet behind him.

George had always found it difficult standing still during Albin's postgame talks. He rocked back and forth from foot to foot. His mind drifted, and he wondered if the man walking up behind the coach was the owner of the Orioles. The man wore a brown suit, brown shoes, and a brown fedora and walked across the grass holding a fat cigar between his teeth, blowing smoke from the corner of his mouth. The guy kept his distance, staring at the ground with his hands clasped behind him, waiting for the coach to finish speaking.

George hadn't heard a thing the coach said. When Brother Albin finished speaking, the players broke up, smiling and congratulating one another, and started the mile-long jaunt back to St. Mary's. George lagged behind, and the man in the brown suit called out to him.

"Ruth, can I talk to you?"

"I don't want to miss dinner," George said.

The man stuck out his hand while tilting his head to duck his own cigar smoke. "The name's Jack Dunn." They shook hands, then walked together behind the team.

"I heard of you. The Orioles, right?"

"Quite a game, son."

"We showed 'em, didn't we?" George flashed a smug grin. "Tell me, Mr. Dunn, what did you think of your star player?"

"Morrisette? You put him in his place."

"Four hits," George said.

"I was more impressed with your pitching," Dunn said. "You're tall, so the ball comes down at an angle. And you throw hard. That's a tough pitch to hit."

"I wonder if anybody kept track of strikeouts?"

"You had twenty-two."

George smiled. "That ain't bad."

"Against a college team? No, it isn't. And you pretty much beat 'em by yourself."

"How much you gonna pay Morrisette?"

"Are *you* interested in playing ball when you leave St. Mary's?" Dunn asked.

"I'd love to, but I don't know if I'll ever leave."

"Sooner or later, they'll have to let you out."

"It's the only real home I've had. I've been thinking of asking Coach Albin if I can stick around and help him. You know, be an assistant coach."

"Would you be willing to put that on hold?" Dunn asked. "The Orioles are just a minor league team right now, but it's the first step to the big leagues, and you'd get paid to play."

———

On Thursday, November 7, 1913, Jack Dunn showed up outside the dining hall at St. Mary's. George recognized him. He stood next to Brother Paul, the headmaster. George passed both men on his way to eat, then waited in line. It was spaghetti night, and he wanted to get his early so he could get a second serving if there were leftovers.

"George," Brother Paul called out. "Come here."

George told one of the older kids to save his place in line, and he dropped back, weaving through the oncoming rush of boys eager for supper.

Brother Paul started talking before George got all the way back to him. "This is Mr. Dunn from the Orioles. He'd like to talk to you. Why don't you use my office."

"I'll lose my place in line," George said.

"I'll be sure they save enough for you," Brother Paul said. "Go on now. My office door is open." George led the way. Dunn sat on a black leather sofa, and George took a wooden chair from a side table, turned it around, then straddled it and folded his arms on the back.

"George, I'm interested in having you play for the Orioles."

"I'd like that, Mr. Dunn. Would I be able to stay here at St. Mary's? I can catch a trolley to the ballpark."

"You'll earn enough to get your own place, if we can work things out."

"What's to work out? Do I have to get my dad's permission?"

"Brother Paul told me your dad signed legal responsibility over to St. Mary's. I can work something out with them."

"Then what is it?"

"Professional baseball has an unwritten law. Negro players aren't allowed."

"What's that got to do with me?"

Dunn sat back and crossed his right leg over his left knee. He fiddled with his pant cuff. "George, you got to be honest with me."

George stood up. "What are you talking about? You don't think I'm a colored boy, do ya? You gotta be jokin'."

"Are you?"

"I never heard anything so crazy. Look at me. I'm white as you."

"No, George, you're not."

"What do you mean I'm not?" George paced back and forth, using his fingers to rake his wavy black hair back behind his ears.

"Settle down, son."

"I won't," George said. "Not till you say you're sorry."

"I'm sorry. The only reason I waited so long to get back to you is because I was afraid you might be."

"Maybe this meeting ought to be over. I'm missing spaghetti because of you. Then you call me a nigger."

"No, I didn't," Dunn said.

"If you weren't who you are, owner of the Orioles and all decked out in a suit, I'd pop you right in the kisser."

"Why are you so angry?"

"Wouldn't you be?" George said.

"I'd probably laugh it off, especially if I knew for sure I wasn't."

"Why would you even ask?"

"Some of your teammates call you Nigger Lips," Dunn said.

"Which ones?"

"That's not important."

"It is to me," George said. He threw his hands in the air. "They're just teasing, the way all ballplayers do."

"Listen, George, we have spring training in Fayetteville. That's in North Carolina." Dunn narrowed his eyes. "They don't know the war's over down there, son. They've been known to hang colored boys."

George looked at the ceiling and inhaled, then stared at the floor. "I never had anybody talk to me like this."

"Where do your mom and dad live?" Dunn asked.

"My mom's dead. My dad lives above the bar where he works, downtown."

"What nationality was your mom?"

George's eyes welled up and his voice trembled. "Why are you doing this?"

"I have a reputation. I sell player contracts to professional teams: the Yankees, the Red Sox, the Philadelphia Athletics, and the Trolley Dodgers. I need to keep their trust, son. I'm a businessman."

"My mom was German. Full-blooded. My dad is too. Maybe he's got some Scotch in 'im. Go see him if you want. Ask him."

"You've got some features that might make some people wonder."

"My lips?" George said. "The fellas are just teasing when they call me that. Ask any of 'em."

"As far as I'm concerned, colored players should play ball at all levels. It's a disgrace they don't, a total shame. But I don't make the rules. And your lips are, shall we say, *full*."

"That doesn't make me colored. A lot of people have big lips."

"Your nose is wide too," Dunn said. "That's common among Africans. And your skin's darker than some. None of that makes you colored, but people are sensitive about things like that. If you've got Negro ancestors, I need to know. I don't want to be the reason you get strung up in some Carolina alley."

"How do I prove I'm not something I'm not?" George asked.

"I'll get hold of your dad."

CHAPTER FIVE

Cammie held her purse in her lap and wore the same gray sweatshirt but had long Levi's on this time. Darwin thought, *if she's going to be here, I'd at least like to see those legs.* She stood up as Darwin walked by with a newspaper under his arm.

"Do you mind that I'm here again?" she asked.

"I didn't know we had an appointment."

"You're mad."

"No, but you're not my only client."

"I'm not?"

His face turned red.

"Nothing till one o'clock," Jody said. She sat behind the receptionist desk and spread crimson lipstick on, looking into a compact mirror.

"Have you heard anything from the police?" Cammie followed him down the hallway and into his office.

"Have a seat." He turned, and she was already sitting with her legs crossed. He sat down behind his desk and pulled up his electronic calendar. "Why do you think they'd call *me*?"

"Just wondered," Cammie said. "They haven't called me either."

"You still don't think it was suicide?"

"I know it wasn't."

"Ms. Griffin, I really like you, and I don't want to sound mean, but I was your *uncle's* attorney. At least, I probably would have accepted him as a client, if he were still alive." He paused. "It depends."

"On what?" she asked.

"Does it make any difference? It's not like I'm going to bill him now."

"It makes a difference to me."

"Are *you* going to pay me?"

"If you'll accept me as a client," she said.

"Why do *you* need an attorney?"

"To help find out who killed Uncle Griff."

"You didn't act that interested when he was telling me about Babe Ruth."

"He's still family. I loved him. I'm not going to let this get swept under some damn carpet just because he was old and black."

Darwin took a deep breath. "I'm not a detective."

"You met him. You could tell, couldn't you?"

"That he was an old man with a big imagination?" Darwin said. "He loved baseball; I love baseball. Look, I'm still not sure why he came to me."

"He was afraid."

"Then he should have gone to the police. I'm a business attorney."

"Do you do wills?"

"I suppose I could, but we have a probate department."

"He had a will," she said. She opened her purse and handed him a one-page handwritten letter on lined yellow paper. It was folded twice.

"At least it's in ink." Darwin scanned the first paragraph, then skipped to the bottom. "And he signed and dated it. Are you sure this is his signature?"

"You think I forged it?"

"A judge might. You got anything else with his signature on it?"

"Will it pass if I do?" she asked.

"If a judge can comprehend it."

"Why wouldn't he?"

"Did your uncle leave any copies?"

"I'm not sure he ever used a copier," Cammie said.

"It could be challenged because you have the only copy and you're listed as the key benefactor. Do you have anything else he wrote?" He pushed the document back across his desk.

"I don't know how much money he's got in his account. There's probably more value in that bat, and he left that to the museum, if they even want it."

"Did the police look at it?"

"They're checking it for fingerprints."

"They won't find any," Darwin said.

"Why do you say that?"

"If he *was* murdered, whoever did it didn't take the bat with them to the garage. They probably never touched it."

"See?" Cammie said. "That's why I need you as my lawyer."

"The police will tell you that."

"They haven't told me a thing. That's another reason I need a lawyer."

"There's nothing that should keep you from getting anything he left you unless somebody challenges the will." Darwin paused.

"How would they do that?"

"Somebody could claim your uncle was despondent and lacked sound mind. They could claim you forced him to name you as the benefactor."

"Nothing was wrong with his mind," she said.

"He told me he couldn't remember what he ate for breakfast."

"We all have those moments. You said that yourself." She looked down, then slowly lifted her head. "So, will you be my lawyer?"

He wondered if she realized the power of her eyes. *No,* he thought. *I can't let that influence me.*

"Will you? If the will's good, maybe I'll have enough to pay you."

"I told you, I'm a business attorney."

She continued staring. The silence made him uncomfortable.

"I'll check with my management team. They're going to ask if you can afford our fees. What do you do for work?"

"I'm a dancer."

———

Darwin stood with his hands folded behind his back and bowed his head, looking at the wet grass clippings clinging to the tops of his polished black dress shoes. The morning sun had dried the surface of the cemetery lawn, but there was still moisture closer to the ground. The recently mowed grass provided a minty scent that gave an otherwise somber occasion a bit of relief.

He wasn't the only Caucasian at the gravesite, but there weren't many in the crowd of thirty-five to forty. The other white guys stood together, and there were only four of them. One was seventy or seventy-five. Another was probably sixty. The other two stood out because they were in their midthirties. Three women between twenty and thirty stood together. One was black, two were white.

The black preacher was stocky and had a deep voice. He read from the Bible—Ecclesiastes 3:2—and wore a green satin stole around his neck, about four inches wide with golden fringe on its ends. It hung evenly over both sides of his chest and down to his waist.

"For everything there is a season," he said, "a time to live and a time to die."

There were few tears except Cammie's. Most people seemed to accept that Choo-choo's time had come and gone. Some looked upward to the blue sky; others stared at the casket. The ceremony took less than fifteen minutes.

As mourners dispersed and drifted toward their cars, Cammie thanked many of them and shook their hands. She hugged others. Darwin looked on, then walked her back to her Toyota. She used tissues to wipe her eyes where mascara had run onto her cheeks, and he used her grief as an opportunity to place an arm around her shoulder. She nestled her head against his shoulder.

"Who were the white guys?" he asked her.

"Probably old ballplayers." She dabbed beneath her swollen eyes again. "Why are you asking about them?"

"They stood out," he said.

"Did it occur to you that maybe *you* stood out?"

"They looked suspicious."

"I thought you weren't a detective?"

"Who were the others?" Darwin asked.

"Some were old ballplayers; some worked or hung out at the museum. One guy owned the corner grocery store."

"The Negro Leagues Baseball Museum?"

"Uncle Griff liked to go there," Cammie said. "On Thursday afternoons, some of the old-timers met and ate lunch. They'd reminisce and play gin rummy."

"What about the others?"

"Maybe relatives of older ballplayers. Some people might have read about the funeral in the obituaries. The three girls dance with me."

———

Cammie sat in the lobby of the law office reading a *People* magazine. Darwin walked in wearing a navy suit with a briefcase strapped over his shoulder. He glanced up at a clock on the wall and nodded to the receptionist, then smiled at Cammie without slowing down.

"Another surprise visit," he said. He turned around. "And so early. Couldn't you sleep last night?"

She stood up. "Do you have time for me?" He motioned and she followed him past Jody, who glanced at them out of the corner of her eye, sizing up Cammie. When they entered his office, he handed Cammie a business card.

"I already have one."

"I thought maybe you'd lost it, since you didn't call first."

"I'm sorry," she said.

"You've got to give me time. And I've got to work on other cases. You have anything new?"

"I went to the bank." She took a seat in front of his desk, and he sat down behind it. "They won't give me access to his account. They won't even tell me if there's anything in it."

"Are you desperate for money?"

"I could use some," she said, "but I was curious more than anything."

"You better slow down. The police might start thinking you had something to do with it, if they ever conclude it was a murder."

"They won't," she said. "I talked to a lieutenant at the police station, a guy named Wilcox."

"Wilson," Darwin said. "That's one of the guys that was at your house."

"The one with the brown suit," Cammie said. "He's the guy that said, 'Why would anybody want to kill an old man?' He meant old *black* man. He said there's no motive."

"You can't get the money until we get a court order. It might take a while, even if nobody challenges the will."

"I could use some cash. Uncle Griff helped me out from time to time."

"It won't help to be too eager. Who do *you* think did it?"

"I don't know," she said, "but somebody smothered him and carried him out to the car."

"Why wouldn't they just leave him in his bedroom?" Darwin asked.

"To make it *look* like suicide. That's another reason I wanted to find out how much is in his account. Maybe somebody wants it. Or maybe it had to do with Babe Ruth."

"Ruth is dead."

"I know that," Cammie said. "You think I'm a bimbo, don't you?" Darwin didn't say anything. "Uncle Griff was obsessed with the Babe at the end. That's why we came to you."

"Maybe it had to do with Barry Bonds and Ruth's home run record. The steroids issue has baseball purists all up in arms."

"No. It had to do with the race issue," Cammie said. "He was anxious to tell somebody, like he was afraid, or like there was a sense of urgency."

"Are you a baseball fan?"

"I don't enjoy watching grown men chase a ball. Anyway, it's boring." She stood up and paced back and forth in front of his desk.

"It's like a chess game," Darwin said, "with more drama and excitement. And it's got a lot of history."

"Uncle Griff talked about that," Cammie said. "I think he felt he'd change history by exposing the truth about Ruth." She stared off. "It's only a game."

"It was your uncle's life," Darwin said, "and it was the *national* game, a major part of American history and culture."

She rolled her eyes and put her hands on her hips.

"Blacks weren't allowed to participate, the same way they weren't allowed to vote, ride in the front of buses, and eat where whites did." Darwin stood up and walked to the window. He stood close to it and looked at an angle to his side, over rooftops to the Missouri River, a mile away. With his back to Cammie, he said, "There may be more Americans that know Babe Ruth than Harry Truman."

"Harry who?" Cammie said. Darwin turned. She was grinning. "I know, Harry Truman, born ten minutes from here: our native son, the atom bomb, the Truman Doctrine."

"Pretty smart for a dancer."

"You got something against dancers?"

"Do you know what the Truman Doctrine was?"

"The U.S. promised to give money to countries opposing communism."

"Not many dancers know that."

"You know a lot of dancers? Would it surprise you to know I have a degree in political science?" She folded her arms. "With a minor in dance."

"Where did you go to college?"

"Po' li'l ol' me? Go to college?" She shook her head. "What kind of dancer do you think I am?"

"I hadn't thought about it much."

"You assumed I work in a nightclub," she said. "A strip joint—with a pole."

He sensed it was a good time to shut up.

"Since I'm black and work at night, you assumed I was a stripper."

"That's not true."

"You're a man," she said. "That's the first thing you thought."

"What other kind of dancer earns a living?"

"Would you like to come and see me perform?" she asked. "You can bring your horny buddies. I'll dance close to the edge of the stage so you can stick dollar bills in my G-string. But excuse me if I don't do lap dances."

"I didn't mean there's anything wrong with it."

"We better talk about something else."

"If your uncle was right, Ruth might have pulled off one of the biggest cultural shams in American history."

"He was just a ballplayer," Cammie said.

"A national hero. And if some people found out he was black, they might be really mad."

"Maybe Ruth didn't know himself."

CHAPTER SIX

1914

A locomotive pulling a long line of passenger cars inched away from Boston's Union Station. It picked up speed as it moved through the drifting snow and for a while seemed to float along the tracks until the click-clack of steel wheels grew louder and faster. The dark windows had fogged up, and he wiped his hand across the chilly glass to see snowflakes blowing sideways under gaslights along West Lexington.

George sat alone in a new gray suit. He hadn't saved enough for an overcoat yet and had wrapped a woolen scarf around his neck. He carried his flat cap wadded in his hand. Other ballplayers were on the train too, but he hadn't met any of them and wasn't sure who was who.

———

The old hotel in Fayetteville was trimmed with dark wood. Morning sunlight beamed in through a line of windows along the east wall of the dining room. George sat at a small table and marveled at the change in weather as he wolfed down jelly rolls and guzzled orange juice. He used the back of his hand to wipe off his chin.

"Hey, roomie," he called out to Roger Pippen. The newspaper reporter was dressed in a tweed sport coat, white shirt, and navy bow tie. He walked George's way with a plate of sugar rolls and a cup of steaming coffee.

"Can I sit with you, Babe?"

"What's with the 'Babe' stuff?" George said.

"Dunnie told me you needed a nickname, and that's what the players are calling you—Dunn's babe—so that's what I reported in the *News-Post*."

"It's better than my last one," George said.

"What was that?"

"Never mind. 'Babe' is better."

"Good, because that's what Baltimore sports fans know you by now. Dunnie said he liked it."

"He owns me. I guess Babe will do." George stuffed the remnants of a jelly roll in his mouth and washed it down with juice. "I know what I'm buying with my first paycheck, Roger." He pointed to a diagram in the Fayetteville newspaper.

"A bicycle?"

"I always wanted one." George studied the diagram. "Why are *you* rooming with me?"

Pippen blew on his coffee, then sipped it. "You're the new guy, and there's an odd number of players. So you get the reporter."

"Are you sure that's it?"

"Why else?" Pippen asked.

"I was worried the fellas might not like me."

"They don't know you."

"I was just wonderin'," George said.

"About the rumor?"

"I don't know what you're talking about."

"Sure you do," Pippen said. "You got Negro blood in you?"

"Hell no." George stood up.

"Sit down, Babe. You don't got to worry about me. The team pays all my travel and motel expenses. Meals, too. I'm not going to report anything bad about you or any other Baltimore player."

"But it ain't true," George said as he sat back down.

"Then stick it out. Play hard. Keep your cool and your mouth shut. A month into the regular season and nobody will even think about it."

"I'm worried about getting through spring training."

"I wouldn't go wandering off alone, not around these parts. And if you're pitching, don't throw too many tight ones."

———

George burst out the back door of the tavern and into the alley. The evening humidity had turned the brick surface wet, and he slipped, tore his new pants, and scraped his knee. Sharp pain bolted up his leg, but it didn't slow him down much. Three men streamed out of the same door after him. He'd been chased many times by older kids in the back streets of Baltimore, and he'd had a few narrow escapes at St. Mary's too. He jumped up and sprinted away.

He remembered what Brother Albin had told him about running to first base. *If you pump your arms faster, your legs will move faster too.* He hoped he was better conditioned than the guys chasing him. He'd never run in a suit before, but his strides were long and smooth. The men no longer shouted obscenities, but he heard their shoes slapping the pavement behind him. He ran a couple more blocks.

He pulled up and bent over with his hands on his knees. He panted, tried to catch his breath, and looked back. He couldn't see anybody. He straightened upright and put his hands on his hips, then grinned.

Suddenly, the three locals rounded the corner, still in pursuit. George turned and sprinted toward the team hotel. He raced up a stairway of the large veranda, slowed down, and walked into the lobby. He buttoned his suit jacket, pushed his hair back, and nodded to a foursome of teammates playing cards at a table near the front desk.

Roger Pippen sat on a sofa reading a copy of the *Baltimore News-Post*. He looked over his shoulder at George.

"What happened to you?"

"Nothing," George said. He tried to look calm.

"Your pants are torn. You're sweating." Pippen smiled. "I warned you not to make any tight pitches."

"It was my first professional game. I couldn't let them make a fool of me."

"You hit two batters."

"They were crowding the plate," George said.

"And you took off alone tonight?"

"I was bored, and none of the guys wanted to come with me."

"I told you it's different in these parts," Pippen said.

"I ruined my suit."

"You're lucky you're not hanging from a lamppost."

———

George pumped his legs as if he were in a race. He had a gleam in his eyes as he steered his bicycle along 33rd Street, dodging trolley rails and trolley cars, avoiding pedestrians, horses, carriages, and automobiles. He smiled and doffed his cap at a couple of young ladies on the street corner at Ellerslie Avenue, then coasted along a sidewalk, standing on a single pedal on the side of his bike. The bike glided along until it slowed and stopped near the player entrance of Oriole Park. Jack Dunn waited outside, smoking a cigar.

"Babe, can I talk to you?" George was taken aback when Dunn used his nickname. "You've been doing a great job, son."

George cracked a smile. "Eight wins; only one loss."

"Terrific." Dunn placed his hand on George's shoulder. "I've been afraid the new team in town might offer to pay you more than I can and steal you away."

"The Terrapins invited me to meet with them, but you've treated me like a father. I'd never turn on you."

"Thanks, Babe." Dunn lowered his head. "I've got some news, and I'm not sure how you're going to take it. Another organization wants to buy your contract and the contracts of a couple other players too."

"Why would you sell any of us when the team's doing so well?"

"I told you before; I'm a businessman. Besides, I built a team that won thirteen straight games, and on that thirteenth, we didn't have two hundred fans pay to sit in the stands. I can't survive at that rate."

"You want some of my pay back?" George asked.

"No, but I appreciate your loyalty. Can we sit down for a minute?" They sat on a brick ledge outside the stadium. "Even though baseball's a game to you, it's a wicked business for the owners. Some of us make a lot of money; others lose their shirts. We're struggling here in Baltimore."

"Do what you think is best," George said. "As long as I'm playing ball somewhere, I'll be happy."

"Nothing's been finalized." They stood up and Dunn patted him on the shoulder again.

"Can I ask a favor?" George asked. "I need six passes for today's game."

"Didn't you hear what I just said? The team's struggling financially."

"I won't give the passes to anyone that can afford 'em. If they don't get passes, they won't come. So you won't be *losing* money,"

George said, "and since you got so many extra seats, I thought I'd help you fill 'em."

"Who for?"

"Some kids at St. Mary's Industrial School."

———

He checked into the Copley Square Hotel on Huntington and walked across the street to Lander's Coffee Shop for breakfast. He sat alone on a stool at the counter, checked the menu, and ordered eggs and bacon.

A quiet, young waitress brought a warm platter and slid it in front of him.

"So what's your name?" he asked.

"Helen."

"They call me Babe. Babe Ruth. I'm a ballplayer. This is my first day with the Boston club."

"Are you famous?"

"Not yet." He smiled. "Maybe you can come and watch me sometime."

"I'd love to see inside the new ballpark."

"I was told it's beautiful and got more seats than most ballparks."

———

George carried a large duffel bag when he walked through the gates of the red brick ballpark. He turned down a long concrete ramp. Several workers swept with wide push brooms, and another one hosed down the thirty-foot-wide walkway. He nodded and made his way to the grassy ball diamond.

He opened a gate next to the first-base dugout and strolled onto the manicured field, then turned and surveyed thousands of empty seats in the grandstand. His body tingled as he thought about playing in front of the huge crowds. *I've made it to the big leagues.*

"I assume you're Ruth," a voice said.

A man in a Red Sox uniform walked toward him from the dugout. He had his hands tucked in his back pockets. His cap was firmly planted down around his ears and the bill was low, shading his eyes.

"I am. Who are you?"

"Name's Carrigan. Bill." He walked closer. "Players call me 'Rough.'"

"I should know, but it all happened so fast. Are you a player or coach?"

"Both," Carrigan said. "I'm a catcher and the head coach."

"I caught the first train last night. I'm not sure Mr. Dunn told me who to look for."

"Where's the other two?" Carrigan asked. "Egan and Shore."

"Ain't seen 'em yet this morning. I got up early and left the hotel. I pretty much go it alone until I'm on the field. How'd you know it was me?"

"I heard you were tall. There isn't another guy on the roster as tall as you. Follow me." Carrigan led George into the dugout and underneath the grandstand to a spic-and-span locker room with polished wooden lockers. Fifteen to twenty players were already suited up. "There's yours. The uniform hanging on the right should fit. Be on the field two hours before game time. You may want to get loose early today, though. You're pitching."

CHAPTER SEVEN

She soared as if suspended by wires, but there were none. She wore pink leotards, ballet shoes, and a short black peasant dress. Her hair was pulled back. She had perfect posture and appeared to float across the stage of the Lyric Theatre, in contrast to the hard beat of the music.

The orchestra performed an upbeat Latin score. Violins wailed; kettledrums pounded. A male dancer lifted her by the waist and above his head, then lowered and swooped her near the floor as she maintained an elegant, still pose, pointing her legs and toes and arching her back. When he released her, she landed gracefully, like a cat, immediately rising onto her toes and striking a statuesque position. Her arms were straight and angled downward behind her, her head erect. The crowd exploded in applause. Darwin smiled and clapped. How did she do it? Her legs were thin and yet so amazingly powerful, her movements so tranquil.

"Excuse me," he said. Voices hummed through the theater. He shuffled sideways out of his row for the intermission. He'd been sitting alone and looked for others he knew as he made his way toward the aisle. One of the partners from the law firm smiled and waved. He reached the aisle and spotted a city councilman he'd frequently seen on television. Next to the councilman was a wealthy businessman and philanthropist for whom he'd drafted a non-profit corporation—one of Bob Flynn's clients. Darwin had only met the man once and wondered if he'd recognize him, but the man looked right by him, then turned away. Two kids were dressed like adults: the boy with slicked hair in a tux, the girl in a pink satin and sequined dress wearing long gloves like the woman next to her.

Darwin stood in line for a soft drink. Others drank champagne in tall glasses. He scanned the crowd for local celebrities or acquaintances, then wandered the foyer. Light shimmered through countless prisms hanging from hundred-year-old chandeliers. An intricate gilded molding of flowers, lions, and maidens adorned the high ceiling. *This is hardly a strip joint,* he thought as he made his way back to his seat.

Horns and stringed instruments tuned up without regard to melody or rhythm, and the audience hummed with quiet conversation. Then, tapping sounded from the orchestra pit and the lights dimmed as soft spotlight highlighted the bottom edge of the maroon stage curtains. A violin prelude led to the same lively Latin melody it had played before, the curtains separated, and a dozen lean women and men in leotards streamed onto the stage performing pirouettes and leaping into the air.

———

Most of the audience had gone. Darwin watched a few stragglers get into a limousine and cruise away. Steam from an iron grate in the sidewalk rose into the night air.

"What did you think?" Cammie said from behind him. She'd walked out of the Lyric Theatre, letting large glass doors close behind her. She wore Levi's that didn't reach all the way to her tennis shoes and a lavender T-shirt that drooped off one shoulder. She carried a worn canvas bag with a strap over her other shoulder.

Darwin turned and smiled. "Not bad."

"I thought the ticket I gave you was close enough you'd come up and stick dollar bills in my tights. How's a dancer going to make any money?"

"It might have looked a bit out of place."

"Let's go have some coffee," she said. "There's a reason I only gave you one ticket."

"Hungry?"

"Can't eat until breakfast. Gotta fit in those tights."

They walked to a Waffle House. Darwin ordered a doughnut, and Cammie picked at it with her fingers. He used a fork and knife, took a couple bites, and slid the rest in front of her.

"I got a phone call today," she said. "Some guy told me to drop it."

"What exactly did he mean by 'it'?"

"He said Uncle Griff didn't know what he was talking about."

"Who was he?"

"Don't know. He wouldn't say. He told me he was a friend of Uncle Griff's. He just called out of the blue. Said he was sorry about Uncle Griff's death."

"What was his name?"

"When I asked, he talked about something else. I could tell he was trying to find out how much I knew."

"Maybe he was just an old friend," Darwin said.

"He asked me if Uncle Griff ever told me anything about the Babe, then asked if he died from natural causes."

"Did you mention asphyxiation?"

"I just said, 'It was probably a heart attack.' He wanted to know if the police asked any questions. I played dumb."

"Maybe he really was just an old friend," Darwin said.

"He told me to be careful what I told the police and said there was no sense raising suspicion that might cause a lot of trouble." Cammie bit her bottom lip and lowered her eyes.

"I'll call Wilson," Darwin said. "He can have the telephone company trace the call."

"It scared me."

"You should be cautious for a while."

———

He gazed out the window from his desk, into the hazy sky. He wondered if there was anything to Cammie's claim about murder. He turned on his computer, and the telephone rang.

"He didn't have his shoes on," she said. "I got a copy of the medical examiner's report."

"How?"

"I phoned Lieutenant Wilson. After I asked a bunch of questions, he said I could have a copy. I drove down first thing this morning."

"Why didn't you demand an autopsy?"

"I didn't know I could."

"You can."

"Does it cost a lot of money?" she asked.

"There's no charge, but not many people ask."

"I saw his shoes but assumed he had his slippers on."

"I go outside all the time in my bare feet," Darwin said.

"Not Uncle Griff," Cammie said. "He always carried on about his tender feet and how cold they got—the way old people do. He wouldn't go to the bathroom without his shoes, or without putting his slippers on."

"I wish we'd asked for an autopsy."

"That's all right," she said. "You're just a business lawyer."

"I'm not sure I like the way you say that."

"He said they don't usually do them on people that old."

"Have you been able to come up with a reason somebody might want him dead?"

"I still think it has something to do with Babe Ruth."

"Have you checked his stuff?" Darwin asked. "Maybe he left a clue, maybe without even knowing it."

"I don't even like going in his room. It's too soon, too eerie."

——•——

Slowly, Cammie opened the bedroom door. She flipped a switch and light shone through a yellowed lampshade. A white brocade bedspread was tucked neatly at the end and lay flat and unwrinkled over a gray iron-framed bed.

"What are we looking for?" she said.

"We won't know until we find it. Then we still may not know."

She opened the top drawer of her uncle's nightstand and pulled out a bunch of old sports magazines and three tattered envelopes that were opened at their ends. Darwin opened the top drawer of a chest of drawers and pulled out a stack of old letters with a red ribbon tied around them. He placed them on the end of the bed and sifted through more drawers.

"Look at this," Cammie said. "A letter from Major League Baseball." She read it silently. "It says there's no record of Babe Ruth being African American."

"When was it written?"

"November 1988. I was six years old." A few moments later she said, "Here's another one." She scanned it quickly. "We have no reason to believe Babe Ruth was a black man. April 1993."

"Was he consumed with the Ruth thing?" Darwin asked.

"He never mentioned it until the last week before he died, and I lived with him almost four years."

Darwin opened a closet door. Eight or ten shirts and a few jackets hung on a single bar. Two old pair of shoes lay on the floor. When he turned around, Cammie was paging through a black spiral notebook. He could see lists of hand-printed names and addresses.

"Some of these are written in fountain pen," she said. "This must be thirty or forty years old." She handed the booklet to Darwin.

"Some of these names are famous," he said. "Satchel Paige, Glendale-1774; Buck O'Neil, Prospect-3709; Josh Gibson; Ernie Banks." He paused. "Listen to these names: Cool Papa Bell, Dizzy Dismukes, Bullet Joe Rogan, Double Duty Radcliffe, Old Soul McDonald, Turkey Stearnes, Showboat Thomas, Bojangles Robinson. You think that's the dancer, Mr. Bojangles?"

"It is. Uncle Griff talked about him. He owned a black team in New York. Uncle Griff used to drag me in front of the TV and make me watch him dance with Shirley Temple in those old black-and-white movies. Some black entertainers owned Negro ball teams. Satchmo Armstrong owned a team from New Orleans."

Darwin turned back to the closet and rummaged through it while Cammie read more letters.

"Look at this old suit," he said. He lifted it off the rod. "It weighs a ton." The brown suit hung on a wooden hanger. It was striped with lines wider and farther apart than most pinstriped suits. The shoulders were padded. "Was your uncle this big when he was younger?"

"That's a zoot suit—from the late thirties. He said Cab Calloway gave it to him. I don't know if he ever wore it or if it was just one Cab Calloway wore." Cammie smiled.

"He knew all those people?"

"The black community was small, so famous and not-so-famous people hung out in the same places. They couldn't get in most restaurants. They took refuge with each other in small out-of-the-way places. Ballplayers traveled from city to city, mostly by bus and car, and hung out in the same spots where other black people did."

"You want to look through those letters?" Darwin asked.

"Those are from my Aunt Phoebe, Uncle Griff's wife. He showed them to me before."

"Check between the mattresses."

Cammie dropped to a knee and stuck her arm between the box springs and mattress. "People don't really hide things between mattresses," she said.

She felt blindly with her eyes turned toward the ceiling, then pulled out an envelope addressed to Mr. LeRoy Griffin with a return address that read "Office of the Commissioner." The envelope was ripped open on the end as the others had been, and she blew in it and slid out a twice-folded ivory piece of stationery. She sat on the edge of the bed again.

> *Dear Mr. Griffin,*
>
> *Your supposition about Babe Ruth is incorrect. Going back in time now that he has passed would be irreverent and damaging to him and the history of the game.*
>
> *My office is pleased Mr. Jackie Robinson was the first Negro American to become a member of the American and/or National League. I expect many more Negro players will become an integral part of our national game.*
>
> *I trust this will finally end your false and potentially destructive allegations.*
>
> *Sincerely,*
>
> *Albert Benjamin "Happy" Chandler*
> *Commissioner of Baseball*

"The date?" Darwin asked.

"Wednesday, October 17, 1945. Who was this 'Happy' guy?"

"Commissioner of baseball. He was the one who allowed Jackie Robinson to cross the color barrier. The Negro baseball museum would probably like to get their hands on that letter."

"I had no idea Uncle Griff dealt with people that important."

 the

"Did he ever talk about Jackie Robinson?"

"He played with him," Cammie said. "Robinson played here in Kansas City, with the Monarchs, before he went into the majors."

"A lot of people think Jackie Robinson, more than anybody, led to the Civil Rights movement."

"Uncle Griff said he gave us hope. Whites might have called that hope uppity." Cammie stared at the floor. "The commissioner must have felt Uncle Griff was important too."

"And afraid what he thought about Ruth could somehow hurt the sport."

"I don't know how," Cammie said.

"Ruth was a national hero. Some historians think baseball was a cultural phenomenon—a constant, a fabric or bond keeping things together, when the rest of the country changed: the automobile, the telephone, air flight, wars, the Depression, segregation, changes in religion, women's rights."

"You might be giving baseball a little too much credit."

"Maybe. But if your job was to promote and protect the image of the sport, who knows how far you'd go to preserve its reputation?"

"You don't think baseball had anything to do with Uncle Griff's death, do you?" Cammie said.

"I won't go that far. But it's a multibillion dollar business. And there're a lot of zealots out there. Also, it's a game of statistics: batting averages, winning records, earned run averages, home run records. Everything in the game is measured with statistics."

"What's that got to do with Ruth?"

"If he was black, he would have been ineligible," Darwin said. "So all of his statistics and records would have been in question."

"But you said the discrimination was unwritten."

"A gentlemen's agreement," Darwin said. "But maybe the powers that be are afraid they'd have to confront the sport's racism all over again. That's a real threat to baseball's history and claim to be the glue that held this country together. For fifty years, it held us apart."

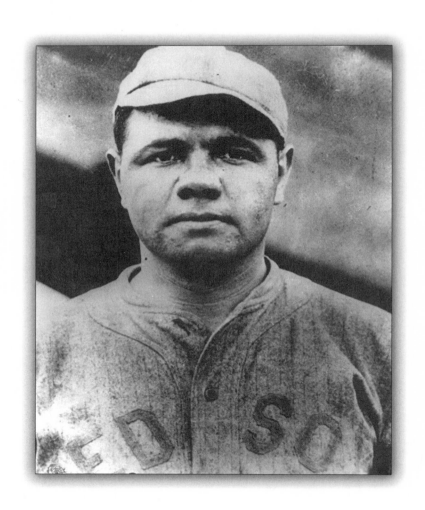

CHAPTER EIGHT

1914

Distance made the relationship difficult. George didn't mind getting assigned to finish the season with the Providence Grays, but the train ride from Providence to Boston most nights was an hour long and had grown old.

"Since that first day you poured me coffee at Lander's, I knew you were special, Helen. Why don't we just get married?"

"Because you're tired of taking the train back and forth?"

"It makes sense, doesn't it?" George said.

"But you still haven't told me why, other than long train rides."

"Hell, we're sleepin' together, aren't we?"

"My parents would die if they found out," she said.

"Then let's make it legal."

"Is there any other reason?"

"There's no reason for me to have another apartment here in Boston. That's for sure."

"Anything else?" she asked.

"If I get a raise next season, you can quit your job."

"George, you're disgusting."

"You want to keep your job?"

"That's not it," Helen said. "You're not very romantic. Haven't you seen any movies?"

"They're bad for my eyes. I gotta protect 'em."

"A girl wants to feel loved."

George lowered himself off the sofa and knelt in front of her. He raised his hands together under his chin like a choirboy.

"I love you. I really do."

"I was beginning to believe you were just using me. You never bring me flowers or treat me any different than one of the guys, until we're in bed."

"I've never been in love before," George said.

"That's so sweet. I knew you had it in you."

"They never had any girls at St. Mary's. We never had anybody to practice on. Or I woulda been practicing all the time."

"From now on, you can only practice on me."

"Then you *will* marry me?" George asked.

"You got to ask my father first."

"Does he like baseball?"

"Not that much," she said.

"I'm goin' back to Baltimore after the season's over. I want you to come with me."

"I have a job, and my parents won't let me just pack up and go away with a man unless I'm married."

"Then let's get married."

"Where would we live?"

"We can live at my dad's place this summer."

———

The Clamdiggers were vying for the championship of the International League, the same league that included Jack Dunn's Baltimore Orioles. In the last week of the season, Dunn's team visited Rhode Island. By this time, someone George knew from

56

his younger days at St. Mary's had signed with Dunn and was playing for the Orioles. His name was Ford Meadows and he'd played at St. Joseph's College, a mile north of St. Mary's.

Meadows sat the bench but must have thought it was funny to ride his old nemesis. Throughout the game he shouted at George.

"Hey, Nigger Lips, couldn't you make it in the big leagues?"

When George rounded third base on his way home, several Oriole players shouted, "Go Nigger Lips! Go!" They laughed.

After the game, George marched over to the Orioles' dugout. He tapped Jack Dunn on his shoulder. "Mr. Dunn, we gotta talk."

"Congratulations," Dunn said. "Good game."

"Your players are riding me pretty hard. I used to play on this team. I'm one of them."

"I'm sorry, son. I thought you'd heard it all before. They didn't mean anything by it."

"You'll always be special to me, Mr. Dunn. But if your players carry on tomorrow, I'll get even."

"You're pretty special to me too, George. I'll do what I can to stop it." Dunn patted him on the back and invited him to sit down on the Oriole bench.

———•———

George stopped on his way into the Providence stadium the next day. A young black kid about eight years old stood outside the gate hawking a shoeshine.

"Babe," the kid called out, "let me shine those shoes." He ran up along George's side. "Please. For you, I'll do it for nothin'."

"How much?" George asked.

"It's free, I told ya."

"How much you usually charge?"

"A nickel," the kid said. "Come over here." George followed the kid about ten yards to a makeshift wooden platform with a couple of scuffed-up chairs on top. George climbed up and sat down. The kid pulled out a wooden shoeshine box and lifted one of George's feet on top of it, then pulled a towel out from under his belt and buffed George's shoes. Then he flipped a small round polish can up in the air. It flipped over about seven or eight times, flickering in the late morning sunlight.

"What's your name, kid?" George asked.

"LeRoy, sir. LeRoy Griffin."

"You're pretty showy, LeRoy."

"Gotta be. I need the money. I'm hopin' you come to me next time, too." LeRoy buffed George's shoes with a flood of energy.

"You play ball, LeRoy?"

"Sure do."

"What position?"

"Outfield, mostly." The kid straightened up and wiped his brow with the back of his forearm. "Hey, Babe, can I ask ya a question? Why do ya let them jackasses call ya 'Nigger Lips?'"

George laughed. "You got in the game yesterday?"

"Through a hole in the fence out back," LeRoy pointed beyond left field. "The cops try to chase us away. Ain't found the hole yet." He buffed and buffed. "Well, why ya let 'em?"

"Aw, it don't make no difference," George said. "They don't mean nothin' bad by it."

"You can't let 'em. It ain't right. They ain't got no respec' for ya, you being a big leaguer and all."

George sat the bench for the first five innings of the game that day, then entered as a pinch hitter and played left field the rest of the game.

"Hey, Babe. Back here." He heard a kid's voice.

George had his hands on his knees and looked over his shoulder, then waved at LeRoy and one of his buddies.

"Don't let 'em call ya no names, Babe."

When he came up to bat and dug into the batter's box, he heard the name again. His face turned red, and other Baltimore players must have seen it because they started shouting at him, too: "What are you doin' in this league, nigger?"

George hit a ball into the gap and loped to second base. He stood on the bag with both hands on his hips.

"Not bad, Nigger Lips," the Oriole second baseman said. "You move those toothpick legs too fast for a white boy."

George took a deep breath, but held his tongue.

"You hear me, nigger?"

A few pitches later, the catcher threw a ball back to the pitcher, but the throw was errant. The pitcher stabbed at it but missed, and the ball rolled toward second. The second baseman trotted in front of the bag, retrieved it, and tossed it back to the pitcher. As he whirled to return to his position, George's fist struck like a lightning bolt, and the guy lay spread-eagled on his back across the green turf.

At first, nothing happened. Not all of the crowd noticed, and players on both benches froze—stunned. Suddenly, the Orioles' bench exploded onto the infield. George stared down at the motionless infielder and grinned.

"How come you're not mouthin' off now?"

George looked up in time to lift his arms against the Oriole players charging toward second base. The Clamdiggers sprinted from their dugout and positions in the field too, and a brawl broke out between the pitcher's mound and second base. Fists flew. Players kicked and tackled opposing players. George had been buried somewhere at the bottom of a pile, pretty much insulated from serious harm.

It took fifteen minutes to calm the disruption. Two Clamdiggers were carried off the field, one unconscious and one too injured to return to the game. Some fans had come onto the diamond too. Umpires and a few police officers tried to restore order. Coaches met with the umpires at home plate after the scuffle and assured the umps their teams were under control.

One of the Oriole offenders came up to bat in the eighth inning, and a pitch got away from the Clamdigger pitcher. The ball hit the batter's thigh, and the Orioles jumped off their bench again. The players rushed to the top step of the dugout, but Jack Dunn and a couple of veterans stretched their arms out and persuaded them not to storm the field again.

CHAPTER NINE

She crossed her legs and placed her elbow on her knee and her chin on her fist. She switched her position several times and glanced repeatedly at a decorative clock in the lobby. She picked up a copy of a magazine, turned some pages, and put it down again.

Darwin came in through an all-glass doorway.

"I just wanted to tell you one thing," she said.

He smiled. "Come on back."

She stood and followed him to his office.

"You could have called."

"You don't want to see me."

"I didn't say that."

"You can charge me. As long as it's not too much."

"And how are you going to pay?"

"You take Visa?" she asked.

"What's your credit line?"

"Five hundred. You don't like me very much, do you?"

"That's not the case," he said. He stopped and turned around. She almost ran into him and stopped suddenly. "And you know it. That's why you take advantage of me."

"I was going to offer to take you to lunch."

"It's not even 8:00 a.m." Darwin said, smiling.

"I'll come back at noon. No, wait. Can you make it earlier? I have practice at 1:00."

"I have lunch plans with my boss."

"I found more stuff," she said. "A shoebox in the basement. I think Uncle Griff had something to do with Jackie Robinson."

"I've got a meeting in about two minutes, and I have to make a call first. Can you make it at 11:00?"

—•—

The sound of traffic blasted through the door when it opened: a bus went by and car horns honked. People stood and waited five deep from the entrance of the downtown coffee shop. Darwin was already seated and drinking a cup of coffee when Cammie walked past the front window and came inside. She wore heels, a tight blouse, and a short skirt. Darwin raised his hand, and she wedged past others waiting for tables.

"Sorry I'm late," she said.

"I thought you had dance practice."

"After lunch."

"Why are you so dressed up?"

"Thanks for noticing." Her breasts appeared fuller than they had behind her dance outfit or when she was wearing her sweatshirt the first time she'd come to his office. She wore a lightweight beige sweater. Her eyelashes were longer than he remembered, and her eyes seemed bigger.

A waitress stopped by their table, holding a pencil in one hand and a small order pad in the other. Cammie ordered a salad; Darwin ordered a Reuben with fries and a chocolate malt.

"The shoebox. It had some interesting stuff in it."

"Threatening letters or clues?"

"Uncle Griff might have been more important than we thought. Have you ever heard of a ballplayer named Dizzy Dismukes? He must have been another Negro ballplayer," Cammie said.

"What's politically correct when we're talking about the old ballplayers? Negro, black, Afro-American, African American? I don't want to offend you."

"It doesn't matter, as long as you don't use the n-word."

"Some people are more sensitive."

"Blacks call the museum the Negro Leagues Baseball Museum."

"Are you a black, Negro, or mulatto?"

"I'm a woman." She repositioned herself slightly in her seat, and he wondered if she'd caught him glancing at her chest.

"You're in pretty good shape," he said.

She raised one eyebrow. "I dance for a living. Are you interested in the shoebox?"

———

They sat beside each other on the edge of LeRoy's bed. The shoebox on her lap contained a stack of yellowed and frayed letters. One was from a soldier serving in Paris in World War II that described the Eiffel Tower and French women. Another was a letter from a young boy who admired LeRoy Griffin. It was hand-printed in pencil and smudged. It said, "I want to play for the Monarchs when I grow up."

She laid the shoebox between them and said, "There're quite a few letters from Dizzy Dismukes."

"Who was he?"

"Just a ballplayer," Cammie said. "Must have been one of Uncle Griff's better friends." Darwin picked up some of the letters and thumbed through them, reading excerpts. He read one out loud.

"Robinson is good enough for the Dodgers, but Chandler's a racist."

Cammie leaned closer. She lifted the shoebox and moved closer to Darwin, looking over his shoulder. Her knee rubbed his.

"A lot of ballplayers probably thought that," she said.

63

"But the letterhead," Darwin said. "It says 'Negro National League.'"

"I'm going to the museum. Uncle Griff hung out there a lot. Want to come with me?"

"Why not search the Internet?"

"We're getting off track," Cammie said. "All this started with Babe Ruth. The old-time players Uncle Griff played cards with are bound to know something."

"They may not open up with a white guy hanging around. You're a relative, and guys of any age will open up more to a pretty woman."

"You're sweet," she said. "Think I'm headed down a dead end?"

"I'm not sure. Can I take this box and read through these letters?"

"You really think I'm attractive?"

"Sure," he said.

"You've probably never dated a black woman."

"I had a black roommate one year in college. He played on the basketball team and thought I was a nerd."

"Did you ever hang around with him?"

"I didn't hang out with anybody." He stood up.

She did too. She cupped her hand around one cheek and kissed his other. He took a step back, but she moved closer and said, "Thanks for saying I'm attractive."

CHAPTER TEN

1918

A black steel gate crisscrossed in front of them and folded together like an accordion when the elevator opened. The operator tipped his hat, and George and his wife walked out and into the lobby of their Harvard Square apartment building. His eyelids were heavy, his eyes red. He swayed, then stumbled and bumped into a floor ashtray. It tipped over and clanged against the marble floor. Tiny sand granules fanned across it.

"Are you okay?" Helen asked.

"I've been celebrating."

"Probably all afternoon."

She wore a mink stole, high heels, and a powder blue hat that matched her dress. His full-length raccoon coat hung open, revealing a stiff white collar, royal blue tie, and double-breasted navy suit. He also wore spats and a tan driving cap.

A doorman waiting outside the glass doors opened one and greeted George and Helen. Their Model T Roadster was parked at the curb and already running.

"Congratulations, Mr. Ruth," the doorman said. He helped Helen into the car, then hustled around to the driver's side, where George had already pulled his door open.

George patted the man's shoulder and said, "Thanks, friend." While holding a fat cigar between his teeth, he handed the doorman a dollar bill.

Helen opened her purse and pulled out a compact. She spread red lipstick on and blotted her mouth with a handkerchief and smacked her lips. "His name's Henry. Why can't you remember?"

"Hell, baby, I don't need to. They all know *me*."

"You won a World Series and think you're more famous than the president."

"More popular." George's speech was slurred. "Hell, they're talkin' 'bout a draft."

"They should, after the *Lusitania*."

"They shoulda bombed the damn Krauts a long time ago."

"*You're* a Kraut," Helen said.

"I'm an American. My parents were German."

"You really think your dad was?"

"Mostly, I guess," said George. "Who knows?"

Their car swerved and hit a curb but veered back into the traffic lane without slowing down.

"You shouldn't be driving."

"I'm fine," he said.

"How many drinks did you have?"

"Hell, I don't know. Nobody was countin'."

Helen braced herself against the dashboard as George drove through a busy intersection, barely missing a horse and buggy.

"Stop, George," she said.

"I drank more than this before and drove."

"That's how you got in that accident in Baltimore."

"That wasn't my fault," he said.

The road had become more congested, but George didn't slow down. They headed onto a bridge over the Charles River, weaving and driving faster than other traffic.

"George, I said pull over!" He stepped on the gas and swerved into the path of another car and a horn blew.

"Let me out," Helen said. She grabbed the door handle.

George yanked the steering wheel to the side and the car tipped, hit another curb, and careened into a lamppost. Steam hissed from the radiator. He stumbled from the car and staggered around to Helen's side. Another vehicle stopped and the driver rushed over. So did several pedestrians. He pressed the back of his hand to his lower lip: it came back bloody.

Helen was unconscious, her forehead gashed. The car window had shattered; the bumper was mangled, and the front grill was dented and bent halfway around the lamppost. George cradled Helen's head in his forearm.

A passerby called out to a man on horseback. "Go get help."

A woman pulled a handkerchief from her purse, reached in front of George, and pressed it against Helen's wound. The lady turned her head away from George and grimaced.

"You smell," she said. She moved in and lifted Helen's head away from him. He backed off and sat on the curb with his head in his hands.

A horse-drawn ambulance arrived, its bell clanging. The driver and a medical assistant jumped down. Several policemen stood by, and a crowd gathered.

"Isn't that Babe?" one man said. "Hey, aren't you Babe Ruth?"

"Leave me alone," George said.

A couple of men knelt down next to him. "He's got a split lip," one said, "and smells like a distillery."

"I only had a couple, for crissakes," George said. "What's a fella s'ppose to do? Hell, we just won the World Series."

His eye had puffed up, his cheekbone was bruised, and one of his hands was bandaged. George stood at Helen's hospital bedside. A white bandage stretched across her forehead. One of her eyes was bruised and swollen shut. A nurse helped her sip water.

"How's the car?" Helen asked.

"I'll buy another one," George said. He wore his raccoon coat and held his driving cap but was now dressed in slacks and a sweater.

"There goes your World Series bonus."

"I promised it to my dad. He's buying a new bar. It's the least I could do."

"What's he ever done for you?" Helen said. "Drop you off at an orphanage for a dozen years?"

George took a deep breath and nibbled on his lower lip. He hated it when she questioned his relationship with his dad.

"I hope you feel better, honey." He turned and walked out of the room and walked out of the Brigham Hospital. Ten minutes later he was in a bar in downtown Boston hailing a barmaid. She brought him a whiskey.

"When you get off, honey?" he asked.

"What makes you think I'd want to go anywhere with you?"

"How much would it take?"

She nodded toward a couple women at a table in the corner. Their dresses were pulled up to their knees. Bright rouge was caked on their cheeks, and their blouses hung low in front. George stood and walked over to their table.

"You girls want to come over to my place?"

One of them folded her arms. "There's no question what's on your mind."

"I'm kind of down on my luck," George said.

"We're down on our luck too, sweetheart. We were just wondering what we could do to make some money."

"I'll pay you both," George said. "How much?"

"You come right to the point." She looked at his bandaged hand. "What happened? Your wife smack you?"

"I got in a wreck," he said.

"Where you want to go?" The woman speaking twirled her finger in a large curl of hair plastered against the side of her head.

"My place."

"What about your wife?"

"She's in the hospital. I'm free."

———

George opened the door, and Helen walked in ahead of him. Dirty clothes were spread over the sofa, dirty glasses were scattered on the coffee table and dining room table, and tin cans that held remnants of beans and corn sat on the counter. A milk bottle sat half full with its lid off, and an empty bourbon bottle sat next to three glasses, two of them holding golden whiskey and doused cigarette butts.

"Have a party, George?"

"A bunch of the guys came over," he said. "We played cards."

"Where's the cards?" She picked up one of the drink glasses. "Did the guys wear lipstick?"

"Their wives dropped by."

"The wives drank and they didn't?" Helen asked.

"Why don't you go lay down?"

She scanned the living room once more and walked into the bedroom. A plate with some crusty baked beans on it sat on the dresser. A pair of George's trousers and three bath towels had been strewn across the wooden floor.

"Get some rest, honey," George said. She stood over the unmade bed. George walked in behind her.

"I think I'll change the sheets," she said.

"I shoulda made the bed."

"One of your buddy's wives sleep here?" she asked. "That's not my perfume I smell." Rouge was on a pillowcase.

"I tried to freshen up the place."

Helen sank to a chair in front of her vanity. A tear ran down her cheek.

"I've heard all the rumors," she said.

"What are you talkin' about?"

"When you're on the road," Helen said, "the way you drink and chase women."

"Some people are jealous and make stuff up. It's not true."

"Don't you have *any* respect for me? For our marriage?"

"Hell yes. I buy you nice things, don't I?"

She looked around the room. "Maybe we got married too young."

"You think I'm lying?"

"You're twenty-one years old and a national hero. You've got more money than most people twice your age. You can have any woman you want."

"I don't want another women," he said.

"You're not ready to settle down."

"I love you, Helen."

"No, you don't. You never had any love when you were a kid. I'm not sure you know what it is." She wiped her cheek. "But things have to change."

CHAPTER ELEVEN

They circled the block slowly and rode past a green parkway with a baseball diamond a block or two in the distance. Darwin wondered how many celebrated ballplayers had set foot on its hallowed ground: Was that where Jackie Robinson picked up ground balls? Was it where Satchel Paige pitched long into his twilight years?

Darwin imagined fans cheering for black players darting around the bases as others dashed to field their batted balls and hurl them back to the infield. Now a bunch of neighborhood kids ran and yelled, probably oblivious to the history of their playground.

The museum was located on 18th Street, five or ten minutes southeast of the KC downtown area. The building looked new and sat among older, mostly redbrick ones. Darwin plugged the meter, and he and Cammie walked inside.

The lobby was spacious and had a tall ceiling. It was modern, something Darwin hadn't expected in a historical district, with bright graphic displays and plenty of photography. Cammie had stopped at a kiosk in front of the jazz museum that shared the building with the baseball museum. He waited, and she caught up with him at a front desk. She folded her hands and placed them on the front counter.

"Where do the old ballplayers hang out?" she asked.

A black woman behind the counter smiled. "There aren't many left."

"I'm Camille Griffin. My uncle LeRoy used to play in the Negro Leagues. He just died. He used to come here and meet some of the old ballplayers. They'd eat lunch and play cards."

The woman placed her hand on Cammie's. "I remember you. I was at the funeral, dear. LeRoy was a wonderful man; we'll miss him." She gave instructions to a restaurant down the street.

Cammie and Darwin walked down the street to the Peach Tree Café.

"I better do this myself," she said. "Go back to my house and wait. I'll walk back; it's not far."

He held out his keys. "I'll walk."

"It's daylight; I know the neighborhood."

"This isn't worth an argument," he said, and she took the keys.

The restaurant was empty except for a heavyset black woman sitting at the counter. Sunlight shone through window blinds and onto her back. She had a cup of coffee in front of her, and smoke rose from a cigarette in a glass ashtray. She swiveled to greet Cammie. "Sit anywhere, honey." The tables and chairs had curved aluminum legs and rested on a well-lacquered wooden floor.

"I'm not here to eat," Cammie told her. "I'm looking for somebody."

"Oh yeah?" The waitress took a puff from her cigarette and exhaled smoke through her nostrils.

"I think my uncle used to meet his buddies here."

"LeRoy," the waitress said.

"Yes, ma'am. LeRoy Griffin."

"My name's Astra."

"Nice to meet you. I'm Cammie."

"We all loved him."

"So, this is the place." Cammie said.

"Through that door, honey. Go ahead." Cammie opened a green wooden door that looked like it had had thirty coats of paint brushed on it over the years. Five elderly men sat around an old wooden table. Smoke rose against light from a small, high window in the back of the room. An old pool hall chandelier hung over the table. None of the men turned to greet her, but an elderly man facing her sat back in his chair and spoke first.

"Can we help you, honey?"

"I'm Camille Griffin."

Several of the others turned.

"You pretty thing," the man said. "I'm so sorry about LeRoy."

"We miss him dearly," another man said. "There's his seat." He nodded toward an empty chair.

"I'm sorry to bother you."

"Don't be silly," the first man said. "My name's Al. Come over here and sit down. We might as well be done anyway. Sammy here has all our money." Sammy smiled. He stood and the others followed his lead. Their chair legs squealed against the cement floor.

"Sit down in your uncle's chair," one of the men said. "You want some coffee or tea?"

"I came to ask about him."

"You checkin' on all those tales he told?" one man asked, grinning.

"I'm not sure he died naturally."

No one said anything. Then Al said, "It wouldn't surprise me if somebody wanted to shut him up." One of the old guys cracked a smile, but the others' faces didn't reveal anything.

"I didn't think he was mouthy or loud," Cammie said. "I can't imagine he'd say anything bad about anybody."

"He knew a lot of people and knew things a lot of people probably wished he didn't."

"What could he have known that would have made a difference? The men all sat silently and looked at one another.

Sammy said, "Let him rest in peace, honey. He was an old man. We're all old. The past is gone. There's no reason to stir it up."

Al seemed like the senior member of the group and their spokesman. "Times is different now," he said. "The past was wonderful." He paused. "And awful bad at the same time. Let's remember the good."

"Do you think somebody murdered him?"

Nobody replied.

"Nothin's going to change nothin'," Sammy said. Two of the five men stood up, said their goodbyes, and walked silently out of the room. The other three sat without speaking. Nothing moved in the room but smoke rising from the table.

"Do any of you know who it was?"

"We don't know anything, honey. Your uncle was a wonderful man and a great friend."

"You obviously suspect something," Cammie said. She examined the three men's eyes.

"It just wouldn't surprise us. We've seen men hung from trees because they were black. Some shot."

"That was years ago. You don't think it was a racial murder or hate crime, do you?"

"Don't know," Al said.

"He was too old to threaten anybody," Sammy said. "There hasn't been a Negro league for a half century. Times is different."

"Are they?" Al said. "He made a lot of people mad back then."

"Colored players was mad because integration ended the Negro leagues," Sammy said.

"You think he was killed by black men?" Cammie asked. "And after all these years?"

"Nobody said it was a black man."

"Then what would a white hold against him?" Cammie asked.

"He helped change pro ball forever. A lot of 'em was replaced by colored players."

"Still, that was long ago," she said.

"Somebody was afraid he'd spill the beans," Sammy said.

"About Babe Ruth?"

"Your uncle was sure he was a Negro, and whites treated Ruth like he was an American god. There's a lot of people, both colors, that think baseball is some kinda religion."

"Do *you* think Ruth was black?"

"Lots of colored players thought so back then," Sammy said. "People forget."

———

Darwin sat on the front steps of Cammie's porch. He watched her pull up the steep driveway, then waited until she walked around front. She sat down next to him.

"I met his buddies. They don't know who did it, but I think they believe it might have been murder."

"Did they have any idea what the motive was?" Darwin asked.

"He knew too much. Apparently, Uncle Griff was involved in a lot of the integration efforts."

"Any idea who?"

"I'd like to talk to one or two of them alone," Cammie said. "I got the idea none of them wanted to open up in front of the others." She wove her fingers together and rested her elbows on her knees. "They pointed out Ruth died soon after Robinson broke the color barrier—within a year."

"He died of cancer."

She wiped her eyes. "I'm tired."

"Or stressed out," Darwin said. "I better get going."

"Don't." She wiped her eyes again. "Are you hungry?" She reached for his hand and pulled him behind her into the house.

"I thought maybe you wanted time alone."

"That's the last thing I want. Macaroni and cheese?"

He sat at her dining room table while she stirred yellow powder from a small packet into a hot pan of wet noodles. Then she sat across from him and they ate in silence.

After dinner, she invited him into her living room. She turned on the television and moved close to him on the sofa.

"Thanks," she said, "for being here."

"I probably should be going."

"Please stay. Just a little bit longer." She placed her head on his shoulder.

CHAPTER TWELVE

1918

George peered through a glass panel that separated him from the discussion. The two men were talking, and he didn't like it. He thought they were talking about him. Ernie Shore was a pitcher and George's roommate on road trips. Shore sat in a wooden chair on the cement floor in a coach's office under the grandstand. They were in Washington DC.

Boston coach "Rough" Carrigan sat at a table jotting down his lineup for that day's game with the Senators. Shore was doing most of the jabbering. *I know they're talking about me,* George thought. *I can tell by the way they keep glancing at me. I can't take it anymore.*

He walked in.

"Hey, Coach, I can't pitch today," George said.

Carrigan crossed his legs and folded his arms. "Why not?"

"My arm's sore."

"Damn it, Babe. You can't walk in here an hour before game time with some cockamamie excuse and tell me how to do my job."

"It's not like I planned it this way."

"You could have given me more warning." Carrigan cocked his arm and threw his pencil against the wall.

Shore sat silently and wouldn't look at George.

"What's going on, Ernie?" George asked.

Carrigan said, "Ernie doesn't want to room with you anymore, Babe."

"Why the hell not?"

"I'm not sure it makes any difference," Carrigan said. "You've already had four roommates, and none of them wants to be around you off the field."

George turned to Shore. "What's the problem?"

"What isn't?" Shore said as he looked away. "Let's just say our lifestyles are different."

"I don't have any problems with you."

Shore slowly turned. "You belch, you walk around naked—all the time. You never flush the toilet. You gorge yourself with food, then leave what's left sittin' around and smellin', and you're up all hours of the night. I can't get any sleep."

"Anything else?"

"You're damn right," Shore said. "I'm tired of the prostitutes."

"I'll share, Ernie. All you gotta do is ask."

"Babe, your last roommate complained about the whores too," Carrigan said.

"They're not all whores," George said.

"Everybody knows you have girls in your room."

"That's a problem?"

Shore stood up. "See, Coach, he doesn't know any better." He turned back to George. "It's my room too, Babe. I came back last night, and you were laying on the floor smoking a cigar with some naked girl on you."

"She woulda done you too."

"You need to grow up."

"You need to relax."

"And quit with all the goddamn pranks," Shore said. "Nailing my shoes to the floor. And what about the cockroach in the ice cube? We're tired of that shit."

"Anything else?" George asked.

Coach Carrigan stepped between them. "You're pitching today, Babe."

"No I ain't," George said.

Shore started out of the office. "Don't you care about the team?"

"I've never felt the team cared about me, Ernie, unless they need somebody to win a game for 'em."

1918

The country cottage sat in the thick forest, thirty miles outside Boston. It was Helen's dream home and George's way of keeping her away from the city and his nightlife after games. The small town of Sudbury had a post office, a combined general store and hardware store, and a two-pump gas station. The new home was supposedly a place to share and be alone together. George had been part of the Boston club for a couple years and had no reason to believe he'd ever play for any other team.

He was called into Fenway Park by the new team owner, Harry Frazee, before the season began.

"Babe, this is the new coach of the Red Sox," the short, stout Frazee said between puffs on his cigar. "Ed Barrows. He's a complete baseball man."

George shook his hand. "Ever played professional ball?"

"Done everything in baseball but that," Barrows said.

"What happened to Carrigan? I was just getting used to him."

"The war," Frazee said. "Half the players in the league were enlisted or drafted."

"Carrigan too?"

"I needed a new man that could do more than just coach. Barrows is a total baseball man, a businessman too."

"I'm not planning to pitch this season," George said.

"You'll do what we need you to do," said Barrows.

Barrows was a tough-minded man trying to establish authority. Early in the season, he made an off-handed remark about George's batting style.

"*You're* going to tell *me* how to hit?" George said.

"Somebody better."

"How many home runs have you hit in the big leagues?"

"I'm the coach, whether you like it or not."

George grinned, then unbuttoned his jersey and took it off, all the time staring at Barrows. Barrows stood his ground. That's when George wadded up his jersey, threw it on the bench, and walked off the field.

"Where you going, Ruth?"

"I'm not playing for you." George headed for the grandstand.

Barrows yelled at him. "You'll be fined."

"Not if I'm not on the team." George took a seat in the stands and watched the rest of the game as a spectator. After the game, he caught a train to Baltimore and arrived at his father's bar on Eutaw at West Lombard.

"So, you're in trouble?" his dad asked.

"I quit," George said. He took a stool at the end of the bar.

His dad wiped the counter off with a wet towel. He wore a long-sleeved white shirt and tie even though it was the first of July and Baltimore was smothered by heat and humidity. Patches of sweat made the older man's shirt cling to his arms and belly.

"I suppose you can tend bar," his dad said, "since *you* paid for the place."

"I lost my temper," George said.

His dad grinned and kept wiping the countertop. "Maybe the Orioles will take you back."

"I'm under contract. If I play ball, it can't be for another professional team. I'm thinking about playing for a company team. They can't stop me from that, and the draft can't get me if I'm working for a shipyard."

"Maybe you ought to enlist."

"I don't take orders very well," George said. "You think something's wrong with me?"

"It's in your blood."

"I can't calm down. I gotta keep moving and my mind won't rest. I can't sleep and never have been able to concentrate."

"Have a beer," his dad said. He slid a mug full of beer in front of George. Foam overflowed and dripped down the glass.

"Some people get tired when they drink. Not me."

"Why isn't Helen with you?"

"She doesn't like to travel."

"What she doesn't like is me," his dad said.

George shrugged. "She blames you for everything wrong with me. How's Martha?"

"I'm lucky she married me. I was lonely after your mom died."

"You weren't around mom that much," George said.

"Probably more than you're around Helen."

"What are you getting at?"

"I'd hate to see you lose her," George Sr. said.

A man wearing round spectacles rushed into the bar. Beads of perspiration had formed on his forehead.

"I'm looking for George Ruth," he said. The cuffs on his pants were high, a couple of inches off the ground. His white socks showed under his light tan suit pants.

George's dad said, "That's me."

"I'm with the *Sun*. A teletype said Babe quit the Sox."

"Maybe they ought to pay him more," the dad said.

"He had a chance to break the single season home run record."

"And just think, the coach only wants him to pitch."

George watched on from the end of the bar. A couple of customers sat at the bar but weren't paying attention to the talk.

Another couple of reporters showed up, and one noticed George. He walked over to George quietly.

"I've been reporting baseball here in Baltimore for years."

"I remember you, kid," George said. He moved to a table, and the three reporters sat around him, taking notes.

"Are you done for good, Babe?"

"I probably made a mistake."

"The team's in Philadelphia," one reporter said. "Will you rejoin them?"

"I don't want to argue with management anymore."

George ate dinner with his dad. George Sr. cooked hash, and they sat at the bar and drank beer into the early morning hours.

"Nobody likes me."

"You're still younger than most players, and you're the star. They probably have trouble with that."

"I try to make friends. More than anything, I just want to be one of the guys. Even at St. Mary's, I was a loner."

"Take care of your marriage, son. Your wife can be your best friend. I know; I never respected my marriage to your mother, and I was awful lonely for years, before and after she died."

"That's not what I mean, Dad. Am I part Negro?"

"Where'd you get an idea like that?"

"I gotta know," George said.

"You couldn't play ball if you were colored."

"I don't know anything about you and mom. And why did I really have to go to St. Mary's? Why haven't I met my grandparents? Do I got black blood in me?"

CHAPTER THIRTEEN

The living room rug was rolled up and pushed to the side. Cammie sat in the middle of the room on the polished wooden floor, then lay down so her body was straight. Her long, thin arms stretched straight above her head and her bruised and crooked toes pointed parallel to the floor. She sat up and touched her toes, then lay back again. She did it again. She wore gray sweatpants and a red tank top. Beads of perspiration dotted her forehead. The stereo blasted so loud that at first she didn't hear the telephone ring.

"Miss Griffin," the older man voice said. "This is Sammy, your uncle's friend from the Peach Tree."

She wiped her forehead with a white hand towel. "I remember."

"I thought maybe we could meet and talk."

She drove downtown near the Negro Baseball Leagues Museum and walked along 18th Street and into the Peach Tree Café. She looked around and saw nobody she recognized. A couple of women sat across from each other at one table; at another, a middle-aged man in a business suit sat alone with a sandwich and cup of coffee. Someone else was reading a newspaper on the other side of the room, but she couldn't see the person's face. She moved that way, and the wrinkled black hands laid the newspaper down.

"Glad you could make it, Miss Griffin. It was hard talkin' in front of the others. Nobody knew what to say or whether to say anything."

"Did somebody kill him?" Cammie asked.

"Hell, I don't know."

"Who is 'they'?"

"Don't know that either, honey. I just wanted to tell you some things. Your uncle was a good man. He tried to help others."

"And that got him in trouble?"

"Coulda. In his day, he was a peacemaker. He tried to integrate baseball, but baseball wasn't ready for that. He wasn't loud, mind you, but he spoke his mind and wouldn't back down. A lotta white men didn't like that."

"Why *now*, after all these years?" Cammie asked.

"He wouldn't keep quiet 'bout Babe Ruth."

"Uncle Griff was old. Who would care what he thought?"

"Ruth's family, old-time white baseball fans that didn't want us playin', those whites that lost their jobs when coloreds come in, Barry Bonds fans, Ku Klux Klan, Major League Baseball people that didn't want the game's history ruined, Yankee fans. I could go on. There's a lot of 'em."

"Did Uncle Griff have any evidence that Ruth was black?"

"I believed him. You ever see Ruth?"

"Did it ever come up when Ruth was playing?"

"All the time. We was jealous. But we didn't want to ruin it for him. We was just hopin' he'd tell the world when he was done."

"So he probably wasn't."

"Mighta been ashamed. He lived in the white man's world. Maybe he didn't want to give it up. Maybe baseball paid him not to tell. Maybe the Yankees paid him not to tell. Hell, maybe he didn't know hisself. Others think maybe he was afraid they'd take his records away 'cuz maybe he woulda been banned. Then there was us."

Cammie tilted her head and said, "The other day, you said some black players were mad."

"Some. If he was, it woulda been nice if he said so. Some Negro players felt stabbed in the back."

"What did Uncle Griff say?" Cammie asked.

"He said Babe was going to tell but put it off, then changed his mind—maybe because of his family, maybe because he was getting paid, maybe because he got sick and died early. Who knows?"

"Why did Uncle Griff think he was black?"

"Ruth told him so," Sammy said, "but asked him not to say anything until after he died."

"That was more than fifty years ago."

"Somethin' made LeRoy wanta tell."

———

Just two types of coffee—regular and decaffeinated. Both strong. No lattes and no mocha or cinnamon. A stale, burnt aroma hovered in the air of the diner. Morning sunlight beamed through open blinds and striped the pale green wall. Breakfast specials were listed above the coffeemaker: #1 was a plate of two eggs—any style, hash browns, bacon, and toast. That's what Darwin and Bob Flynn each ordered.

Darwin glanced at Flynn several times and stirred creamer into his cup. He watched the coffee turn pale brown and wondered why his boss wanted to meet outside the office.

Flynn had recently been promoted to partner. He raked his thick brown hair back in place with his fingers. His navy pants had sharp creases down to oxblood shoes that were polished like fenders at a classic car show. His burgundy necktie was a perfect triangle beneath his starched white collar. Darwin looked away from him and stared at the line of eight or ten people waiting for tables.

Two men wore gray work pants and matching jackets. They looked like Maytag repairmen. Another man stood with his hands in the pockets of his Levi's and wore a red T-shirt with "Chiefs" scrolled in yellow and white across the front. He was unshaven and had uncombed black hair.

Two women emerged from the group. They wore dark slacks, white blouses, and business jackets.

"Hi, Bob," one drawled as she strutted by. She appeared to be in her late twenties.

"Hey, sweetheart."

Another woman, in her early forties, rose from a couple tables down and walked by on her way out.

"Peg, how are you?" Flynn asked. He made a half-hearted attempt to wave and she turned away. He lowered his voice, "Have a nice day." He pushed his chair back, stretched his legs out, and folded his arms. He sized up a couple more women and rolled a toothpick over his tongue.

"You're quite the celebrity here," Darwin said.

"I come here a lot," Flynn said. "Good-looking women. Don't you think?"

"Why did you want to meet?" Darwin asked.

"I'm your mentor. I'm supposed to meet with you from time to time and see if everything is going okay."

"I think so."

"I'm concerned a bit about your billable hours. This business is all about money, you know. Remember that."

"Money rarely came up in law school."

"You can take all that theoretical bullshit you learned in your fancy schools and flush it down the toilet," Flynn said. He drank some coffee and pushed his plate away.

Darwin nodded.

"There isn't a judge in Missouri—or Kansas—that's going to look at your résumé," Flynn said. "It's all about bringing money into the firm. The partners will constantly review your hours. They want to know how much revenue you're bringing in."

A waitress came by with a pot of coffee. "What line of bullshit are you feeding this poor kid?" she asked. She topped off their cups.

"Mary, honey. You know me better than that."

"That's why I mentioned bullshit." She walked away.

"Apparently she's not one of your fans," Darwin said. Flynn signaled her back over and she slid the tab onto their table. "I wish I was as smooth and confident around women as you are."

"Stick around. I'll teach you the ropes."

Darwin had grown up in Shawnee Mission, Kansas, a small town later gobbled up by Kansas City. He'd gone east to Dartmouth, then Cornell Law School.

Flynn reached in his pocket and pulled out a money clip holding a stack of folded twenty-dollar bills.

"What's with the Griffin chick?" Flynn asked. "Pretty hot."

"She's a walk-in. Her uncle died, and she thinks the death was suspicious."

"We're not detectives." Flynn followed another woman out of the restaurant with his eyes, then said, "I review your client billing reports. A lot of your nonbillable hours have been devoted to her."

"She shows up without making appointments."

"You got something going with her?"

"Not at all," Darwin said.

"It's all right if you're banging her on the side, if we're not billing her."

"I wouldn't."

"She's foxy." Flynn said. He pulled a *Kansas City Star* from the tabletop and turned to the front page.

"She's a dancer," Darwin said.

"Doesn't surprise me. We ought to go see her some night."

"For the Kansas City Ballet."

"I thought you meant a stripper," Flynn said. He didn't look up from the newspaper. "What a waste."

CHAPTER FOURTEEN

George Sr. considered his son's question. He didn't know where to begin. *How am I going to explain why Kate and I gave him up to an orphanage?* he thought. *Do I tell him everything?*

"I guess it all started when my friend Archie introduced me to your mom. I was tending bar down by the harbor."

The lanky blond dockworker had bustled into the bar.

"George, they're coming. Die fraulein. Right behind me."

George stood behind the bar washing mugs. The door opened and two attractive young women walked in. They were consumed in conversation. One was taller and had straight blond hair. She used her hands to talk to the other woman. The other one wore her brown hair shorter. Her eyes were big. She just listened.

Archie smiled. "Hannah. Kate. Happy you came. This is my friend George." The women nodded. "Can we get the ladies something to drink, George?"

George carried three mugs to a table where Archie and the girls sat. Archie leaned toward Hannah with his chin propped on his fist and stared, ignoring Kate. Hannah kept talking to Kate, ignoring him.

George stood over them. He felt awkward and turned to the quieter Kate. "You live around here?"

"Yah."

"You're German."

"Yah."

"You don't say much."

She blushed.

"I'll be right back." He walked to the bar, served several customers, and returned and pulled up a chair next to Kate. "Where do you live?"

"At the tavern: the Brauhaus."

"You live at the tavern?"

"My father," Kate said, "he owns it."

"You were made in heaven." A broad smile spread across George's face. He turned to Archie. "Her dad owns a pub." Archie didn't respond; his back was turned and he was absorbed in conversation with Hannah. George turned back to the quiet girl. "My shift is over in twenty minutes. Will you wait around?"

———

George yawned as he wiped the bar top with a damp towel. He tilted his head and looked at it. Lanterns hanging from the ceiling reflected off the dark wooden grain.

"Seen Kate?"

He glanced up at Hannah. "Not many girls visit the bar alone. It's kind of a rough area."

"I thought Kate would be here."

"She waited for a long time, then went home to help her dad."

"Can I get a drink?"

"Anything for a pretty woman."

"You think I'm pretty, George?"

"Hell, yes. I'd chase you around this barroom if it weren't for Archie." Hannah blushed. "What it'll be?"

"Gin and limewater," she said. "What about Kate?"

"And if it weren't for her."

"You two are getting pretty thick," Hannah said.

"I like her a lot. Where's Archie?"

"I can't keep track of him. He'll probably come by. Mind if I wait?" She took a seat at the end of the bar, and George slid a glass of gin with a couple of lime slices hung over the edge.

Some uniformed sailors approached Hannah. She talked with them and smiled. One of them bought her another drink, and George poured her more gin, then waited on other customers and tidied up behind the bar. More customers came in. An occasional roar of laughter broke out.

"George?" Hannah shouted from the end of the counter. "Can I have another?"

He moved closer to her. "You think that's a good idea?"

"I can handle it." Her eyes wouldn't focus.

"I don't think Archie's going to make it," George said.

"Probably not," she said. "Maybe I'll have one of these sailors escort me home."

"I'll take you home, honey," one of them said.

"Hannah, you've had too much to drink," George said.

"I knew you'd take care of me," she told George.

One of the sailors whispered in her ear. She laughed and pecked him on the cheek, and he put his arm around her. She laughed some more and he tried to pull her up from her stool.

"Come on, sweetheart," he said.

George came back over and intervened. "You really want me to take care of you?"

"I'd love it," she said.

"Listen, friend, this is my buddy's girl. She's had too much to drink. I'll buy *you* another one—on the house, but I can't let her leave with you when she's like this."

"What are you? Her father?"

"Just a friend."

"Come on, honey. Let's go," the sailor said again.

"George, will you walk me home?" she asked.

George nodded and the sailor shrugged and walked away.

Hannah leaned her elbows on the counter. Her eyelids drooped above her blank stare. George cleaned up behind the counter, balanced the cash register, and escorted her out of the tavern. She stumbled a couple of times.

"I better sit down," she said. Her knees buckled and she plopped onto the curb.

"How far to your place?" George asked.

"Two blocks." He let her sit for a couple seconds, then picked her up and cradled her in his arms. She placed her head on his shoulder, and he carried her down the sidewalk.

"You really know how to take care of a girl," she said.

"You shouldn't come to the bar by yourself, Hannah."

"I knew you'd take care of me. That's my apartment, down there." He went down several steps into a dark passageway to a basement apartment, then propped her against the brick wall while she rummaged through her purse for a key. She shoved the purse at George. "You find it."

The sunken alcove provided no light. He felt inside her purse until he pulled out a copper key. She swiped at it but knocked it out of his hand.

"Damn." She giggled.

George bent over and patted the ground until he found it.

"You open it," she said and put her arm around his shoulders. "Help me in."

He shoved the door open and walked inside with her.

"Don't leave, George."

———————

Archie staggered into the tavern. His eyes were red. He couldn't focus. George held up a mug and examined it for spots, then looked at Archie and smiled.

"George, there's another guy," Archie slurred. "Hannah. She doesn't act the same. She never has time for me anymore."

"Women." George shook his head. "They're hard to understand. Be patient."

"She won't let me touch her."

"Give her some time and space."

"I love her, George. I asked her to marry me and she wouldn't answer."

"She didn't say no, did she? That's good."

Archie slumped over the counter and buried his face in his hands. He raked his wavy hair back with his palms. "What am I doing wrong?"

"You're probably smothering her," George said. He paused. "I'll talk with her next time she's with Kate and see what I can find out."

"Would you? Don't make it obvious, George. And she probably won't say much in front of Kate. Maybe you can corner her alone."

CHAPTER FIFTEEN

He explored shelves of books that reached to the ceiling and lined both sides of the narrow aisle, then homed in on a section that matched the numbers he'd written on his pad. He pulled down another hardback and added it to the four he already carried under his arm and walked back to a walnut library table. More books about Negro baseball and Babe Ruth were stacked there.

He examined rolls of microfilm, then went online and perused electronic files. He found an old tub file of index cards and searched for books no longer in print. Then he pored over anything he could find in the Kansas City Library that had anything to do with Babe Ruth.

Someone tapped his shoulder. "Is this how you spend your weekends?"

"How'd you find me?"

"It wasn't easy," Cammie said.

Darwin checked his wristwatch. "The time got away."

She sat down across from him, put her purse on a chair, and whispered. "You're two hours late. You stood me up."

"I can't believe how much stuff there is on Ruth. I could spend a week here."

"You won't find anything that says he was black."

"They called him 'Nigger Lips' and 'nigger' when he played for Providence, and later when he was with Pawtucket," Darwin said.

"I guarantee," Cammie said, "he wasn't black."

"Why do you say that?"

"You ever called a black man 'nigger'?"

"I wouldn't."

"You wouldn't because most black men would kick your ass."

"Did I offend you?"

"You're not offending me, sweetheart." She grinned. "I'm just saying not many white men call blacks 'nigger,' not to their face, anyway."

"Maybe he didn't know he was black," Darwin said. "And I've got a feeling whites could get away with more back then."

She turned up the corner of her mouth and shook her head. "I'm sure a lot was different back then."

"This book is by a guy named William Mitchell." Darwin held up a book called *Baseball's Pivotal Era*. "It says over 75 percent of all blacks lived in the South before World War II when segregation was legal and accepted." He opened the book and pointed: "A gentleman's agreement between owners segregated the game by the time the U.S. Supreme Court rendered its 'separate but equal' doctrine in the *Plessy v. Ferguson* decision of 1896."

"You *sound* like a lawyer," Cammie said.

"I'm surprised by what I read about Ruth. He was a bully—a bum. More like a spoiled child that never grew up." Darwin grabbed another book, Ken Sobol's *Babe Ruth and the American Dream*, and began reading aloud: "He was a mess. He was foul-mouthed, a show-off, very distasteful to have around."

"What's this got to do with my uncle?" she said.

"I'm learning a lot I didn't know."

"You're a rich white kid," she said.

"What if I said 30 percent of blacks in America were descended from Caucasian fathers?"

"That wouldn't surprise me," Cammie said. "A lot of female slaves were helpless, I'm sure."

"*USA Today*, February 2, 2006." He slid a copy of a newspaper page in front of her.

She leaned forward in her chair and put her elbows on the table. "Don't you think slave owners forced themselves on slave women regularly? They had the power, and there was no repercussion."

"I don't like to think about it," Darwin said.

"You mean, talk about it."

"The next logical question is, what percentage of Caucasians in America have African American blood?"

"A lot," Cammie said.

"Ten to twenty percent, according to what I've been reading. It wouldn't be unreasonable to believe Ruth was one of them."

"He looks black," Cammie said. She picked up an open book with a photograph of Ruth in it.

"That's not politically correct," he said.

"I'm black; I can get away with it." She grinned.

"But why the secret?" Darwin asked.

"So he could get paid big money for playing a kid's game." She sat back in her chair and folded her arms. "Plus, it's always been more acceptable to be white."

"Would you lie about your race if you were told you couldn't dance unless you were white?"

"Damn right."

He picked up a copy of Robert Creamer's *Babe: The Legend Comes to Life* and summarized a story Creamer told about Ruth and another Yankee player. "They went over to the other team's locker-room after a game. Ruth was mad because players called him a nigger during the game. There were some angry words exchanged and Ruth started to leave." Darwin lowered his eyes to an open page and read, "'Don't get me wrong fellows,' Ruth said,

'I don't mind being called a prick or a cocksucker or things like that. Buy lay off the personal stuff.'"

"'Prick' and 'cocksucker' aren't personal?" Cammie said.

"I guess not, if you believe you're not a prick or cocksucker."

"Now you're insinuating he knew he was black."

"Listen to this." He thumbed to another page in Creamer's biography of Ruth. "Ruth was called 'nigger' so often that many people assumed he was indeed partly black and that at some point in time he, or an immediate ancestor, had managed to cross the color line. Even players in the Negro baseball leagues that flourished then believed this and generally wished the Babe, whom they considered a secret brother, well in his conquest of white baseball."

"I'm convinced baseball couldn't afford to let him be black." She stood up and grabbed Darwin under the arm. "Let's go. I'm hungry, and you're not looking for the right stuff, anyway."

"What do you mean?"

"If you want to find more about Uncle Griff, you should be investigating Jackie Robinson."

"You said it was all about Ruth," Darwin said.

"But Sammy said Uncle Griff was involved with integration."

"Now I'm more confused."

"That's how we like you," she said. They left the books on the table and walked out of the library.

"Blacks want me confused?"

"Women."

———

The Investigations Bureau of the Kansas City Police Department was located on Linwood, about a mile and a half south of downtown. Darwin pulled his small red sports car into the parking lot and went inside.

He waited on a bench in a dull gray, government-sterile lobby. The only wall hangings were photographs of the police station and several high-ranking officers. Two flags stood next to a double door, a Missouri state flag and the stars and stripes. A man in a brown suit shoved one of the glass doors open.

"I'm Lieutenant Clark Wilson." He stood in front of Darwin with his hands on his hips. "What do ya need?"

"We met," Darwin said.

"The old man: LeRoy Griffin. I remember."

"Anything new?"

"I told you," Wilson said, "we're not treating it as a homicide."

"I hoped our conversation might have raised your curiosity."

"There's no motive," the detective said.

"We think somebody was trying to shut him up."

"About what? He was an old man."

"You have to admit the death was suspicious," Darwin said. "The cane, his glasses, his bare feet. What was he doing in the car? He hadn't had a driver's license in sixteen years."

"It was an easy, painless way to end his life. It happens all the time."

"Would you be treating the same if he'd been fifty?"

"Probably not," the detective said. "You think he was smothered."

"Yes, I do. Why wasn't there an autopsy?"

"We rarely perform them," Wilson said. "Less than 10 percent of the time. You want us to dig him up? It isn't going to happen." The detective looked to both sides as people passed in the hallway. His jaw tightened, his eyes narrowed, and he took a step closer to Darwin. He placed one foot on the bench next to him and lowered his voice. "We have twenty-four detectives investigating approximately a hundred and twenty real murders a year. Come to me with a motive, some details, and maybe a suspect, and I'll spend some time on it."

"Are you a baseball fan, detective?"

"I go to a couple Royals games a year."

"Ever been to the Negro Leagues Baseball Museum down on 18th?"

"Nope," the detective said. "Why?"

"LeRoy Griffin is part of that history. He played and was a controversial figure in the move for integration. There was a time when he challenged authority, the baseball establishment. He helped change America, socially and politically."

"Playing baseball?"

"It's the American game," Darwin said. "You've heard of Jackie Robinson, I presume."

"That was fifty or sixty years ago," Wilson said.

"Griffin knew something that threatened to change history."

"So you *don't* think the old man's death was racially motivated. You know what they say," the detective said. "It's only a game."

"I'm concerned about the girl," Darwin said. "She's shook up."

"She was pretty close to the old guy, huh?"

"It's more than that," Darwin said. "If she's right, the guys that did it were in her house. Could you at least have somebody drive by, maybe drop in every once in a while?"

"We're not convinced a crime occurred," Wilson said.

"Maybe you could just keep an eye on her place the next couple days or so."

"I can't afford a stakeout. My resources are thin. I'd advise her to inform her neighbors. Let them know and ask them to watch for anything suspicious."

"Sure," Darwin said. "But if you'd have a patrolman stop by."

"We'll see. She can always call 911 if there's a problem."

CHAPTER SIXTEEN

1893

George walked away from the bar carrying an empty crate and disappeared down a hallway that led out back. The door slammed. Kate stood up from her barroom table, taking long, purposeful strides as if to follow, but waited inside. When he came back through the door, she cornered him.

"What are we going to do?" she asked. "I'll start showing any day now."

"Why do you think you're pregnant?" George asked.

"A woman knows."

"I can't tell any difference."

"You gotta make a decision," she said.

"You know I love you, Kate. I'm just waiting until I get a little more money."

"By then the baby will be born."

"I don't like the pressure," he said. "Maybe you've got the flu. Sure, that's it." He wiped his hands on his apron and walked back toward the bar. She followed him.

"Father is going to be angry if I start showing and I'm not married." She looked to the side to see if anyone heard her or was watching. He whirled.

"Can't you see I'm working?"

"He might fire you. Don't you have any honor?"

"Let's wait and see."

"I can't afford the humiliation."

He turned his back on her and smiled at a customer waiting at the bar. "What will it be, friend?"

"Beer," the man said.

She stormed toward the door, her face red.

"Kate, honey. Wait," George shouted above the barroom buzz. She slowed down and waited until he caught up. He rushed up behind her and placed both hands on her shoulders. She refused to turn around. "Kate, don't tell your dad."

Still, without facing him she said, "Either you announce you're going to marry me and get me something that resembles a ring, or I'm going to my father."

He gritted his teeth and paused while he inhaled deeply. "I'll marry you. Okay? Just wait." She turned.

"You've got until Sunday," she said. "And you better speak to Father first, like a man."

"Where am I going to get enough money for a ring?"

"That's your problem," Kate said. "Talk to Father. He'll give you an advance. Or borrow it."

"I'm getting a new side job: selling lightning rods. I'll get paid commission for each one."

"When do you start?"

"Next week, honey. Really."

"Sunday, George." She turned away again and walked out the door.

———

Hannah was the only woman in the barroom. She sat in the back with Archie and three of his buddies. She smiled, waiting for one of his friends to get to the punch line of a joke. Then the entire table burst into laughter.

It was close to six, and the Conway Street Bar was full of regulars hanging out after work. The dockworkers and sailors were loud and boisterous. Men shouted back and forth across the smoke-clouded room. George balanced a tray of beers over a shoulder, then placed them on the tabletop one by one. He waited to be paid while one of the men launched into another yarn. Archie and another man pulled cash from their pockets and plunked it down, and George scooped it up and started away when Hannah reached over and tucked at his sleeve. She said something, but George couldn't hear her above the barroom clamor. He bent toward her, and she spoke louder.

"I've got to talk to you."

"I'm kind of busy right now," he said.

She put her hand up to the side of her mouth. "When you get off work, come to my place."

He glanced at Archie, who was staring but not laughing anymore.

"I can't, Hannah. I start a new job tonight."

"George, don't ignore me." Another round of laughter erupted at the table. He started away, but she yanked at his shirtsleeve again. He turned and saw Archie's angry stare. "Don't put me off."

"I can't help it. There's a lot of thirsty customers, and I can't be late for my new job."

George was still asleep the next morning when there was a banging at his door. He staggered to answer it and stood barefoot in his boxers and sleeveless undershirt. He rubbed his eyes.

The silhouette of a tall, willowy female appeared in the doorway. She leaned against the doorjamb with her arms folded and stared at his groggy, unshaven face. The bright sunlight shone over her shoulder and into his eyes. He was slow to speak, and she didn't wait. She moved into his one-room apartment.

"I'm surprised you're alone," Hannah said.

"What are you doing here?"

"This is your baby. *I* should be living here." She sat on the edge of his bed, crossed her legs, and looked around the one-room flat. His paunchy belly stuck out from under his shirt and hung over his low-riding boxers. "This place is a pit," she said. "You ever clean?"

He stood silently, struggling to hold his eyes open.

"What are we going to do?"

"I don't know."

"This baby's gonna need a father."

"Archie's probably your best bet," George said.

"I told you, I'm not marrying him."

"Kate thinks she's pregnant too."

After a long silence, she said, "So you're going to marry *her*?"

"She wants me to." He lifted a glass half full of warm scotch from an end table and downed it.

Hannah stood and paced. "Damn it, George." She placed her hands on her hips. "You no good piece of crap. How many other pregnant women you got out there?"

"None, I hope."

"I thought Kate and I were best friends," Hannah said as she lit a cigarette and sat on the edge of his bed. "Why didn't she tell me she was pregnant?"

"Did you tell her you are?"

"I was afraid she might ask who the father was." She took a drag and slowly exhaled the smoke. "Damn it, George. You've got us all in a horrible fix."

"I didn't do it alone."

Hannah's eyes welled up.

"I'm hoping one of you is wrong."

"About being pregnant?" Hannah said. "I'm not." There was silence and she stood up again and paced. "Do you care about me at all?"

"Sure I do, but I already promised Kate I'd marry her."

———————

Kate wore an ivory muslin dress that covered her shoulders and fell to the floor, brushing the tops of her shoes. A thin veil dropped from her matching pillbox hat and a beaded border circled her high neckline. Her mother, Johanna, had pinned a red rose to the dress, right over Kate's heart. The late-June Sunday afternoon service was held at the Fulton Street Baptist Church.

"I love you, honey," Johanna said. "Don't worry about your father. He'll get over it."

"But I do," Kate said.

"He just wants you to be happy."

George wore a dark suit coat borrowed from Kate's father, Pius Schamberger. The jacket was snug around his broad shoulders and the sleeves hung an inch and a half above George's hands. His necktie covered the open shirt that wouldn't button around his eighteen-inch neck.

Hannah and Archie were bridesmaid and best man. Hannah wore a full-length muslin dress too.

"Yours looks like a wedding dress too," Archie said.

"Maybe someday."

Other than the Reverend Alonzo Barron and Kate's parents, Kate's younger sister, Lena, rounded out the wedding party.

"Mom and Dad will never forgive you for not getting married at St. Peter, Katie," Lena said before the service.

"The baby will be baptized there," Kate said. "I've known Father O'Brien my whole life and couldn't face him if he knew the baby was illegitimate."

Lena lowered her voice as she stood behind her sister and tucked in part of the excess material that had been patched and sewn into seam of the dress. "Father will hold this against George forever."

Reverend Barron read two psalms Kate and her mother had chosen, then skipped directly to the vows. "George, do you promise to be Catherine's solemn partner, in sickness and health, in good times and bad?"

"Sure," he said. He wedged his finger between his neck and collar and tugged.

"Catherine, do you promise to love George unconditionally, to honor and obey him, until death do you part?"

"I do."

The wedding party walked to Pius Schamberger's bar on Conway Street. It was closed, and Kate's mom boiled brats while her dad served drinks. Kate hugged him. He wouldn't let go and wiped a tear from his eye.

"Thanks for the room upstairs," she said. "It's a wonderful wedding present and will save us so much money."

Pius Schamberger squeezed her again, smiled for the first time, and said, "I figured George will have no excuse for being late to work if he just has to walk downstairs."

After he loosened his tie and downed a couple beers, George wandered down a long hallway and out back to an outhouse behind the building. On his way back, he looked down, still fastening a button over his crotch when he ran into Hannah.

"I'm late," she whispered.

He smiled and said, "It's right around the corner."

"That special time of the month, George. It never came." His smile disappeared. "I'm definitely pregnant," she said.

His face grew red and he faked a smile. "Good for you. You and Archie can be next."

"I haven't slept with him for six months."

George looked over Hannah's shoulder, back toward the bar-room where his wife and in-laws were smiling. Without another word, he walked past Hannah and into the barroom. Minutes later, she returned to Archie. Her eyes were red. She stood by him and nudged his ribs. She whispered in his ear, and they got up to leave.

"Why so soon?" Kate asked.

"I'm not feeling well, honey," Hannah said. "Anyway, this is *your* day."

Kate reached down and lifted a locket that hung around Hannah's neck. Her name was engraved on the back.

"This is new. Where did you get it?"

"Archie gave it to me," Hannah said. "He says he loves me."

"It's beautiful. You're lucky he cares so much."

"I guess."

"Come back tomorrow," Kate said. "I'll be right upstairs."

"She seemed quiet," Kate's mom said about Hannah, after she and Archie left.

"She's not feeling well, Mamma," Kate said, "and I think she's sad she's not getting married too."

"Archie wants to marry her," George said.

"She doesn't love him."

"I think she'll marry him," George said.

"I wish your parents could have been here, George. I want to meet them."

"Someday," he said.

"Did you even write?"

"I don't write that good."

"Kate could have written for you," Johanna said.

CHAPTER SEVENTEEN

By the time Darwin arrived at the diner, his boss was already at a table. Darwin wedged through a handful of people waiting to be seated. Flynn sat back in his chair with his thumbs wedged into the top of his pants.

"About time," Flynn said.

"I had to run an errand."

"For that black chick."

"I ran by the courthouse and filed a petition for Goldberg," Darwin said.

"What's her name again?"

Darwin pulled off his suit jacket and hung it over the back of his chair. "Camille Griffin."

"You were going to introduce her to me."

"You told me to spend less time with her."

"Still doing work for her?" Flynn asked.

"A little."

"Then introduce her to me."

"I have to wrap up some things."

"Don't waste your time. She'll never pay," Flynn said.

"Because she's black?"

"You said she was a dancer. Dancers don't have money."

"Ballet. Remember?"

"Too bad," Flynn said. "I'd like to stick a buck in *her* G-string." He stared at a couple of young women sitting at a table on the other side of the restaurant.

Darwin shook his head. "Why are we meeting?"

"Because we're supposed to and because I'm your mentor."

The women stood up. Both of them wore dark slacks, heels, and business jackets. One lagged behind, examining the bill and leaving some money on the table, while the other walked out toward the door. As she passed by, Flynn smiled.

"Hey babe," he said. She ignored him and kept walking. The second one came by, and he said, "Good morning, Nancy. Are we going to have dinner, again—sometime soon?"

"Don't count on it," she said.

The waitress slapped a couple of menus on the table.

"You've still got it, Flynn," the waitress said.

"Thank you, Mary."

"And apparently nobody wants it. Coffee?"

———

Cammie sat in the lobby on a leather sofa, beneath the golden letters that read "Law Offices of Goldberg, McIntosh, Hartwood & Flynn." Her chin was cupped in her hand and her elbow rested on her knee.

Flynn walked in ahead of Darwin and nodded. Darwin stopped. She didn't look at him.

"Good morning. I didn't know you were coming."

"You don't want me here."

"That's not true. I just wish you'd call first."

She slowly turned her head. A bruise, still purple, stretched down from her swollen eye. The white of her eye had turned red. Darwin knelt beside her.

"Tell me what happened."

"Somebody met me outside the dance studio and warned me to keep quiet."

"Have you been to a doctor?" Darwin asked.

"I'll be all right."

"Let's go." He stood up and tugged her gently to her feet. "You could have a concussion or lose sight in that eye."

"I said I'm all right." She yanked her arm back.

"There's a clinic right down the street."

"It's nothing a little makeup won't cover."

Darwin turned to the receptionist. "Jody, call Mr. Sherman, please. Tell him something came up and I'm going to have to reschedule."

"Why are you so concerned all of the sudden?" Cammie asked as they left the lobby toward the elevators.

"You're my client."

"I should have figured as much," she said. They got on the elevator. He raised his hand to touch the side of her face, but she grimaced and turned her head.

"He didn't try to take your purse?"

"I would have given it to him rather than get bashed alongside the head."

"I want to know exactly what he said."

"He told me I better learn to keep quiet, then he hit me," she said. "I fell down and covered my head. When I looked up, he was gone."

"What did he look like?"

"White, tall. Unshaven. He wore a navy or black stocking cap. I'd guess he was in his midforties. It happened so fast, and I was stunned at first."

"Ever see him before?"

"I don't think so."

"Cammie, do you have any friends or relatives in Kansas City?"

"Just dancers."

Darwin held her elbow and ushered her into the clinic. A heavyset thirty-something woman and her child sat at the end of a row of chairs, and an elderly man sat across from them. The woman looked at Cammie, then Darwin, then shook her head slowly and turned up the corner of her mouth. The man's eyes narrowed, and he glared at Darwin. Darwin looked away, then turned back to see the woman's arms crossed.

Darwin read a *Forbes* magazine while Cammie visited with the doctor. When she came back out, she held an icepack over her cheek.

"He said I should call the police."

———————

She ran in place on the wooden floor of her living room. She wore her sweats and perspired as her legs pumped up and down. The music was loud. Then the telephone rang.

"I told you to keep quiet," the caller said.

"Who is this?"

"Maybe I should pay you another visit."

"I haven't said anything to anybody," Cammie said.

"You went to your lawyer's office."

"I already had the appointment. It would have been more suspicious if I didn't."

"What did you tell him?" the caller asked.

"That I got hurt practicing dance."

"You went to the doctor too."

"I was hurt," Cammie said. "Are you *following* me?"

"I know everything you do, and I'll keep knowing until I'm sure you've learned to shut up."

"What is it you want me to keep quiet?"

"Take a guess."

"Is it about my uncle's death?" Cammie asked.

"Bingo."

"Did you do it?"

"Do what?"

"Kill him."

"I thought he left the car running in the garage."

"Then what are you afraid of?"

"Your uncle was a great man. He did a lot for this country," the caller said. "He lived a long life. Now, let him be."

"What are you talking about?" Cammie said. "What are you trying to hide?"

"Keep the police out of it. And stay away from the lawyer."

"The lawyer and I have a *personal* relationship."

"Does he know that?"

"He's cute. He's the closest I have to a boyfriend."

"And the press: nobody better go to them or you'll be sorry."

"Sorry?"

"Dead."

CHAPTER EIGHTEEN

1893

Autumn sunlight shone through the open windows of the corner tavern, and specks of dust floated and sparkled in its still beams. The sounds of the city made their way inside as well: horse hoofs thumped the hard-packed dirt streets; delivery wagons and carriage traffic squeaked and rattled; and pedestrians shouted over it all. Hannah came by before the after-work bar crowd gathered.

George was serving drinks to a couple of elderly regulars, and the noise from traffic outside muted her footsteps when she walked in. She took a barstool, waited until he saw her, and signaled him over. He wiped his hands on his apron and took his time making his way over to her.

"Where's Kate?" she asked.

"Upstairs taking a nap."

"We have to talk," Hannah said.

"Again?"

"Yes, damn it. You're not getting out of this."

"Is there a chance it might be Archie's?"

"Women keep track of stuff like this. Anyway, it's not like we only did it once."

"Are you sure you want to be here without Archie? That's how we got into all this confusion."

"There's no confusion," Hannah said, raising her voice above the city noise. "It's your baby."

He looked around to see if anybody heard. "Be careful, Hannah. I'm married now." He sighed and looked down at the countertop. "We won't tell anybody and you can marry Archie."

"I don't *want* to marry him."

"You're a great couple and he loves you to death."

"What did you say?" Hannah asked above the noise.

"He loves you to death."

"It's too difficult to talk here. Come over tonight after you're off work."

"I got to go upstairs to Kate," he said.

"Just for a while. Pregnant women get tired. She'll never know."

———

Customers stomped to shake snow from their boots. Kate swabbed the wooden planks of the floor where a drunk had vomited the night before. She bent over her balloonlike belly and wrung the mop into a pale of grungy water.

A few men entered the bar laughing and one accidentally bumped into her on the way to a table.

"Sorry, sweetheart," he said.

She wiped her brow with her forearm and blew away hair that had fallen from the bun on her head. She walked over to George. "I don't think I can do this anymore. I'm dizzy."

"I'll walk you upstairs, honey. Rest a while."

"Give me a minute." She sat down and leaned back in a chair while straightening her legs. "I can't do this anymore."

"Your mom said she'd help out when you can't work. Hell, I can get along by myself, if need be."

"You might have to," Kate said. "I'm moving in with my mother and father."

"You're leavin' me?"

"Just until the baby's born. I can't get any rest here with all the noise, and the steps are too steep. They kill my back. You don't mind, do you?"

"I'll miss you."

"You can come over too," she said.

"I'm not sure your parents want me there."

"You're my husband and the baby's father, for heaven's sake."

"Your dad probably wants me to stay close by and watch over his bar."

"Hannah told me she'd stop by and check up on you."

———

George threw his apron on the counter and darted out of the bar. He pulled his cap out of his coat pocket while he sprinted the first three blocks. Then he lost his wind, slowed down, and walked. His warm breath sent foggy clouds into the frigid winter air. He jogged the final block to Emory Street, burst into the Schamberger house, and climbed up a steep flight of stairs to the second floor.

Kate lay in bed with a red, wrinkled baby in her arms. The baby was wrapped in a white towel. Minnie Graf, the neighborhood midwife, sat in a rocking chair next to Kate's bed and smiled when George entered. Johanna Schamberger had followed him in and stood at the foot of the bed, examining her daughter's tired, solemn face.

"Is everything okay?" George asked.

Kate's eyes opened and sparkled. "You have a son, George." He grinned.

"He's awful big," his mother-in-law said. "Kate had a difficult time. I'm worried about her."

"Are you feeling all right, honey?" he asked.

"She's tired," Minnie said. Kate looked at him, then closed her eyes. "I'm more concerned about the baby. He's weak and doesn't respond well. The delivery was rough on him too."

"This is no place for a man right now, George," his mother-in-law said. "We'll take care of her." She placed her palm on George's back and ushered him out of the bedroom.

"Did she decide on a name?" he asked.

"She'll probably call him Pius."

"We never talked about that one." He looked at the floor.

"It's a wonderful name," Johanna said, "and she worships her father."

"Sure," George said. The door opened before he reached it. Hannah looked up at him. He froze.

"How's she doing, George?"

"Not too good, I guess."

"I stopped by the bar, and they said you left in a hurry," Hannah said. "I knew it was time."

"Kate will be glad you did."

"She'll be all right, George. There's no such thing as an easy birth. Go back to the bar. I told Archie to buy some cigars."

"You're seeing him again?"

"For now," she said, "but I'm starting to show."

"When are *you* due?" He looked at her stomach.

"Three or four months. It's getting uncomfortable."

"I can tell," he said. He put on his hat and started out the door, then turned and said, "I'm sorry about all this."

Hannah reached out to hug him and whispered in his ear. "I'll always love you, George."

He looked over her shoulder and saw his mother-in-law watching.

A group of mourners gathered in a small chapel off the main sanctuary at St. Peter the Apostle Catholic Church. The body of the infant lay in a homemade wooden casket. The casket was draped in white and placed on a table next to the baptismal font. Father O'Brien conducted the service.

Kate sat in a pew next to Lena and her mother. Kate and her mother wore black dresses and dark veils. Kate sobbed. Her father, her sister, Lena, her best friend, Hannah, and George gathered around the other side of the casket and bowed their heads. George fought to hold back tears, but he couldn't hide his red and swollen eyes. Father O'Brien sprinkled holy water over the casket. The child was baptized and buried the same afternoon, March 1, 1895.

Pius Schamberger had borrowed a buckboard to haul his wife, two daughters, and the casket to the church. He'd rigged a wooden plank behind the front bench for Kate and Lena, and Hannah squeezed in and huddled with them on the makeshift bench. George had pulled down the back gate and sat in the rear of the wagon with his feet dangling. He rested an arm over the casket so it wouldn't shake and move.

Kate was too frail to travel the distance from the church to the cemetery, especially in the cold, and she wanted her family by her side. So George volunteered to bury the baby.

After Archie got off work, he met George at the Schamberger house, and the two of them rode the buckboard four miles to the Louden Park Cemetery. The sun was setting and the temperature had fallen by the time they arrived. They lifted the casket off the back of the wagon, then used ropes to help a gravedigger lower it into an open grave. The gravedigger shoveled loose dirt onto the casket as George and Archie stood by. George wept. Archie pulled a bottle of whiskey from his coat pocket and offered him a swig.

"Give me a minute," George said. Archie walked over to the wagon and climbed aboard. George wiped his eyes and watched the gravedigger shovel more dirt. A sliver of light blue sky remained on the horizon.

"Let's go, George," Archie said. "It's too cold." Except for the sound of clopping horse hoofs and the squeaking and rattling of the old wagon, they rode the four miles back to Emory Street in silence.

By the time they got back, the other mourners had disbanded. Kate had gone to bed early, and her sister had walked around the corner to her house on Portland Street. Hannah had gone, and Pius was reading a book next to the fireplace. Johanna was washing dishes in the kitchen.

Archie took off to find Hannah, and George walked the other way toward the Conway Street Bar. He pulled his collar up and placed his hands inside the pockets of his heavy woolen coat. He stared at the sidewalk under kerosene streetlights as snowflakes fell and closed in around him.

CHAPTER NINETEEN

Leaves had turned maroon and brown and blew sideways across the backyard, gathering in piles along the fence. Most of the year, Cammie couldn't see the sky from the back window because of the tall maple trees. Now, the wind had stripped them, and a bright gray sky glowed from above.

She walked out back to the garage. She'd made the short trek hundreds of times before and it had never bothered her, but she'd never been threatened before, either. She lifted one of the two heavy wooden garage doors so it wouldn't drag and swung it to the side. It squeaked like it always had, but this time the sound seemed louder. And when the wind rattled a garbage can, she flinched and her eyes darted from side to side.

She peeked inside, then took a couple of deliberate steps and craned her neck. She looked over the hood of the car and into a dark corner, then opened the other door and glanced behind her, moving quickly to get in the car. She slammed the car door and pressed the lock button.

The engine started when she turned the key, but the radio blasted and she jumped. "Damn it."

A shadow moved across the rearview mirror, and the garage grew darker. There was a loud bang. Her muscles tightened, her body and neck became taut. She looked over her shoulder. One of the garage doors had blown shut. She sighed and rested her forehead against her forearms on the steering wheel, then lifted her head and looked behind her one more time. Nobody was there, and she unlocked the car and got out.

She placed a brick against the bottom of the door, hurried back inside the car, and backed out.

She constantly checked her rearview mirror on her way to the Peach Tree Café. The same waitress was there.

"Astra. Right?" Cammie asked. "Remember me?"

"Sure I do, honey. It's good to see you."

"It's good to be seen."

"What's wrong, honey?"

"Weird things. I've been threatened; I'm kind of jittery." The waitress gave a curious look and started to say something, but Cammie kept talking. "Are the guys in back?"

"Not today, honey."

"I thought they always met on Thursdays."

"Most the time, they do. Ain't seen any of 'em today, though."

"I was hoping to speak with Sammy."

"He lives right up the street. Go on up there."

The waitress pulled a phone book from under the counter. She looked up his address and wrote it on the back of a blank order form and handed it to Cammie.

Cammie thanked her and turned to leave, but three men stood on the sidewalk outside. She hesitated and turned back to Astra.

"They're regulars," Astra said. "You're safe."

Cammie walked up 18th Street past several buildings. Another couple of men stood talking outside the Negro Baseball Leagues Museum. They watched her, and she stared back with that "don't-even-think-about-it" glare.

She kept looking back. A man in a dark suit and white shirt stood about a half block behind her on the corner. She walked another block to Woodland Street and turned around again. The same man was still a half block behind her, and again he was peering into a window.

She turned north on Woodland, walked down it, and crossed the street, still looking back. She walked into a small apartment complex called Parade Park Homes. The buildings had gray clapboard siding. They were new or remodeled and contrasted with the older neighborhood. She knocked on the door that matched the address Astra had written down. Nobody answered.

A man in his early thirties walked by from the other direction and smiled. He had a bounce in his gait and an unlit cigarette in his lips.

"Looking for Sammy?" he said.

"Have you seen him?"

"He must be out of town," the guy said. "I ain't seen him all week. He might be visiting his sister in St. Louis. She comes up and gets him every now and then." He walked on.

Cammie watched him walk away, and he turned to catch another glimpse of her too. Their eyes met, and they both looked away at the same time. Then, she saw the man in the business suit. He stood on the sidewalk out on Woodland Street, looking down the street.

"Hey," she called to the man that had just walked by and spoken to her. He turned. "What's your name?"

"Eddie. Why?"

"You know Sammy well?"

"He's friendly." The guy started walking back toward her. "We all like him and kind of watch over him."

"You think he's all there?" she asked.

"Mentally? I think so. Why?"

"He seems to have a good memory," Cammie said. "He was a friend of my uncle."

"Sammy's pretty sharp."

"Everybody likes him then, huh?"

"Oh, yeah. How can you not? I gotta go, ma'am." He turned and started away.

"You know that guy over there?" He turned back and she nodded toward Woodland Street.

"The guy in the suit? No. Why?"

"Just wondered," Cammie said. "He might be following me."

"You want me to talk to him?"

"Can I walk that way with you?" Cammie asked.

She and Eddie walked toward Woodland as the stranger in the suit walked further down the same street, away from 18th Street.

Eddie shouted to him. "Hey buddy. You want something?"

The stranger continued in the opposite direction, then stopped and looked back at Cammie and Eddie. Eddie accompanied Cammie to the corner. She felt more comfortable on 18th Street a busy main drag. Eddie remained by her side, and they walked toward her car. Then she stopped quickly. Somebody stood in the street by the driver's side of her car.

"It's a policeman," Eddie said.

"Trouble, officer?" Cammie asked.

The policeman smiled. "You forgot to load the meter."

"I stayed longer than I thought."

"Sorry," he said. He handed her a citation, tipped his hat, and started away.

"Officer? Can you watch while I drive off? There's a man around here. I think he's following me."

"Oh, yeah. He's following her, all right."

She thanked Eddie and the policeman, got in her car, and locked her doors. She opened her purse and rummaged for her keys, then dropped them. They fell between her seat and the console. "Darn it," she said. She reached down, but couldn't see or feel the keys. She moved her seat back and bent forward, wedging her arm farther down between the seats. The policeman still stood beside her car, and when she rose back up, she was startled to see him still there.

"Are you all right, miss?" the officer asked.

"Yes, thank you. Just a little nervous."

She drove off, looking in all directions.

———

Much of downtown Kansas City is on a hill, and Darwin's office building—the Commerce Tower—was on the riverside of that hill, on Main Street. Cammie didn't have change for a meter, so she pulled into a parking garage, then pulled her cell phone out of her purse and dialed.

"I'm in the parking garage of your building. I know you don't like it when I just drop in, so I can go back home if you want."

"I'd like to see you."

"You would?"

"Does that surprise you?"

"Kind of," she said. She looked from side to side, then gasped.

"What's wrong?" he said.

She took a deep breath. "Nothing, I guess. Some guy just walked past the back of my car."

"Are you all right?"

"I think he went in the building."

"What level of the garage?"

"Four," she said.

"Wait there." He raced down the hallway and lunged between elevator doors about to close. The numbers over the door lit up one at a time as the elevator descended fifteen stories, much too slowly. He darted out and down a concrete tunnel into the garage. Cammie unlocked her car door, got out, and threw her arms around him. She kissed his neck, then his cheek a few times.

"I'm sorry," she said, still holding on.

He didn't say anything but relaxed his grip and pulled back and wiped a tear from her cheek. She pulled him closer.

"I'm sorry," she said. "Again."

"It's all right." He kissed her cheek. "There's no charge until you get to my office."

She wiped her own cheek and forced a smile. Then her face turned sober again. "I need a gun."

CHAPTER TWENTY

1895

A half glass of bourbon lay on the counter of the bar, and a lit cigar rested on the edge of a round clear-glass ashtray. The *Baltimore Sun* was spread out in front of George. The date on it was the same as his baby's death, but three months later.

He turned when he heard feet shuffling along the wooden floor. Hannah leaned back to carry the load of her unborn child. Her hair was long and stringy, and her breasts were twice the size they were when George first met her. Her stomach stuck out so far she wobbled back and forth with each step.

She pulled out a chair that had been tucked under a table and sat down, spreading her legs and leaning back so that her belly puffed upward, becoming even more prominent.

"I hate you for this, George," she said.

"It's not all my fault."

"Are you ever going to tell Kate?"

"Hell, no," he said. "And you better not either."

"I guess that means I'll be left alone to raise *our* kid?"

"Archie thinks it's his," George said. "Why don't you make it easy on everybody?"

She rolled her eyes, then said, "I don't know how I'm supposed to feed and clothe the poor thing."

"Archie's no slacker. He's got more money than me."

"If I marry him, it'll be *just* for the money."

"You used to like him."

"He was fun at first; it got old," Hannah said. "He makes me crazy now." She struggled to rise from the chair. "I think I'll go see Kate. Is she out of bed yet?"

"She's still at her mom's. She still sleeps a lot. She's not her old self yet."

"You asshole." Hannah turned and wobbled toward the door.

"What'd I do now?"

"You're just an uncaring bull. How many other women are laid up and stranded because of you?"

———

George walked into the Schamberger house and stuffed his hat in his pocket. He nodded silently to Johanna, and she motioned him upstairs. He tipped his head and climbed the narrow stairway. When he reached the top, he looked up just in time. A plate sailed toward him. He raised his arms. It hit his forearm and crashed to the floor.

"Get away from me." Kate sat on the edge of her bed. "I don't want to see you," she said.

"What did I do?"

"Hannah was here. Does that give you a clue?"

"What did she say?"

"Just leave," Kate said, burying her head in her hands and crying.

"Honey." He stepped toward her, and she raised her hand. He froze. "You can't believe everything *she* says."

"So you know what she said."

"I just don't like her. She's trouble."

"Leave, George."

———————

George banged on the door. He put his ear to the door. He banged again. Finally, Hannah opened it.

"What in hell did you tell Kate?"

"What are *you* doing here, George?"

"Kate's really mad. You told her you're carrying my baby, didn't you?"

Hannah's eyes grew larger, and she looked to the side. Archie sat in her kitchenette.

"You're the guy?" Archie asked.

Hannah broke the icy silence. "Don't be silly, Archie."

"No wonder you're naming the baby after George," Archie said.

"I'm naming my baby out of respect for Kate's baby. Not after George. It's the least I can do for my best friend."

"Bullshit," Archie said. He stood up and came toward George.

George put his hand up. "You've gotta be crazy. Kate and Hannah are best friends."

Hannah came from the side and put her hand on Archie's shoulder. "I told her we could share my baby."

George's face was red. "Damn, Arch, I ain't been spending time with your girl. Kate got mad. That's all."

"Then why would Hannah tell her she was carrying your baby?"

"I didn't," Hannah said.

"All I know is Kate was mad," George said. "I figured maybe Hannah was joking around and Kate thought she was serious."

"I came here to ask Hannah to marry me," Archie said, "once and for all."

"Good," George said. "Did you tell him yes, Hannah?"

"I didn't have time. You came and ruined the moment."

"Well?" Archie asked Hannah.

———•———

The bar was closed on Sunday. George sat at the counter with the justice of the peace. They both drank bourbon. Archie pounded on the door from outside and George let him in. He bounded in with a bouquet of roses. He tossed them on the bar, reached in his pocket, and pulled out a small box.

"Here you go, George. You're the best man."

George opened the box. "Where'd you get this?"

"My mom gave it to me. She wore it for thirty-eight years."

"She died, right?" George said.

"That's why I'm using it. Where's the girls?"

Kate had moved back into the room above the bar. She helped Hannah get ready for the ceremony. Hannah wore a long navy dress and a pearl necklace.

"I can't believe you're wearing a dark dress," Kate said.

"It's a symbol of the death of my lifestyle. Besides, I hate being this fat; I'm trying to hide it."

Kate laughed. "I don't think you can."

George and Archie waited downstairs. Archie fidgeted. His face was red and he was perspiring. George kept handing him more shots of whiskey.

Upstairs, Hannah faced Kate and placed her hands on her elbows. "Do you think I'm doing the right thing?"

"The baby needs a father," Kate said, "and you need a man."

"It's money I need."

"You got one, you got the other," Kate said, grinning.

"I can't believe *you* said that." Hannah smiled.

"I'm not sure how you got by this long," Kate said.

A grandfather clock ticked and exaggerated the silence. "You really know, don't you?"

"I figured your dad sent you money from Pennsylvania."

"You're so innocent," Hannah said. "How do you think I met Archie in the first place?"

"At the bar, I guess."

"That much is right," Hannah said, "but not many women go to bars."

"You're not like most women."

"He was a customer."

"He's here a lot," Kate said.

Hannah paused, then said, "*My* customer."

"What do you mean?"

"We had an understanding, and I got paid."

Kate's face turned pale. She took a deep breath. "Was he the *only one* you had an understanding with?"

"Since I got pregnant," Hannah said.

"That's dreadful, Hannah. How could you? George wasn't ever a customer, was he?"

"He was *your* guy, Kate."

"Then who?"

"Sometimes two or three men a week. At their places, mostly," Hannah said. "Remember Joey?"

"Really?" Kate asked.

"He makes a lot of money and bought me jewelry and clothes."

"How come I never knew?" Kate said.

"I didn't advertise it. Anyway, you're so religious. I was afraid what you'd think."

"Are you sure it's Archie's baby?"

"He doesn't know there was anybody else. He has suspicions, but he wants it to be his, and I won't hurt him."

CHAPTER TWENTY-ONE

Cammie pulled into the driveway and got out to open the garage. A car pulled in behind her. It sat still, waiting with its lights on. It was only 6:30, but that was dusk in Kansas City during late October. The headlights exaggerated her shadow against the back wall of the garage.

Darwin got out of his car. She pulled him inside the house behind her, turning on lights room by room that hadn't already been left on.

"You're still frightened," he said.

"You think I've been faking it?"

The doorbell rang.

"You get it," Cammie said.

He opened the door, and two kids yelled, "Trick or treat."

She put her hands to her mouth. "I forgot."

"Got any candy?" Darwin asked.

"I'm a dancer."

"Dancers can't eat candy?" He pulled a couple of one-dollar bills out of his pocket and opened the door. One kid wore a cheap black store-bought outfit with a white skeleton painted on front. It was impossible to tell whether the kid was a boy or girl. Darwin assumed it was a he. The other one was a girl dressed in pink tights, a tutu, and a sequined skin-tight top. She wore a sparkly crown and had glitter on her tiny dark face. Her eyes were bright.

Cammie sighed. "I had a costume like that when I was her age." A smiling woman stood behind the two children. Cammie held up both hands. "Wait here. Don't go anywhere."

The woman moved closer to her kids and reached down to hold their hands. Cammie rushed back into her kitchen, where she reached on top of her refrigerator and pulled down an envelope. She stepped back into the living room and opened the door, handing the woman what looked like four tickets.

"Please use these. I had a chance to see a ballet when I was her age, and it made all the difference."

"What are they for?"

"Tickets to the ballet's next performance. Please come. The kids will love it."

"We ain't ever been to a ballet."

"What's your name?"

"I'm Vera. This is Alicia and Robert," she said as she placed her hand on each kid's head.

"Do you like ballet, honey?" Cammie asked Alicia.

"I think so. I don't know."

"There's only three of us," the mom said.

"You can come with Darwin," Cammie said. Darwin rolled his eyes. "You'll have a wonderful time."

"She's dancing in it," Darwin said.

"You are?" the woman asked.

"Let's go see her, Mama," the little girl said. Robert stood silently.

"Here come more kids," Darwin said, "and I don't have anymore cash."

"Kids, give back the dollar bills," Vera said. "We got the tickets."

The little girl reached in her pillowcase. The skeleton wasn't following what was going on.

"That's all right," Darwin said. "Keep it."

The mother, skeleton, and miniature ballet dancer turned and shuffled down the porch steps as two more kids ran up.

"Trick or treat," they said in unison.

"You got any ones?" he asked Cammie. She didn't, and it cost him all of his change. The older kids, both dressed like hobos, turned and rushed down the stairs. Cammie switched off the porch light, as well as the lights in the rooms in the front of the house. She pulled him closer to her.

"I can't stay here alone tonight," she said. Streetlights beamed through the front window onto her face. "You're going to have to stay here."

"I've got to work in the morning."

"Please," Cammie said. "You can sleep in Griff's room."

"You're going to have to come to my place."

"How many bedrooms?"

"One," he said.

"Got a couch?"

———

Darwin walked in first, turning on lights. The wooden floors were smooth and polished. The furniture was sleek, blacks and browns, a lot of leather. Everything was in its place. Magazines on the end table were stacked perfectly. There were no empty glasses or dirty plates. No clothing on the floors.

Ceiling-to-floor sheer draperies formed one whole wall of his living room. He pulled them open, and the city's buildings seemed close enough to touch. Cammie moved closer and peered down at the nighttime traffic eight stories below. He lifted a remote control and turned on a flat-screen TV mounted on the wall, then laid the remote back down and disappeared into his bedroom.

He walked out with a blanket and pillow and dropped them on the sofa.

"Thanks," Cammie said.

"*You're* sleeping in the bedroom."

"No way. This is *your* home. But I could use one of your old shirts—the larger the better. I forgot my pajamas."

"Something warm, I presume," he said.

"Got an old flannel shirt?"

He disappeared again and returned carrying a red-and-black plaid flannel shirt. He dropped it on the couch.

"You're mad," she said.

"I never had a client stay overnight."

"I won't tell anybody. Where's the bathroom?" He pointed, and a minute later, she came back out, buttoning his long shirt. The tails almost reached her knees. Her legs and feet were bare. "Can I build a fire?"

He flipped a switch on the wall. The fireplace flickered on.

"Natural gas," he said.

"Neat. You want to watch a little television?" She sat on the sofa, and he sat on the opposite end. "I'm sorry about this. I thought maybe you'd like to stay at my place." She swung her legs up under her bottom and the shirt rode up.

He inhaled and tapped his fingers on the arm of the sofa. She blushed.

"You got any wine?" Cammie asked. "I need something to help me sleep."

"Grape juice or Bud Light."

"I'm not into beer. I'll have grape juice."

He walked into the kitchen and opened the refrigerator, bending over and pulling out a plastic bottle of Welch's. When he closed the door and looked up, she was standing next to him.

"You're afraid too," Cammie said. "Of me." She wrapped her arms around his waist and kissed the side of his mouth. He put his arms around her and blindly placed the grape juice on the counter. He hugged her without saying anything, then poured another glass of juice. They retreated into the living room, arm in arm.

"I think I'll go to bed now," he said.

"It's early." She kissed his cheek again, and he started toward the bedroom. "I brought my dance stuff. Can I just hang out around here in the morning until practice?"

He turned back. She sat on the sofa with her long, silky legs stretched out toward him. The top button of the flannel shirt was unbuttoned. She reached behind her neck with both hands and unhooked the thin golden chain at her neck, holding it by one end and lowering it into a circle on the coffee table.

"I've got to wake up early," he said. "My boss wants me to meet him for breakfast."

She lifted her eyebrows and reminded him of Margaret Keane's paintings of children with oversized eyes. She didn't say anything. He walked in his bedroom and stood by his nightstand, setting his alarm for 6:45 a.m. He felt her presence and turned. She leaned against the doorjamb. Those same big eyes.

CHAPTER TWENTY-TWO

Archie strained. He carried a wicker basket over his arm as he walked into the Conway Street Bar. His face glowed as he looked around the barroom to see if anyone was watching. Hannah straggled behind him and pulled up a chair. The wooden legs scraped against the planks of the floor. George, who had been wiping the top of a table with a wet rag, looked up.

"She had to get out of the apartment," Archie said.

"First time?" George asked.

"I couldn't stand it any longer," Hannah said. "I needed fresh air and wanted to talk to adults. Other than Minnie the first couple days, I haven't talked with anybody but Archie."

"His eyes are open," George said. "This is the first time I've seen him when he wasn't all squished up and red."

"Isn't he beautiful, George?"

"He's starting to look like a real person. You're so lucky," George said. He swallowed hard and wiped his eyes.

"I'm sorry," Hannah said. "I shoulda known better."

"That's all right. I'm happy for you."

"Kate will have another baby."

Archie squatted down next to Hannah and put his hand on her shoulder. He looked at the baby, then up at George. "It's not like

you're going to give her much rest until she's pregnant again."
Archie grinned.

"I'm going to run up and get her." George walked to a staircase
behind the bar and lumbered upstairs. "Kate, Hannah and Archie
are downstairs. Come and see their baby?"

"No, thanks."

"I think they came to show the baby off."

"You heard me."

"But Kate."

"Leave me alone," she snapped. "*You* go see it."

George turned away.

"Does it look like you, George?"

He turned back. "It's a baby. It doesn't look like anybody."

"I'll bet its eyes turn brown," she said

"They're more gray."

"Babies' eyes turn color after six or seven months."

"What's that got to do with anything?" he said.

"We'll see."

"Damn it, Kate. Why are you in such a lousy mood? Isn't
Hannah your friend?"

"I don't know. Is she?"

"What do you want me to tell her? That you're not interested
in her kid?"

"Tell her what you want, George."

He hesitated halfway down the staircase. "She's in bed already,"
he said.

Hannah shrugged. "She didn't *want* to come down, did she?"

———

George ambled down Washington Boulevard. The gray afternoon
didn't diminish his spirit. He waved at a policeman walking his
beat and stopped to pet a scraggly dog that accompanied a boy
hawking newspapers. A trolley bell rang, and George rushed

across the brick street, hopping over steel rails. Then he turned and smiled at the conductor, shaking his head.

He stopped at the entrance to a grocery store and tipped his hat to an elderly woman, then walked inside and picked an apple out of a bin. As he reached in his pocket for some change, he heard his name. He turned.

"Hannah, where you been?"

"Kate didn't seem to want my friendship anymore, and you wouldn't lay an eye on me because I was still fat after having *your* kid. You wouldn't even come over to see your own son."

"You're looking great." He chomped into the apple and eyed her up and down. "Where's Archie?"

"At home with the baby," she said. "Why don't you come over?"

"It's too uncomfortable," George said. "Archie gets all huffy."

"I miss her," Hannah said. She looked off into the distance, then back at George. "Come over in the morning after Archie leaves."

"I'd just get in trouble. Come by the bar, if you want."

"Archie doesn't want me to, and I'm not going to beg Kate to be my friend."

"She's never happy anymore," George said.

"You're not getting any, huh?" Hannah grinned. "Neither is Archie. He drives me nuts. I don't think it's going to work."

"I'd like to see the baby."

"He's your spittin' image."

"What color are his eyes?" George asked.

"Brown."

———————

Morning fog hugged the rooftops of buildings. Bells and foghorns sounded from the harbor. The streets and sidewalks were wet from last evening's frost. The predawn sky was pale, and streetlights were still on. George stood with his hands in his pockets. He'd pulled the earflaps down from inside his hat and yanked the collar of his coat up around his neck. He leaned against the brick wall of an apartment building, then peeked around the corner. He looked again.

Finally, Archie loped up the concrete stairway from his basement flat, less than a hundred yards away, and walked the opposite direction toward the harbor. George waited an extra minute until Archie was out of sight, then walked at a brisk pace toward the flat.

He rushed along the sidewalk, then stepped down several stairs to the sunken entrance and knocked lightly on the door. He heard a dead bolt turn and the chain from the door rattle. Hannah opened the door, and he swooped her up and onto her unmade bed. The baby cried, but that didn't stop them.

What stopped them was Archie, standing behind them in the doorway and staring down on George, whose pants were dropped to his ankles. He was on top of Hannah, whose nightgown was pulled up to her neckline.

Hannah saw Archie first. Her body went limp. George looked into her eyes, then turned over. Archie stood still, breathing hard. He took several steps toward them. George rolled off the bed and struggled to pull his trousers up at the same time. Archie froze, as if he wasn't sure who deserved his fury most. That gave George enough time to rise to his feet.

Archie dove at him, putting his shoulder into George's ribs, knocking him back and against a wall. They both fell to the floor. Hannah stood up and moved to the opposite side of the room. She picked up the baby, covered him with her arms, and held him against her chest.

Archie swung at George over and over. George covered his head with his arms but didn't hit back.

"You son of a bitch. I knew it," Archie said. "I knew it."

Hannah turned and cowered in the corner. The baby cried.

Suddenly, Archie stopped swinging. He stood up. George remained on the floor staring up at him. Archie looked at Hannah and the baby.

"Why?" he said. Then he turned and ran out of the flat, slamming the door behind him.

———————

The women made eye contact but didn't speak. Hannah carried little George in a basket. She placed him on the bar next to several empty beer mugs. Kate had been swabbing the wooden floor, but when she saw Hannah, she put the mop in a pail of water, left it there, and walked up the back stairway. George folded his arms and stood behind the bar.

"I'm leaving, George," Hannah said.

"It would probably make Kate feel better."

"For good."

"You can't do that. Where would you go?"

"Probably Boston," Hannah said. "Maybe New York. A big city."

"With Archie?"

"I don't love him," she said, "and he shouldn't love me. Anyway, I haven't seen him since that morning."

"He'll be back," George said.

"I went down by the harbor. They said he hadn't shown up for work for over a week. He mighta gone to sea; he talked about it."

"How you going to get by?"

"I don't know. I'll turn tricks if I have to, at least until I meet somebody with promise. I still look pretty good. Don't you think?"

"Like a million." George cleared the counter of two empty glasses, then reached in the basket and pulled the blanket away from the baby's face. George smiled while he touched its chin with his forefinger.

Hannah placed her hand over his.

"You love me, don't you, George?"

He looked over his shoulder then back into her eyes. "Don't you know I do?"

She stood up and grabbed the basket and baby off the counter. She gave a faint smile. "That's all I needed to hear." She turned and pushed the door open.

"Don't go, Hannah."

"I got no choice," she said.

"Then give it some time, but come back."

"That wouldn't be good for either of us. Or the baby." She turned her back on him and walked outside into the daylight.

———

George rushed to clean up the bar before closing time. He coaxed the last few customers out, then locked the door and extinguished the lanterns hanging from the ceiling beams, ignoring the dirty mugs on the bar. Then he ran up the stairs two at a time. Kate was reading a book, sitting in their only upholstered chair.

"I was thinking all day about you."

"What's up your sleeve, George?"

"I want to take you somewhere this Sunday," George said. "I sold some lightning rods to bar customers, and I've got a couple extra bucks."

"Where in the world would we go?"

"Mr. Schmidt said he'd let me borrow his buckboard. I thought I'd drive you up to that little bed and breakfast by Clifton Park. We can have lunch and just ride around."

"What do you want, George?"

"Just to be with you, honey. To get away from the bar and get some sunlight and fresh air."

"Can we go to church?" Kate asked.

"Would I have to wear a tie?"

"I'm tired. Let's go to bed."

———

One of the regulars came into the bar with a wicker basket hanging from his forearm. The basket looked like the one Hannah used to carry little George. He lifted it onto the counter, and bawling came from inside.

"I was told to give this to you," the man said. "I guess you're going to be a father now." The man chuckled. Several other nearby customers listened. They looked on and laughed.

"Hey George, you a father now?" one asked.

"Give the poor kid a drink," another one said. "Maybe it'll shut him up."

"You get deliveries like this often, George?"

"Most parents have to wait nine months for a new kid; you get one delivered on your doorstep."

George's expression remained stonelike. A piece of paper was wedged between the folds of the blanket around the baby. He picked it up. "George Herman Ruth—with love forever, Mom."

CHAPTER TWENTY-THREE

She wore the long flannel shirt and floated through Darwin's kitchen like a swan, as she swayed to the music from his stereo. She stopped only to wait for his toast to pop up, then lifted her foot and scratched her calf. Every move was graceful, quiet, and smooth.

She buttered his toast and cut the pieces into triangles. She didn't ask him how he liked it, but everything she did seemed just right. She poured him coffee and pulled a plastic milk container out of the refrigerator, then put just a little into his cup and stirred it with a spoon.

"How did you know I use cream?"

She returned a half smile as if her answer wasn't necessary, then cupped her warm hand around his chin, bent down, and kissed his cheek. Her lips were warm and soft. Her cleavage was at his eye level, and he considered calling in sick.

"What time is it?" he said. "I'm late." He stood up.

"Mind if I shower?"

"Go ahead." She wasn't that much shorter than he was, but she stood on her toes and kissed his cheek again, then turned down the hallway toward his bathroom.

He opened the door but looked over his shoulder once more. She'd unbuttoned his shirt, tossed it in his room, and looked back over her shoulder. She stood naked and turned just enough. She batted her eyes just once and stared.

———

The same pale green walls. The same specials; they never changed. And the same smell of burnt coffee. Flynn sat alone at a four-top when Darwin rushed in twenty minutes late. He leaned back in his chair with his arms folded. The top button of his starched white shirt was unbuttoned, and his navy tie was loose around his neck. He used his tongue to push a toothpick from side to side in his mouth.

Darwin took off his overcoat, folded it neatly, and laid it over the metal chair on his side. "Sorry," he said.

"I don't get any respect."

"I had a visitor this morning."

Flynn grinned. "Okay. Give me five." He held his hand up.

"It's not like you think."

"Your mother? A brother? Your college roommate?"

"It was a little better than that," Darwin said.

"Good for you. Then I'm not even mad that you blew me off. But I already ate, buddy." Flynn waved the waitress over. "Hey, Mary."

She came over with a coffee pot and poured more into Flynn's cup.

"He finally came, hey?" she said. She looked at Darwin and pulled a pencil from behind her ear. "What can I get you, honey?" Darwin ordered eggs and toast, and she stuck her pencil back behind her ear and walked away.

"I'm going to need your help with the Hallmark interrogatories," Flynn said. "I need you to draft responses. I've got two depositions today."

"When do you need it?"

"This afternoon."

"I hope I can get it done."

"We've got no choice," Flynn said as he peered over Darwin's shoulder. "Look at those legs."

Darwin turned. A thin woman in spiked heels was walking away. Her heels clicked in a methodical, rhythmic way, and other men looked at her too.

"That reminds me," Flynn said. "When you going to introduce me to that black dancer chick? You done with her yet?"

"You mean with her *legal* work?"

Flynn smiled. "Is there something you're not telling me?"

Mary brought Darwin's breakfast. He grabbed his knife and fork, punctured his over-easy eggs, then sliced his toast and mixed it all together.

"I hope you're billing her. I haven't looked at the report lately, but the partners are watching that shit."

Darwin didn't say anything and kept eating.

"You are, aren't you?"

"Probably not as much as I should," Darwin said.

"You banging her or feeling sorry for her?"

Again, he didn't say anything.

"Hell, Darwin, you got to bill her. If she doesn't pay, it's her fault. If you don't bill her, it's yours."

———

She watched the elevator lights above the door. When it opened, she walked across the concrete floor to her car. She wore white tennis shoes, Levi's, a sweatshirt, and a long scarf. Her purse was hanging over her shoulder.

The garage was cool and had that tunnel-like echo. Every sound was magnified. She heard a distant car door slam and a car squeal on the pavement in another part of the garage.

She passed a Chevy Impala with a man sitting at the wheel. She sped up, almost jogging. She got in her car, locked the doors, backed up, and pulled away.

She looked in her rearview mirror and saw the man who had followed her away from the Peach Tree Café. He wore the same dark suit and walked toward the back of her car as she drove away. He waved as if he was trying to stop her. Her car squealed away.

She phoned Darwin's office. He wasn't in yet. She tried his cell phone, but he didn't answer that. She pulled around the corner and slammed on her brakes. She waited. No one was following her. She stepped on the gas.

She pulled up in front of the Peach Tree Café, parked, and went inside.

"I know it's early," she said.

"Not for me," Astra, said. "I been here since 6:30."

"I'm still looking for Sammy."

"Didn't you hear?" Cammie watched Astra walk behind the cash register and examine an order form. "He died," she said without looking up.

Cammie's mouth hung open.

"They found him in his apartment," Astra said.

"I went up there after I talked to you."

"You might be getting a phone call, then."

"His neighbor said he went to St. Louis. Do the police suspect anything?"

"He was old," Astra said.

———

Cammie called Darwin from her cell phone. He'd been in his office all morning working on a response to the Hallmark interrogatory. Composing the legal response was more than writing a blanket denial. He had to research his answers. And the document had to address all allegations of the plaintiff with denials consistent with specific points of law. Each allegation had to be denied in a way that Flynn could defend Hallmark if the matter ever reached court.

143

"Sammy's dead," she said.

"He's the guy you went to see?"

"I'm afraid, Darwin."

"I know, honey." He paused. "I didn't mean to sound mushy."

"Don't apologize," Cammie said.

"What are you going to do?

"Go see Detective Wilson. I'm hoping maybe he'll do an autopsy this time."

"I'll meet you there," Darwin said. He made some quick notes on the legal papers and stacked them neatly on the corner of his desk.

———

Wilson walked into the gray, sterile hallway.

"Come on in," he said. "I want to talk to you."

Darwin and Cammie followed him back to a bullpen of desks. Several officers were on telephones. Others looked at computer screens. Some were filling out reports. Wilson pulled two metal chairs over to the edge of his desk.

"Have a seat," he said.

"When was the last time you saw him?" Wilson asked Cammie.

"A week ago. I tried to see him a couple days ago, but his neighbor said he went to St. Louis."

"His neighbor?"

"A guy named Eddie, a nice guy."

The detective made some notes. "Is that the guy you were with outside Sammy's place?"

"How did you know?" Cammie asked.

"Your attorney here asked us to watch over you, so we've been trying to—when we have the manpower. Detective Gilmore tried to wave you down this morning."

She looked back and forth, at Wilson, then Darwin, and lowered her eyes to the floor. "The guy in the garage."

Darwin felt blood rush to his face. He figured they knew Cammie had stayed overnight.

"I thought he was stalking me," Cammie said.

"He was protecting you." Wilson picked up his phone and dialed a number. "Gilmore, you got a minute?"

"It would have been nice if he told me."

"He said he tried to this morning," Wilson said.

"I didn't know. I thought he was dangerous."

"We tried to be inconspicuous," Wilson said. "We were afraid you might get careless if you knew we were watching over you."

"I guess we should thank you," Darwin said.

"Any idea who threatened me?" Cammie asked.

"I'm still guessing it was harmless," Wilson said. "Somebody was probably overreacting to your uncle's death."

The guy who had followed Cammie walked through a double door into the bullpen. He nodded.

"Camille Griffin, meet Rodney Gilmore."

"Call me Rod. How do you do, ma'am?"

"This is her boyfriend, the attorney," Wilson said. Gilmore seemed to be a pleasant, quiet man. He reached out to shake Darwin's hand.

"Nobody needs to know she stayed at my place, do they?" Darwin asked.

"Not at all," Gilmore said.

"Are you ashamed of me?" Cammie asked.

"It's my office," Darwin said. "They don't understand our relationship."

Cammie turned up the corner of her mouth, then stood up and put her hands on her hips. "What about Sammy? Do you assume he died a natural death too?"

"Do you know something we don't?" Wilson asked.

"I don't believe this. You can't believe Sammy's death was a coincidence."

"We don't know."

"Have you heard anymore from this Eddie guy?" Gilmore asked.

"Why?"

"We don't know who he is. Nobody at the complex knows who he is, either."

"He knew Sammy."

"That's why we're curious," Wilson said.

CHAPTER TWENTY-FOUR

George heard footsteps coming downstairs. He closed his eyes. He knew it was Kate. He swung his pocket watch over the baby's face, trying to calm him.

"Don't cry, Georgie," he said. "Shhh."

The baby in the basket sat on the bar. Kate took a couple steps toward it, then scanned the room.

"Where is she?"

George didn't answer. He glued his eyes on the baby. He didn't want to face Kate.

"You heard me."

"I don't know, Kate. I'm sure she'll be back soon."

"What did she say?"

"I didn't talk to her." The men who had teased him earlier now sat still. They looked away from Kate, but she stared at each of them, one at a time, and zeroed in on several of them sitting together ten feet away.

"What's going on, George?" Kate asked.

"I'm not sure, I told you."

"We are not taking care of her baby while she gallivants around town chasing men."

"Hell no," George said.

"I'm going to see Mama." Kate stormed toward the door.

"What should I do with the baby?"

"He's your namesake," Kate said, "and your problem."

"How do I make him stop crying?"

"Feed him."

———

The apartment was dark except for dim moonlight seeping through a couple windows. George and Kate were in bed. Their apartment above the bar consisted of two rooms. One was a kitchenette with a small table and two chairs, a queen-sized bed, a dresser, and a brown upholstered chair. The other room—the bathroom—had a toilet, a small sink, and a bathtub.

The baby cried. Kate rolled over. George lay still with his eyes open, staring at a blank, shadowy wall. Kate tossed and turned again.

Daylight came too soon, and George rose and sat on the edge of the bed in his undershirt and shorts while he held the sides of his head and stared at the floor. Kate was dressed and moving about the room picking up dirty clothes. The baby bawled. Kate jerked open the dresser, pulled out some clothes, and threw them on the bed. Then she slammed the drawers, stuffed the clothes into a garment bag, and slipped on a jacket.

"Where you going?" George asked above the crying.

"I'm moving in with my parents."

"Kate, don't blame me. She's got to come back soon."

She opened another drawer and flung a folded sweater at her bag. "Do you think I'm a fool?"

"It's not *my* fault."

"Find her, George." She closed her bag, gripped it, and walked downstairs. "Maybe you should live with *her*. I never want to see her again, and I'm not sure I want to see you. I definitely don't want to take care of *her* baby."

"But Kate, things have been going so well."

"In your mind, maybe. If you've got a woman in your bed, *you* think things are going well. Obviously, it doesn't make a lot of difference who it is."

———

George carried the baby in the basket Hannah had left him. He walked down Portland Street and up the steps to the door of a brick row house. The fronts of the homes butted directly against the sidewalk. He knocked.

"Minnie Graf?"

"I remember you, Mr. Ruth. Who's in the basket?"

"It's a baby, ma'am. But not mine."

"I know," Minnie said. "I recognize the baby. It's Hannah's child, isn't it?"

"It's a long story, ma'am, and I don't have a lot of time, except to say it was abandoned and Kate and I have been taking care of it. But I need to go get Kate."

"I talked to her two days ago," Minnie said. "She came by. She wants me to help with your next infant."

"I don't understand."

"Maybe I spilled the beans."

"She's pregnant again?" George asked.

"I presumed she told you."

The color left George's face. "Can you watch this baby until I get back?"

———

Kate made the trek to her parents' home again, but this time she was in pain. She stopped on the sidewalk and doubled over.

"Are you all right, lady?" a man asked.

She dropped to her knees on the brick. Several more people gathered around her. A woman in her midthirties knelt down next to Kate.

"I need a doctor." Kate turned, still gripping her stomach. She pulled her knees up. A man ran down the street and hailed a policeman on horseback.

By the time he arrived, two men had lifted Kate into the back of a wagon. The woman who had knelt down next to her climbed aboard and cradled Kate's head in her lap. The policeman escorted the wagon two miles to the new Johns Hopkins Hospital on Wolfe Street, and although the driver maintained a steady pace, the trip over brick and rutted streets jostled her up and down. She moaned.

———

"I'm sorry, Mrs. Ruth." the doctor said. "We're not able to save the baby."

Kate lay in a pale green hospital room. Nurses were uniformed in white dresses, long white stockings, and caps with bands around them that reminded George of the sailors that hung out at the bar. The sterile smell of the place was nauseating and etherlike, and the place was quieter than a church.

George squeezed his hat in his hands. He walked slowly. He looked over the room and couldn't see her. A nurse came up behind him and pointed to a bed in the corner. As if she felt his presence, Kate rolled over and faced him. Her eyes were glazed and red, her expression blank, her lips dry and cracked.

"I came as soon as I heard," George said. He knelt down next to her low bed.

"Where's little George?"

"With Minnie," he said.

"I don't hate little George," Kate said. "I'm just jealous and angry and hurt that I can't have a baby like him."

"Don't worry about it," George said.

Her lower lip puffed up and her eyes narrowed as if she was going to cry, but no tears were shed. "I wanted a baby of our own."

"We'll keep trying, and if we never have a baby, I'll still love you."

150

———•———

George sat at an empty table in his father-in-law's empty bar. Late-morning sunlight lit the room enough for him to read. He unfolded the newspaper, page by page, and read the headlines, stopping to read a couple of stories. Then he turned to the back page. Next to the obituaries was a story about a woman found floating facedown in the harbor. Her body was bruised—beaten and thrown in the water. Authorities identified her from an engraving on a locket she'd worn.

George skimmed through the rest of the article, then rolled up the newspaper and gazed out a window. Suddenly, he popped up and ran upstairs.

"Kate." He hopped up a couple of more stairs to the top landing. "Kate, what was Hannah's last name?"

Kate sat in their only upholstered chair and looked up from her darning. Little George crawled on the floor and played with wooden blocks.

"Tell me you're kidding," she said.

"Was it Wilhart?"

"George, do you know how disgusting that is?"

He panted from the quick climb. "Was it?"

"You didn't even know her last name?"

"She was *your* friend," he said.

"For God's sake, George." She shook her head. "Yes, it was Wilhart."

CHAPTER TWENTY-FIVE

They walked out of the police station and into the parking lot. Cammie opened her car door while Darwin continued to his sports car.

"I've got to get back to the office." He glanced at his watch.

"I don't feel safe going back to the house," she said.

"Meet me at my place. Go there now, if you want."

"I don't have a key."

He told her the numbers to his security code, ducked into his car, and sped away.

At 7:30 p.m., he brought home Chinese food: fried rice, General Tso's chicken, chow mein, and noodles. He put the white cartons on the table and tossed her one of two fortune cookies.

"You didn't bring hot tea?"

"Didn't think about it," Darwin said.

"Next time, remember. You didn't bring chop sticks either."

"Didn't think about them." He used a stainless steel fork to shovel limp noodles into his mouth. "You hear anything from Detective Wilson?"

"I thought I'd give him a day or two. He's got to be more suspicious with Sammy gone."

Cammie got up and walked into the kitchen. She filled two glasses with ice and tap water and brought them back to the dinette table.

"I'm sorry if I embarrassed you," she said. "The detectives obviously knew I stayed overnight."

"I don't care about that," Darwin said.

"You acted like you did."

"I don't want it getting back to my office."

"Because I'm black?"

"My boss has been getting on me about not billing you. He's got an idea I'm spending more time with you than I'm reporting."

They sat silently for a while, then Cammie said, "Does it bother you that I'm black?"

"You're not that dark."

"Darwin, honey, I'm black." She grinned. "If I were a guy, I wouldn't have been able to play Major League Baseball when my uncle did, and I would have been a slave before the Civil War."

"I don't think of you as black."

"So, there's something wrong with being black?"

"I didn't say that either."

"I can't help but be sensitive about it."

"Don't be."

"It's all right. It's not like I turned black yesterday."

"I never thought about it."

"You didn't notice?"

"Sure I did."

"I don't know that much about you, but you look like a spoiled rich kid from the suburbs. You never dated a black girl, did you?"

"You're right about that," Darwin said.

"What would your parents think?"

"They'd be shocked but not upset." He thought back to his teenage days. Every night his family had eaten dinner at the same time. His mom was a full-time homemaker and fixed a warm meal and had it ready promptly at six o'clock. There had been a rhythm to his family's meals, and a sound: the hush before grace, a sudden rush of voices, the clanging of dinnerware, then more silence right before his father began his routine queries. The questions rarely changed, and he couldn't remember them ever addressing racial matters.

"Billy, how was practice? Darwin, did your car run all right? Kelly, did that boy at school quit bothering you? Susie, did you take your puppy to show-and-tell? Marian, did you play bridge, and was that nosy new neighbor lady there?"

Order had always been part of Darwin's life. Spirituality and Darwin's attendance at Good Shepherd Catholic Church became an integral part of his life back then. He felt guilty if he didn't get an A in each course or if he wasn't home before midnight on a weekend evening. After he graduated from Shawnee Mission North High, he didn't think about doing anything other than what his parents wanted, so he prepared to be a lawyer like his uncle in Chicago.

He'd only had two girlfriends, April and Melanie. April was a long-haired redhead and his high school sweetheart. He received a "Dear John" letter from her in the autumn of his sophomore year in college and was crushed until he met Melanie, a blond Dartmouth coed from a wealthy family in Poughkeepsie. There were few African American students at Dartmouth.

"I haven't been around many black people," he said, "at least not in a close way. But I'm not embarrassed about being with you. I wouldn't want my office to know about us, regardless of your race. It's a professional thing. I'm not supposed to fall for clients."

"I was afraid you were just a horny white boy that had a chance to hop in the sack with an easy black girl."

"You're not easy," Darwin said.

"I probably seem like it," Cammie said.

"I don't want to talk about this anymore."

"I don't want you sleeping with me for the wrong reasons."

"Is this discussion about race or sex?" he asked.

"I'm sensitive about both."

———

Cammie fixed Darwin breakfast again. She poured orange juice and coffee and made him toast.

"I think I should go back to the house tonight," she said. "I've been here too long."

"I'm getting used to it."

"Wilson was probably right. I was probably overreacting."

"Maybe whoever threatened you thinks the threats worked. You haven't done anymore to question your uncle's death."

"I'm going back to the library today," Cammie said. "I spent most of yesterday there. I've been reading up on Ruth and Jackie Robinson."

"Can't you let it go?"

"I loved Uncle Griff. Why would anyone hurt him?" She stared out the window.

Darwin stood up and finished off his coffee. Then he placed his hand on Cammie's shoulder. She gazed up. He bent over to kiss her goodbye. "Be careful."

She stood up and wrapped her arms around him.

———

Darwin checked his messages. No calls. He finished redlining a draft of an employee handbook for Warren Trucking, then reviewed some depositions taken by Flynn regarding a workers' compensation case.

"Darwin?" the receptionist's voice came through his phone set. "That girl, Camille Griffin, called while you were at lunch."

"Any message?"

"I thought it might be personal."

"Why would you think that?" Darwin asked.

"I kind of got the idea you two had become friends. She wants you to call her right away—on her cell."

He dialed her number.

"Somebody broke into my house," Cammie said.

"Are *you* all right?"

"I'm a mess," she said. "They were looking for something."

"A lot of damage?"

"Trashed," she said.

"I'm more concerned about you."

"Can you come over?"

"I'm on my way."

CHAPTER TWENTY-SIX

1902

Kate Ruth tried every way she could to make residing above the bar more tolerable. She moved the bed from the center of the room against the wall to provide more play space for little George. She painted the walls, made new draperies, and borrowed a rug from her father.

Little George was growing bigger, almost seven, and his body seemed to grow faster than his coordination. He was always tearing around a corner and bumping into a person or piece of furniture and breaking vases or keepsakes, slamming doors when Kate was trying to rest, or knocking a plate off the kitchen table. He was perpetually moving, and the apartment was too small. And Kate was pregnant again.

She'd just finished doing the dishes, and her back was aching from standing too long with the added weight of the unborn child. As she walked toward the upholstered chair, she heard feet rushing up the stairway. The door burst open. George darted in. He cackled as he ran from another boy chasing him. He looked back toward the other boy and ran into Kate. His cannonball body brushed her hip and knocked her off her feet. She landed against a kitchen cupboard and flew to the floor. Her head cracked against the baseboard.

Her head pounded, but she held her hands to her stomach and the unborn baby. She didn't want to lose another one. Little George hadn't slowed down. He ran into the bathroom and slammed the door. The other boy, a bit older, stopped and tried to help Kate up.

"Sorry, Mrs. Ruth."

She didn't respond at first. She was groggy. The boy did his best to help her up and onto the edge of the bed.

"*Your* son just about killed me today," Kate said to her husband later. "I hope the baby's not hurt."

"Damn kid. I'll talk to him."

"I don't know what to do about him."

"I've got good news," George said. "The lightning rod business has been so good that I've been able to buy our *own* business," George said.

"You think that's best for our family? Do you want the additional risk?"

"I can't wait," George said, "and we can finally move into a house."

"I don't want to move. Not right now."

"I already took out a loan and put money down on the building."

"We need a building to store lightning rods?"

"It's a bar. It's always been a dream to own my own bar."

Kate glared at him.

"That's selfish. If the lightning rod business is so good, why do you want to open a bar?"

"Everything will be fine," George said. "I hate sales work, and I'll have more time for you and the kids. I won't be away from home at night selling those damn lightning rods."

"No," she said. "You'll be down in the bar, surrounded by drunks. What kind of life is that for the kids?"

"It's best this way. You'll see. We won't have to live above a bar anymore."

"I'm trapped," she said. She turned away and folded her arms. "If it wasn't for the church."

"You'd never make it without me, Kate. What kind of job can a woman get? Besides, who'd take care of the kids?"

"Where's the bar?" Kate asked.

"On West Camden."

"By the waterfront?"

"That's where all the customers are. Dockworkers and sailors spend everything they've got on liquor and broads."

She sobbed. "Booze and loose women. You'll love that, won't you, George?"

"I want to make more money and be with you and the kids more."

"If there's any more women, George, I'll leave you. I promise. I'll go live with Father."

———

Little George tore down the sidewalk with an apple in his hand. He turned the corner and ran into a stout policeman.

"Whoa, son. Where you going so fast?"

"Home," George said. He was dirty. His shirt hung loose and he'd torn the knee of his knickers. He wore no socks, and his shoes were scuffed.

"Where did you get that apple?"

"From the store."

"Did you pay for it?" the cop asked.

"I'm going home to get the money right now."

"I'll go with you and talk to your mom."

"My mom's busy."

"She's not at home?"

"She's working," George said.

The officer walked along West Camden Street with George at his side, but after a half block, the kid dashed away and ran into his parents' bar.

The policeman walked in and approached the bar.

"Can I help you, officer?" Kate Ruth asked from the side. She had her hair in a bun and wore an apron.

"A kid ran in here."

"What did he do now?" she asked.

"I think he stole an apple."

"I'm sorry. I'm his mother."

"Don't worry about it, ma'am. It happens around here. You're George's wife?" the policeman asked. "Where is he?"

"He worked the late shift last night."

The policeman said, "The kid seems pretty street-smart, but he's going to end up in trouble. I thought you should know." The officer left the bar.

Kate walked behind the counter and stooped over. She walked the length of the bar, then stopped and tugged little George out from behind a cooler. "Where's the apple?" she asked.

"What apple?"

"The policeman is looking for you."

"He's a dirty copper and a liar."

"Let's go hear his side of the story." She grabbed his shirt collar and dragged George out from behind the bar. He wiggled and broke away. He ran toward the front door but was blocked by his grandfather, Pius Schamberger, who had just walked in the bar. Pius grabbed his arm.

"What are *you* doing here?" Kate asked.

"Your mother's sick, Kate. You better come over, right away."

———•———

Kate had been working alone, and the place was filling up with thirsty customers. Mugs sat unwashed. Tables were messy with empties, as well as cigarette and cigar stubs. She stood behind the counter with her hands covering her face; she cried. George came into the bar to relieve her.

"Are you all right?"

"Leave me alone," she said.

"Talk to me, honey."

"I can't do it anymore, George. I can't work your bar, feed the kids, have your children, take care of the little bastard, and be your whore." Her voice carried throughout the bar. The customers' eyes were on her.

"Calm down," George said. He stood at her side holding her hand and pulling a chair over for her. She pulled away.

"I can't," she shouted. She grabbed a dirty mug and flung it. Some customers ducked; others raised their arms. The mug exploded against a wall.

George held both hands up.

"Calm down, honey."

"I can't," she said.

He put his arms around her, but she twisted away.

"I hate you, George Ruth, and I hate this bar."

He attempted to restrain her again, but she flailed her arms and screamed until he wrestled her against the wall. The entire room watched in silence.

He bent over and threw his arms around her waist, then picked her up and carried her out the door. He put her down, but she continued to struggle. He pinned her against the wall. Her breathing sped up until she passed out. She dropped to the sidewalk. He ran back into the bar and shouted, "My wife fainted. Does anybody know what to do?"

A sailor rushed forward.

"I might be able to help," he said. They hurried outside. He used his fingers to pry open one of her eyes, then held her wrist and felt her pulse. "I think she'll be all right. She must have hyperventilated."

"What does that mean?" George asked.

"I'm a medical assistant on a ship, not a doctor." Both men waited by her side. George knelt and lifted her head and shoulders.

"I watched her inside," the sailor said. "She's pretty stressed."

"We have a new baby at home. We've lost three."

"She's had four babies die?"

"It's been tough. And we've got a boy at home that's pretty wild. Plus, she's workin' in the bar full time."

Her eyes opened. They were glazed. She closed them again. Her breathing had slowed.

"Maybe you need to hire somebody to help her out at home."

"We don't have the money," George said.

"You better do something."

"That's what her father says. He wants me to get rid of my boy. Take him to an orphanage."

CHAPTER TWENTY-SEVEN

He sped up Prospect and swerved into Cammie's driveway. The bottom of his car scraped the driveway pavement when he zipped up the narrow, steep incline. He stomped on the brake and ran to the back door. He pounded. Nobody answered, but the door swung open.

"They broke the lock," Cammie said. She'd walked up behind him. "The door was wide open."

"Where've you been?"

"In the 'hood," she said. "I was hoping somebody saw something." She walked in the house ahead of Darwin and took a seat. She held up a photograph of LeRoy Griffin. The frame was broken, the glass cracked.

"It was my only picture of him." A sunlike pattern of cracks fanned out from the center.

"We can fix it," Darwin said. "Are *you* all right?"

Cammie stared off silently, then stood up. "Why don't they leave me alone? I'm not a threat to anybody."

"I'm calling Wilson."

"Don't," she said.

"Why not, for God's sake?"

"I got a phone call after I talked with you. I was told not to get the police involved."

"The caller probably *did* all this," Darwin said.

"I think I should listen." She walked into the living room, and Darwin followed. Drawers were pulled out and overturned on the floor. The front glass on a china cabinet was shattered. A dark antique rolltop desk was on its side.

"Any idea what they were looking for?"

"No, I told you."

"Detective Wilson can have this stuff dusted."

She looked up.

"Fingerprinted," he said.

"I'm afraid to get the police involved."

"You'll have to stay at my place."

"I'm staying here," she said.

"I *want* you to."

"It's not necessary," she said. She reached in her purse and pulled out a steel gray pistol. She placed it on the table.

"Where'd you get that?"

"Down the street. Twenty bucks. Now, I hope that son of a bitch comes back."

His cell phone rang and he pulled it out from inside his suit jacket. "I'm at her place now. It's pretty bad." He pressed the call button and put the phone back in his suit pocket. "That was Wilson. He's on his way."

She placed her hands on her hips.

"I'd already called him," Darwin said. "Before I got here."

———————

Wilson and Gilmore walked through the living room, looking at the mess. Wilson had his hands in his pockets. Gilmore pulled plastic gloves from inside his suit coat and slipped them on. He cleared a path and picked up drawers, papers, and broken glass off of the floor and set it all neatly on the dining room table.

"What's this?" Gilmore said.

"It's for protection," Cammie said. She put her gun back in her purse.

"Have you had any training with that thing?" Wilson asked.

"A guy down the street. He said, 'Squeeze, don't pull or yank.'"

"I recommend you give me the gun, Miss Griffin."

"No."

"Is it registered? Do you have a permit?"

"I will," she said.

"Bad things happen when untrained people have firearms."

"Bad things already have."

"I had no idea it would be this bad," Wilson said. "You didn't get mad and do this yourself, did you?"

"Are you crazy?"

"I had to ask," Wilson said. "Any idea who did?"

"The same guy that's been threatening me."

"You sure there's only one?"

"I prefer to think it's a nut rather than a conspiracy."

"That's a word I don't want to hear."

Darwin interrupted. "What's wrong with the word *conspiracy*?

"It usually involves the FBI, and we try to keep them out of local matters. They slow things down. Too many chefs in the kitchen."

"Conspiracies suggest plots that reach across state lines?"

"The FBI doesn't have enough to do," Wilson said. "They try to justify their existence by making things harder than they need to be." He turned to Cammie. "Anything missing, Miss Griffin?"

"I don't know yet. I wish I knew what they were looking for."

"When did this happen?"

Cammie looked at Darwin, then back at Wilson. "I assume last night. I'm not sure."

"You've been staying at Mr. Barney's place."

"Does that have anything to do with the crime?" she asked.

"Just that you weren't here for a while. The more recent the prints, the more likely we'll get good ones."

"It makes a difference?" Darwin said.

"The temperature, humidity, time," Wilson said. "They all make a difference."

Somebody knocked at the front door. Two men with white, knee-length jackets entered and put on plastic gloves. They were part of a mobile forensics lab.

"When you discovered the damage, did you move anything, ma'am?" one asked. He was quick to explain. "It's all right if you did. We just need to know."

"I started to, yes. I tried to pick up that old desk, and I've been holding this photograph."

"Have you ever been fingerprinted?" the technician asked.

"Why?"

"We better do it now."

"You think *I* did this?" Cammie said.

"Not at all, ma'am. But how are we supposed to know if we get a suspicious print or one of yours?"

The guys in the lab coats used flashlights to find fingerprints, then dipped brushes in a fine powder and lightly spread the white dust on the prints. Then they pressed clear tape onto the prints and lifted the residue from the surfaces of items touched. After transferring the tape to white index cards, the technicians made notes and drew pictures by hand on the cards to identify where the prints were found.

While one technician labeled an index card, the other pulled an aerosol can out of a bag and lightly sprayed some papers.

"I picked up most of these papers and stacked them," Cammie said. "Can you get fingerprints from paper?"

"Sometimes," the man said.

Wilson and his partner left, and Darwin and Cammie waited around until the fingerprinting was done.

"I'm getting tired," she said to Darwin. "And stressed."

———

The Lyric Theatre was built in 1926 and was originally designed for opera and vaudeville. Its eighty-foot ceilings, rounded archways, and crystal chandeliers created an air of sophistication and excitement.

Darwin wore a business suit. Vera wore a floor-length purple velvet dress with a long pearl necklace. Her hair was shiny and stiff and sat high on her head.

The kids were dressed up too. Alicia showed off a pink chiffon dress. Robert's hair was jelled. He wore a white shirt and long black pants.

The symphony warmed up. People moved toward their seats under a hum of conversation. Most men wore tuxedos; women dressed in long, formal gowns.

"Darwin, how you doing?" He turned.

"Hey, Bob. I'm fine. I didn't know you would be here."

"I came for the wrestling match," Flynn said. He looked over Darwin's shoulder and made a point of letting him know he was scanning the auditorium. "This is where they're wrestling tonight, isn't it?"

Darwin grinned and Flynn laughed. "Nothing you do surprises me, Bob."

"Who are you with? Introduce me."

"This is Vera, Alicia, and Robert." Vera smiled and nodded. The kids weren't paying attention.

"My first time," Vera said before bending over to speak with her kids.

"Darwin, this is my date, Shelly." Flynn had a blond hanging on his arm. She wore a short red satin dress and a blush to match. She smiled. Flynn leaned toward Darwin.

"Who's the woman and kids? Your client's family?"

"Friends," Darwin said.

"Where's your girlfriend?"

"I'm not sure who you're talking about."

"The dancer," Flynn said. He leaned closer again and out of the corner of his mouth said, "The black chick. This her mother?"

"You mean Ms. Griffin."

"Is she here tonight?"

"Remember," Darwin said, "she's a dancer."

Flynn nodded toward the stage. "Up there?"

CHAPTER TWENTY-EIGHT

1919

A message was taped to George's locker. He climbed a long stairway to the top floor of the redbrick stadium and knocked on the office door.

"I'm the new owner of the Red Sox, Babe."

"We were told about you, Mr. Frazee," George said.

"Call me Harry. Anything good?"

"That you're from New York, that you're a song and dance man."

"I produce Broadway plays, but that's a small part of what I do. I'm an entertainment man. If it makes people clap or cheer, I'm interested in producing it. That's why I invested in baseball."

"I was told you don't know much about the game," George said.

"I know it's in trouble, Babe. Smaller crowds because of the war; we lost a lot of players to the draft and the flu epidemic."

"Why'd you invest in a sport that's losing money?"

"The team was in trouble. It was cheap, and I'm bettin' on the come. I'm hopin' players like you can help turn it around and make it bigger than ever."

"It's only a game."

"Sure it will. The newspapers have been reporting nothing but the war. Now that it's over, people will want to get out again. I intend to promote baseball just like I do Broadway plays, and you're going to be one of my main attractions."

Frazee sat in a leather swivel chair behind his desk. A cloud of smoke hung in the air. The only light shined in from a single window overlooking the playing field. A small lamp with a green lampshade sat on the center edge of the desk. It reminded George of Brother Matthias's office at St. Mary's. But Frazee was a short man, and he smoked a pipe.

"You can start with more money. I want $20,000 this season."

"You've already got a contract," Frazee said. "Anyway, fans aren't coming out to the ballpark like they used to."

"Those that are, come to see me," George said.

"There's complaints that you're not a team player, that you're always bellyachin'."

"I don't like how I'm used. The coach wants me to pitch. The fans want to see me hit home runs."

"That coach just won Boston a World Series. He must be doing something right," Frazee said. "He says you don't listen and you're a loudmouth. He calls you incorrigible."

George stood up to leave. "I don't even know what that means. But I know one thing: I don't *have* to play for the Red Sox."

"I can sell you to another team."

"You wouldn't dare," George said.

"I borrowed a lot of money to buy this team. If fans don't start showing up, I'll have to unload more expensive players to pay off the debt."

"Anything else?"

"Do you have Negro blood?"

"Goddamnit, Frazee." George leaned closer, bracing himself with both hands on Frazee's desktop. "I don't have to listen to crap like that from you or anybody else."

"I was just wondering, Babe. There's been a lot of talk."

"Shove it up your ass," George said.

"Why are you so sensitive about it?" Frazee had a tongue-in-cheek grin and leaned forward with his elbows on the desk.

George grabbed him by his lapels, lifting him out of his chair. "I don't like being called a nigger. That's why." Then he shoved him back in his leather swivel chair.

Frazee straightened his collar and pulled down his tie. He spun slowly in his chair. He relit his pipe, then puffed a couple times and looked out the window onto the playing field. "You can't play for *any* team in this league if you're colored."

George backed off and stood breathing hard. "You son of a bitch."

———

All gates into the ballpark were closed from October through March, except one turnstile that allowed ballplayers, coaches, and the whittled-down administrative staff to come and go to conduct off-season business.

A short, stocky man in a brown suit sat on a cement step outside the main concourse under the Fenway Park grandstands. He wore a tan business hat pinched together in front. A horseracing ticket was stuck in the headband. He thumbed through a newspaper. When George passed him coming out of the stadium, the man hopped up in pursuit.

"Hey, Babe. What's going on?"

"Who are you?"

"Ed Martin, *Boston Globe*."

"You guys ever take a break?" George asked. Martin coughed and bent over at his waist with his hands on his knees.

"Damn it, man. Stay away." George walked faster. The reporter jogged to catch up.

"It's not the flu, Babe. I smoke too much." He opened his suit jacket and pulled out a pack of Camels.

"The whole fuckin' country's sick," George said. "I ain't taking no chances."

"Rumor has it you're going down to Chester, Pennsylvania, to work in a shipyard."

"Not anymore. This damn epidemic is too dangerous. I'm hiding out all winter in my country home. That'll keep the missus happy."

"You think there's going to be a baseball season next year?"

"Ask Frazee," George said, and he kept walking along Jersey Street. "If that greedy bastard doesn't make a million, he'd just as soon keep the game from all the kids in America."

"Can I print that?"

"All I know is I'm not playing next year unless I get paid more."

"Some are saying you don't get along with the coach."

"I'm not pitching next year either," George said.

The reporter rushed along George's side, scratching notes in a spiral notepad. George opened his car door and slid behind the steering wheel.

"One more question, Babe," the reporter said.

"Crank me up," George said as he pulled the clutch open. The reporter walked in front of the car and placed his notepad under his arm. He slipped his pencil behind his ear, bent over, and turned a lever under the radiator. The car rumbled, shook, and vibrated to a hum.

"Hey, Babe," Martin yelled over the car's hood. "What do you think of the rumors about the White Sox throwing the series?"

"It's bullshit," George said.

"Some say the White Sox owner treated them like dirt and they were just getting back at him."

"I don't believe it. Shoeless Joe's a friend of mine. He only knows how to play one way—hard."

———

172

Snow sifted down from a gray sky. He looked out a window onto the frozen pond. The ground was covered with fresh snow, and no footprints had disturbed the picture-perfect setting. George slipped on his boots and buttoned his hunting jacket, then pulled a rifle from the wall.

"I can't sit here any longer," he said. "I'll go crazy."

"If you shoot a turkey, I'll cook him," Helen said.

"Can you cook a neighbor?" he said. "There's getting to be too many of 'em. Pretty soon, I won't be able to hunt at all."

———

He trudged back to the house with three turkeys strung over his shoulder. He stomped his snowy boots and plopped his trophies on the counter next to the kitchen sink. Helen plucked feathers as George pulled his boots off.

"It's nice having you home," she said.

"I'm home half the season."

"You've got games almost every day and you're out late most nights."

"That's the sacrifice we make for living in the country."

"Sometimes I think that's why you wanted to live this far out."

"I like being home," George said, "but I got to answer to coaches and management and the fans and my teammates."

"They're all more important to you than *I* am." Helen had her back turned to him as she continued cleaning the birds. "So are the booze and your nightlife."

George stood up in his stocking feet and pulled off his hunting jacket, then dropped it on the table and moved behind Helen. He wrapped his arms around her and kissed the back of her neck.

"I love you."

"I want you home more. I was thinking we could move some-place closer to the ballpark. Maybe Watertown or Brighton. Or even Brookline."

"I couldn't go out in my backyard and get dinner in Brookline," he said.

"Once the season starts, I never see you."

"It'll be different this year. I promise."

"When does spring training start?" Helen asked.

"Unless Frazee doubles my salary, I'll skip spring training."

"Will they let you play if you do?"

"They need me," George said.

"Don't *you* need them?"

CHAPTER TWENTY-NINE

The lobby of the theater had grown dark. Darwin waited out front.

He buried his hands in his pockets to help ward off the late November chill. He had pulled his suit coat up around his neck, and he shifted from one foot to the other as his breath rose.

He reached inside his pocket and pulled out the cell phone he'd turned off before the performance. He'd missed a call and listened to his voice mail.

"This is Lieutenant Clark Wilson. I got a call from the lab. Miss Griffin was right; the ol' guy—Sammy—*was* smothered."

Darwin listened to the message again, then checked to be sure he kept Wilson's cell number on speed dial.

The lights deep inside the auditorium went off; only a few dim security lights shone. A couple of uniformed guards came outside. One turned to lock the doors while the other one zipped up his jacket.

"I think there's still somebody in there," Darwin said.

"Ain't nobody in there," one guard said.

"My girlfriend's in the dance company." Darwin said. "She hasn't come out yet."

"Must have gone out the stage door. Most of 'em do," the other guard said.

Darwin pulled out his cell phone and dialed her number. No answer. He tried again, and again he heard her recording.

"This is Cammie," the message said. "I'm not using my cell phone right now. Please call me at home."

He trotted down an alley and around to the rear of the building. He banged on the stage door. No one answered. He looked down the street both ways. The only movement came from a car three blocks away and steam rising from a manhole cover. He jogged across the street to the parking garage where Cammie normally parked.

He scanned the first floor of the four-level garage. He couldn't see her car. Only five cars were parked on that level. He ran upstairs, panting. Five or six more cars, including his. Not hers. He leaned forward with his hands on his knees and took several deep breaths, then turned and ran up a cement stairwell to the third level. Her maroon Taurus sat three stalls from the top of the stairs. Her pullover green sweater was wadded in the back seat.

He yanked his cell phone out again. She didn't answer either of her numbers. He moved to a waist-high wall on the perimeter of the garage. A few cars passed along the downtown street below.

A thin woman walked toward the garage, almost a block away. He couldn't see her well. She was on the same side of the street and partially blocked by some trees in the parkway. He ran back downstairs to the main level and out onto the sidewalk. The woman's heels clicked on the pavement as she came closer. He walked out from the garage and she flinched. It wasn't Cammie.

"I'm sorry. I thought you were somebody else," he said.

She gave him a strange look. "Are you looking for a date?"

"I thought you were my girlfriend."

"Are you a policeman?"

"I'm not interested." She wore tight jeans and a furry coat that fell to her waist. She kept walking, turned back, and smiled. Darwin looked up and down the street. "Ma'am," he called out to her.

She stopped and turned around, then put one hand on her hip. "Change your mind?"

"I was wondering. Are there are any late-night diners or restaurants around here that are still open?"

"I can keep you warm."

"Thanks, but I'm looking for somebody."

"You don't need anybody else, honey," she said.

———•———

Darwin moved back inside the garage and up to his car. He got in and sped away, down Broadway, onto I-35 East, then south on I-70. He tried his cell phone again. Still no answer. He keyed the numbers for the phone at his apartment. No answer there either. He pulled off of the freeway and drove up Prospect Avenue.

The lights at Cammie's house were off. He pulled into her driveway. He jumped out and knocked on her back door. No answer.

He walked back to his car and dialed her number again. No answer. He headed toward his place and called Wilson.

"She told me to wait. I can't find her and she doesn't answer her cell phone."

"I'll call the station," Wilson said, "and see if there's been anything reported. You two didn't have a fight, did you?"

"No. Why?"

"She's not just mad and refusing to answer your call, is she?"

"I wish that was it," Darwin said. "You try calling her."

"I will. I'll call you back after I check with the station."

———•———

His cell phone played "The Star Spangled Banner." He assumed it was Wilson calling back, but Cammie's number showed up on his display.

"Where are you?"

"I'm hurt, Darwin. Come and get me," she said. Her voice trembled. "On Front Street." She gave him instructions.

He raced his car along I-70 to I-35 and headed north toward the river. He pulled off and drove past the casino. Blue and red strobe lights flashed on top of a police car, and an officer stood outside of it, next to Cammie. She sat on an old telephone pole lying on the ground, twenty feet back from the road. Darwin's car slid to a halt on the gravel and sandy dirt along the road. He hopped out.

"Is this him, ma'am?" the policeman asked.

"Are you all right, Cammie? What happened?" Darwin asked. Her right eye was puffy and red. Her lip was split in two places and blood had dried on her chin and under her nose. Her cheekbone was bruised. There was a torn hole in the knee of her black pants. Her arm was scraped raw, and she was holding her elbow.

"Eddie told me you were waiting outside."

"Who is Eddie?" the police officer said.

"He helped me when I was looking for Sammy," she told Darwin.

"He did this, ma'am?" the officer asked.

"Not Eddie. He was backstage. He said you were outside, Darwin. I followed him out back, and somebody smacked me on the side of the head."

"Where's this Eddie character?" the policeman asked.

"I guess he ran away when I got hit," she said.

"Eddie wasn't with the guy that hit you?"

"I don't think so," she said.

"He told you I was waiting outside in the alley?" Darwin asked.

"That's right."

"I don't know Eddie; I've never seen him," Darwin said, "and I sure as heck didn't talk to anybody outside the theater. I was waiting in front."

"Tell us what happened, ma'am," the officer said as another police car pulled up with its overhead lights spinning.

Cammie buried her head in her hands. Darwin sat down on the telephone pole next to her and put his arm around her. She shivered.

"I just want to go home," she said.

"Ma'am," the officer said. "I've got to make out a report, and you need to be checked by a physician."

"I'm fine," she said. She sat in the police cruiser and answered questions. Then Darwin drove her to St. Luke's Hospital. A police car followed. A doctor checked her over, and she limped out of the examination room into the waiting room where Darwin and the officer waited. Detective Wilson walked in.

"You don't look too great," Wilson said.

She glanced up at him, but didn't say anything.

"Apparently, you didn't use that pistol of yours."

"I forgot I had it in my purse."

"You better not go home tonight," Wilson said.

"I'm taking her with me," Darwin said.

"Do you believe me now, Lieutenant?" she asked. "They told me to shut up and let it be."

"I believe you, honey," Wilson said.

"They said, 'Next time we'll *accidentally* break your leg.' Do you know what I do for a living?"

CHAPTER THIRTY

George's spindlelike legs moved with short, stiff strides around the bases. No other player had ever hit as many home runs as he did in 1919, and he was just twenty-six. He and many other ballplayers assumed the following season would never be played because the game had taken such a hit during the war and flu epidemic. After the last game, George left a handwritten note on top of a bundle of Red Sox uniforms outside Harry Frazee's office door.

"Babe, I'd like to talk to you," Frazee said. George had walked away and was halfway down the stairway. He turned and looked back up at Frazee.

"About my salary?" Frazee motioned, and George retraced his steps upstairs to the owner's office.

"I can't afford to pay you more," Frazee said. "The team lost money this year. I'd like you to be patient."

"I'm going barnstorming this fall, and I'll play all winter in California. I make more money in the off-season than I do working for the Red Sox."

George and Helen rented a luxury bungalow behind a swank hotel in rural Beverly Hills. When George came back to the hotel early one evening, they took a taxi into Hollywood and ate outside on a small restaurant patio.

"I never thought I'd get tired of a swimming pool," she said. "While you're gallivanting around, I get lonely."

"Relax, honey. You're on vacation."

"I get bored."

"Go to the beach," George said. "Go shopping."

"Hollywood's six miles away—down a dusty desert road. Los Angeles is farther, and it's hot, and there's nothing there." Helen shook her head. "And how am I supposed to get around?" She crossed her arms. "I'm surrounded by bean fields."

"Would you rather be back in Watertown?"

"I want you to come back to the hotel at night."

"They pay me too much," George said. "I got to stick around and sign autographs and chat with the fans, and it's too late and too far to travel back to the hotel every night."

"Then I'm going with you."

"You'd get more bored and hot sitting on bleachers all day," he said.

"You want me here. You drink and carouse all night. I know you do."

"I'm scheduled here for another month."

"We've been here a month already," she said, "and you've only been with me a couple of nights."

"I'm going to meet with Jack Dempsey tomorrow. Do you know what that means?"

"Another night of booze?"

"He invited me to his home," George said. "He said I can fight him. What would fancy-pants Frazee think of that?"

Helen's face turned red. She closed her eyes and took a deep breath. "Are you a complete fool?"

"I'd be the underdog," George said. "They'd cheer for me."

"You're such a child—anything to be accepted."

"It's the money," George said.

"You'll humiliate yourself. Maybe end your baseball career."

"I don't plan to lose."

"Let's go, George." Helen stood up.

"I'm not done eating," he said.

"You're gaining weight. What will Mr. Frazee think of that?"

"The hell with Frazee."

———

Both men were in their midfifties and wore dark suits, perfectly pressed. Both had pocket watches with gold chains dangling from their vests, and both owned the New York Yankees. They were sitting together in the Oak Room of the Plaza Hotel. Jake Ruppert and Tillinghast Huston were known as the colonels. Ruppert had earned his title in the New York National Guard but had been born into aristocracy. His family was wealthy and had earned its money in the brewery business. Huston had actually fought in the Spanish-American War, but he was an engineer. And after the war, he'd stayed in Cuba and made a bundle of money leading a project to dredge the harbors of Havana and other neighboring cities.

Dark wood contrasted with the light gray smoke rising from the many cigars and pipes in the room.

"He'll be here any minute," Huston said.

"I'm against it," Ruppert said in a Germanic accent. "How do you know him?"

"He's a New Yorker. You'll recognize him when you see him. He makes the circuit of local bars and restaurants."

"I don't understand why he owns the Red Sox," Ruppert said.

"We wanted the Giants and ended up with the Yankees. He's a promoter: prizefights, tours, and Broadway plays. He probably got a good bargain."

Frazee walked into the Oak Room carrying a thin cane with an arched silver handle. White spats covered all but the tips of his shiny black shoes. He had a gold pocket watch too and wore lamb-chop sideburns low on the side of his red cheeks.

"Harry, meet Jake Ruppert." They shook hands, and the three of them moved to a round table.

"Three weeks left before Prohibition," Ruppert said. "Can we buy you a scotch, Harry?"

"I would feel honored, gentlemen."

"Why in hell do you want to get rid of Ruth?"

"He doesn't get along with my coach," Frazee said.

"It would be less expensive to get rid of the coach," Ruppert said.

"Babe doesn't get along with me either," Frazee said. Then he shrugged. "I'm short of funds, and I still carry debt from buying the team. I need cash."

"Harry's got a girlfriend," Huston said. "Louise Groody."

"The Broadway singer?" Ruppert asked. Frazee blushed.

"He cares more about Broadway than baseball," Huston said.

"I'm turning a play into a musical," Frazee said. "I'd also like a loan to help with that."

"Miss Groody going to be in it?"

Frazee blushed again.

"You're thinking with your heart, Harry." Ruppert said as he lit up his pipe. "How much?"

"$125,000 plus a $300,000 loan."

"That's twice what anybody ever spent for a ballplayer." Ruppert blew smoke, then ducked his own cloud. "Will you put up Fenway Park as collateral?"

"I'd rather not," Frazee said.

"Coach Huggins wants Ruth, Jake," Huston said.

"He's a smart little guy," Frazee said. "College educated, isn't he?"

"A lawyer," Huston said.

"We better have him speak with Ruth. He's not worth the investment if he won't play for us."

—■—

Huggins stepped off the train at Union Station in downtown Los Angeles. He was only 5'3" and wore a pinstriped blue double-breasted suit, a stiff rounded collar on his white shirt, and a gray business hat. He walked along the platform between trains. Steam from Union Pacific locomotives rose from the tracks and surrounded his feet. When he returned to the main rotunda of the station, a voice called out.

"Hey, midget. Over here."

Huggins walked over to a long wooden bench that looked like a church pew.

"Hello, Babe." The men shook hands. George and a woman next to him remained sitting. "Is this your wife?"

"This is Juanita. My wife went back to Boston."

———•———

He'd met her in El Jardin, the upscale lounge and restaurant. She had raven hair, longer than was customary on the East Coast. He attributed her flowing hairstyle to the loose and out-of-touch California way of life, a lifestyle he favored now that his wife had gone back home.

Her clear skin and long, lean figure gave her the look of a woman in her mid-to-late twenties. Her brown eyes and soft Mexican skin tone highlighted the white of her dress and clear eyes. Embroidered red roses covered her tight dress and matched the real one stuck in her hair above an ear. She dipped her chin and turned slightly to the side, not looking directly into anyone's eyes. And she batted her own in an effortless way.

She had been the only female in the lounge filled with men in posh suits, sport jackets, or flowery silk shirts. No less than three men surrounded her at any time, and rambunctious George Ruth sat quietly, as if in awe of her grace, or intimidated by the many surrounding her.

Then, suddenly, as if the room were vacant except for her, he stood and walked a straight line to her.

"I'm George." He stared at her, and other men backed away. He stepped forward. "You're beautiful."

"Como se dice?" she asked.

"George."

She had a Hispanic dialect like the maids who had cleaned his bungalow. It was a distinctive dialect, one he'd not heard in baseball, one not prevalent in the Baltimore or Boston.

"What's your name?"

"Juanita Jennings."

"Do you work here?"

"En el cine," she said.

"In the movies?"

"Si."

"I guess you don't need to talk in movies."

"No, señor." She smiled and her bright teeth glowed.

"You want to come to my bungalow?"

She tilted her head slightly. "No comprendo."

"My little house out back?" he explained.

"Su casa?"

"I guess that's what you call it in Mexican."

"No." She shook her head and blushed.

"Can I buy you a drink?" He raised his hand. "Hey barkeep, another drink for the lady."

A balding man in a white shirt and bow tie behind the counter motioned and mouthed the words, "What does she want?"

"Hell, I don't know. Whatever Mexican broads drink."

George grabbed Juanita's hand and pulled her behind him through the crowd. She took short, quick steps in strapped heels.

Three men had taken his table and were eating peanuts and drinking highballs, so he turned back, still holding onto Juanita, and passed through a glass door outside and onto a brick patio.

They sat on a stone step under a canopy stretching out from the building's roofline. A red clay fountain sprayed water into the air in the center of a small courtyard.

"I'm a famous baseball player, honey."

"Beisbol? We play en Mejico."

"What did *you* do in Mexico?"

The bartender walked out onto the patio, wearing a green apron, wiping one hand on it as he handed George a drink glass half full of yellow liquid. George gave it to Juanita.

"What is it?" George asked.

"Tequila and orange juice," the bartender said, "for the señorita."

She blushed as he handed it to her.

"Enjoy it, ma'am, it'll be the last alcoholic drink you'll ever have at the Beverly Hills Hotel."

"Hey Mack, you shuttin' her off?" George asked.

"You too, Babe. Tomorrow's the 16th—Prohibition."

"I forgot about that. Damn feds," George said. "Can I buy a couple bottles of scotch for my bungalow?"

"As long as we deliver before midnight. Anything else?"

"How 'bout some tequila and a pitcher of orange juice for the señorita?"

CHAPTER THIRTY-ONE

She sat in a nightgown and folded her legs up underneath her. She rested her elbow on the arm of the sofa and stared out the window onto the hazy morning skyline. Darwin wore his business suit and walked into the living room behind her.

"Are you going to be all right?" he asked.

She didn't turn or say anything.

He put his hands on her shoulders and bent down to kiss the nape of her neck. She reached down and picked up a cup of coffee, took a sip. "I'll be here until I go to dance practice."

"Are you stiff? You going to be able to move well enough?"

"I have to," she said. "*The Nutcracker's* coming up."

"I can come home to take you to practice."

"I'll get a ride from one of the other dancers."

He started for the door, then turned slowly.

"I'm worried about you," he said.

"Don't be."

"You're so quiet."

"Next time I'll be ready. I've got a gun."

"You had it last time."

"In my purse. From now on I'll carry it around my neck and have my hand on it anytime I'm alone and going somewhere." She finally turned and looked at him. "I'm not afraid. Really. I'm just trying to figure out the Babe Ruth connection."

"We've probably spent too much time researching him rather than your uncle."

"That's a good point," she said. She flashed a smile. "Go on now. I'll be fine."

"Call me." He walked out the front door. She got up and turned the dead bolt behind him, then sat back down and stared out the window again.

Her cell phone rang, and she followed the sound to her purse.

"Good morning, Miss Griffin," Lieutenant Wilson said. "There's no Eddie living in the apartment complex. Is that a nickname?"

"I don't know," she said.

"We checked for Eddie, Edward, Ed, and even anything that sounded like it. There's a Fred, but he's sixty-eight years old and lives with his wife."

"It's Eddie. I'm sure of it."

"Can I come over and talk with you?" Wilson said.

"I'm at Darwin's place."

"I know."

———————

Lieutenant Wilson pulled open the passenger door of his unmarked police car. Cammie got out and looked up and down 18th Street. They entered the foyer of the Negro Leagues Baseball Museum. A woman sat at the front desk.

"Good morning, ma'am," Wilson said. "Do you know Eddie?"

"I don't know anybody named Eddie."

Wilson showed his ID and said, "Can you direct us to the person in charge of the museum?"

"That's Mr. Kendrick."

A tall black man in a suit walked out front.

"I don't know anybody around here named Eddie. There've been a few Eddies that played ball in the Negro leagues."

"We're looking for a younger guy, one that might have been involved recently in some way with Sammy Haynes."

"That was sad, wasn't it?" Kendrick said. "Sammy was one of the last. There aren't many players from the Negro leagues still alive." He shook his head. "No, I don't know anyone named Eddie. I recommend you check down at the Peach Tree."

"Mr. Kendrick, what do you know about Babe Ruth?" Cammie said.

"He was a great ballplayer."

"Was he a black man?"

He grinned. "There was a lot of talk about that back in his early years. Quite a few players in the Negro Leagues thought he was, but there was never any proof, and whites wouldn't hear of it. He was too big, too great. So the notion was lost in time. Back then, before Jackie and civil rights, the black man didn't have a voice."

———

They walked east on 18th and into the offices of the apartment complex on Woodland Avenue. The manager came to the front desk. He was a black man, about fifty-five or sixty. He had a pot-belly and wore suspenders and a long-sleeved button-down shirt.

"I don't know who you're talking about," the manager said.

"He said his name was Eddie," Cammie said.

"A lot of people hang out around here: visitors, tourists, and all. Gets pretty wild some weekends with the jazz museum and restaurants around the corner. But I can't think of anybody named Eddie. I've looked through our resident list. What did he look like?"

"He was thin," she said. "Probably 5'8". He had a thin mustache, more like he hadn't shaved in awhile. He smiled a lot."

"How old was he?" the manager asked.

"Probably twenty-eight to thirty."

"That fits a lot of people. Any tattoos? A lot of people wear tattoos these days."

"None I saw," she said. Cammie turned and wandered up by the apartment where Sammy died. Wilson and the manager followed. "He came up the sidewalk from that way. I assumed he lived there."

"That's Earl and Delores Greene's apartment there, and that's Michael Thompson's place. Around the corner is Jerome Stevens's and Belinda Southwell's."

"Earl Greene," Wilson said. "What's his age?"

"Probably sixty-six to sixty-eight."

"What about Thompson and Stevens?" Wilson asked.

"Thompson's probably forty, and chubby. Stevens is tall. He played basketball for UMKC." The manager rubbed his chin. "I can't figure out who it would be."

"What about *your* relatives?" Wilson asked. "Any sons, son-in-laws, cousins, or anybody else that might meet the description?"

"Got three sons. None of 'em in KC."

"Any of them been around lately?"

"Not since last July. And none of 'em named Eddie."

Wilson and Cammie walked down 18th Street toward Wilson's unmarked navy Pontiac. Cammie moved slowly, with a perceptible limp.

"Can you make it to the Peach Tree?" Wilson asked.

"I'm a bit sore," Cammie said, "but I'm determined to find Eddie."

———

The Peach Tree Café was a block away. Astra sat on the same chair at the counter she'd occupied before. She turned slowly when they came through the front door. "Hello, Cammie." She stood up and opened her arms. "It's so good to see you, honey."

Cammie smiled as Astra hugged her. "This is Lieutenant Wilson."

Wilson reached forward to shake her hand as she said, "Am I in trouble?"

"It's about Sammy," Cammie said.

"Ain't it just horrible? First your uncle; now Sammy."

"Some think there might have been a connection," Cammie said. "Sammy was smothered."

"Murdered?" Astra asked.

"Let's just say the death was abnormal," Wilson said. "Do you know anybody named Eddie?"

"Sure do. My Uncle Eddie."

"Does he hang out around here?"

"Hell no," Astra said. "He's older than dirt. He ain't been out of his rocker in fifteen years, and he lives in Arkansas."

"A young black man has been seen in this neighborhood. A small guy, kind of wiry. He told Miss Griffin his name's Eddie."

"You met this guy?" Astra asked Cammie.

"He was nice to me. He said he lived up on Woodland in the same complex where Sammy did."

"And he killed *our* Sammy?" She lowered her brow.

"He's merely a person of interest," Wilson said. "We want to talk to him."

"You got a picture?" Astra asked.

Cammie described him in detail.

"I ain't seen nobody like that. Least that I remember."

Wilson handed one of his cards to Astra. "Keep this in the cash register," he said. "If a guy like Miss Griffin described comes around here, or you hear anyone talk about him, phone me."

CHAPTER THIRTY-TWO

1920

A line of luxury vehicles waited to unload celebrities—one car at a time, each car a showpiece: Crossleys, several Ford Touring Cars, a Packard Roadster, a Cleveland Roadster, a Mercer two-seater, a Studebaker Special-Six, several Pierce-Arrows, and a Cadillac Limousine.

The cars pulled gradually up the long, winding driveway, and silver-screen stars and starlets emerged one at a time. Famous actors in tuxedos served primarily as attendants to actresses wearing black velvet and crepe, crimson charmeuse, and beige satin. Their dresses rose six inches above their ankles and were heavily laden with brocade, taffeta, or lace and had hip sashes of wide ribbon, tulle, and net.

The fashion procession ascended the magnificent limestone steps of a copper-roofed Tudor mansion.

George wore a rented tux and had driven a rented Packard Roadster. He walked around to the other side of the car, tugging at the stiff white collar snug around his thick neck. He opened the door and offered his arm. Juanita emerged from the passenger side like a flower unfolding in time-lapse photography. A glow from inside the country estate brushed her face and bare shoulders, highlighting her golden brown skin. She smiled and moved smoothly, comfortably.

A tall, slender gentleman with a perfect thin mustache stood on the stone terrace. A smiling younger woman stood next to him. Her big round eyes, overly long eyelashes, powdered face, and plastered curls gave her the look of a life-sized porcelain doll.

"Welcome to Pickfair, Mr. Ruth. I'm Douglas Fairbanks."

"Wouldn't miss it for nothin'." He glanced up at the tall green gables. "Nice shack." Fairbanks grinned and placed one hand on George's shoulder and shook his hand with the other.

"A year ago, this was a hunting lodge. It's not quite done yet." Fairbanks turned to Juanita and bowed his head ever so slightly. "I'm glad you came, darling. I'm honored and hope you'll christen our home for all of Mexico."

"Gracias," Juanita said.

"You met Juanita before?" George asked.

"She's a Mexican beauty," Fairbanks said. He turned to the cherub-faced doll next to him. "Darling, this is Juanita Elias. Her father's the Secretary of Commerce in Mexico. She's one of our next screen stars. Juanita, this is Mary Pickford."

Juanita leaned forward and touched Miss Pickford's cheek with her own, then repeated the gesture on the other side. In the foyer, George leaned toward Juanita.

"I thought your name was Jennings."

"Me llamo—como se dice—stage,'" she said. "Stage name."

A six-member jazz band in the corner played "I'm Always Chasing Rainbows." The large room had a wooden floor, and the furniture had been moved to the outer edges, leaving an ample area for dancing. But the guests had not loosened up yet. They were drinking, and four or five servers with short white jackets carried trays with champagne and weaved through the celebrity crowd. A table along one wall had fifty or sixty green bottles with yellow labels that read "Dewar's Scotch." A bartender poured liquor onto ice in glasses lined in four or five rows, each eight or ten deep. Pitchers of water sat on the end of the table.

At least one hundred people filled the room and sprawled along a wide stairway, looking down. Music blared and voices hummed. People laughed and occasionally called out to others. An older man with eyeglasses and long, thinning black hair combed straight back stood halfway up the staircase. His eyes met George's, and he and his female companion moved down toward George and Juanita.

"Hey Babe, I'm Fred Niblo. This is my wife, Enid. I hear you might want to be in the movies."

"Are you an actor?" George asked.

"I just directed Doug in *Mark of Zorro*."

"I oughta see that one."

"Seen many of Doug's or Mary's pictures?" Niblo asked.

"I don't go to movies much," George said, "because of my eyes. I got to take care of 'em."

"You think you can act?"

"I'll play myself in a movie next summer," George said.

"Here's my card. Get ahold of me," Niblo said. "You know any of these people?"

"It's my first trip to California."

"There's Noah Beery and Claire McDowell. That's Constance Talmadge over there. And Buster Keaton; you've heard of him."

"I've seen posters, but I didn't recognize him without his hat," George said. "Is that little thing over there in movies?"

"That's Gloria Swanson," Niblo said. "She looks taller on screen." Niblo took a swig of his drink. "There's Harold Lloyd—another comedian—and two industry gods: Charlie Chaplin and the director D. W. Griffith."

Fairbanks and Mary Pickford strolled by, arm in arm. He maintained his perfect posture and puffed a pipe. Ms. Pickford smiled and batted her eyelids.

"Mr. Fairbanks," George said. "Where'd you get all the liquor?"

"You're from Boston. So is he." Fairbanks motioned toward a tall, slender man in round glasses who stood in the corner next to Gloria Swanson. She leaned against the same wall, gazing at him.

"Is he an actor?" George asked.

"He wants to be a producer. He seems to have a lot of connections and does a little bit of everything, including getting our booze."

"I don't recognize him."

"I'll introduce you," Fairbanks said. They started walking. Juanita tagged along. Mary Pickford came too, still hooked onto Fairbanks' arm. "He claims he's a banker. Seems to be a real wheeler-dealer. Supposedly, his wife's dad was mayor of Boston. His family was in the liquor business; that's how we got the booze."

"Hey Joe, I want to introduce you to Babe Ruth," Fairbanks said. Gloria Swanson smiled, sipped her drink, then slinked away without saying anything.

"I actually met you before, Babe," the impeccably dressed man said. He had a distinctive Bostonian accent.

"I'm not good at remembering names and faces."

They shook hands. "I'm Joe Kennedy."

"Glad to meet you, Kennedy," George said. "I think you and me are the only ones here that aren't famous movie people."

———

George's debonair maroon sweater-vest went well with his flashy white flannel knickers and matched the three-inch-tall diamonds on his maroon-and-yellow knee-high stockings. He loved playing golf, and that's what he did while the rest of his

Yankee teammates attended the first day of spring training in Jacksonville.

He smoked a fat stogy and tipped his flat golf cap back on his head so his black, shiny hair curled over his forehead. He completed all eighteen holes before having dinner in the clubhouse with the rest of his foursome.

"Didn't you have practice today?" one of the golfers asked.

George didn't look up as he sawed his steak, then gored it with a fork and stuffed it into his mouth.

"It was optional," George said.

"All the other Yankees went?"

"Optional for me."

"Huggins gave you the day off?"

"I needed to get accustomed to the warm weather," George said. "And I don't need as much time as the rest of the fellas to get ready for the season."

———

Coach Huggins gathered the players and explained the day's routine, then sent them to their various workout stations.

"Ruth, I want to talk to you," he said.

George put his hands on his hips and tucked his ball glove under his armpit. He pulled his baseball cap off and wiped his forehead with the forearm of his shirt liner.

"What ya want, flea?"

"I really don't care what you think of me, as long as you follow team rules and do your job. You act like you think you're better than other players, better than me, and like you're not serious about the game."

"I *am* better than them," George said. "And it's still a game, ain't it? Ain't it supposed to be fun?"

"You're overweight, Babe."

"That's what spring training's for."

"Most players show up in shape," Huggins said.

"I wanted to make the trip worthwhile. So I waited till I got here. Come April 1, I'll be ready."

"What were you doing out late last night, Babe? That's no way to get in shape. What kind of lesson is that for the others?"

"That's how I get in shape." George grinned. "Anyway, you haven't set a curfew."

"I want to treat the players like adults. If I respect them, maybe they'll respect me."

"Respect? I thought you wanted home runs."

"I'm going to invite your wife down so you get some sleep and live a more normal lifestyle."

"Don't you dare," George said.

"You're acting like a big kid."

"Maybe I never had a chance to be one. You ever live in a reform school?"

———

The Yankees played in Chicago against the White Sox at Comiskey Park, and George had just taken batting practice before the game. He was walking back to the Yankee dugout.

"Nice hittin', Babe." Shoeless Joe Jackson stood with his legs crossed and his ball cap pulled down low over his brow.

"Hey Joe. How ya doin'?" Jackson had wandered over and stood at the on-deck circle just outside the Yankee dugout.

"Not so good," Jackson said, "with all the rumors."

"You didn't do it, did ya?"

"Me, cheat?"

"I didn't think so," George said.

"I ain't s'pose to talk about it. My lawyer says," Jackson said. "There's talk 'bout throwing us out of baseball."

"That wouldn't be right."

"You're doin' good, Babe," Jackson said. "Hittin' all those long shots."

"A lot of it's because of the new rules. Plus, the balls are wound tighter."

"Not for the rest of us," Jackson said.

"You're still the best, Joe."

"It's changing, thanks to you." Jackson looked down and kicked the dirt.

"You gonna be all right, Joe?" Babe patted his shoulder.

"I love the game, Babe. I don't know what I'll do if I can't play anymore." Jackson bit his lower lip. "It's all I think about."

"Hang in there, pal."

———

He stood in front of the long mirror over a row of sinks. Players walked behind him bare-chested with towels wrapped around their waists as he combed his hair. Then, he grabbed his own towel, wiped his face, and strolled back to his locker. He sat on a small stool, loading his duffel bag, when Coach Huggins tapped him on the shoulder and handed him a telegram envelope. George folded it over and stuffed it in his back pocket.

When he returned to his hotel room, he reached for his billfold and pulled out the telegram too. He tore it open and studied the message, then walked down to the lobby. He waved a bellman over and showed him the message.

"Anybody around here speak Mexican?" he asked.

"Take it to the concierge."

He grabbed a copy of the *Chicago Tribune* from the front counter and walked to a woman sitting at a desk in another part of the lobby.

"I need help with this telegram," he said.

"Have a seat." She grabbed the message. "I'll be right back." He sat in an armchair, stuck an unlit cigar in his mouth, and scanned his newspaper. He crossed his legs and opened the *Tribune*, skipping to the sports section.

The lead article read, "Grand Jury Investigates White Sox Players." He read the first few paragraphs. The grand jury planned to probe an allegation by a New York Giants player that four White Sox players had colluded to fix the 1919 World Series. He was pleased to see Joe Jackson's name wasn't one of those mentioned. He had his head buried in the newspaper when the concierge returned.

"You're Babe Ruth, aren't you?" she asked, taking her seat.

"That's me." He moved his cigar from one side of his mouth to the other. "What's your name, honey?"

"Who's George?"

He pulled the cigar from his mouth, smiled. "That's my real name."

"Congratulations, Mr. Ruth. You have a new baby daughter. Her name's Dorothea. "

The cigar drooped from the corner of his mouth.

"Mr. Ruth?"

"The Mexican broad," he said.

The concierge said, "The message is from Juanita Jennings."

"I could read that much."

CHAPTER THIRTY-THREE

Cammie's eyes roamed from face to face, but no one looked up at her. The room was quiet except for the occasional sound of serving spoons meeting china as food was passed. Eight people sat at the formal dining room table, three on each side, with Darwin's parents at each end. Voices were low, almost whispering, and came from those asking for the food.

A sixteen-pound turkey sat in the center of the table with more food than twice that many could eat: scalloped corn, mashed potatoes, gravy, homemade bread, cranberry slices, a fresh-fruit salad, a punch bowl full of Romaine lettuce, and a tray of cut vegetables along with dips and warm, creamy sauces, all spread over a formal white linen tablecloth.

Darwin's mother was tall and thin with shoulder-length dish-water blonde hair marked by occasional strands of gray.

"Michele, will you say grace?"

Darwin's seventeen-year-old sister recited a short prayer; it was followed by a silence that seemed loud and awkward to him compared with the conversations that usually crisscrossed over the table.

"Marian, do we have any butter for the bread?" Darwin's father asked. He was 6'2" with a receding hairline. He wore glasses.

Darwin's mother pushed her seat back. "I forgot it."

"I'll get it, mom," Kelly, another one of Darwin's sisters, said and stood quickly and walked into the kitchen. She was twenty-one and home from college.

The other three at the table were Darwin's younger brother, sixteen-year-old Billy, his younger sister Susie, a nineteen-year-old, also home from college, and Cammie.

"Darwin tells me you're a dancer," his mother said. "Is that a hobby or a career?"

"Dancing is my job, ma'am."

"Wonderful."

"You're a dancer?" Billy asked. "Like in a nightclub?"

"No." Darwin said. "She's with the Kansas City Ballet. She dances to the symphony. Maybe when you grow up and experience some culture, you'll have an opportunity to see her. Of course, you'd probably have to wear something other than jeans and a T-shirt to get in."

"Hey, mom said this would be all right," Billy said. "I didn't know we were having company."

"How long have you two been dating?" Kelly asked.

"They're not dating," Darwin's dad said.

"Actually, we are, Dad."

Cammie grinned.

"I thought she was a client," Mr. Barney said.

"That's how we met."

"Doesn't that cross the line?"

"The professional line, Mr. Barney?" Cammie said. "Or the color line?"

"I'm sorry, dear," Darwin's father said. "I didn't mean that."

"This is embarrassing," Darwin said. "I wanted Cammie to meet my family. Maybe it was a mistake."

"I didn't mean to suggest anything about color. I was concerned you might get in trouble at the office. You know, for dating a client."

"That's all right, Mr. Barney," said Cammie. "I'm used to it."

"Tell us about your dancing," Darwin's mother said.

"Why don't you come and see?" Cammie said. "We perform *The Nutcracker* starting next week."

"She's Clara," Darwin said.

"Really?" Susie said.

"She's the best dancer."

"Can we get tickets this late?" Darwin's mom asked.

"I'll get you some," Cammie said.

"You don't need to do that."

"I get an allotment, and I don't have anybody to give them to but Darwin."

"Don't you have family in town, dear?"

"I had an uncle, but he died. That's how I met Darwin."

"You didn't grow up around here?" Mr. Barney asked.

"I moved here after I graduated."

"From high school?"

"From dance school," Cammie said.

"You didn't have a chance go to college?"

"Dad," Darwin said, shaking his head. "She graduated from UC-Berkeley and went to Julliard."

Susie sat forward with her elbow on the table and rested her chin on her fist. "I've never met anybody that went to Julliard." She turned to her father. "That's the Harvard of fine arts."

"I know what Julliard is," he said. "More turkey, anybody?"

———

The fireplace crackled. Shadows danced on the opposite wall. Mr. Barney crossed his legs and tasted his clear German wine. He sat in a beige stuffed chair. His wife sat in a matching one on the opposite end of the hearth. Cammie and Darwin sat next to each other on the sofa. She reached for his hand and held it on her thigh. Marian Barney smiled.

"I'm sorry, Cammie," Mr. Barney said.

"There's nothing to apologize for."

"I guess I wasn't ready for Darwin bringing a black girl home, but I know better."

"Blame it on Babe Ruth," Cammie said.

"You're the one? Darwin told me a client thought Babe Ruth was black. I hadn't put two and two together."

"Actually, my Uncle Griff *was*," Cammie said.

"Her uncle played for the Monarchs," Darwin said.

"So did Jackie Robinson," Mr. Barney said. "Wouldn't it have been difficult for Ruth to play for the Yankees—when blacks weren't allowed?"

"He meant too much to the game," Darwin said. "They needed him after the Black Sox scandal almost ruined the game."

"They?"

"The owners. The commissioner. The media. The fans," Darwin said. "He was what Michael Jordan was to basketball. He saved baseball like Muhammad Ali saved boxing."

Darwin's dad sat back in his chair.

"After you mentioned it, I saw a picture of Ruth. He looks black." Mr. Barney said. "Am I making a fool of myself again?"

"No need to be politically correct around me," Cammie said.

"He had more Negro features than you."

"Except for color," Cammie said.

"He was pretty dark."

"All games were played during the daytime," Darwin said. "No lights. They probably assumed he was suntanned. To a large degree, he probably was."

"That didn't account for his nose and lips," Cammie said.

"That's probably *not* politically correct," Darwin's dad said.

"*I* can get away with it."

"How about his kids?" Marian Barney asked.

"He only had one," Darwin said, "and she was adopted."

"Wasn't that convenient?" Mr. Barney said. "No DNA unless they dig up Ruth."

———

She did a pirouette, then leaped and floated through the air. A pink organdy tutu, pink leotards, and ballet slippers enhanced her sleek elegance. She landed gracefully in the hands of a male dancer.

The audience clapped as the orchestra performed Tchaikovsky's "Dance of the Sugar Plum Fairy." Cammie had a serious, porcelainlike glow on her painted face and turned her head slowly, like a mechanical doll.

Darwin sat forward and clapped. He smiled and turned to his parents. His mother beamed; his father nodded in approval.

The expression on Cammie's face suddenly changed. She glared off the stage. Darwin followed her line of sight to a thin black man, the only man standing in the far aisle. The man leaned against the wall just off the edge of the stage. Lighting dimly illuminated his slender outline.

Darwin stood up and shuffled sideways out of his row.

"Excuse me," he said. "Excuse me."

"Where are you going?" his mother whispered.

He rushed to the back of the auditorium, into and through the foyer, and around to the end aisle where the man had been standing. He hurried, but the man was gone.

CHAPTER THIRTY-FOUR

She surprised him at Grand Central Station. Yankee players and coaches walked up the platform between trains in suits and ties—their normal travel attire. Most of them carried duffel bags or small suitcases. A couple of porters pulled railway wagons with the rest of the players' luggage and equipment.

George was halfway back in the pack and waved when he saw her. He put his arm around her as they walked into the main rotunda. Other players dispersed, some with their wives or girl-friends, the rest moving outside in groups of two or three to catch cabs.

"I thought we could have dinner downtown," Helen said.

They took a taxi to Jack and Charlie's on West 49th so George could order his favorite ribs and get a drink from the speakeasy in the basement.

"I've decided to barnstorm again this fall, Helen."

"Not if I have anything to say about it."

"I'll make the decisions regarding my career."

"Not if you want me to be your wife."

George fell silent. He took a couple bites of his food and drank several swigs from a glass of scotch on ice.

"Are you threatening to leave me?" he asked.

"It's not a threat. You go to California again and I'll go back to Boston—and stay there. Decide whether I'm important."

George lowered his voice. "You'd divorce me?"

"Catholics don't divorce."

"I love you, Helen."

"Until I'm out of sight," she said.

———

George threw a sport jacket over his shoulder, left the locker room, and took the long tunnel underneath the grandstands. He hurried to his car, then drove across the George Washington Bridge and north along a dark road winding high above the Hudson River. Moonlight flickered on the pavement through the thick trees as he sped north. The waterway shined like a silk ribbon below.

At Haverstraw, he pulled up next to the same building he had the night before, and the night before that. He rushed inside.

"Get your makeup on, Babe," the director said. George knew the routine. He sat back in a chair that resembled his barber's. A woman in her sixties tossed a white sheet over his torso and it floated down over his chest. She tucked it in around his neck.

The director walked in on him and the lady smoothing powder on his cheeks.

"Is he ready yet?"

George remained still. The makeup lady said, "In a minute," and the director walked out. She brushed powder on his face, then used two fingers to rub it in.

"Have they decided on a title yet?" George asked her.

"*Headin' Home*," the makeup artist said. "Have you been paid anything yet?" She smoothed a light cream under his eyes.

"Mr. Kessel gave me a check up-front; I got a bigger one comin' when we're finished."

"You're lucky," she said. "Most of us haven't been paid a thing. We have to wait until the end." She ripped off the linen sheet and patted his shoulder. "You're done."

George hustled into a makeshift dressing room and emerged in his costume—a white baseball uniform with red trim, no letters on the front, no number on the back. He played the part of a naïve, small-town baseball player who had become famous overnight but had fallen in love with the hometown sweetheart. The lead actress was younger than he was and no one he'd ever heard of before. She had big round eyes, like Mary Pickford, and her name was Maggie.

The shooting usually lasted until one in the morning. That night, they continued until three.

"Babe, what time can you be ready tomorrow night?" the director asked.

"Probably later, maybe around 7:00."

"Then that's when we'll start."

"I got a road trip next Monday," George said.

"We'll shoot the entire movie before then."

Most of the crew rushed off as soon as they were done that night. George waited in the shadows outside Maggie's dressing room. He sat on a wooden crate that had been used to transport one of the cameras. Maggie came out, closed the door, and started away.

"Hey, honey," George said.

She turned. "You don't even remember my name."

"Sure I do." She waited.

"You've kissed me on set and don't even know my *real* name."

"You're a good kisser. Maybe we should rehearse more." George grinned.

"My name's Maggie," she said.

"Honey, I'm sorry." He kicked the ground. "Bet you don't know my name."

She blushed. "Everybody does, Mr. Ruth."

"What's my first name?" he asked.

"Babe."

"Nope; it's George. I can't believe you kissed me and didn't even know my name."

She smiled. A janitor came by and pulled out a key chain.

"We're just leaving," she said.

"Can I give you a lift?" George asked. He pushed a door open and they walked outside.

"I'm staying at the motel next door. Most of us are."

"I got a bottle of gin out back in my coupe."

"And you'd share it with me?" she said.

"I don't kiss just anyone."

"Shame on you," Maggie said, "but I can't stay long."

The car rocked and swayed in the moonlight.

———

Waite Hoyt stared at him as he paced back and forth in the dugout. Hoyt had pitched the night before and sat in the dugout with his uniform on, even though it was his day off. He'd watched George for most of five innings, and when he came in from the outfield between innings, he thundered down the dugout steps.

"What the fuck's wrong with you guys?" George shouted to his teammates. "Do I got a carry the fuckin' load all the time? Somebody get up there and get a fuckin' hit." Then he punctuated his sentence with his favorite word. "Fuck."

Hoyt didn't react. He'd been on the Red Sox team with George, then was traded to the New York Yankees the year after George was. He'd watched George for years and sat quietly observing him again.

George put his hands on his hips and paced the dugout again. He was restless and rarely sat down between innings. Hoyt folded his arms. George didn't pay attention to him and yelled at the batter on deck. "Come on kid, get a fuckin' hit."

Carl May was in the dugout that day too. He was also a pitcher not playing that day.

"Hey Ruth, why do you call everybody 'kid'?" May asked.

"I can't remember everybody's name."

"You just don't care about anybody else."

"Fuck you," George snapped. "They don't care about me, do they?"

"They might if you showed *you* cared." May sat on the bench with a warm-up jacket hanging over one arm.

"Maybe I don't."

May turned to Waite Hoyt sitting six feet away.

"What are you lookin' at Hoyt?" Hoyt kept gazing at George.

"Him."

"Mad?"

"I don't know," Hoyt said in a monotone. "Amazed, I guess."

"At Babe?"

"I've been watching him for a long time. I don't understand."

"What are you muttering about?"

Hoyt's eyes followed George climbing to the top of the dugout steps and walking toward the on-deck circle.

"I can't figure him out," Hoyt said. "He's amazing and a piece of crap, all in one. He's superhuman and an ignorant, selfish child. He acts like a saint around kids and treats women like a heathen."

"He can have any woman," Carl May. "I hate him."

"He treats them all the same and sometimes screws two or three a night. I couldn't do that even if I wanted. It's like he's addicted." Hoyt paused. "I almost feel sorry for him."

"Hell, he's addicted to everything," May said. "Women, food, booze, cigars." May paused. "Two or three a night?"

"If he isn't passed out drunk. But then he gets up in the middle of the night and goes down to the lobby or calls a hooker. I've seen him do three hookers in a row while we were in his room. He doesn't care." Hoyt said. "That's why Ernie quit being his roommate. And Babe doesn't care if they're fat and ugly, a teenager, or a grandmother." Hoyt stared off.

"You hate him. I can tell."

"He has his good sides too," Hoyt said. "Sometimes, it seems all he cares about is getting more money. Then, he gambles it away—or gives it away to any Tom, Dick, or Harry who's down on his luck." Hoyt narrowed his eyes and stared at George in the batting box, ready to hit. "Did you see what he did for the orphanage that burned down? He paid for every kid in the band to travel, eat, and stay in hotels. Then, he donated thousands to help rebuild the school."

"I hate him," May said. "He's a wretch."

"And a god. He's a thick-headed village idiot and one of the smartest guys I know. He never sleeps, and he's one of the healthiest guys around. But he's lazy, overweight, and pays no attention to what he eats and drinks, and he stays out all night smokin' and drinkin' and screwin' every dame he can."

George dug his spiked shoes into the batter's box and focused on the pitcher.

"So what's your point?" May asked.

"How's he do it? He's a paradox."

"What's that?"

"He's the most despicable person I know. Still, I kinda like him and admire him. I just don't understand how he does it."

CHAPTER THIRTY-FIVE

The *Nutcracker* characters were still in costume. They mingled, constantly looking toward Cammie. She stood on stage in the middle of a circle of people including two policemen, Gilmore, Darwin, his parents, and the director of the show.

Stagehands moved sets. One backdrop was an entire German village with forty-foot storefronts. It rolled by, a couple of men on each end. The lights in the theater had been turned down, but a few floods were aimed at the center of the stage and remained bright enough for uniformed officers to walk the aisles. They carried flashlights and searched alcoves, back rooms, and even the concession areas out front. A couple shined them along the floor and in between the long rows of seats.

They checked closets, storage rooms, and dressing rooms downstairs, beneath the stage. A janitor walked with one cop, showing him spaces that could hide a lingering assailant. Together they unlocked a storage closet with mops and cleaning materials, then another closet filled with portable racks of costumes.

The sound of footsteps clanked above, and Darwin, his parents, and Cammie looked up to see a policeman on a catwalk, six stories up. His flashlight beamed to the side and down into the back corners of the deep stage.

"We'll wait until you leave, Ms. Griffin," Gilmore said, "and walk you to your car."

"I'm taking her with me," Darwin said. He glanced at his mom and dad. His mom nodded in approval. His dad kept silent and peered at Darwin as if he were proud of him.

"You poor thing," Mrs. Barney said to Cammie. She hugged her. "I don't know how you finished the performance."

"We practiced enough," Cammie said. "I just went through the motions. I feel like I cheated the audience."

"Nobody could tell," the director said. "In fact, it was your best performance yet. You were unconscious. It all just flowed."

"How many more performances will you have?" Gilmore asked.

The director answered for Cammie. "Eight, including two each next Saturday and Sunday."

"He surely won't come back here after the way you swarmed the place tonight," Mr. Barney said.

"There's no way to be sure," Gilmore said.

"I don't think I scared him," Darwin said.

Gilmore put his forefinger and thumb to his chin and rubbed up and down. "Are you sure this guy isn't a stalker? You think he might be attracted to you, Ms. Griffin?"

"I wasn't in tights the first time I saw him. I wore jeans and a baggy sweatshirt," she said. "You were there. You saw him," she said to Gilmore.

"Maybe he'd seen you before then."

Five cops converged on the stage and joined the circle around Cammie. One of them said, "There ain't nobody left in here." Gilmore asked them to move outside, circle the Music Hall, and be sure nobody was lurking outside.

Footsteps slapped against the wooden stage floor and everybody in the circle turned at once to see Lieutenant Wilson.

"Looks like I missed all the fun," he said.

"You missed all the drama," Gilmore said.

"I saw another one," Wilson said. "My daughter was Mary in her school play—over at Holy Cross."

"Eddie was here, standing right over there."

"Sorry I didn't get here sooner. Mary's mother wanted me there for Jesus' birth. She thought it was a pretty big deal." Wilson came closer to Cammie. "You all right, honey?"

"Just scared."

"I doubt he'll come around here again," Darwin said. His dad stepped closer and put his arm around Darwin's shoulders.

"The fact he came at this time shows he's not afraid of crowds," Wilson said. "Maybe he likes the excitement."

"He won't get away with anything at a theater," Darwin's dad said.

"You ever hear of John Wilkes Booth?"

———

Cammie received roses on stage after Sunday evening's last performance. The cast stood in a line across the stage and bowed. Policemen stood in the aisles below each end of the stage. Cammie and the male lead stepped forward to bow and thank the crowd. She blew kisses. The director carried a dozen red roses to the stage behind the row of performers and handed them forward to the man who played the Nutcracker. He then gave them to Cammie. She curtsied and blew another kiss to the audience.

Darwin walked backstage after the spectators thinned. Cammie had tears in her eyes and smiled. She took several quick steps toward Darwin and threw her arms around him, pecking his cheek.

"I'm so lucky," she said. "Will you come to the after party?"

The party was in the foyer of the Music Hall. Hors d'oeuvres and champagne were served to performers, the stage crew, and musicians. They congratulated each other, hugged, and wished each other happy holidays. Cammie held Darwin's hand and pulled him around as she introduced him to the other cast members. One was the Nutcracker himself. He wore dark slacks with a dressy, narrow black belt, shiny black loafers, and a black turtleneck. Cammie smiled and hugged him. He swung her back and forth with her feet off the ground.

"This is my other man, Darwin," she said. "I've probably spent more time with Gerald over the past month than you."

"I'm jealous," Darwin said.

"Don't be," Gerald said. "This is my roommate, David." Another man stepped forward. He held a glass of champagne in one hand and stuck out his other to shake Darwin's. Darwin looked over his shoulder and nodded to Rodney Gilmore, standing discreetly in the corner of the room. Gilmore nodded back.

Cammie introduced Darwin to several of the stage crew, then told Darwin, "We have to leave now."

"You don't want to wait until the end?"

"There's kind of a tradition," she said. "Because I have the lead role, I have to leave early."

"I'll go get my car."

He pulled up front and left the parking lights blinking, then walked back in the lobby. He couldn't see Cammie. He scanned the crowd. Gilmore was absent too. Then Darwin walked over to the Snowflake Fairy, one of the dancers he'd met earlier.

"Have you seen Cammie?"

"She was just here." The dancer stood on her toes and panned the gathering, then turned back to Darwin. "I heard her say she'd forgotten her bag in the dressing room."

Darwin walked back toward the auditorium. A security guard stood outside a set of double doors.

"Did a young woman come this way?"

"Miss Griffin? She went down to the dressing room."

———

The lights were dim; the dark, empty theater was quiet. He walked away from the security guard, down the center aisle, and crossed over toward the corner of the stage. The cavernous auditorium was pierced by her scream. He sprinted down the aisle and yelled Cammie's name, lunging through a draped entrance leading backstage.

A man's head popped up from the stairwell leading down to the dressing room. Darwin darted toward him, and the man ran the other way. Cammie sat on a step rubbing her neck—halfway down the stairway.

"Are you all right?" Darwin asked.

She held her throat but nodded, and he ran backstage after the assailant. But the stage door was closed and chained. The assailant wheeled and both men froze; then the thin black man bolted onto the wooden floor of the stage. He looked out over the empty rows of seats as the security guard was moving down the center aisle. He looked back at Darwin, then ran up a metal stairway in back of the stage. Darwin tore after him. They ran up several flights, zigzagging back and forth, the assailant two flights ahead. At the top, he leaped onto a catwalk high over the stage floor. Darwin examined the iron grating, peered through the latticework to the security man standing far below, then stepped onto the swaying catwalk too.

Midway over the stage, the man grabbed a rope that hung from a pulley high above. He hopped over the railing of the catwalk, clutching the rope, but the weights on the other end of the rope were nowhere near his body weight, and he plummeted to the floor. He rose slowly and hobbled toward the front of the stage, only a few feet from the security guard.

He shoved him to the side, and the security guard fell to his knees. The fleeing man lowered himself off the front of the stage and staggered toward the auditorium exit.

Darwin hurried back down to Cammie, who by this time had made her way onto the stage. He hugged her, then backed up a step and looked at her neck. A thin bruise circled her throat.

"Why did you go down there alone?"

"The security guy didn't want to go into the women's dressing room." She coughed and rubbed her neck again.

"Where's Gilmore?"

"I don't know," Cammie said. She motioned to the stairway where she'd been assaulted. "That's what he wrapped around my neck." Darwin walked down three steps and picked up a piece of 12-gauge copper wire. The ends were twisted around two round pieces of wood, one on each end.

"That was Eddie, right?"

"Now you've seen him too," she said. They walked to the front of the stage and up the aisle and back toward the lobby. Outside the double doors, a disheveled Gilmore stood with a cell phone to his ear. His hair was messed, his tie was crooked, and his shirt had come untucked in front.

"I need backup," he said.

Eddie sat on the marble floor with one of his hands over his head, handcuffed to a metal bar on a door.

"Where were you?" Cammie asked.

"Even superheroes like me have to take a leak from time to time. Couldn't you have waited a minute?"

"I thought you left, so I asked the security guy for help."

Gilmore motioned toward the corner. The security guard sat on the edge of an antique love seat. He wiped his brow, then bent forward with his elbows on his knees.

"What happened to him?" Darwin asked.

"He got tired watching me wrestle this asshole to the floor," Gilmore said. Eddie squirmed but didn't say anything, then kicked the door in frustration.

Red and blue strobe lights flashed outside and several uniformed police officers came running down the hallway. They slid to a halt, and two of them lifted Eddie to his feet as static crackled from the two-way radios clipped to their belts. Performers, musicians, and the stage crew gathered, many of them still holding wine glasses and hors d'oeuvres.

——— • ———

Eddie sat at a bare metal table. Wilson lifted his foot onto an empty chair and rested his elbow on his knee. A single bright light hung overhead and a one-way window lined most of a wall. Darwin and Cammie sat on the other side of the window as Wilson read the suspect his Miranda rights.

"You sure you don't want an attorney?" Wilson asked.

"I can't afford one," Eddie said.

"The court will appoint one."

"One of your cronies? No thanks."

"What's your real name?" Wilson asked.

"Eddie."

"No it's not."

"That's what *you* can call me."

"If you got a record, we'll ID you from your prints."

Eddie shrugged and looked away.

"Where you from and who do you work for?" Wilson asked.

"Chicago. I don't know who paid me. All my orders come by mail," Eddie said. "The money too."

"Don't give me that bullshit."

"It's always cash." He pulled a pack of cigarettes out of his front shirt pocket and lit one.

"Ever *seen* your boss?" Gilmore asked.

"Nope." He blew smoke slowly from the corner of his mouth.

"How'd he contact you the first time?" Gilmore asked.

"He phoned me."

"So it's a man," Wilson said. He paused and looked down at the concrete floor. "Why did you kill the old man?"

"What old man?"

"Why did you try to keep Miss Griffin quiet?"

"I didn't mean to hurt her."

Gilmore stepped forward. "You tried to strangle her. Why, damn it?"

"It was my orders," Eddie said. He looked up at Gilmore. "Back off." He slid his chair away and turned toward the window. "Is she on the other side? I like her; she's cute." He blew a kiss and waved at the glass. "I was nice to her. I went to see her dance and tried to watch out for her."

"Have you ever been in her house?" Wilson asked.

"I don't even know where she lives."

———

Darwin had his arm around Cammie as they shared a bowl of home-cooked popcorn. The only light in the room came from the television. Darwin had his feet out straight and resting on his coffee table. Cammie's were pulled up and tucked underneath her.

"I suppose it's safe to go back to the house," she said.

"I'm getting used to you here."

"Maybe you can come over to my place."

"Or you can sell it," Darwin said.

"Then what?"

"Stay here until you decide."

"What would your boss think? And what about your parents?"

The phone rang. The cordless was on the coffee table. Cammie reached over and handed it to him.

"I don't believe it," Darwin said. He sat forward on the sofa. "Who did it?" There was more silence. "Now what?" More silence again. "I'll tell her." He looked at Cammie, still with the cordless to his ear. "She's here right now." He placed the cordless back on the coffee table and rubbed his fingers through his hair.

"He's dead," Darwin said. "They found him in his cell. His real name's Elijah Parks."

"Suicide?"

Darwin stared at the floor. "They found him at dinnertime. I don't know all the details."

"Shot? Poisoned?" Cammie asked. "What was it?"

Darwin raised his head. "Strangled—with wire."

CHAPTER THIRTY-SIX

The new twelve-cylinder maroon Packard was nicknamed "the torpedo" by George's teammates. He drove it to 57th Street at 5th Avenue and parked outside the stone mansion on the corner. A tall wrought-iron fence bordered the home, now surrounded by downtown Manhattan and its skyscrapers. Still, it remained stately, partly because of its owners—the Vanderbilts.

The midsummer sky was still bright at 8:00 p.m. A doorman stood at the curb and opened his door. George walked around to the passenger side, and Juanita placed her arm over his forearm. She had excellent posture, and her flowing black hair made her look taller than she was. She wore a single strand of pearls George had purchased for her in California two years earlier.

From outside, the home resembled a medieval castle, but natural light shone inside and brightened the interior. An ornate crystal chandelier sparkled overhead next to a sweeping stairway with curved railings. A reception line with Mr. and Mrs. Vanderbilt and local politicians had formed inside the foyer.

The hostess introduced herself. "I'm Consuelo Vanderbilt, Duchess of Marlborough." She bowed her head slightly as if trying to prevent her jeweled golden crown from tipping off her bouffant hairdo. She appeared to be in her midforties and wore long beige gloves that matched her floor-length satin dress. Diamonds flashed from her neckline and wrists. She offered her hand to George, tipping her fingers forward.

"How ya doin', ma'am," he said, and he shook it up and down vigorously. "Is that a Mexican name, because Juanita here is Mexican."

"My mother was born in Puerto Rico," Consuelo said.

"I thought maybe you two could talk, because Juanita speaks mostly Mexican and I don't know it too good."

"Spanish is *one* of the languages I know. Como estas, Juanita?" Consuelo Vanderbilt reached out, and Juanita took her hand in both of hers, then dipped into a mild curtsy.

"Bien, gracias," Juanita said. Consuelo and Juanita spoke to each other in Spanish and spent much of the next hour circulating together, while George hung out in a corner where other guests came to him. He laughed, drank a lot, and told baseball stories.

"Let's go, honey," he said to Juanita. "Most of these people don't know much about baseball." George accompanied her outside, and they drove to his suite at the Ansonia Hotel on the Upper West Side. They took a gated elevator up to his floor.

"I want to stay in New York," she said in Spanish.

"You can stay with me, as long as Helen doesn't come down from Boston."

———

A man wearing a sport coat and tie appeared behind him in the lockerroom mirror. He stared as George patted green after-shave lotion on his cheeks. George waited for him to move or say something and lifted a comb to his hair.

"Can I help you?" George asked.

"I got a great idea."

"Who the hell are you?"

"Hugh Fullerton, *Times*."

"I can't keep all you guys straight. How'd you get in here?"

"I told 'em we had a meeting."

"Do we?" George asked.

They shared a taxi and rode to the Commodore Hotel. They waited in the lobby for a table in the dining room. George rested in a high-backed upholstered chair, puffing on a fat, half-burned stogy. Fullerton sat on a sofa across from him. A cloud hung over the marble-topped coffee table between them.

"They'll wire you up and test your reaction speed." Fullerton sipped coffee. "Then, they'll put you through tests to compare you to normal people."

"I *am* normal." George had four empty bottles of Red Rock Cola on an end table and drank the next one in two swallows.

Fullerton fidgeted and pulled a folded newspaper from out of his back pocket. He opened it up and spread it out on the table. The headline in the editorial section read, "Babe Ruth: Nation's #1 Hero."

"Maybe I should run for president," George said.

"You're more popular than he is."

"I had a better year."

"A couple of psychologists at Columbia University want to test you," Fullerton said. "All you got to do is show up."

"What do you expect the tests will show?"

"That you're superhuman," Fullerton said.

"When I played in Boston, a reporter tried to make me out to be some kind of gorilla. You aren't going to make me out to be some ape or nigger, are you?"

"I wouldn't, and neither will they."

"If you're trying to make me the butt of some joke."

"I want to show you're *more* advanced than the average Joe," Fullerton said. "Who was the reporter?"

"Some guy from the *Boston Globe*. I can't remember his name."

"Ed Martin?"

"How'd you know?" George asked.

"He died," Fullerton said. "Caught the Spanish flu and died—over a year ago."

George looked down. "Poor guy. He didn't deserve that."

———

They wore white lab coats. Joe Holmes was heavyset and wore thick glasses. Al Johansen was thin with a receding hairline. He rarely spoke. The room was sterile, gray, and bare, except for several contraptions with leather straps and a desk-sized black rectangular box with wires, clocks, and blinking lights.

"This is a Hipp Chronoscope," Holmes said. Its wires ran to a baseball bat. He fastened a tube around George's chest. "Go ahead and swing."

They ran him through a succession of tests, and George was intent on beating the performances of anyone they'd tested before. Some of the tests measured his hearing, some measured his aptitude, others his sight.

"How'd I do?" George kept asking. "Let me try again. I can do better." He perspired and gritted his teeth. "Was that faster?"

"You're definitely superior to most humans in reaction speed and eye-to-hand coordination."

"That's good, isn't it?" George asked.

"Fullerton wants to report it in the *New York Times*," Holmes said.

"We won't release the results, if you don't want."

"Why wouldn't I?"

Holmes and Johansen looked at each other, then Holmes said, "There's always a chance people will compare you to animals."

"I thought you said I'm superhuman."

"It's common knowledge among scientists that some animals have better eye-to-hand coordination than most adult humans."

"I don't get it," George said.

"Humans can't jump from tree limb to tree limb."

"What the hell are you saying?"

"There's a lot of talk these days about evolution. Southern states won't let schoolteachers mention it."

"Are you saying I'm an ape?"

"Not at all," Johansen said, "but I'm afraid how the *New York Times* might make it sound."

———

They sat next to each other and swayed back and forth as the train rocked and clicked over the tracks. Helen looked at him and smiled. George patted her knee. The train slowed and they stepped down onto the platform. George wore a dark suit, white shirt and tie, and a driver's cap and held a suitcase in each hand. He watched the porter unload more suitcases onto a railway baggage cart.

"Where are we?" he asked Helen.

"Syracuse."

"A different town every day," George said. They walked inside the depot: a rough wooden floor, a clock on the wall, a ticket window with black steel bars.

"Rochester on Wednesday, then Buffalo on Thursday."

He walked outside and pulled their suitcases off the baggage cart. His breath rose in the autumn air.

"Hey, Babe, can I get an autograph?" a man asked. Others heard him and a small gathering formed.

"One at a time," he said. He pulled a fountain pen from the inside pocket of his suit coat. Helen turned her back and walked out of the station. The bottom of her skirt brushed the tops of her shoes. A short woolen jacket hung open over her white ruffled blouse.

A policeman escorted George and Helen to a taxi, and George loaded their luggage behind the seat. They sat in the back.

"She's the cutest thing you've ever seen," he said. "I almost brought her home."

"She's not a pet," Helen said. "I'd like to see her. Do you know anything about her family?"

"They passed away, I guess," George said.

"Who's taking care of her?"

"A Mexican woman," he said. "Poor little kid."

"You're sure she's available for adoption?" Helen asked.

"The lady said I could have her."

"What lady would give up her child?"

"Juanita," George said, "the lady whose kid it is."

Helen looked deep into George's eyes, then laughed and said, "That's crazy. Why would this woman want to give up her child?"

"She can't afford to keep her," George said. "She's trying to get a job but doesn't speak English too good." He hesitated. "A kid might help our marriage. You know I love kids."

Helen raised an eyebrow. George waited for her to say something.

"It sounds too good to be true," she said.

He patted her knee again. "I thought so too, but there's nothing wrong with this one. Most kids you can adopt got somethin' wrong with 'em."

"Not necessarily."

"I heard it's hard to find good babies for adoption."

CHAPTER THIRTY-SEVEN

Darwin had his back to Cammie. She drank coffee and sat on the sofa with her legs curled underneath her. His arms were folded as he stood at the picture window, staring over the nighttime skyline.

"Did you see it?" Darwin asked.

"They didn't try to make the connection." She picked up a folded *Kansas City Star* from the cushion next to her.

"Between your uncle and Ruth?"

She opened up the front section and started perusing the article. "I want this over. They made Eddie sound like a maniac."

"There'll be more," he said.

"Articles?"

"It was too dramatic—in the theater and all. And there're too many loose ends."

"Is there any way we can keep them quiet?" Cammie said.

"I asked Wilson not to say anything. He did us a favor. But reporters won't let it die."

"I just want to get on with my life."

Darwin looked down onto 27th Street. He turned.

"You're not really his niece," he said.

"Are you just *now* figuring that out?"

"The age difference: it's too great. I never thought about it before."

"It was a term of affection. I've called him that since I was a kid."

"Were you even related?"

"He was my mom's uncle. Really, my mom's great-uncle."

"What's your mom's name?"

"Pearl," she said.

"And your grandmother's name?"

"Kamaile. It's an African name."

"You were named after her?"

"That's right," Cammie said.

"I'm confused. I've got to write all this down." Darwin opened a drawer in an end table and pulled out a pen and pad. He sat at the dining room table and drew brackets. Cammie stood up, walked over, and looked over his shoulder. "So your mom was Pearl, and she was born when?"

"May 12, 1951," Cammie said.

"Her mom was Cammie Sr."

"Kamaile." She spelled it.

"That was your Uncle Griff's sister?"

"My grandmother. Isadora was his sister. They called her Issie for short, and she was my great-grandmother."

"When was she born?" Darwin asked.

"I'm not sure." Cammie looked at the ceiling and did some calculations in her head. "About 1908 or 1909."

"Then she was alive when Babe Ruth was famous."

"What are you getting at?"

"That day in my office," Darwin said. "Your Uncle Griff said, '*You* more than anybody.' You."

"I was his only blood relative left. He meant I owed him allegiance. He wanted me to believe him."

"Maybe he meant something more."

"Like what?"

"I don't know," Darwin said. He stood up and paced slowly.

"*You* don't know?" She smiled.

He lay his pen down and wrapped his arms around her. "Not yet." He kissed her and still had his arms around her.

She pulled back six inches from his face. "You think Granny Issie got knocked up by Babe Ruth?"

"Did you ever meet her?"

"She died when I was twelve."

"What do you know about her?"

"She was the outcast of our family, a real rebel. She never married and never attended church."

"She had at least one kid."

"My grandmother," Cammie said. "Kamaile."

"Who was your great-grandfather?"

"I don't know."

"Help me fill in these brackets." He turned back to the table and sat down. She pulled up a chair next to him and grabbed the pen, then filled in all the empty spaces, except the one next to her great-grandmother, Issie.

—————

Cammie opened the door and walked onto a wooden landing, then pulled a string overhead and a single light bulb came on. She held onto a wooden railing, slowly descending the creaking stairs into the dark, moist basement. The brick walls had been painted or whitewashed once, but in the many years following, it had faded and worn off. Cobwebs hung in the darkness, and she raised her hands to bat them away. Each stair step was a single 2 x 12-inch board. Some were cracked. They all had dark, open spaces between them.

Cammie had lived with her Uncle Griff for almost five years and had only been down here three times, once to take extra winter clothing she'd never retrieved since and a suitcase filled with memorabilia her mother had given her, and once to replace a filter on the furnace. The third time, she'd gone down at her Uncle Griff's request to get him an old issue of *Life* magazine with Jackie Robinson on the cover. Her uncle had been a collector of magazines and had stacks of old issues of *National Geographic*, *Life*, and *Look*, as well as piles of yellowed issues of *Sporting News*. The *Sporting News* issues were bunched by year and tied vertically and horizontally with string.

This time, she was after the suitcase. She'd forgotten the floor was dirt, and she'd never been down here in the evening. During the daytime, a couple of windows high on the brick walls had allowed sunlight in. Now it was dark, and shadows from the single lightbulb made the one-room basement seem even smaller.

Headlights from a car shined through the basement windows and streaked across a brick wall. Cammie took a long step over a stack of *Sporting News* issues and grabbed the handle of an old but small suitcase and yanked it out of a corner, then turned and rushed upstairs. By the time she got to the landing, she heard the back door open. She stopped and pulled the string that turned out the basement light. She waited.

A light in the kitchen came on. She didn't move.

"Cammie?" It was Darwin. She walked out from the stairwell landing.

"What are you doing here?" she asked.

"What are *you* doing here? You think you're safe because Eddie's gone?"

"I was hoping so."

"You're not," Darwin said. "Maybe somebody hired him."

"I had to get this." She held up the suitcase. It was tan with brown stripes and leather trim and had brass fasteners.

"What's in it?"

"I can't remember; it's been a while. Mostly hand-me-down relics from my grandmother and great-grandmother. A couple of things from when my mom was young." She laid it on the table and finagled a brass opener. "When Uncle Griff died, I never thought about this stuff, until you brought up my ancestry."

The top popped open, and yellowed and browned stationery and envelopes cast a musty scent. She lifted papers out and spread them over the tablecloth, then reached down inside the walls of the suitcase. Pleated ivory silk lined the interior of the suitcase. She pulled out a golden necklace strung through an old wedding band, a silver brooch, several black-and-white photographs, dozens of negatives, and layers of aged papers with handwriting.

She strategically grouped the photographs.

"This is my mother," Cammie said. "Isn't she beautiful?" She placed her to the right.

"You look like her."

"God, I hope so." She pulled out another photograph. "This is my grandmother and her husband." She placed the second picture in the center of the table an arm's length away.

"You look like her too," Darwin said. Cammie smiled again. Then she pulled out a handful of eight or ten more photographs and examined them one by one, sorting them into the piles.

"How about her?" she asked. She held a single black-and-white photo in both hands and turned it toward Darwin. "Do I look like her?"

"She's much darker," he said.

"That's Great-Grandma Issie." Cammie started a third pile for Issie.

"You sure she didn't have a husband?" he asked.

"Never had one," Cammie said. "At least none we knew of. Mom said she never seemed to miss one either. I remember; she always had that cat-caught-the-canary sparkle in her eye."

"And your great-grandmother outlived your grandmother?"

"Shows what a man can do to a woman."

"I've got to get up early in the morning," Darwin said. "Why don't you bring the suitcase back to the apartment?"

"Stay here tonight."

CHAPTER THIRTY-EIGHT

Colonel Ruppert talked on his telephone. George sat on the other side of his desk and leaned forward. He pushed his hair behind his ears, then stood up and paced back and forth before sitting back down again.

"We want to be sure he's cleared this time," Ruppert said. Then he paused. "He's right here." Ruppert handed the receiver to George.

"This is George Ruth. Mr. Commissioner?" He listened. "I don't want to get suspended again." He listened again, then handed the phone back to Ruppert. "He said I'm clear to go."

Colonel Ruppert took the phone and put it to his ear.

"Yes sir," he said. "No sir. Yes sir."

"What was all that about?" George asked.

"He says you're a disgrace to the game and asked if you have any African ancestors."

"He doesn't like me."

"He's a racist, George—a damn racist," Ruppert said, "and he's out to get you, I'm telling you."

"What can I do?"

Now Ruppert stood up and paced. He puffed on his pipe.

"Stop all the controversy. Stop acting like a big kid, damn it." Ruppert looked out the window then turned back to George. "Listen, Babe. I don't care if you're black, red, yellow, or green. I'm a businessman trying to sell tickets to ballgames. But there's only so much I can do." He put both hands on his desk and leaned closer. "Time has come when the only person that can help you is you."

"I'm not sure anything I do will get him to leave me alone."

"Give him a chance."

"Can't he see I'm not colored?" George asked.

"Hell, sixty years ago you would have been sold as a slave if you had even a drop of black blood."

"But I don't," George said. "Don't you think I'd know?"

"Landis thinks your grandfather or grandmother was colored. Do you even know the truth? Have you seen your grandfather or grandmother?" Then Ruppert held his hand up. "Never mind. I don't think I want to know."

"I'm sure my dad would have told me."

"How about that reform school you went to? Do they have any records?"

"I'll make a call," George said. "Mr. Ruppert, you don't really think I'm colored, do you?

"Get me the number. I'll call them."

"Sure, but I think I'd know."

"The owners want you to play. They know attendance goes up when you're on the field. I think you're safe as long as you keep your conduct clean on and off the field."

"I'll do my best," George said.

———

They were a month into their barnstorming tour when they reached Springfield, Illinois. The exhibition game was played at the state fair grounds. George hit two home runs and pitched a couple of innings before he walked off the playing field and climbed into the wooden grandstand behind home plate. He sat among the fans and signed autographs for thirty minutes. Local photographers asked him to pose with the mayor, with a couple of corporate officials that sponsored the event, and with kids.

More than one hundred people, mainly young fans, gathered around him. They carried fountain pens and pencils and programs and baseballs, hoping to get autographs. None of them failed. They closed in on him, and George smiled and laughed. He shook everyone's hand. He held two smaller boys, one on each knee.

"Great hittin', Babe," one kid said.

"You're the greatest," said another.

"Thanks for comin', Babe."

A photographer representing a local orphanage asked George to pose with a group of the kids. George paid special attention to a ten-year-old boy with crutches. When the boy couldn't get through the swarm of bodies, George got up and went to him. He picked the boy up and carried him back and signed the kid's ball cap, then autographed one of his crutches.

Twenty-five feet away, an elderly man wearing a union soldier's infantry coat and a Yankee ball cap stood watching. He smiled as George entertained the young fans.

When the sun began to set and the number of kids dwindled, George stood up to leave. The old man had remained, almost as if he were at attention, except he carried a cane and continued smiling.

"Hey old-timer. I like that hat," George said. The old man grinned and glanced upward, as if he'd forgotten he'd worn it. George started walking away.

"My grandson plays for the Yankees," the man said.

George looked back over his shoulder and said, "Who's that?"

"George Ruth."

George spun and stared at the man.

"That's me. Who are you?"

"John Rhoadie," the man said.

"My last name's Ruth." George started walking away again. The old man took a step forward.

"Your dad never told you about us?"

George turned and looked back. His smile faded. He tilted his head. "He didn't tell me about you, old-timer."

"Remember the bar in Baltimore? Remember how you crawled under the counter to hide? Remember the outhouse with orange walls? And what about your mother's golden locket, the heart-shaped one."

"She did have a necklace like that."

"Your grandmother sent it to her."

"I don't remember my grandparents coming to visit."

"I came a couple of times," the old man said, "but your dad didn't want us around. And we'd moved back here—so far away."

"Where do you live now?"

"North of St. Louis. A town called Fidelity. We traveled almost fifty miles to see you play."

"Why'd you move so far away?"

"It was easier living back here, under the circumstances. And we could get a homestead."

"We?"

"Your grandmother and me."

"Is she here?"

"Up there." The man pointed up into the covered grandstands. She wore a scarf. The sun had fallen and the wooden roof over the bleachers behind her cast a shadow.

"Why doesn't she come down?"

"She'd like to; she's afraid."

George looked back into the grandstands.

"He never told you, did he?"

George didn't say anything. He turned back to Rhoadie, then and took a deep breath. "Have her come down."

"Would you mind coming with me up to see *her*?"

George said his goodbyes to a few lingering fans, then walked with the elderly man. He cupped his hand under the man's elbow, helping him up the bleachers one step at a time.

The woman sat on the top row. Her arms were folded. Then she raised a hand over her mouth as her eyes sparkled from tears reflecting the faint moonlight. She stood up and reached out. The dark woman put her arms around George's neck. She held on more than hugged him. She was frail. She whimpered. Neither of them spoke. Her arms trembled, but he felt the softness and sincerity of her grip. He drew her closer and patted her on the back.

"Sit with me," she said.

George and the frail black woman sat on a bleacher. The old man circled behind them and sat on the other side of his wife.

"I don't know what to say," George said.

"It's not your fault, son," Rhoadie said. "Your father was ashamed."

"I wish he woulda told me."

"He thought it was better this way," the woman said. "Don't blame him."

"What is your name?" George asked her.

"Becca, short for Rebecca. Becca Rhoadie."

"But mine is Ruth."

"I gave that name to your father. John was away at war. I never thought he'd marry a slave girl."

"Did we ever meet? Why didn't you come and visit?"

"Baltimore was too far south," Becca said. "We found a home far away from all that hate. And your father didn't want anybody knowing."

"Did Mom know?"

"I doubt it," John said.

George rested his elbows on his knees, folded his hands, and looked down. "They'll kick me out of baseball."

"Nobody needs to know," John said, "and we won't tell."

"If we were goin' to tell," Becca said, "we woulda done it long ago. I been wantin' to see you all these years." A tear ran down her cheek.

"Tell me everything. Where you're from, how you met, and how you came up with the name Ruth. I never really had any family."

"It could take awhile," Becca said.

"I got all night."

CHAPTER THIRTY-NINE

Darwin flipped the light switch on. No one was there. The suit-case lay open on the dining room table. Memorabilia was scattered over the dinette table, on chairs, and on the living room floor: letters in stacks, photographs in small piles, trinkets and odds and ends that were souvenirs of Cammie's ancestral past.

He picked up a small golden locket. There was nothing inside and no initials engraved on it. He picked up a wedding band. Nothing engraved on it either. He thumbed through several black-and-white photographs and read handwritten comments on the back of some of them. Then an electronic rendition of "The Star Spangled Banner" sounded from inside his suit coat. He pulled out his cell phone.

"These guys want to know what I know," she said.

"Who are they?"

"I don't know."

"Where are you?" he asked.

"Harry's—at the River Market."

"Alone?"

"I was."

"I'm on my way." He started out the front door. "Ask them who they are."

"I did, for God's sake," Cammie said. "One's in the restroom. The other one's on his cell phone by the counter." She paused. "I'm afraid, Darwin. It was in the newspaper. Did you see it?"

"About your uncle?" Darwin picked up his pace.

"Maybe these guys saw it."

"Did they follow you?"

"I don't know," Cammie said. "I didn't see them. They must have. Hurry, Darwin." He was racing to his car. Cammie spoke faster.

"One guy's coming over here."

"I'll call the police," Darwin said.

"Hurry." She hung up.

———

The taller of the two men walked out of the restroom and slid into her booth next to her, blocking her way out. The other man, still on his cell phone, started toward her booth too, then lingered while he finished his call.

"Who are you?" Cammie asked the first man, the one sitting next to her. He stared ahead and didn't look at her. "What do you want?"

"We're with the FBI."

"Show me some ID," she said. He ignored her.

"We're just trying to find out more about your great uncle." He spread the morning *Star* on the table. The other man closed his cell phone, stuck it in his suit pocket, and sat down also.

"What do you know about LeRoy Griffin?" the taller man asked.

"Not a lot. He was a private man," Cammie said. "I want to know who you are."

"Not that private," the talker said. "The article said he was key in helping blacks play in the major leagues."

"You're thinking of Jackie Robinson," Cammie said. "What are you guys? Ku Klux Klan? Let me out."

"We're reporters for *Sports Illustrated*."

The other man came and sat down across from them.

"And I'm Venus Williams," Cammie said.

"Spunky little thing," the other man said.

"I'll make a scene. Let me out." She pushed against the man beside her, and he moved over and stood up. She slid out, stood up, and threw her purse over her shoulder.

"It's been memorable, gentlemen." She turned to leave.

"We tried to be nice," one man said. She looked back.

"Nice would have been introducing yourselves."

"We'll talk again," he said. "Later."

"The police are on their way."

———

Darwin paced back and forth in front of the picture window. His suit coat had been tossed over the back of the sofa. His sleeves were rolled up. The television was on, but he hadn't watched or listened to it and the volume was low.

The door opened, and Cammie walked in.

"That was strange," she said.

"Who were they?"

"I still don't know."

"Why didn't you ask them?"

"I did." She flopped her purse down on a chair. She wore a maroon jogging suit and white tennis shoes. "They wouldn't tell me."

"Did they threaten you?"

"No," she said.

"Then why didn't you just leave?"

"I wanted to know who they were. Then I decided to let them know I don't know anything about Uncle Griff."

Darwin asked more questions. Cammie told him that the men had been dressed in white shirts and business suits, were "arrogant" and "almost" condescending," and that they were both white.

239

They'd approached her after her dance practice. She'd gone into a small market to get eyeliner and a pack of gum, then stopped for a pick-me-up fruit smoothie.

"At first, I thought maybe they were policemen. They wanted to know what I knew about Uncle Griff. Then I thought maybe they were reporters."

"What did you say?"

She threw her arms up. "*You're* worse than they were."

"What did you tell them?"

"Nothing. Okay? It was just odd. They didn't tell me who they were or how they knew who I was."

Darwin paced faster. "I'm calling Wilson."

"Calm down. I'll be all right."

"I'm supposed to be your attorney."

"You're too emotionally involved."

"Fine," he said. "You want another attorney?"

"No, damn it. But back off."

"You were almost killed, and I'm supposed to relax when two strange guys corner you and give you the third degree?"

"I used to like being around you—to escape the stress."

Darwin raised his voice. "I'm sorry I care."

She paused and spoke softly. "Did you look through any of this stuff?" She motioned to the items from the suitcase.

"No."

"I shouldn't get mad," she said. He walked over and put his arm around her. She turned away.

"I'm not trying to take your clothes off." He walked into the kitchen.

"You're right. I'm sorry. Maybe that's what I need," she said.

He came out of the kitchen holding a Coke. The top of his shirt was unbuttoned.

"I don't know as much about women as I'd like," he said. "I don't want you thinking I'm sex-crazed."

She took two steps toward him and grabbed both sides of his shirt collar and pulled him closer. Then she ripped his shirt open. Buttons popped in several directions and rattled on the hardwood floor. She kissed him over and over. Without looking, he placed his bottle down on an end table.

He unzipped the top of her jogging suit and she helped yank it off. Then he reached for the collar on her blouse.

"Don't even think about it," she said and unbuttoned it methodically.

He slipped the bottoms of her running suit down over her hips. She cooperated and stepped out of them, unbuckling his belt and unzipping his suit pants at the same time.

"Want to take your tennis shoes off?" he asked.

"Can't you get caught up in the moment?"

He brushed the suitcase off the dining room table. It slammed to the floor and ten or twelve photographs flew along with it. Then she spun and faced him again while placing her hands behind her as he lifted her bare bottom onto the table.

"I've never," he said.

"Shut up."

CHAPTER FORTY

1920

The sun reflected off George's dark glasses. He stretched out on an orange beach towel spread unevenly over the hot sand. His birdlike legs stuck out from his round torso as he dosed in a striped tank top and navy swimsuit.

Helen rested next to him on a mint-green towel under a beach umbrella. She'd propped herself up against a canvas-backed beach chair and was reading Edith Wharton's *Age of Innocence*.

"You're going to burn," she said in a monotone without looking at him.

He twitched and swatted the air above his nose as if it were a fly. "I don't burn. I'm in the sun every day."

"It's hotter here, and it hits places your uniform covers."

He lay still.

"I've been thinking about the baby," she said. "Can we stop and see her on the way back to Boston?"

"I'll call ahead." He opened his eyes but didn't move.

Helen closed her novel and placed it on her lap.

"This is so much nicer than California," she said. "We're right next to the beach, the water's warmer, and there are shops nearby."

George didn't reply at first, then rolled onto his belly. "And there's gambling here." He pushed himself up off the ground. "It's too hot. I'm going to get a highball. Want one?"

"That's another thing about Cuba. We can buy liquor," she said. "Sure, I'll have one."

He was gone for half an hour, and Helen walked back to their room. She unlocked the door and found George next to their bed rummaging through his suitcase.

"Where have you been?" she asked.

"I stopped in the casino."

"What are you doing?"

"I need more money," he said.

"I knew you'd go overboard. Don't go back down there."

"I won. Close to a thousand."

"Don't go George. Please."

"You're afraid I'll *win* too much?" George counted bills.

"You won't know when to quit."

"I'm not a fool," he said.

"You're compulsive. Please, George. Come shopping with me."

"Then I'll lose money for sure. I'll be back before dinner." He handed her a twenty. "Here; go shopping."

When he returned to their room, Helen was eating from a food cart that had been rolled into their room and placed at the foot of their bed.

"I couldn't wait any longer," she said. "Did you win?"

He didn't say anything.

"Well?"

"I came *so* close to winning a hundred-thousand-dollar pot."

"I guess that means you bet that much."

"I got cheated." He looked out a window. "Things are different down here."

"Do we have enough to get home?" she asked.

"I still got a check in my wallet from that movie I was in up in Haverstraw."

"Why did you wait so long to cash it?"

"It was nice having it in my wallet," he said. "It reminded me I was a movie star."

"You showed it off, didn't you?"

"It was fun showin' the fellas—and some of their wives."

"Everything else is gone?" she asked.

"Pretty much."

The next morning he got up early and walked to the front desk. When he returned, Helen was in her robe in front of the bathroom mirror, powdering her face.

"They wouldn't cash it," he said.

"Maybe you need to go to a bank."

"I did. They said it wasn't any good."

"It's a bad check?"

"They talked in Mexican," he said. "I couldn't understand everything."

"Do you know anybody in Havana?"

"We already got our boat and train tickets. You still got that twenty I gave you?"

———

The sun shone down between the tall buildings as George and Helen walked out of St. Patrick's Cathedral. They stood on the long stone steps and gazed down Madison Avenue, then caught a taxi back to the Ansonia.

"Why is she staying in your apartment, George?"

"I thought you wanted to meet her," he said.

"I did, and Dorothy's a beautiful child. I love her," Helen said. "I'm talking about Juanita."

"The baby couldn't stay there alone."

"Where do they live?"

George stared out the front window and swallowed hard. "I thought it would be easier if they came to the Ansonia and stayed with us. I thought you'd want to spend time with the baby before you decide."

"I think I have."

Babe turned quickly.

"I want to adopt her, George."

They walked into the lobby and caught the elevator upstairs. When they walked through the door, Juanita came out of a bedroom. Her long black hair cascaded down the front of her patterned ivory dress. She reached down to her side and held the tiny hand of little Dorothy. The toddler wobbled when she walked and moved uncertainly toward George and Helen.

George bent down and lifted her into his arms. He smiled and poked her in the belly.

"Coochy-coochy," he said, then looked at Juanita. She was all made up, her hair brushed softly, her lips bright red. "Good news. Helen said yes."

Juanita's smile wilted. She bit her lower lip. She turned and disappeared into a back bedroom.

"She doesn't want to give her up," Helen said. "I knew this was too good to be true."

"She'll get over it. She can't afford to take care of a baby. Anyway, she wants to go back to Mexico."

"Is it *her* baby?"

"She got to like her just like you did," George said. "Don't worry about it."

Helen walked into the back bedroom. Juanita was sobbing quietly, sitting on the edge of a bed. Helen sat next to her.

"You love the baby, don't you?" Helen said.

Juanita nodded. "Si." She wiped her eyes with the back of her hand.

"Maybe you can come to Boston and help take care of her."

"Vamos a Boston?" Juanita asked.

George walked in holding Dorothy. He handed the child over to Helen. She placed the child on her lap, but the baby reached for Juanita.

"I got to go meet the boss," George said.

"On Sunday?" Helen asked.

"I got to get an advance, and he wants to talk to me."

George walked out of the bedroom and the apartment.

Helen spoke to Juanita. "I'm going to stay in our new home, just outside of Boston. I like it up there. You come too."

Juanita hugged the baby and put her hand over her heart. "Si. Yo tambien. Me too."

———

George walked into Colonel Ruppert's office wearing his camel-hair overcoat and matching driver's cap. Colonel Ruppert wore a suit and sat behind his desk, smoking a pipe.

"Where's Huston?" George asked.

"I bought him out," Ruppert said.

"I kind of liked the ol' guy. He was German like me."

"You've got somebody else you have to worry about now."

George took a seat opposite Ruppert. Ruppert leaned back in his leather chair and stuck his thumbs in the small pockets of his vest. He spoke out of the corner of his mouth while he held his pipe between his teeth.

"Judge Kenesaw Mountain Landis, the most powerful man in baseball. He's like a king. And he's a tough old lawyer that won't take any shit from anybody."

"What's that got to do with me?"

"Two weeks ago, the owners met and appointed Landis the new commissioner." Ruppert said. "Hell, Babe, even I report to him.

It's because of the scandal. The White Sox: they threw the World Series. Eight men are suspended for life."

"Joe Jackson?" George asked.

"He's one."

"Damn." George shook his head in disbelief. "He's a nice guy, Jake. Dumber than dirt but a great player and honest as the day is long."

"You'll never see him in a ballpark again."

"It ain't fair." George paused. "What did you want to talk about?"

"Landis."

"You answer to him," George said. "Not me. I was wonderin' if I could get an advance."

"You gambled, didn't you, Babe?"

"How'd you know?"

"John McGraw. Word spreads."

"I got cheated," George said.

"Have you heard anything I said? Shoeless Joe got thrown out of baseball for gambling. So did seven others, and more, maybe."

"I didn't bet on baseball. It's legal in Cuba."

"I don't want to hear about it. It's time you grow up and take some responsibility."

"So, will you give me an advance?" George asked.

"Not unless you agree to change."

"Okay, I agree."

"In writing," Ruppert said. He placed a small stack of papers in front of George. "What would you do if you didn't play baseball, Babe?"

"I been thinkin' about the movies. I starred in one already. I also been thinkin' about boxing."

"Go ahead, Babe," Ruppert said.

George sat, waiting for Ruppert to say more, but he didn't. Finally, George gave in, losing the battle of silence.

"What about my advance?"

"How much you want?" Ruppert said.

"Ten thousand."

"I'll write a check right now. Ten or twenty thousand if you want, but first, read this contract and sign it."

George pulled the contract in front of him.

"Listen, Babe, I want you to play for the Yankees. We're building a new ballpark just for you. But you've got to start following rules," Ruppert said. "If you don't, you'll end up like Shoeless Joe.

"Landis won't give you any slack. He was hired to clean up the game and help baseball improve its image. He'll watch your every move. He's already upset with you."

"What did I do?" George asked.

"You didn't follow rules about barnstorming."

"He can't make rules in the off-season or off the ball field."

"Yes he can, as long as you're in baseball."

Ruppert slid a fountain pen across his desk to George, and he signed the contract.

"Can I get my advance now?"

"You didn't read it," Ruppert said.

"I heard what you said. I trust you."

"I want to be your friend. So does Coach Huggins."

George sat quietly and stared at Ruppert.

"You've got to know there are people out there that think you're a Negro."

George took a deep breath and stood up. He turned away and said, "That's bullshit, and I'm tired of it."

"It's true, isn't it?"

"No, damn it," George said. He turned back around. "Where'd you come up with that?"

"Hell, Babe: the owners, for one. We meet regularly. Frazee thinks you're African." Ruppert leaned forward and put his elbows on his desk. He folded his hands and said, "A lot of people still think he got rid of you because he was afraid you'd get kicked out of baseball and he'd be stuck with a bad investment."

"Fuck him. I'm as white as he is."

"Maybe," Ruppert said. "But the rumor's out there."

"It's a lie."

"You're lucky we pay the way we do for sports reporters."

"They're a bunch of jerks," George said, then stood up.

"Babe, sit back down."

George had teared up.

"You bring thousands of fans to the ballpark, and that's money in *both* of our pockets."

"Then why do you say things like that?"

"Because a lot of people believe it."

CHAPTER FORTY-ONE

Cammie wore one of his long white dress shirts. The tails reached down to the middle of her calves and she glided over the shiny wooden floor in her bare feet, swaying to the rhythm and sound of "Lady in Red." Darwin was on his knees picking up scattered photographs. As she rocked back and forth, she swooped downward and lifted the old suitcase from the floor and in one motion swung it onto the dining room table. Something fell and slid across the floor.

Darwin reached under the sofa and pulled out an autographed baseball card. Cammie was lost in the music; her eyes were closed. She kept dancing.

He stood up and tapped her on the shoulder, showing her what had come from the suitcase.

"Where did you get this?" she asked. She flipped the cover of the suitcase open. It was empty. She felt along the inside walls and stuck her fingers under a gathering that formed a satin lining.

"Pockets," she said. "I didn't notice them before." She ran her fingertips along the interior walls and pulled out a folded hand-written letter.

Dear Issie,

Wish I was there. Good luck with the kid.
Don't think she is mine, but here's some
money to keep it secret. I'll visit you
next time I come to Kanses.

George

"You think George is the Babe?"
Darwin nodded.
"Think he ever made it back to Kansas?"
"Look at the handwriting. Same as the card."
"Looks like the same ink too. Think it's authentic?"
"It's famous," Darwin said. "See the *B* and *R*?"
"But the card says 'Babe.' The letter says 'George.'"
"Babe was his celebrity name—like a stage name. He used the more personal form in the letter."
"The son of a bitch," Cammie said. "I bet he never saw her again. She probably waited most of her adult life. Poor Issie."
"That makes you his great-granddaughter."
"It makes my grandmother a bastard child."
"Maybe that's why she had lighter skin." Darwin said.
Cammie stared into space.
"The letter's probably worth a lot." he said.
"I don't want anyone seeing it."
"It doesn't make *you* illegitimate."
"But it's my great-grandmother's secret," Cammie said. "He probably had little bambinos sprinkled all over the country."
"That wouldn't make *you* any less related."
The telephone rang, and Darwin picked up.
"I was just thinking of calling you, Lieutenant," he said. Then he listened. "Sure, we'll come down." He hung up and turned to Cammie. "They've got some stuff about Eddie."

"You go," Cammie said. "I'm not in the mood."

"Depressed?"

"Kind of," she said.

"You just found out you're related to a great American hero."

"I feel sorry for Issie. I wonder if my mom or grandma knew. I wonder if they read this letter."

"It's not like Ruth spent a lot of time in Kansas," Darwin said. "He barnstormed across the country a bunch of times and probably spent one night or a couple hours with her."

"You don't understand," Cammie said.

"I don't mean to be irreverent, but she got knocked up and the guy left town. She was probably pissed off."

"You're talking about my great-grandmother. You're a typical male."

"She probably got caught up in the moment, like we just did."

"What we did wasn't important?"

"Darn important," Darwin said. "But I didn't just meet you this afternoon, and I'm not hopping on a train tomorrow and leaving. I *love* you."

———

Numerous desks were lined along a wall. Lieutenant Wilson sat at his. Fluorescent lighting was on in only half the room, and his desk sat partway in the shadows. He examined papers in a folder and looked at a computer screen. He turned as Darwin walked in.

"You're here late," Darwin said.

"Where's Cammie?"

"She wasn't in the mood."

"I thought she'd be curious," Wilson said.

"What do you got?"

"Eddie's real name was Elijah Parks. He's from Brooklyn. Apparently, he was just visiting."

"Any suspicious ties?" Darwin asked.

"If you're talking about connections to the underworld or extremist organizations, we haven't found anything. But I wanted to show you these." He pulled a folder from the corner of his desk and opened it. He spread six 8 x 10-inch photographs on his desk. "These are pictures of the walls in his apartment. They were attached to an e-mail sent by NYPD."

"Looks kind of cramped," Darwin said.

"He had season tickets to Yankees games, though they were in his dad's name and the old man died eleven years ago."

"Must have had money if he could afford season tickets?"

"You'd think so," Wilson said, "but he drove a cab."

"Taxi drivers make a lot of money in New York. Right?"

"Compared to KC. Look at his walls."

The apartment walls had been plastered with old Dodger photographs and articles from sports pages. There were no bare spots and a lot of pictures of Jackie Robinson.

"The guy was obsessed," Darwin said.

"Apparently, he had been treated for obsessive-compulsive disorder. He saw a shrink."

"Wouldn't that indicate he had another source of income?"

"That's what we're thinking," Wilson said, "but we haven't found the source yet."

"Did he have a life outside of baseball?"

"Cab driver and an officer in a Brooklyn Dodger fan club. His cell phone records showed he was pretty much a loner."

"Who'd he go to games with?" Darwin asked.

"Nobody. He had two reserved seats but sat alone."

"What did his parents do? Were they the ones that established the trust fund?"

"His dad was a doctor, but we're not sure he was the key source for the money Eddie lived on. However, we haven't been able to establish any kind of conspiracy or link to anyone else. Not yet anyway. My hunch is we won't."

Darwin took a chair from an adjacent desk and turned it around. He crossed his forearms on the back of the chair.

"Two guys cornered Cammie in the River Market today. She handled it pretty well," Darwin said, "but they wouldn't tell her who they were and whether or not they were acting on their own."

"What'd they say?"

"They wanted to know what she'd said to others, whether she'd told anybody about her uncle."

"What was there to tell?" Wilson asked.

"They told her he had something to do with integrating pro sports."

"We're learning more all the time."

"We're trying to find out if there might have been a blood link between Cammie and Babe Ruth."

"That'd surprise a lot of people," Wilson said.

"Who knows? He might have just had a relationship with a black woman."

"If he was black, what about all of his records? Blacks weren't allowed to play back then."

"Blacks weren't outlawed in writing," said Darwin.

Wilson put his feet on his desk and crossed his legs. "What about the two guys? Did they threaten her?"

"I guess not; they were in public. She walked away, but she was bothered."

"What'd she tell them?" Wilson asked.

"To leave her alone."

CHAPTER FORTY-TWO

1865

Hartford Road was lined with spectators three and four deep. They cheered and shouted congratulations at the Union troops marching in loose formation south into in Baltimore. Children tossed confetti, men raised their fists, and women smiled through their tears while searching for their sons or husbands. Drums beat and the cadence of footsteps rumbled, while flutes played "When Johnny Comes Marching Home."

A woman in a powder blue dress broke from the crowd and lunged at a soldier. He opened his arms and they hugged and kissed before she pointed back toward the bystanders to an older woman with a baby. The soldier darted into the crowd and lifted the child into one arm while reaching back to hug his wife. He beamed, then handed the crying infant to its mother and scurried back into formation. He turned once more and waved.

Becca watched from a stone staircase leading to an apartment building. Hundreds of Union soldiers passed by. The music faded, but the pulse of the drum corps lingered as the marchers pounded the cobblestone road. The cheers seemed muffled as her thoughts drifted back to John Rhoadie. She, too, held an infant in her arms.

A father spotted his son in the ranks, and the young infantry-man broke formation to greet and hug him. The older man's eyes dripped tears. The boy smiled at first, but his eyes narrowed as he searched for someone that never appeared.

Becca scanned the endless rows of Union soldiers as another line of drummers approached. The beat intensified. Her eyes fell on a thin marching man with a sad, empty stare.

"John Rhoadie," she shouted. "Up here."

His eyes searched for the person shouting. Then his face lit up and he waved. She stepped down to the street and he rushed to meet her. They both hesitated; then he moved closer and she reached out with a free arm. He hugged her as several parade viewers gave curious looks.

"Yuh r'member me?" she asked.

"I didn't know if you were still in Baltimore." He looked into the brown eyes of the infant. "Who's this?"

"George," she said.

"Are you a mammy?"

She conceded a weak smile. She wanted him to hug *her* or at least ask about her.

"I gotta go," he said as he backed away. "I'll be back. We're going to Fort McHenry."

"Dat ain't nothin' but a war jail."

"War's over. Prisoners was graycoats," he said. "Where can I find you?"

"I work 'round the corner. At Montebello."

He turned and jogged back to his unit but shouted over his shoulder. "I'll find you. Can I come by?"

———•———

John walked along a redbrick sidewalk parallel to a narrow dirt road bordered by long stone curbs. The smell of salt water hung in the air. The young man wore a clean Union Army coat and carried a large pink peony blossom. He stopped to examine a castlelike stone home perched on a hill. A black wrought-iron fence surrounded it and its sprawling green lawn. The front gate was open, and he walked up a cobblestone carriage path to a wide stone stairway. He climbed the steps and used a large brass knocker on one of two tall doors.

No one answered. He was retreating down the stairway when he heard the door open. He turned.

"Hello, John Rhoadie. Whut yuh doin' in dis parta town?"

"I come to call on you."

"Don' you give a woman warnin'?" Becca's brown hair was tied on top of her head. She wore a white apron and carried a broom.

"I didn't know how. And if I was to deliver a note, I might just as well stop and say hello." He hesitated. "I can come back another time."

"Maybe yuh should."

"Okay then, but I'm not sure how much longer I'll be at Fort McHenry. I'll probably be goin' back up north."

"Yuh said Baltimore was yo' home."

"If I can't see you, I just might head *farther* north to Philadelphia."

"I ain't dressed for company." She leaned closer and whispered. "I ain't a slave no mo', but I still gotta work."

"You look wonderful to me."

"Wait," she said and closed the door. He paced, then sat on the second granite step, still holding the peony. After a few minutes, the door opened again. Becca's long dress swooshed as she sashayed down the steps. Her apron was gone; her hair was down. She sat next to him.

"I work and live here now," she said. "Mr. Garrett, he's my boss. He's the president of the railroad, yuh know."

"You live here alone with him?"

"He gots a family."

"That's better," John said. "Will you walk with me?"

"Where yuh wanna go?" she asked as she got up. He reached back for her hand, and they strolled away from the house and onto the massive, manicured lawn. The sun shone on her brown, smooth face. Her lips were ruby. He led her into a thick grove of mature trees near the six-foot-tall wrought-iron fence. He pressed her against a large oak and kissed her. She twisted her shoulders and turned her head. "Quit it, John. I ain't that kinda woman."

"I been away at war. Aren't you glad to see me?"

"I guess," she said, "but yuh gotta show respec'."

He held the peony up. She smiled and took it; then he kissed her again and she was less resistant. He lifted her dress.

"John. No." She brushed his hands away and stepped back. "Not here. I gots a good job. I can't have nobody seein' me carryin' on wid a soldier, even if yuh is a bluecoat."

"Can we go inside?"

"Miss Rachel's in dere wid her kids."

"Damn, Becca," he said. "I'm so excited to see you."

"Come wid me," she said. She took his hand and led him around the house into the backyard where there was a large carriage house. They opened a side door and climbed a steep wooden staircase into a second-floor hayloft above some draught horses and a couple of fancy buckboards. Heat and wet air accentuated the stench of horses.

Becca turned and puckered her lips. John pushed against her shoulders, and she fell back into a pile of loose hay. He lowered himself on top of her.

—■—

She pushed the door of the carriage house open, and she and John emerged onto the shady grass courtyard behind the house. She pushed her dress down and brushed hay from it. They sat on the back stoop.

The back door opened and a thin brunette in a long pink chiffon dress carried a tray with two tall glasses of lemonade.

"You might enjoy something cool," the woman said. Her hair was perfectly combed and wrapped on top of her head. Her face was powdered and her eyelashes extra long.

"Thank you, ma'am," John said.

"I'm Rachel Garrett."

"John Rhoadie, ma'am. I'm a friend of Becca."

"I can tell."

"Ah motty sorry, Miss Rachel," Becca said. "Yuh should not wait on me."

"Just returning the favor, my dear," the soft-speaking woman said with a smile. "Anyway, you're entertaining a soldier. It's my patriotic duty." She retreated back inside.

"You really live here?" John asked.

"On da third floor. It's motty hot up dere."

"Do they know you're a slave?"

"Ah'm not," Becca said.

"That you were?"

"War's over."

"Maybe not," John said. "A telegraph came into the fort this morning."

"But Lee surrendered," Becca said. "And da parade."

"Lincoln was shot last night. Killed."

"Dat can't be true."

"The *Baltimore Sun* printed an extra. I saw it on the way here."

Becca stood up and took a few steps away from him.

"You're safe," John said.

"I don' want to go through it anymo'."

"Don't ever go back to the South, Becca."

"Dere's mo'," she said. "Ah gots a baby."

"Your own?"

"Yuh saw it. At the parade."

"It was white," he said.

"Da daddy is white."

"I didn't know." He lowered his head.

"Yuh didn't know what?"

"That you'd been with another man," he said.

"I ain't."

CHAPTER FORTY-THREE

Darwin's office door was open, and he thought that was odd. He had walked into the lobby of the law offices, said hello to Jody, stopped and picked up a fresh cup of coffee, grabbed a section of the morning newspaper, then walked to his office. Bob Flynn sat inside reading the sports section and didn't look up when Darwin came in. Darwin put his coffee cup down and took his chair.

"We need to talk," Flynn said. He folded up the newspaper and tossed it on the corner of Darwin's desk. "I understand your affair with the black chick has become the talk of the office."

"I didn't know that."

"I overheard the girls huddling around the water cooler."

"We have a water cooler?"

"Okay, the microwave," Flynn said. "Anyway, it shouldn't be any of my business. Except that I'm jealous. On the other hand, it is my business because you report to me and she's a client."

"Was I supposed to get permission?"

"Yes, particularly if the client hasn't paid us a dime."

"I'll check into it. She'll make a payment."

"That's not really the point either," Flynn said. He slouched back in his chair so that he was almost reclining. The top of his shirt was unbuttoned and his fingers were interlocked across his chest. "I suspect you're spending a lot of time working on affairs—and I use that word loosely—having to do with the client in question, and you're not billing for all the time."

"You're probably right."

"I usually am," Flynn said. "Listen, good buddy, you're still new to this firm, and the partners are worried you don't have your priorities in line."

"Not enough billable hours?"

"There you go," Flynn said. "We've talked about this before and I can only cover for you so long."

"I appreciate it."

"I'm under the gun, and I could use your help. And it would help you increase your billable hours."

"Sure," Darwin said. "That would be great."

"I think I can save your ass, but you better figure out a way to collect more money from your girlfriend or stop spending so much time on her stuff. What's going on there, anyway?"

"Since her uncle died, she's been threatened. He had some connection to Babe Ruth, and apparently the Bambino was part black."

"No way," Flynn said.

"There are some pretty clear indications, and Cammie might be related to him."

"Any chance she'll get an inheritance?"

"Nothing like that," Darwin said.

"Too bad. Maybe she'd pay her bill." Flynn stood up and knocked on Darwin's desk twice with his knuckles. "Anyway, come into my office after lunch. I need help." He backed out of Darwin's office. "And you can spend your evenings with what's-her-name."

"Cammie."

"Right, Cammie." Flynn disappeared.

"Hey, Bob." Flynn stuck his head back inside Darwin's door. "Am I really the talk of the office?"

"I asked and Jody told me it wasn't any of my business."

"Are the partners *really* upset about my hours?" Darwin asked.

"It might be worse than I let on."

———

The warm sun felt good against Cammie's cheeks. The air had a spring scent of lilac from bushes lining the parkway. A city bus drove by and gas fumes overpowered the lilac smell.

Cars honked, a siren sounded in the distance, truck engines groaned, and a far-off jackhammer pounded as she walked along the downtown street.

A duffel bag hung over her shoulder. Her hair was pulled back. She took long strides. She stopped at the corner and looked to both sides, then behind her. A tall man followed her. He wore an open trench coat and had his hands in his pockets. She grinned when she recognized it was Detective Gilmore, and she waited for him to catch up.

"Is this coincidence or are you watching out for me again?"

"Not officially," he said. "I'm not guarding you. I'm what you might call *observing*."

They kept walking, now together.

"What's the difference?" she asked.

"I can't be responsible for safeguarding you. But occasionally, when I'm not busy with other cases, I can *observe*." He smiled. "It's a casual thing."

"Everywhere?"

"Rarely anywhere," he said. "In other words, don't get used to it, and don't rely on someone like me looking out for you. You're pretty much on your own."

"How'd you know where I was?" Cammie asked.

"I've been apprised of your routine: dance practice every day from 10:00 until 2:00, with a half-hour lunch break."

"Apprised?"

"Informed, made aware of."

They stopped at the corner and waited for the light to change.

"I didn't realize a cop would use such sophisticated vocabulary."

"It's one of the ten words they taught us at the police academy to impress people."

"I appreciate that you're watching out for me."

"But I'm not," he insisted. "I'm just checking up on you."

"Why now? Why in the middle of the day?"

"That's when you're most prone. You're most predictable in the daytime. And that's when most assailants strike. They learn your pattern and can wait and watch for you."

"So I don't have to worry as much at night?"

"You're usually with someone at night, aren't you?"

They crossed the street and a man wearing a business suit approached them.

"Excuse me," he said. They guy directed his question to Gilmore. "Can you tell me how to get to the Mystique Steakhouse?"

Gilmore started giving directions. "Broadway is two streetlights up." The guy asked more questions, and Cammie waved and kept walking.

"Thank you," she said. "See you later." She disappeared into a parking garage. Instead of taking the elevator, she jogged up two flights of stairs.

A man stood in her path, one of the same men she'd run into at Harry's after dance practice the day before.

"Remember me?" he said.

"Yeah, KKK."

"Smartass. Come with me." A black four-door Mercedes sat on the ramp of the parking garage. Its engine was running, and a driver sat behind its tinted windows.

"Not on your life," Cammie said.

He grabbed her elbow and pulled her behind him. She jerked her arm back, but he didn't let go.

"Don't even think about it," she said.

"Let's talk." He pulled her again.

"No."

The driver got out of the Mercedes. He left his car door open. The car was running. He opened the back door and assisted his partner. Together, they lifted Cammie off the ground and hauled her into the backseat. The first guy held onto her while the driver got in and closed his door. They sped down the parking-garage ramp and out onto the busy street. They stopped at the curb, and the guy that had asked Gilmore for directions climbed in the front seat on the passenger side and slammed his car door.

Cammie squirmed and yelled, flailed her arms, and kicked.

"Let me go, damn it. Help. Somebody."

When the car was speeding along 12th Street, heading west, she finally realized the futility of struggling and stopped.

"What do you want?" She sat up straight, and the guy let go.

"Stop fighting. We just want to ask some questions."

Cammie stared out the backseat car window as they sped south on I-35.

"You've just crossed the state line," Cammie said. "Now it's a federal offense."

The guy sitting next to her in the back seat acted as though he didn't care. He sat still and didn't even look at her. The driver and passenger up front just stared ahead.

"We're in Kansas now," she said

"We're not kidnapping you. We just want to talk."

"You could have talked to me back in the parking lot."

"Not without your detective friend getting in the way."

"What do you want?" Cammie asked.

"We tried to talk to you the other day and you walked away."

"Maybe it's the way you came across."

"Can we talk now?" the man asked.

"Do I have any choice?"

CHAPTER FOURTY-FOUR

1300

John's gray shirt was saturated with perspiration. He lifted one end of a large wooden crate from the hull of the freighter, and a muscular man holding the other end strained to help swing the load onto a platform. He'd been quiet and deep in thought.

"You going to marry her?" the muscular man asked. He wiped his brow with the back of his gloved hand.

"I don't have much choice."

"Just leave."

"I can't do that, Lukas."

"Hell, John. She's a nigger."

John dropped his end of the crate and swung his fist into Lukas' jaw. He fell back against other crates. John held both fists in front of his face and gritted his teeth, but Lukas merely raised a hand to his face, grimaced, and moved his jaw back and forth.

"Jesus, man, what are you doing? I'm your friend."

"She's *not* a nigger."

"I was just trying to say nobody would hold it against you if you moved out."

"I couldn't live with myself," John said.

"She's a damn handsome woman. And she ain't that dark. Kinda looks like one of those pretty Latin women. You know, the ones that dance down at Sully's on the weekend."

"I don't even see the color. I think I love her."

"Then marry her, for Christ's sake."

"She says I got to or move out."

"Then you gots to."

"And there's the kid."

"You sure it's yours?"

"Becca certainly is."

Lukas cupped his hand around his jaw and opened his mouth to test it. He squinted and tilted his head slightly to the side. "I can tell you feel strong about her."

———————

The noisy barroom was dark. The crowd was primarily dock-workers. Men shouted and laughed. A few black musicians played instruments in the back. One played a piano. A tall, thin black man plucked a mouth harp and swayed to the melody. Another man played a wooden cornet, while yet another performer sat on a stool and thumped hand-carved drumsticks on a small military drum between his knees. The music was hard to hear over the buzz of voices.

A smell of kerosene and beer filled the air, the kerosene from lanterns lighting the room, the beer from the wooden planks of the barroom floor.

A huge mirror behind the bar intensified the dim, flickering light and helped the male audience view a thin, Latin woman slink through cigarette smoke along a runway three feet off the floor. She had on a one-piece dance costume with ruffles around her rear end and bosom. She waved a long feather in front of her low-cut top. Lukas and John Rhoadie watched and drank luke-warm beer.

"I can't decide if I should marry her, Lukas."

"You goin' to hit me again if I say what I think?"

"I better get used to that kind of comment."

"Hell, John, she works and brings in money. That's a bonus."

"But it wouldn't be right to let her work if we're married."

"Let her work."

"She says the Garretts will let her bring the baby with her."

"Maybe *you* should work for them too."

"Maybe I will," John said. He looked at Lukas, but Lukas was staring at the dancer. "You think she's pretty?"

"Becca or the dancer?"

"The dancer's pretty dark," John said.

"I think it makes her more mysterious and exciting." Lukas waved her nearer and tucked a couple of wadded bills over the frills that bordered her cleavage.

———

The small Episcopalian church sat on a corner, just north of Baltimore. The wedding party was small. Other than the priest, only John and Becca, their infant child, John's best man, Lukas, and Becca's maid of honor, Rachel Garrett, were there. Becca held George in her arms. The ceremony took less than five minutes.

"How'd you come up with the name George?" Lukas asked.

"He wuz da man dat set me free," Becca said.

"The minister called him George Ruth."

"Who woulda knowed Ah wuz to see John again, and Ah like da book of Ruth in da Bible."

"We can change his last name," John said.

"We can have mo' kids. He been George Ruth for mo' than a year. He been wid no daddy mos' a dat time."

1891

George was tall enough that when he stood behind the bar at the Ropewalk Tavern, he could comfortably rest one foot on top of the cooler and lean forward with his elbow against that same knee. He read the newspaper and puffed a fat cigar.

"Pour me a cool one, George."

"How you doing, Mr. Booth. You want something for the girls?" The plump middle-aged man wore a white fedora. A golden chain dangled from a pocket in the vest of his business suit. He had a woman hanging on each arm.

"Ladies?"

"I'll have one," one of the women said. They both wore dresses with low necklines and had on thick red lipstick. Cheap jewelry dripped from their necks, ears, and wrists.

"Me too," the other said.

"Anything really new in that paper?" Booth asked.

"I was reading 'bout the Indian massacre. The cavalry wiped out a couple hundred of 'em. Some reservation out west—a place called Wounded Knee."

"Redskins started it, I bet."

"The cavalry did," George said. "They killed women and children too. Wiped 'em out."

"That's not fair," one of the floozies said.

"George, come sit with us," Booth said. "I can't handle both these fine ladies."

"Yeah, Georgie," one woman said. "Come sit with us." She batted her eyelids. "I want to hear more about the Injuns."

"I got to work, honey." He grinned and rinsed out the inside of a mug.

"How late you work, Georgie?"

"Until the bar closes. I kick everybody out 'bout 2:00."

She lingered by the bar and talked to George as Booth and the other woman took seats at a table near the back.

"Can I sit up here?"

"We don't have many women come in here." George waited on customers and tried to keep enough mugs clean to meet the steady demand from after-work regulars.

"Are you married?"

"No, ma'am. How 'bout you?"

"My husband's a sailor; he's at sea." She ran her hand over her shoulder-length hair and put on more lipstick. "Seems like it's been forever."

"What's that, ma'am?"

"Since he's been home," she said.

"You must miss him." He took more beer orders and slid some sudsy mugs a couple feet down the countertop.

"In some ways I do." She batted her eyes again.

When her mug was empty, George offered her another one.

"Ladies don't normally drink beer."

"How about coffee?" George said.

"Gin," she said. He served her a drink, and she sat at the counter until closing, talking with George anytime he wasn't busy with customers. "You live around here?" she asked him.

"I got a room upstairs."

"I'd like to see it."

———

Four sailors came into the tavern and sat at a back table. After sundown, they were still there. George sauntered around the bar-room, trying to keep the place clean, and he cleared their table of empty mugs. He wore a long-sleeved white shirt and tie and a clean white apron that made his brown skin appear darker. He carried a couple of mugs in one hand and slid his finger inside another to pick it up too. The glass had a little beer in it.

"Hey, I'm not done with that," one of the sailors said. George put the mug back on the table.

"Sorry, friend."

The sailor raised his voice. "I don't want it now that you put your nigger finger in it," he said with a southern drawl.

"I'll get you another one."

"Fuckin' nigger. You bet your black ass you will."

George froze and stared at the man. "I'm no more black than you are, friend. I said I'll get you another beer—on me."

"You bet your black ass you will."

"Maybe you should leave," George said. The other men at the table were now silent, watching him.

"I ain't goin' nowhere. Get my beer."

George turned away and started back to the bar.

"Fuckin' nigger," the sailor said.

George returned with a fresh mug of beer.

"Your mama a slave bitch?" the drunken sailor said.

George inhaled and said, "You can stand and walk out or I can help you out."

"Over your mama's dead body."

George reached for the beer he'd just set on the table and poured it into the crotch of the sailor. The sailor jumped up and yelled. "Fuckin' nigger!" He came at George.

George punched him in the jaw and he fell back and slid across the floor. George grabbed the back of his pants and shirt collar, lifted him up, and carried him to the door, then used his head as a battering ram and tossed him outside.

———

John Rhoadie walked into the tavern and sat at the bar. He was older now. His gnarled fingers were folded in front of him on the counter, his head dropping forward, his face weathered and wrinkled by long hours of farming in the sun. George didn't recognize him at first, then felt a sudden lump in the pit of his chest and put a beer in front of him.

"What brings you to town?" George asked.

"I decided to give myself a birthday present. I wanted to see my son."

"How old are you? Forty-three? Forty-four?"

"Forty-six."

"I shoulda sent a card," George said.

"You've *never* sent your mom or me so much as a letter, all the time we've lived in Illinois. If I hadn't come to Baltimore, I'd never hear from you. But that's not why I'm here. It's your mom. She's getting older and she worries about you."

"I thought about traveling to visit you, but I got this job. Is that why you came this far? To tell me to write?"

"Her birthday's coming up," Rhoadie said, "and it would be nice if you'd traveled to see her once before she dies."

"She's dying?"

"She's sad. At least buy her a gift and send it—on time and with a card. Let her know you think of her."

"I'll go see her," George said.

"We'd love to have you, but I know that's unlikely."

"I meant to write but never got around to it." George looked down at the countertop, then lifted his eyes to meet his father's. "It's good to see you."

"Bullshit. If you never saw us again, you'd be just as happy."

"When's her birthday? I forgot."

"June first."

George leaned nearer to his dad. "Nobody here knows."

"About your mom? You're ashamed, aren't you?"

"I'm seeing a German woman, kinda steady."

"And you're afraid she'll leave you if she learns you got Negro blood? Hell, George, the war's been over for more than twenty-five years."

"This is Maryland, not Illinois."

"That's why we moved away," Rhoadie said. "But what's important is what's in your heart. If nobody ever finds out about your bloodline, you still have to remember and love your mom for the life she gave you."

"Life will be better if people here don't know," George said. "I still care about her and miss her."

"Do you really think people care about skin color anymore?"

"Maybe by 1900 or 1925 things might be different. But my girlfriend's family is pretty old-fashioned."

"We all have *red* blood, George," John said. "I fought in the war to be sure people know that. I saw the blood of white men and black men—from the North and the South; it's all one color. All one color, George."

CHAPTER FORTY-FIVE

The man in the backseat reminded Cammie of a minister. He crossed his legs and folded his hands on his knee. He'd straightened his tie and unbuttoned his suit jacket. She could tell his black hair had been freshly trimmed; his skin was whiter around the edges of his hairline.

"Pull over, Frank," he said to the driver. "Into that Burger King. You want something to drink, honey?" The car veered onto an exit ramp.

"I didn't know we were dining together."

"Want a Coke?"

"No, thanks," she said. The car pulled into the parking lot.

"Frank, go inside and get me a Coke." The driver got out of the car and walked into the restaurant.

"We're patriots," the man in the backseat said. "Just all-American citizens concerned about the history of our nation. What can you tell us about your uncle?"

"He was a nice old man," she said. "He never did anything wrong in his life. He never hurt anybody."

"You must have cared a lot for him," the man said.

"I loved him." Cammie looked away, out the window.

"Did he ever talk about his past, about baseball?"

"All the time. It was the most important thing in his life."

"What did he tell you?"

"About baseball or Babe Ruth?" she asked.

"Since *you* brought up Ruth, let's start there."

"He thought he was part black. Anything wrong with that?"

"Only that it's wrong," the man said. "Ruth wasn't black."

"It was almost a hundred years ago. What difference does it make?"

"There's no reason to rewrite American history."

"Why do you care? Are you a fascist or just a racist?"

"It seems a lot of people want to change history these days. They attack anything that's been near and dear to America. They change history to fit what they *wish* it was."

"Ruth's race is near and dear to America?"

"Baseball's the national game. It's been a constant thread that helped hold this nation together throughout most of our history."

"Or apart, if you were black," Cammie said. "Never mind."

"Never mind what?"

"My question. You're a fascist."

—————

The black Mercedes sat in the far corner of the parking lot under a tree near a large garbage container. The tinted windows were rolled up. Two guys up front ate burgers from cardboard trays that held fries and soft drinks. The guy in the back with Cammie drank a Coke from a straw.

"Want some?" he said.

"I want some gum." She reached in her purse and felt the cool metal of her handgun. She kept her hand in the purse. "Are you going to let me go?" she asked. "Or are you going to beat me or kill me?"

The man grinned. His thick black hair was oily and combed back. His white shirt collar was stiff and his navy suit looked tailored. His shoes were shiny. By appearance, Cammie thought he was the boss. The other two guys didn't say anything.

"We don't want to hurt you. We just want your cooperation."

"It might be easier to kill me," Cammie said.

"Aren't you even a little bit afraid?"

"I don't even know your names."

"Call me Max. The driver's Frank." The driver raised his drink cup. "That's Crawdad. He's from Louisiana." Crawdad was scrawny, wore a diamond in his ear, and hadn't shaved that morning. He also hadn't talked yet or acknowledged he'd heard a thing.

"Who do you work for?"

"Ourselves," Max said. "You might say we're independent contractors. You sure you don't want something to eat or drink?"

"Who's paying you to hush me up?"

"Can't tell you."

"Why not?" Cammie asked.

Crawdad turned around. His eyes were beady, his jaw tight. He stared at Max.

"Get on with it," Crawdad said. "Quit all the bullshit."

"Max don't know who's paying us, honey," Frank said without turning around. Frank was stocky, the oldest of the three, probably sixty. He wore a brown suit.

"That's right," Max said. "We get our orders from a bowling alley. We used to get them from the airport, but since 9/11, they don't have lockers anymore."

Crawdad turned back around and took a bite out of his burger.

"I don't understand," Cammie said.

"Orders come in envelopes—with money," Max said. "We been told we can give you money if you agree to keep quiet." He waited for a response. She said nothing. "You can be an independent contractor too. It's legal and everything."

"Kidnapping me isn't," Cammie said.

"You can get out and leave if you want," Max said. "Nobody's stopping you."

"Right now," she said.

"If you want. Or we can give you a ride back to your car."

"How much are you offering?" Cammie asked.

"How much will it take?"

"What are the stipulations?"

"You got to keep quiet about your uncle and Babe Ruth, and you got to give us all the stuff your uncle left behind: letters, notes, any hints about the past. Everything."

"What did he do that's got you so worried?" Cammie asked.

"Don't know, exactly," Max said, "but we've been told he was pretty important. Helped blacks get into the major leagues."

"Where did you get the money?"

"I told you," Max said. "In a bowling alley."

"But where? What city?"

"New York."

"So it was the Yankees?"

"Coulda been. But there's a lot of people in New York that might want to keep this quiet," Max said. "Major League Baseball has an office on Park Avenue. The Yankees. Hell, some of Ruth's relatives live nearby in Connecticut. New York's kind of the center of the world."

"A million dollars," Cammie said.

Max grinned and took a sip of his Coke.

"Two million," she said.

He shook his head.

"Okay," Cammie said. "Just a million."

"We were told to offer you five thousand and ten if you held out."

Crawdad turned in his seat again.

"God fuckin' damn it. I said get on with it. Quit all the bullshit."

"Calm down," Frank said before he stuck a handful of fries in his mouth.

277

"Did you guys have anything to do with Eddie?" Cammie asked.

"That guy was loony," Max said. "A real freak. He was a Brooklyn Dodger fan, afraid Jackie Robinson would be less famous if people found out Ruth was really the first black. Hell, he mighta been a relative of Jackie, for all I know."

"How'd you learn about him?" Cammie asked.

"You ask way too many questions. The boss told me. I was curious, just like you, and didn't want to get into something that involved hurting anybody."

"I thought you got your instructions from a locker in a bowling alley."

"Did. But somebody had to tell us which bowling alley. That's when I started asking questions. You know, to be sure we weren't getting into anything dangerous or illegal."

"So you're not going to hurt me?" Cammie asked.

"There's no need for anybody to get hurt." She relaxed her grip on the gun.

Crawdad whirled. In an instant, he rose onto his knees and pointed a long pistol with a silencer at Max. A poof sounded, and air in the car seemed to suck inward. Cammie gasped. There was silence until Crawdad muttered, "Fucker talked too much."

Cammie looked at Max. He had fallen back into the corner of the backseat. His eyes gaped in a cold, blank stare. He had a small bullet hole, clean and round, in the center of his forehead. A bright circle of light glowed in the tinted glass of the back windshield. Blood trickled from the corner of Max's mouth.

She wanted his eyes to close. She turned back toward the front. Frank had turned to look at Max. Crawdad flashed a crazy glare at Cammie, and his eyes locked onto hers.

"What the hell did you do that for?" Frank said.

Cammie wrapped her finger around the trigger.

"Shut the fuck up," Crawdad said. "You want it too?" He pointed his gun at Frank. Without pulling it out of her purse,

Cammie squeezed the trigger of her own gun. Pop. The bullet hole on the side of Crawdad's head wasn't as clean as the one in Max's. The side of his head had ripped open. Blood had splattered against the dashboard and front and side windshield. The force of the shot knocked him against the console. He fell limp, partly on the floor and partly on the front seat.

Frank was sprayed with blood. He pulled pink gooey tissue from his cheek and wiped his sleeve across his face.

"Jesus Christ," was all he said.

The silence seemed to last forever. Frank looked around, then down at Cammie's purse. She turned toward him.

"Don't shoot. Please."

"I thought he was going to shoot you," said Cammie.

"Where's the briefcase?" Frank rose onto his knees and reached into the backseat. He pulled Max's black satchel into the front and yanked it open. He reached inside and pulled out a large envelope. He held two small stacks of bills and fanned them as if he wanted to be sure they were all real.

He handed Cammie a bundle of hundreds, evenly stacked and wrapped with a bank label that read "$10,000." He took the other bundle and shoved it inside the chest pocket of his suit coat.

"Don't ever mention anything about Babe Ruth being black," he said. "Not ever; not to nobody."

He turned away and opened his car door, then got out and slammed it. He walked away, weaving between cars waiting to place their orders at the drive-through speaker, and disappeared toward Rainbow Boulevard.

CHAPTER FORTY-SIX

1925

The train whistle was deafening as it pulled into a large depot. George and Bob Meusel walked up a flight of marble steps into a depot with a domed ceiling eighty feet above their heads. People sat along wooden benches and stood in lines in front of ticket windows.

"Where are we?" Meusel asked.

"I don't know." George looked up. The city's name was etched in granite above the revolving door heading outside: "Omaha."

From Springfield, they'd traveled to Peoria, Illinois; then Davenport and Dubuque, Iowa; Rochester, and Minneapolis, Minnesota; and Des Moines, Iowa, sometimes sleeping on the train, other nights in hotels.

"Who do we play here?" Meusel asked. "Another company team?"

"I think so. But we stay over and play a colored team from Kansas City on Sunday."

"Good. I get tired of clowning around. We need competition, even if we have to play niggers."

"I don't think you should call 'em that," George said. Meusel gave him a curious glance.

———

George and a bunch of the other Yankees took a streetcar south along a brick street on a high bluff over looking the Missouri River. They had worn their uniforms from the hotel and walked the final two blocks to the ball field carrying their duffel bags with their spiked shoes, gloves, and extra shirts and socks. Bats were slung over their shoulders. One player carried a canvas bag full of baseballs.

Commissioner Landis and Yankee owner Jake Ruppert wouldn't let them wear their Yankees gear on barnstorming trips, so players brought custom uniforms they'd had made, and the uniforms didn't match. Neither did their hats. George's uniform was trimmed in royal blue. Each letter was sewn individually, and together they stretched across his chest to form the words "Bustin' Babe." Meusel's nickname, "Long Bob," was stitched across his jersey too, but his uniform was edged with red-and-black piping.

The barnstorming teammates looked like a bunch of misfits. Their mismatched shirts were unbuttoned and untucked. Shirts ranged from white with blue lettering to gray with red stitching. Some wore hats; others didn't; and none of the hats looked the same. A couple of players wore slippers. Others wore dress shoes over their baseball stockings. They ambled down a gravel road to a lush green ball diamond in a hollow.

Twenty black players sat in the first-base dugout. They wore matching Kansas City Monarchs uniforms. All of their hats had crimson stripes that met at the crown. Each uniform had a big "K" stitched on the right chest and a "C" on the left side. Their pants each had a single stripe running down the side of their legs, and they all wore red-and-white striped woolen stockings.

When it came time to warm up, the white players joked and smiled and tossed balls back and forth in half-hearted, lazy ways.

The expressions of the black players were serious. They sprinted out to their positions and ran through a sharp pregame practice routine. They threw as if baseballs were shot from cannons—in straight, low trajectories. Two or three balls were in flight at any one time in different parts of the field. Their routine was sharp and smooth, as if choreographed. The players caught, spun, and fluidly threw. The balls zipped around the diamond.

A couple of white boys about twelve years old sat behind the fenced-in bench of Babe and his teammates. They drank from Pepsi bottles. Two black girls in their late teens sat in the grandstands behind the Monarchs' bench.

One umpire was dressed in a navy jacket and ball cap. He stood behind home plate and wore a wire mask and chest protector; another was dressed in street clothes and stood behind first base.

After the KC players finished their pregame practice routine and retreated from the field, the Yankee players, along with a few professional players they'd recruited from other teams at the end of the season, took the field. They trotted out to their positions, and the umpire behind the plate yelled, "Play ball!"

———

The Monarchs jumped out to a lead, up 4–1. By the fifth inning, the KC team increased its score to 7, while the barnstorming Yankees had managed to score only 2. George came in to pitch and held the Monarchs scoreless, and the Yankees eventually scored three more runs: 7–5, KC in the lead.

In the final inning, George came to bat with two outs and two teammates on base. He'd struck out twice before. He stepped up and smiled at the pitcher, then stepped out of the batter's box and pointed his bat over the right-field fence. The pitcher stepped off the mound and put his hands on his hips, his glove in one hand, the baseball in the other. He turned and rolled his eyes at the second baseman. Meusel, the base runner, smiled.

George lunged toward the first pitched ball and swung with a powerful whiff. His body twisted like a pretzel until he faced the umpire behind him, who called out, "Strike one."

The pitcher grinned. George's eyes narrowed, and he coiled his bat back for the next pitch. Again he lunged forward and swung with plenty of air between his bat and the ball. The pitcher's expression had become stern and determined. The first baseman trotted to the mound and said something, then retreated back to his position. Babe wiped his brow with his forearm.

The final pitch was low and inside. George connected and sent the ball sailing far over the right-field fence. He trotted slowly around the bases and tipped his hat at the pitcher, who again had his hands on his hips, his hat tipped back, the corner of his mouth turned up. The white players gathered around home plate, smiling and waiting for George to complete his round trip. His final step was a small leap with both feet together, landing on home plate.

"Way to go, Babe," one teammate said.

"Nothin' to it, Babe," another said.

———

Players from both teams, twenty-five in all, sat in the grass— spread out in the shade under several tall maple trees outside of the left-field fence. Some of them lay resting on their elbows. Others sat with their legs crossed, leaning back on their duffel bags. Most drank Falstaff beer from thin-necked brown bottles.

"I thought we had you," the black pitcher said.

"I thought you did too," Meusel said.

George laughed and threw his hat at Bob Meusel. "You didn't think I could do it?"

"You're so lucky."

"I never seen anybody hit a ball that far," the Negro pitcher said, "'cept for Josh Gibson. Did anybody go look for it?"

"Those two boys in the stands," Meusel said.

Before long, the two kids walked from behind the right-field fence toward the players lounging in the shade. One of them carried a baseball in his hand.

"You want this ball?" the kid asked.

"Bring it here," George said.

The kid shrugged and handed it over.

"You want it signed?"

"You gonna let us keep it?"

"Sure," George said. "Toss my bag over here," he said to one of the other barnstormers. "I got a fountain pen in it."

"Sign it for the pitcher," Meusel said. "Give another one to the kid."

George pulled out a pen and a second ball. He signed both of them and flipped one to the kid.

The kid's mouth fell open. "You're Babe Ruth?"

George signed and tossed the home-run ball to the pitcher.

"Thanks a lot, Babe."

"I never had a fella thank me for hittin' a home run off 'em."

"Ain't enough like me that get to pitch agains' yuh."

"And it's a shame," George said. "You got better players on this team than most professional teams."

Only eight players remained under the maple trees finishing off the beer. Most of the barnstorming team had walked up the hill to wait for streetcars back to their hotel. Some of the black players had piled into cars sitting in a dirt parking lot outlined with telephone poles lying on the ground. Several shoeless feet with red-and-white stockings stuck out from car windows and doors as a few Monarch players reclined on car seats.

Two thin black girls strolled toward the remaining beer drinkers.

"Who's the broads?" George asked.

"My sister and her friend," one of the younger black players said. "They rode up with us. My sister's one of your biggest fans."

"Tell 'em to come on over," George said. "What's *your* name, kid?"

"LeRoy. Most the guys call me Choo-choo."

"Everybody's gotta have a nickname," George said. Then he called out, "Come on over, girls."

The girls looked at each other, then took a few steps closer.

Bob Meusel stood up, brushed off his pants, and said, "Let's go George. I don't want to miss the last streetcar."

"Go ahead," George said, and Bob walked toward the hill. George turned to the girls. They had long legs and big eyes. "You girls want a signed ball?"

One of the girls said, "I'd love to have one."

"I ain't got anymore here, but if you girls talk your brother and his friends into giving me a ride back to my hotel, I'll get you one."

"We ain't got enough room," LeRoy said.

"The girls can sit on my lap." The girls smiled, and George said, "What's your names?"

One said, "Rachel."

"Issie," said the other, "short for Isadora."

The girls walked toward the cars. They turned around and looked back a couple of times. LeRoy lingered behind with George and a couple of Monarchs players.

"I once shined your shoes, Mr. Ruth—back in Providence, when you comed down to play for the Clamdiggers."

"That was a long time ago," George said, "my first year."

"I was jus' a kid. Me and my brothers hung outside the stadium and shined shoes. You was always nice to us kids and darkies."

"You never know," George said. "I might be part darky."

LeRoy laughed. George didn't.

———

The dusty Model T wobbled over bricks and streetcar tracks. George rubbed Issie's leg. She smiled. They pulled up outside the Flatiron Hotel in downtown Omaha. The girls crawled out first, then George. The black players stayed put.

"Come on in," George said.

The three black ballplayers and the two girls looked at one another as if searching for the right answer.

"We can't go inside," LeRoy said.

"Sure you can."

"Not unless we work there. Then we got to go in the back."

"You're my guests," George said, but there was no response. "Come on, girls."

Issie walked up beside him. "Come on, Rachel," she said.

"You go," Rachel said. "I'm waitin' here."

"Suit yourself. Most they can do is tell me to leave." She turned and hooked her arm around George's. He grinned and escorted her inside the front lobby.

"Good evening, Mr. Ruth," a uniformed doorman said. George raised his hand and gave the man an informal salute. Issie hung on to George and raised her chin, staring back at the guests and hotel employees in the lobby who were watching her. She and George got on an elevator and rode up to his floor.

Almost forty-five minutes later, Issie came back downstairs by herself. She strutted through the lobby, gazing right back at anyone who looked her way. Once outside, she flipped a signed baseball up in the air several times and caught it, then waved it over her head, swung her hips, smiled, and raised her eyebrows.

LeRoy and one of the other ballplayers sat on the running board of the Model T. Again, red-and-white striped stocking feet stuck out the back window. Rachel leaned her rear end against the front fender and folded her arms.

"What took you so long?" she asked.

"I got his autograph," Issie said, flaunting her baseball again.

"What'd you have to do to get it?"

"I got my ball, and the rest will always be my little secret."

"Did he kiss you?" Rachel asked.

"I ain't tellin'"

"More?"

"None of your business."

CHAPTER FORTY-SEVEN

Cammie stood outside the University of Kansas Medical Center on Rainbow Boulevard, across the street from the Burger King. A taxi pulled up. She opened the back door and got in, and the taxi drove away.

Darwin phoned. She looked at his number on her cell phone and didn't answer.

———

Legal files were spread across his desk. He placed his elbow on his desktop and his hand to his forehead. He reviewed a draft of a legal brief and jotted notes in the margins. He looked at his watch, then read more of the document.

Flynn knocked on his open office door and walked in.

"Thanks for all your help," Flynn said. "Why don't you go home? It's almost seven."

"I'm waiting to hear from Cammie. I've still got some work I can do. Go ahead. I'll see you in the morning."

"Here's a copy of that invoice." Flynn flicked it on Darwin's desk, on top of the brief he was revising. "If she can even pay a portion of it, I can stave off the pit bulls."

"I'll see what I can do."

"Are you all right?"

"Just tired," Darwin said.

"Hey, good buddy. Everything's going to be all right."

"Thanks, Bob." Flynn walked out.

Darwin tried to call Cammie again. Still no answer. At 9:20 p.m., he left the office and headed home. She wasn't there. At 11:00, he drove to her place. She wasn't there either. He called Wilson on his cell phone as he drove down Prospect Avenue.

"Have you heard anything about Cammie?"

"Nope," Wilson said. "Gilmore talked to her this afternoon but lost track of her."

——————

He walked into the lobby of the law offices, said hello to Jody, stopped at the kitchenette for a cup of coffee, and walked to his office.

Jody walked in with a Federal Express envelope.

"Heard from her yet?"

"Not yet," Darwin said.

"This came for you yesterday afternoon." She handed him the FedEx envelope. "How long has it been?"

"Almost a month," he said.

"What do the police say?"

"They've looked everywhere but the bottom of the river."

"She's probably just confused. Take it from me," Jody said. "Women get that way. She probably just needed space and time."

Darwin sat with his elbows on his desk, propping his chin on his fists. Jody sat down in a chair across from him.

"You think she was concerned about the black-white issue?"

"I don't think so," Darwin said. "I probably was more sensitive about it than she was—at first, anyway. I'm worried about her safety."

"I know you are."

Darwin opened the FedEx envelope, and Jody stood up to leave.

"The detective working on her case contacted the real estate company selling her house," he said. "She signed an agent agreement. But the communications are all one way, from her to them. The police think she's just hiding out. They won't spend any more time on it."

A plain white business envelope was inside the FedEx package, and inside that was cash.

"What's this?" he said. Jody was almost out the door and turned.

"Any note?" she asked.

He kept counting. "Four thousand two hundred and twenty dollars."

"Somebody paying you off?"

Darwin reached in a side desk drawer and pulled out a copy of an invoice.

"She's all right," he said.

"It's from her?"

"Exactly what she owed." He pulled the air bill out of the plastic sleeve on the FedEx envelope.

"Where's it from?" Jody asked.

"Strange. It doesn't say. The spaces under the 'From' portion of the air bill are blank."

"Give it to me." Jody walked around to Darwin's side of the desk. "Move over." He slid his chair over and she bent over at his computer screen. Her keystrokes sounded like a woodpecker at his keyboard. She didn't say anything but gazed at the screen and keyed in more data. A Federal Express Web site came up, and she pulled the air bill closer and keyed in the tracking number. Darwin watched over her shoulder.

"She's in New York," Jody said. "At least that's where the package came from. She must have gone to a Federal Express store, maybe a copy center, and paid cash."

"Maybe I'll make a trip to New York City."

"It shouldn't be too hard to find her there." Jody rolled her eyes. "Want an airline reservation?"

"I wouldn't know where to start," Darwin said.

"Does she have any relatives there?"

"I don't know; I don't think so."

"Her mom doesn't live there, does she? Girls down in the dumps like to talk to their moms. Or a girlfriend."

"She wanted to dance on Broadway," Darwin said. "Maybe even sing."

"There can't be *that* many Broadway productions."

"Why would she use Federal Express?"

"The envelopes are stiffer," Jody said. "She probably thought it was more reliable for sending cash. And if she paid cash, she wouldn't have to write down a return address."

"But she had to know we could track it back to New York."

"You didn't."

He turned up the corner of his mouth.

"Maybe she wants you to know where she is."

"If that was the case, she would have put her name and address on it. Or she would have just called me."

"She's probably unsure of herself and hoping you'll care enough to search for her," Jody said.

———

Flynn walked into Darwin's office. His suit coat was off, and his sleeves were rolled up. He wore reading glasses and carried a computer printout.

"Damn, Darwin. Your girlfriend made a payment. She finally come home?"

"I haven't heard from her. She sent cash."

"Where from?"

"New York City."

"Hell, that's just an island. You ought to be able to find her there."

"Fourteen million people. And she's probably using a different name."

"Women," Flynn said. "They never make it easy."

"Can I have a couple days off?"

"The good news is that since she's been gone, you've had more billable hours. And now that she's made a payment, the partners will be off my ass."

"Is that a yes?"

"Take a couple days off before Labor Day," Flynn said. "Make it a four- or five-day weekend."

———

Darwin got out of a taxi on West 45th Street and paid the driver. He walked up to the entrance of the Minskoff Theatre and looked at the billboard for *The Lion King*. He walked down to the Schoenfeld and looked over the billboard for *Chorus Line*. He didn't recognize any of the names, and Camille Griffin wasn't listed on either of them.

He walked over to 44th Street and checked *Les Misérables* at the Broadhurst, then *Beauty and the Beast* at the Lunt-Fontanne. He went to the Ambassador on West 49th Street and asked about female dancers in the musical *Chicago*, then walked up Broadway to the Brooks Atkinson and Broadway theaters. He couldn't find any clues that might lead to Cammie.

He purchased a ticket for the Thursday evening performance of *Chorus Line*, Friday evening for *Lion King*, Saturday afternoon for *Beauty and the Beast*, and Saturday evening for *The Color Purple*.

I should have come here first, he thought Saturday evening as he watched *The Color Purple*. There she was, singing the blues, dancing, and playing the part of Shug Avery. He looked in the program but didn't recognize the name: Elisabeth Withers.

He tried to walk backstage after the performance, but a security guard stopped him.

"I want to see Elisabeth Withers," Darwin said. "She's a friend of mine."

"Just a minute," the guard said. He turned and walked away. Then another man came to the door, a big man.

"Miss Withers isn't here tonight."

"Who played Shug?" Darwin asked.

"Millie Stinson. She's an extra."

"That's who I want to see."

"Sir, if you didn't even know who she was."

"I do," Darwin said. "She's a good friend."

"I'm sorry." He closed the door.

Darwin turned and lowered his head, then walked outside and explored, looking for the backstage door. He walked down an alley and passed a couple of bums. One held a brown paper bag the shape of a bottle. Neither of them said anything, but they both stared at him.

He turned around and walked out front. He waited. Several casually dressed people came out; they looked like performers, crew, or theater workers.

"Has Millie Stinson come out yet?" he asked one woman. She looked him up and down and kept walking. A couple of others came out, but not Cammie. He waited longer. He cupped his hands around his eyes and peered inside a glass door but couldn't see anyone.

He walked next door and leaned against a building. Traffic was still heavy, mostly yellow taxis. Pedestrians paraded past him: every kind of character, from tourists to hookers. An unshaven man wearing a dirty tweed sport coat, gray polyester pants, and grubby tennis shoes approached Darwin.

"Hey, bud, you got any extra change?"

Darwin reached his pocket and gave the man some coins.

"How about a couple of those dollars?" the man said. Darwin glanced to the side. Cammie came out of the theater and walked the other way. He gave the man what was in his hand and trotted after her.

He reached for her arm. She turned. He could see the confusion in her face. She started to smile, but then, as if she'd remembered she wasn't supposed to care for him anymore, she pulled away, stepped back, and glared at him.

"What are you doing here?" she said.

"I came after you."

"You shouldn't have."

"I want you to come home," Darwin said.

"It isn't going to work. I'm a different person now. And I am home."

CHAPTER FORTY-EIGHT

Hot water bubbled up around him. Steam rose. Perspiration beaded on his forehead. He leaned against the boulders of the hot springs pool, shut his eyes, and inhaled the fresh mountain air.

"You're Babe Ruth, aren't you?"

He opened his eyes. A brunette sat across from him. Her eyes glowed from daylight reflecting off the water.

"Who's asking?"

"I'm from New York too," she said. "My name's Claire. I recognize you from pictures in the newspapers."

"What brings you down to Arkansas?"

"I'm an actress trying to break into the movies. Cameras make a girl look bigger than she is, so I came down here to shed some extra pounds."

"You don't look heavy."

"Why are you here?" she asked.

"I been coming here every spring before training camp. I work out in the mornings and play golf in the afternoons."

"You're so tall and strong. You don't need to lose weight."

"My coach thinks so," he said. "Say, I been in a movie and got some Hollywood friends. I came here from Hollywood. Maybe I can introduce you to some of them."

"Would you?" Claire said.

"If you have dinner with me tonight, we can talk about it."

———

A fire blazed above the stone hearth next to their table. "Don't you have a wife?" Claire asked.

"I don't know what I'm going to do about that," George said. "I never see her anymore. She lives outside Boston, and I have a place in Manhattan during the season. I just got back from a three-month exhibition tour, and she didn't come. Now I'm going south to spring training for a month."

"Doesn't sound like much of a marriage."

"And a fella has needs."

1925

The ball exploded off his bat. Players on the field stopped and watched it soar. Everyone in the park had their eyes riveted to the speck whizzing through the sky, over the outfielders' heads, over the outfield fence, and still rising. The ball disappeared over the tall palm trees swaying gently in the breeze.

George walked out of the mobile batting cage. Several coaches had been watching as George took his practice cuts.

"Three in a row," George said. "Are you still wondering if I can hit?"

"You're overweight again," Miller Huggins said.

"It gives me more power." George grinned; Huggins didn't.

"Power's never been your problem. You've got to be able to chase balls in the outfield and run the bases too."

"Don't worry about it," George said to Huggins. "This is my comeback year."

"I hope so, because it wasn't pretty last year."

George walked closer to Huggins and put his arm around him. "You're not really worried, are you?"

"Ruppert thinks you're done—a pinch hitter at best. He says you abuse yourself and it's finally caught up with you."

"I'm not even thirty," George said.

"You've got the body of a fifty-year-old, Babe."

"What about the new stadium? The *fans* will want to see me."

"We know that, and we want you to play," Huggins said. "But we're worried. The colonel thinks it's all about filling seats, and if you play like you did last year, they'll be empty."

"I was suspended three times, almost a third of the season. I never got my timing. It wasn't a normal year."

"I hope you're right," Huggins said. "Get your glove and shag some fly balls."

George headed toward the dugout.

"George." Helen stood in the empty grandstands holding little Dorothy's hand. He opened a metal gate and walked up the cement stairs. He hugged Helen and bent down and kissed Dorothy on the cheek, then lifted her into his arms.

"What are you doing down here?" he asked.

"We decided to surprise you."

"Where you staying?"

"In the same hotel as the team."

"You've already checked in?" George asked.

"I told them we'd stay in your room, but the guy at the front desk said you already have a roommate. I thought you roomed alone."

"Usually, I do." He paused. "The coach had an odd number of players and asked me to take in one of the new guys until the roster's final."

"Maybe you can stay with us," Helen said.

"How long you goin' to be here?"

"You don't want us to leave, do you?"

"It's just—I wasn't expecting you," he said.

"It was so cold on the farm, and we weren't sure when we'd see you again. I thought this might be a good time."

"Sure, but I got a lot going on."

"What besides baseball?"

"Don't worry." George put his arm around Helen's shoulders. "I'll find time for my two favorite gals."

"We wondered if you missed us anymore. It's been so long."

———

He hesitated outside his room, planning what to say, then unlocked the door.

Claire sat on the bed with several pillows fluffed up behind her shoulders. The window was open, and a breeze blew against the thin, translucent draperies. She wore a taupe silk slip showing her legs and bare shoulders. One of her hands held a book open on her lap; the other was wrapped around a gin gimlet on a nightstand.

"I'm hot," she said.

The door behind him slammed shut from the same breeze that blew the draperies. She closed her book. He unbuckled his trousers.

———

They lay on the bed together. George opened his eyes. Hers were already open. She smiled.

"Claire, I can't eat dinner with you tonight."

"I'll wait in the room," she said. She rubbed the tips of her fingers across his brow. "How late will you be?"

"It's more complicated than that. Helen's in town."

Claire sat up and swung her feet around to the floor. "I thought you were separated."

"I haven't seen her in months. I had no idea she'd come down."

"Where is she?" Claire asked.

"In the hotel."

Claire stood up and walked to the closet. "I'm leaving."

"Don't, Claire. I love you. Helen and I don't have anything in common anymore."

"Then why are you afraid of her?" Claire said. "And by the way, whose bed were you planning to sleep in tonight?"

George knocked on the door. Helen opened it. She was dressed in a long, flowery dress and batted her eyes. He stooped down to pick up Dorothy.

"Are you hungry, honey?" he asked the child.

"She already ate," Helen said. "I thought we needed some time together alone."

"Who will watch her?"

"Juanita," Helen said.

Juanita walked out of a side room, sticking a bobby pin in her hair. She looked up and stopped. She dropped her hands and folded them together at her waist. She smiled. George blushed. Her big bright eyes contrasted with her dark features. Her long eyelashes helped make those eyes appear exotic.

"Did you bring your things?" Helen asked George. His eyes were still glued to Juanita.

"Is there room for me here?" he asked.

"This is a suite. Dorothy can stay in Juanita's room."

"I wasn't sure you'd have space for me. I'll get them after dinner." Juanita gave him a shy grin and walked closer, taking Dorothy from him and resting the child on her hip. "I wasn't sure I'd ever see *you* again," he said.

Helen grabbed his arm. "Let's go, George."

A streetlight shone through an open window onto the face of the ticking alarm clock. The small hand pointed at two. George crawled out of bed quietly. He tiptoed out of the room, grabbing his clothes before he closed the door gently behind him. He rushed to put them on and left the suite, buckling his belt once he was outside. His shoes remained untied.

He took the elevator upstairs and used his key to open the other hotel room. The lights there were out there too, and he began undressing.

"Don't bother," came Claire's voice.

"Sorry I'm so late. I told her how it had to be."

"Forget it, George. It's too late. You're not sleeping with me when your wife's downstairs. I'm not some slut."

"But honey."

"Don't 'honey' me," Claire said. "When you're divorced, look me up. I'm in the New York City telephone book."

George turned on a lamp.

"Where am I supposed to sleep?"

"I don't really care," Claire said, rubbing her eyes. "Maybe with your wife?" She paused. "Or have you done that already?"

George reached out to her and bent down over the bed. She slapped his hands away. "Don't even think about it."

"I don't have anywhere to go," he said.

"That's not my problem. I'm leaving in the morning. You can sleep here after I'm gone." She turned out the lamp.

"I want to sleep with you, Claire. I love you."

"I'll call security."

"It's my room," he said. He left and took the elevator back downstairs. He knocked on the door of Helen's suite. No answer. He knocked again. Finally, the door opened just a crack. Then it opened further and light from the hallway shone on Juanita standing in a robe. She shielded her eyes.

"I don't have a key," he whispered.

He walked in and moved toward Helen's room. Juanita walked the other direction, where she and Dorothy were staying. George spun around. She looked back over her shoulder and saw him staring, then stopped. He walked back to her and threw his arms around her. She hugged him back and gave him a brief kiss. He guided her backward into her room. The baby was asleep and the room was dark. He unbuckled his belt.

"No, George," Juanita said.

He answered in a low, soft voice. "You're the one I *should* be with. You're the mother of my child."

———

The lights were off. The blinds had been pulled up, and a warm Florida breeze poured through the window. The cord knocked against the oak window frame.

George's trousers were down around his ankles. He lay atop Juanita. He grunted into the silence; she moaned softly. The door behind them opened.

Juanita's eyes bulged. George flipped over. Light shone in from the living room, and Helen's silhouette filled the doorway, the wind blowing against her white gown.

She didn't say anything. No one did. George pushed off the mattress, stood, and yanked his pants up. Juanita cowered under the covers and pulled them up around her shoulders. Helen walked methodically to the baby's crib and pulled Dorothy up and into her arms, then walked out of the room without a word.

Juanita's face was now drawn and pale. George followed Helen, but she'd locked her bedroom door.

"Helen, I can explain," he said. She didn't respond. He banged on the door. "Open up, Helen." Still no response. He banged again. "Helen." He lowered his shoulder and exploded through the doorway, the door smashing against her bedroom floor.

He took two steps and stood on the door, his arms at his side. Helen had retreated into a corner, shielding little Dorothy in her arms. Tears rolled down her cheeks. The child cried.

"She's my daughter too," George said.

"You don't love her, and you don't love me."

"I do."

"Leave us alone."

"I'm sorry," he said.

"It's too late."

"No, it isn't."

"I came down here to give it one last chance."

"I want another one," he said. Now tears were in his eyes.

"You'll never change."

He stepped toward her. She pulled back and turned her face to the corner. She pulled the baby closer.

George sank to his knees. "Please, Helen. I'll do anything."

"I'm going back to Boston."

———

Juanita's heels tapped the floor. That was the only sound as they walked down the long, sterile hallway. The building manager hobbled with a pronounced limp, and the hem on his short leg was frayed in back. He unlocked the door. Juanita walked in first, then George and the manager.

"It's furnished," George said. "This will do." He relaxed a hand in his trouser pocket, looked around the living room, and wandered over to a large window overlooking Riverside Drive and the Hudson River. "What do you think, Juanita?"

"Es good. Muy bien."

"Shall I put it under your name?" the manager asked George.

"That's fine."

"Will you be residing here?"

"Sometimes, but it's mostly for her," George said.

"Who's responsible for the rent?

"Me," George said. Juanita moved next to him.

"Why don't you go down and get the contract ready," he said to the manager.

"Right away, Mr. Ruth." The manager limped out of the apartment and closed the door.

"Juanita, what's wrong?"

"Quiero Dorothy," she said. Her eyes welled up. George put his arm around her.

"I'll get her back, next time we play in Boston. I'll bring her back," George said. "She's our kid."

CHAPTER FORTY-NINE

Cammie turned her back on Darwin and walked away, heading down Broadway. Darwin followed and walked beside her, but she wouldn't look at him. She kept her eyes straight ahead and didn't slow down.

"I came two thousand miles," he said.

"You shouldn't have."

"What happened?" He asked. "Can you slow down? Can we at least talk?"

"Give it a break, buddy," a passerby said. "Leave her alone."

She stopped and whirled. "Yeah, leave me alone." Then she walked away again.

"No," he said. "I deserve more than this." And he caught up to her again.

"So it's about you."

"Okay, it's about me. I love you."

"It isn't going to work; it never was."

"What changed?"

"You're white; I'm black. You're a lawyer; I'm a dancer. We were raised differently."

She crossed Broadway and started down the stairway of the 50th Street subway station.

"You're not taking the subway at night, are you?"

"Every night," she said. "See, we're different."

"Is it safe?"

"It is for me. If you keep on like this, it may not be for you."

He grabbed her arm halfway down the stairway. She turned.

"Please, Cammie."

"That's not my name anymore," she said. She gave him a serious you-*better*-believe-me glare. "Don't blow my cover."

"I'm sorry. Can we stop and talk?"

"Follow me," she said. She reversed her course and marched back up the steps, then led him to an indoor newspaper stand and ordered two coffees. "You better give us some cream for his," she said.

"You remembered."

"It hasn't been that long." She finally broke into a grin. "I just remembered you don't like your coffee *or women* too black."

They walked to a fountain near the Gershwin Theatre and sat on a ledge around it.

"Darwin, honey, it's over. It isn't going to be like it was. We had a great time, and I'm thankful. Let's just leave it at that."

"I can't," he said.

"I don't love you anymore."

"You do too."

"What makes you so sure of yourself all of the sudden?" She crossed her legs and took a sip of her coffee.

"What happened, Cammie?"

She fought to hold back tears. "You don't know?"

"No," he said. "Tell me."

"I killed a man."

——◆——

Cammie recounted everything that had happened that afternoon in Kansas City, how she'd squeezed the trigger and shot Crawdad.

"I don't remember reading about it in the newspaper or seeing it on TV," Darwin said. "I'm surprised they didn't trace the gun."

"I never registered it. It was just a Saturday-night special, that cheap gun I got in the neighborhood."

"What did you do with it?"

"I threw it off the Broadway Bridge," Cammie said. "In Kansas City. It's somewhere on the bottom of the Missouri River."

"Why didn't you go to Wilson or Gilmore?"

"I killed a man. I used an illegal gun." She blew in her coffee. "And for all I know, they're still after me."

"Two of them are dead, and the other guy sounds like he's more afraid than you."

"There'll be somebody else," she said. "More of them." She looked up in the air and exhaled, then closed her eyes. There was silence for a few seconds. "That's why I changed my name."

"How did you do that?"

"You can get anything in this town. Remember, I had $10,000 in cash. I just needed $500 to get a fake license, picture and all. With that I went across the river to Jersey and got a real one. Then I came back over here and got a real one with the Jersey license, and the rest is history: Millie Stinson, New York, New York."

"Come back to Kansas City," Darwin said. "We'll explain it to Wilson."

"Then I'll be in the newspaper, it'll start all over again, and I'll probably have to get a lawyer."

"Thanks for paying the bill, by the way," said Darwin.

"I thought you'd like that. Anyway, I'm not going back to KC. I'd probably get arrested."

"I don't think so. You were the victim."

"I'm a poor black girl. I shot a white man at a hamburger joint. Doesn't sound good."

"What about us?"

She sighed. "I missed you."

He started to put his arm around her.

"No, Darwin. Don't."

"Where do you live?"

"Way north. 157th Street. In an apartment, not too far from Yankee Stadium. I went to a game. It was fun. The fans are hilarious."

"By yourself?"

"With my roommate," Cammie said.

"A girl, I hope."

"Another dancer."

"Can I buy you dinner?"

She shook her head. "No thanks."

"Will you come up to my hotel?"

She shook her head again. "I better go." She stood up.

"Cammie. It can't end this way."

She gave a faint smile. "It must."

"I'll move to New York," Darwin said.

"No you won't. One of the things that makes you so sweet is the Kansas in you."

She hugged him, then turned and walked away.

"Will I see you again?"

She shook her head again, that silent no. Then she walked away.

———

He walked the busy New York streets, a mile back to his hotel room. He had a difficult time sleeping that night and ended up watching an old black-and-white movie, *Double Indemnity,* with Fred MacMurray and Barbara Stanwyck. He couldn't help wondering if there was a way he could clear Cammie so she could come back to KC. He couldn't just give up.

———

The old suitcase Cammie had brought up from her basement still lay in his apartment, in the corner of the dining room. Darwin couldn't shake that eerie loneliness. He sat down and ate a bowl of cornflakes.

———

He walked into Flynn's office.

"Ever done any criminal work?"

"Erickson does most of that," Flynn said. "Sometimes Bennett. Why?"

Flynn was sitting at his desk. Darwin sat down on the other side.

"Did you find her?"

Darwin nodded.

"Damn. How'd you do it?"

"Just like you said. I visited a bunch of the theaters and eventually found her dancing and singing."

"Wonderful," Flynn said. "Is she coming back?"

"She's too afraid." Darwin crossed one leg over the top of the other and fidgeted with the cuff of his pants.

"Sorry to hear it, kid."

"That's why I need criminal advice."

"Doesn't sound good. But you know Erickson. Talk to him."

"Not that well," said Darwin.

"Come on, buddy." Flynn stood up. "Let's go. Right now." He walked toward his office door and tapped Darwin's shoulder on his way out. Darwin got up and followed him down a long hallway and into Neil Erickson's open office. Erickson sat at a side table reviewing some documents. He was in his midfifties, graying at the temples, and wore reading glasses and a gray pin-striped suit.

"Erickson, we got a legal question for you," Flynn said.

"Have a seat."

"You know Darwin, right?"

"How you doing, son," Erickson said. "What's the question?"

"This is where I take leave. Darwin?" Flynn turned and walked out of the office but looked back at Erickson. "Thanks, Neil. We owe you."

Erickson's glasses perched on the end of his nose. "What is it?"

"Let's say, hypothetically, that my girlfriend killed somebody."

Erickson sat calmly. "Murder or self-defense?"

"Self-defense."

"My first piece of advice: don't make her mad." He grinned. Darwin didn't, but it was the first time he'd seen a friendly side of Erickson.

"You're serious about this?" the older lawyer said.

"Yes, sir." Darwin explained what happened.

"I remember the incident." Erickson said. "It read like a gangland type of thing."

"Any chance she could get away without going through a major ordeal?"

"I'll see the Johnson County Prosecutor on Thursday. Let me feel him out."

"Could she get in trouble for fleeing the scene?"

"She could," Erickson said, "but let me do a little probing and get back to you."

"Do you need her name?"

"Not yet. I just want to ask some theoretical questions—find out whether or not there has to be a grand jury investigation. I'd hate to see her go through all that and have something go haywire. Then she gets accused and it gets drawn out over the next three years."

"That's what frightens her. And she's afraid media coverage would make her a bigger target."

"I don't blame her."

"The dead guys were trying to shut her up."

"She was lucky to get away alive."

"They probably didn't expect she'd have a gun in her purse."

CHAPTER FIFTY

1926

George pounded on the door. He'd tried his key twice; it didn't work. He pounded again. He walked around back. Nothing in the distance but forest. He cupped his hands against the window and looked inside.

"Helen, are you in there?" he called out.

He took off his driving cap, then his sport coat. He folded the jacket and placed it on top of a woodpile next to the backdoor, propped the screen door open, took three steps back, then lowered his shoulder. The door broke away from the jam.

He rubbed his shoulder.

"You didn't have to do that," Helen said. There she stood, ten feet away. Dorothy was in the hallway behind her.

"Why didn't you let me in?"

"What are you doing here?" Helen asked.

"I live here." He waved at four-year-old Dorothy, fluttering his fingers. "Hi honey." He started toward her, but Helen stepped in his path.

"I want you to leave," she said. "You don't live here anymore. You've got an apartment in New York—two from what I understand. You winter in California and vacation in Arkansas. And when you're not in one of those places, you're gallivanting around the country in trains and hotels, sleeping with whores and who knows who else."

"Helen, not in front of Dorothy."

"You haven't been here in six months," she said.

"But I own the house. And you're my wife." He paused. "I still love you, Helen."

"Is that why you're living with Juanita?"

"You kicked her out. I felt sorry for her and helped her get an apartment. That's all."

"It's in your name," Helen said. "You're paying for it and staying overnight there, aren't you?"

"Hell no. Where'd you hear that?"

"I hired a man to check up on you after I hadn't heard from you in six weeks. Not even a phone call."

"You coulda called me," he said.

"I did, George. You're never home."

"We have a series against the Red Sox." He brushed past Helen and squatted in front of Dorothy. "Hey, Baby. Can you give Daddy a hug?" She did, and he picked her up. Then he sniffed the air and walked around the corner into the living room. A man smoking a pipe sat in an armchair with his hands folded on his lap.

"Who are you?" George asked as he lowered his daughter to the floor.

Helen interrupted. "He's my dentist and a good friend."

"How good?"

"None of your business," she said.

The man in the chair stood up. He was a couple of inches shorter than George and lean, with thick brown hair. He wore a dark sport coat over a gray sweater-vest. He offered his hand to George.

"My name's Kinder," the younger man said, shaking George's hand. "Ed Kinder."

"You livin' here now?" George asked.

"I have a home in Watertown." Dorothy reached out to him, and he took her in his arms. George turned back to Helen.

"What the hell's going on? I don't feel welcome in my own home." He looked first to Helen, then to Kinder. "I'm staying here tonight, you know."

"That's probably not a good idea," Helen said.

"We got to talk—alone."

"It's been a long time since we did that," she said. "It's too late, George. I'm sorry."

George stared at her, then at Kinder and Dorothy. He turned and started out the front door but stopped and looked back at Helen. His eyes glistened.

Then he said, "Want me to fix the back door?"

———

His legs trembled. The train rocked back and forth as it rolled along the tracks. He held his stomach. He perspired and wiped his forehead with the back of his hand, then fell to one knee.

His teammate Steve O'Neill came by and leaned over him.

"You all right, Babe?"

"I'm sick as hell," George said.

When they arrived at the train depot, O'Neill and another teammate helped George into the station. They made their way into the waiting room and sat on a bench. George doubled over and moaned. Railroad patrons watched. Some moved closer.

"Get me out of here," he said. He rose and took three steps, then fell against a radiator. O'Neill and another man rushed to his side.

At the hotel, George ordered an airplane to fly him back to New York City. "I don't care if it drops," he said. "I just want to get home and see my doctor."

The Yankees sent him home the next morning on another train. Before they left, the Yankee scout Paul Krichell accompanied George into a washroom. George's face was pasty.

"I want to freshen up before we get to Penn Station," he said, "in case any fans show up."

"Anything I can do for you?" Krichell asked.

"Go get me some Wrigley's. My mouth smells from throwin' up." Krichell walked out of the washroom. When he returned, George was sprawled out cold with his head bleeding onto the white tile floor.

"Call an ambulance," the depot manager told one of his aides.

"No," Krichell demanded. "I'm taking him into the city, where he can see his own doctor and the team physician. Got a stretcher?"

George was carried onto the train, and he made the journey into the city in a sleeping berth, still unconscious. At Penn Station, an ambulance crew hoisted him from the sleeping berth through a window and carried George on another stretcher through the hectic depot crowd to a freight elevator. He went into convulsions, and an ambulance took him two miles to St. Vincent's Hospital.

Two hours later, he sat up in his hospital bed.

"That's the press for you," George said. "They think I'm dead and I'm fine. But I lost everything I ate. I'm hungry again. How 'bout a steak and some mashed potatoes?"

———

"George's condition is not serious," his doctor, Ed King, said. "He'll be out of the hospital in a couple days."

The *New York Tribune's* headline read, "The Bellyache Heard Round the World".

Helen traveled all the way from Boston.

"They told me he was going to die," she told Dr. King. "I got down here as soon as I could."

"We thought it was just gluttony at first, but he's got a high fever, and it doesn't seem to be coming down. We're still doing tests."

Helen walked in George's hospital room.

"I didn't think you cared anymore," George said.

"I'll always love you, George. I just can't live with you."

———

Three weeks later, George remained in his room at St. Vincent's, and Dr. King was forced to hold a press conference and answer reporters' questions.

"He's not going to be released yet," King said. "In fact, Mr. Ruth had minor surgery this morning. He had an abscess in his stomach. He's expected to be fine, and he'll be here one more week."

"What was it, really?" Helen asked Dr. King by telephone. "I'm his wife; I should know."

"I'm a doctor, but I also represent the Yankees, Mrs. Ruth, and they've made it clear the public is not to know any details."

"I'm not the public," she said. "Some newspapers said he's got gonorrhea or syphilis."

"Those are infections," the doctor said, "and an abscess can be a result of an infection."

"Which was it? Gonorrhea or syphilis?"

"I wouldn't tell reporters a detail like that," Dr. King said, "even if it was."

"But it was, wasn't it?" Helen prodded.

"I've heard rumors that you and your husband are separated."

"What business of that is yours?"

"Divorces can get messy," the doctor said, "and if settled in court, messy details become public."

"George and I are Catholic. There will never be a divorce."

———•———

The door cracked, then opened a bit farther. A man scanned the hospital room. George's eyes were closed. His sheets and a blanket were pulled up around his shoulders. The man walked in and pulled a chair up next to the bed. He pulled a newspaper from under his arm and started reading it.

A nurse came in and filled a pitcher of water next to George's bed.

"Can I help you?" she asked the man.

"I'm just waiting for him to wake up."

"Are you family?"

"This is Babe Ruth." George stirred and rubbed his eyes.

"I know who *he* is. Who are you?"

"I'm here to guard him. I'm with his employer, the Yankees, and they want to be sure reporters, overzealous fans, and other undesirables don't bother him."

"There hasn't been anybody here in three weeks but doctors and his wife," the nurse said. "I'll look into this." She walked out of the room.

"What are you doing here?" George said, squinting from sunlight coming through the windows.

The man stood up and moved closer to the bed.

"Hugh Fullerton, the *Times*."

"How'd you get up here?"

"The stairway," Fullerton said. "I'm a reporter. It's part of my job to get into places like this."

"I'm glad you came. I get bored, and I hate reading."

"What's wrong with you, Babe?"

"Hell, I don't know," George said. "They're still doing tests. They keep stickin' needles in me."

"Those tests at the university—Columbia. Remember?"

"They want more?"

"The commissioner does. But he doesn't want *you* tested. He wants a bunch of Negroes tested—only Negroes. He's putting them through the same tests."

"Why?" George asked. "And what's it got to do with me?"

"He's trying to prove you're colored. He's hoping the new test show your results are closer to theirs."

"What the hell?" George said. "How'd you find out?"

"I ran into Al Johansen, one of the guys that tested you."

"Landis doesn't like me. He thinks I'm no good for the game."

"Hell, Babe, all those fans aren't coming out to see *him*," Fullerton said. "They come out to see you hit home runs. What do the Yankees think about Landis?"

"The owners are afraid of him." George stared out the window. "Hey, you want to do an article about me?"

"I can always submit it to my editor. What about?"

"I want you to tell how my relatives are all from Germany and how I treat little kids good and stuff like that."

"Sure, but first I got to know why you're *really* here."

"They call it 'gluttony,'" George said. "Too much of a good thing."

CHAPTER FIFTY-ONE

Darwin felt uncomfortable around Erickson. He didn't say a lot and seldom smiled. He often wore reading glasses and peered over them while the corners of his mouth drooped. He was lanky and walked with long slow strides. A quiet man.

"Got a minute?" he asked. He'd taken a step into Darwin's office.

"Have a seat," Darwin said.

Erickson leaned back in a chair, crossed his legs, and interlocked his fingers over his belt buckle.

"I think we can get her off, but we'll have to go through the motions."

"Will she have to spend time in jail?"

"We can post bail," Erickson said, "but it won't be much, assuming she doesn't have a record."

"How much?"

"I'd guess five or ten thousand. Will she turn herself in?"

"I'm not sure," Darwin said. "She's afraid and doesn't have a lot of money."

"Unless there's something you're not telling me, there'll never be an indictment."

"What about the fees?"

"Too bad you're not married," Erickson said. "On something like this, we'd probably waive them."

"There doesn't seem to be much chance of that."

"That's probably good. It sounds like she's got problems you wouldn't want to inherit."

"Is there something I don't know?" Darwin asked.

"I don't know many attorneys with wives or girlfriends that carry guns, then change their names and hide out."

"It's not her fault. A bunch of thugs kidnapped her."

"I'll be glad to take care of it if you can get her in here." Erickson stood up and walked toward the door, then turned. "The two dead guys had records as long as they were tall. The police didn't know anybody else was involved. They think some joker named Quatrocelli was involved, but he and one of the guns are missing."

"She called him Frank."

"Frank Quatrocelli."

"He's still out there. That won't make Cammie feel any safer."

"What's her name?" Erickson said.

"Never mind."

"I understand."

"We don't have to defend her, you know. The grand jury would need enough evidence to indict her, and the prosecuting attorney told me they don't have it."

"Could that change?" Darwin asked.

"You never know." Erickson walked out.

———

Darwin got back on a plane and flew to New York. He waited outside the Broadway Theatre, but Cammie didn't come out. Finally, the lights went out inside. A security guard locked the doors from the inside.

Darwin knocked on the glass of one of the theater doors and the security man mouthed the words, "We're closed."

"I'm looking for my girlfriend. She hasn't come out yet."

He could barely make out the guard's words. "Nobody left in here."

He walked to the subway entrance where he'd last seen Cammie. She'd disappeared down the stairs, under the street. He walked down himself and examined a subway map. The red line traveled into the Upper West Side, and the next morning, he took a taxi there. He handed the driver some cash and walked around a neighborhood full of tall apartment buildings. He went inside one of them and looked at the mailboxes. None of the names looked familiar until his eyes stopped on *Stinson*. He went up an elevator and knocked.

"I'm looking for a Millie Stinson."

"She's not here," a young woman said. "Are you Darwin?"

"How did you know?"

"She told me about you. I'm her roommate, Sally." She wore rubber gloves as if she'd been cleaning a sink or toilet. Her hair was bunched on top of her head, and she blew out of the corner of her mouth to keep loose strands of hair out of her eyes. "I'd invite you in, but she's not here."

"I really need to talk to her."

"You ought to take her back to Kansas with you."

"I would if I could," said Darwin.

"Don't give up, honey. She's just afraid and confused."

"I didn't think anybody here knew."

"Nobody but me," Sally said. "She's playin' softball in Central Park."

———

Cammie stood close to the plate, her bat cocked, her legs spread apart. She bent slightly forward at the hips. Darwin stood twenty feet behind the backstop with eight to ten other spectators. There were no bleachers. The only seats were the player benches.

She swung so hard at the first pitch that she almost fell over. After she missed and whirled, she stuck the fat end of the bat on the ground behind her to keep from falling. She hit the next pitch solidly, high into the air and far over the right fielder's head.

She tore around first base. There was no fence, so she just kept running. As she rounded second, she turned to see if a fielder had the ball yet. No one had picked it up, and she slowed down, then trotted around third and into home.

After she crossed home plate, her teammates surrounded her and congratulated her. She smiled and jumped up and down with her hands over her mouth. Then she looked behind the backstop and saw Darwin. She walked back to the bench and looked over to him. He walked closer.

"What are you dong here?" she said through the fence next to the dugout.

"We've got to talk."

"I told you; it's over."

"I found you an attorney. He said he can get you off."

"I'm not willing to go through it all," she said. "Besides, I've got a new life. There's no reason to go back to KC."

"What about me?"

"You were one of the sacrifices." She turned to walk away.

"But, Cammie."

"No, Darwin," she said, looking over her shoulder. "It's over."

"I'll wait until after the game," he said. "I want to tell you what I found out."

She kept walking.

"Can you give me your telephone number?"

"I've got a game to play." She took a couple of steps and turned, then grabbed a glove and jogged toward the outfield.

"What if you're cleared?" he yelled.

"I still wouldn't leave New York," she said. She seemed like a different person. Cool, unsympathetic.

"I came all this way," he said.

"Go home, Darwin. Stay in KC."

———

He didn't hear the doorbell. The music was turned up too high. Classical music: a piano sonata. He was pouring himself a glass of merlot when the chime sounded again. He walked to the foyer to answer it.

"I need an attorney," she said. She wore dark glasses even though it was evening.

"What are you doing here?"

"Uncle Griff's house sold."

"Come on in," he said. He held the door open.

"I better not."

"You could have had the papers faxed or sent overnight and executed them in front of a notary."

"All my ID says Millie Stinson."

"What did you do with your old driver's license?"

"I threw it away," Cammie said. "Forgot I'd need it again. Besides, I left in a hurry. There are things in the house I want."

"It's silly talking in the hallway."

She took a few steps inside, and he let the door close.

"I probably overreacted a bit," she said. "I threw everything away except my birth certificate, and it's at the house."

"Do you want me to go over and get it?"

"You can come with me," she said.

Darwin placed his hand on her arm, and she pulled away.

"Sorry," he said.

"I don't want to be distracted. I need to be back in New York in three days."

"Glass of wine?"

"Water would be nice," she said. "What's the music? Beethoven?"

"Chopin," Darwin said. He walked in the kitchen. "Like it?

"Too loud."

He pulled a bottle of spring water from the refrigerator, then walked to his stereo receiver and turned down the volume. She scanned the headlines on a copy of the evening *Star* that lay on the dinette table. He moved behind her and reached around her, handing her the water. He wrapped his other arm around her waist. She turned and pulled her head back. "Don't, Darwin."

"I still love you, Cammie."

"You're just horny."

She let him remove her sunglasses. He placed them on the table, then put his palms on her cheeks. She showed no resistance, and he kissed her.

She seemed to enjoy it, then turned her head again. "I'm not here for that."

"It can't hurt."

"Yes, it can." She pushed him away.

CHAPTER FIFTY-TWO

George stood outside looking in and scanned the display window: watches, necklaces, and jeweled purses, even china. Engagement rings were displayed on black velvet and gleamed in the morning sun. Gold and silver settings with diamonds, emeralds, rubies, and sapphires. He walked inside, and a male clerk approached him.

"I'm looking for a ring," George said.

"Engagement?"

"I guess."

"In what price range?" the clerk asked.

"I don't know. I never bought one before."

He walked out of Tiffany's with a light blue box stuffed in the front pocket of his trousers and took a taxi to Juanita's apartment. He knocked on the door. Nobody answered. He used his key and walked inside.

"Juanita?"

He searched the bedroom and kitchen. An envelope with his name on it was taped to the icebox. He couldn't read all of the Spanish words in the note and left carrying it folded in his shirt pocket. He hailed another taxi and asked the driver to take him to Yankee Stadium.

"You're here early, Babe," Coach Huggins said.

"Where's that Mexican groundskeeper?"

"Carlos?"

"I can't remember his name."

George walked through the dugout, up the steps, and onto the field. Carlos was tamping dirt on the pitcher's mound.

"Hello, Señor Babe."

"Read this for me, will you? I can't read Mexican."

Carlos read the letter silently.

"She is going back to Ciudad de Mexico—Mexico City. Her father is importante: Plutarco Elias." Carlos looked up from the letter.

"Go on," George said.

"She says she loves you and misses her baby. She says her family needs her in Mexico. She wants to help them and says she will come back to America one day."

"When?"

"She does not say," Carlos said. "She says she is sorry about el apartamento."

"I bet she'll never come back."

———

He looked weak in his now-baggy uniform. He'd lost thirty-five pounds and wasn't allowed to play when he first returned after his stay in the hospital. Before games, he jogged in the outfield and took batting practice, but gone were the home runs and sharp, explosive hits. During games, he sat on the end of the bench next to a male nurse assigned to him by the Yankees' doctor, and none of the players sat near him.

"Are you here to protect me or them?" George asked the nurse.

"Dr. King wants me to be sure other players don't use the same towels you do, and you have to wait to take your shower after they're all done. When you drink water, he wants me to get it for you in a cup; he doesn't want you to drink from the same fountain as other players."

"I thought I was all right," George said.

"It's just a precaution."

"They all stay away from me anyway. Hell, they don't even talk to me."

Miller Huggins walked by with his hands in his back pockets.

"Hey, Coach, who's the new guy at first?" George asked.

"Lou Gehrig. Some say he might be the next Babe Ruth."

"He's too slow," George said.

"You aren't that fast anymore, Babe."

"But can he hit the long ball?"

"Haven't you been following the team?" Huggins stood about ten feet away, still holding his hands in the back pockets of his baseball pants. "Visit me in my office after the game."

The Yankees lost again, and the nurse escorted George into the coach's office. The nurse stood by the door and George sat in a chair in front of Huggins' desk. When the coach walked in, he threw his baseball cap on top of a metal file cabinet and sat down. He leaned back in his chair with his feet on his desk and his hands folded behind his head.

"This is the worst team I've ever had."

"Then put me back in the lineup," George said.

"I'd like to, but first we've got to get the rules straight."

"What rules?"

"The same rules every other player has followed over the last six years when you haven't," Huggins said.

"I've done pretty good without rules."

"I'm tired, Babe. Tired of the stress, tired of fighting with you, tired of you ignoring team rules and curfews. It's your last chance. Or we'll trade you."

"Colonel Ruppert wouldn't let you," George said.

"It's *his* idea. He thinks you're done. He wants to trade you while he can still recoup some of his investment."

"Get me back in the lineup. I'll show him."

"You've missed almost two months. We've been paying you the highest salary on the team and getting nothing for it. Follow rules or you're done. You'll play on June 1st, next week. Get in shape, or else."

———

He sat alone in his Ansonia Hotel suite on upper Broadway. He looked at his watch, then counted the number of taxis that went by in a minute. A half hour later, he was still gazing out the window. He dialed the telephone.

"I want to see you," he said.

"I don't think so," she said.

"My wife stays in Boston all the time now. She moved out of our house, and she's living with some dentist in Watertown. Can I take you to dinner?"

Claire had a bit part in a Broadway play, a musical comedy called *The Vagabond King.* George attended a performance and met her afterward at a restaurant in the Roosevelt Hotel.

"I'm lonely," George said, "and I remember the fun times we had."

"Get a divorce and I'll see you again."

"We're Catholic. My wife refuses."

"I don't mind meeting you for lunch or dinner once in a while," Claire said, "but I won't be the second woman."

"Will you come back to my place?"

"That's not the kind of relationship I want."

———

St. Louis. Live jazz was too loud in the background. Thinly clad women sashayed past him on the runway. A paper bib was tied around his neck, and he used a fork and knife to attack an eighteen-ounce porterhouse steak. The madam of the House of the Good Shepard, a woman in her fifties, carried a bottle of red wine to his table. She pressed a corkscrew into the top, twisted it, and popped the bottle open. She had to raise her voice above the music.

"It's on the house, Babe. We haven't seen you in a long time."

"I shouldn't be here," he said.

"Why the hell not, honey?"

"I get in too much trouble."

"You're special here. We'll take care of you," the buxom blond said. "Is that guy over there with you?"

"Never seen him before."

"Just wondering," she said. "I ain't seen him either, and he came in right behind you." She watched the newcomer for a few seconds. "Which one of my pretty ladies do you want tonight, Babe?"

"I can't stay," he said. "I got a curfew."

———————

George strolled into the visitors' locker room just an hour before game time. Other Yankee players were already on the field and had gone through their pregame practice routines.

George yanked off his loose tie and hung it over a hook in his locker. He pulled off his sport coat and placed it over a hanger, then unbuckled his belt, sat down, and pulled off his shoes. Miller Huggins pushed open the door from the field.

"Don't bother, Babe."

"I'll be out in a minute."

"You're suspended."

"I said I'll be out in a minute."

"I warned you," Huggins said.

"You can't suspend me."

"I just did," Huggins said.

"I'll go to Ruppert, and if he doesn't do something, I'll go to Judge Landis."

"You'll certainly have enough time."

"Goddamn it. You can't treat me like this."

"Ruppert already approved it," Huggins said. "He's the one that hired the detective that followed you into your whorehouse last night. For the past five years Landis has been looking for an excuse to throw you out of baseball. He thinks you're colored."

"You just started winning games again—when I came back."

"We're building for the future, Babe. Unless you change your ways for good in the off-season, you won't be part of it."

Huggins started away, and George stood up and lunged at him. He grabbed the back of his jersey and spun him around.

"I'll kill you, you son of a bitch."

Huggins was crumpled against the wall, his feet off the floor.

"Don't do it, Babe. You still have a chance to play. Just not today and tomorrow."

"If I don't play ball, I don't have anything else to do."

"I know," Huggins said, "and I want you to play."

George lowered Huggins to the floor and let go of his jersey, then put his hands over his own eyes. "I'm sorry."

"I believe you." Huggins tugged his jersey back in place and stretched his neck. "You need some time off."

"No, I don't." Tears formed in George's eyes.

"For once, let me be your friend, Babe. Take time off. Learn to relax—without women or booze. Spend some time alone and figure out what you want to do with the rest of your life."

"I've spent my whole life alone. I'm tired of it; I don't want to be alone anymore."

CHAPTER FIFTY-THREE

They piled the furniture in the driveway. They were hot and sweaty. Darwin wiped his brow with his forearm. Cammie walked back into the house. He straightened a dresser, then followed her inside, where she stirred lemonade and poured some into a glass and handed it to him.

"I still have to pack everything I'm taking with me," she said. "I'm not planning to come back." He didn't like hearing that. He hoped she was trying to convince herself.

"Take a break."

"I've got to be in New York in three days. I'll give away everything I don't sell in the garage sale," she said. "Will you help me with the bed?"

"Do you have a screwdriver? I have to take it apart."

"In the pantry."

They stacked the mattress and box springs against the wall, and he kneeled inside the frame. She pulled Uncle Griff's clothes out of drawers and placed them in cardboard boxes.

"Are you keeping anything?" he asked.

"I already took what I wanted. Uncle Griff's clothes might fit the old guy down the street. I'm just keeping the picture on the dresser," she said. She had her back to him and bent over the bottom drawers of her old dresser. Her shorts were tight, her legs smooth.

He sat on the floor and leaned against the headboard, then placed the screwdriver next to him on the hardwood floor. He watched her yank folded shirts and pants from a bottom drawer and stack them in a box. She turned and looked at him.

"Why are you resting?" she said.

"Why should I rush to help you leave me?"

"You know I can't stay."

"No," Darwin said. "I don't."

She stood up and reached for a glass of lemonade on the top of a nightstand. She took a long swallow, then set it back down and pulled a piece of ice out of the glass. She lowered herself onto the floor next to Darwin and held the ice cube above her face, letting it drip onto her face.

"God, I'm hot," Cammie said.

"What are you going to do with the rug?"

"You want it?"

"If you don't," he said.

"It would cost too much to ship. You can have it."

She held the melting ice above her face again. It dripped onto her chest. He used the back of his hand to wipe the droplets from her cleavage, then pulled her closer. They kissed and he lifted her blouse. She raised her arms and he slid it over her shoulders. They laid back on the area rug. She unbuckled his belt. He pulled her shorts off. They made love on the floor.

"Okay, are you satisfied?" she asked. She traced his lips with her finger.

"Not until you tell me you'll stay."

"I'll stay." She reached for her blouse and pulled it back over her shoulders, then stood up and yanked her tight shorts back on. He pulled his pants on too and zipped them. She tossed his T-shirt at him.

"You will?" he asked.

She smiled. "Help me with this bed."

He picked up the screwdriver and proceeded to take the frame apart. The wooden slats, the headboard, the sides, and the foot of the bed were stacked against the wall, and Cammie began rolling up the area rug. It had covered most of her uncle's bedroom floor, except for the perimeter of the room. Darwin had hauled several boxes of clothing outside and had come back inside to help with the remaining bedroom furniture.

An old envelope lay on the floor where the area rug had been. He picked it up and opened it.

"What's that?" Cammie said.

Darwin read the typed letter out loud. Cammie moved closer. "It's dated April 2, 1947," he said.

> *Dear Mr. Chandler,*
>
> *Judge Landis thought I was colored and wanted to throw me out of baseball. He hated anybody different than him.*
>
> *Now I have little time left and feel I must do what I can. I love baseball and don't want to change the history of the game or any of its records. But you must let colored fellows play.*
>
> *I gave this letter to LeRoy Griffin and told him to pass it on to anyone he wants if colored players are not allowed to play in the big leagues before I pass away. My time is short. Colored players should play.*
>
> *My grandmother was a slave. I was afraid I would be kicked out of the game I love and my records taken away. If I help remove the wall that keeps colored players from baseball, I will give more to the game and America than all of my home runs and records ever did.*
>
> *Babe Ruth*

Darwin looked up. A tear slid down Cammie's cheek.

"You really think that's Ruth's signature?" she asked.

"It sure looks like it, and his name is printed on the stationery."

"I guess that's what they wanted."

"They?"

"The men that ransacked the house," she said. "The guys that kidnapped me."

"Probably," he said. "Maybe with all the steroid issues and negative publicity, they just didn't want any more controversy."

"But who are they?"

"Does it really make any difference? Blacks are playing and have been for a half century. Nobody needs to know about this."

"My pride wants me to tell the world," Cammie said.

"Your great-grandfather's pride prevented him from telling anyone."

"But was that good?"

"He was a hero. His color shouldn't change that."

———— • ————

Cammie wore dark glasses when she visited her own garage sale. Her friends from the neighborhood sat at the bottom of the driveway at one of four eight-foot-long folding tables, one of them borrowed from the Sacred Mission Baptist Church on Benton Boulevard. Two black ladies held up clothes that had been folded and placed on one of the tables.

"The clothes are selling good," one of the friends said, "and a couple of men went to get a pickup truck. They bought those dressers and that bed."

"Thanks for doing this," Cammie said. "You two get half of all you take in."

"No we ain't. We just want to be neighborly."

"I insist on paying you for all the time you're spending."

A car stopped across the street. Two white men got out and walked across Prospect Avenue toward the sale items. They were dressed casually and seemed to be in no hurry.

"I'm going to leave now," Cammie said. "I'll see you later, girls."

"Go on now. We'll take care of everything," one woman said. "What we don't sell today, we'll get rid of tomorrow. Saturdays is better for garage sales."

Her cell phone rang. Darwin was on the line.

"Sold anything?"

"I'm ready for lunch. Want to meet me?"

"The Peach Tree?" Darwin said.

"I don't feel safe there. How 'bout the Plaza?"

They met at P.F. Chang's and sat in a booth. Cammie sipped hot tea.

"I don't want you to leave," Darwin said. "Stay in Kansas City."

"I've got a job back there—and a new name. I feel safer. Anyway, the house is sold, and by tomorrow all my furniture will be too."

"Live with me," Darwin said.

Cammie drank more hot tea. "That wouldn't be a good idea. Anyway, it would never work out. Your parents would go crazy. You, shackin' up with a black girl."

"It's the twenty-first century, Cammie."

"You're Hitler's wet dream," she said, grinning. "A blond with blue eyes."

"I'm not blond, and my eyes aren't blue. You look like my high-school girlfriend after she'd been baking in the sun at the pool. Who knows what our kids would look like?"

"I'm a dancer," Cammie said. "I got a couple more years before I start thinking about kids. Anyway, I'm not having kids unless I'm married."

"Well then?"

"Are you proposing?" she asked.

"You're the best friend I've got. I don't want to lose you."

"Friends don't have kids."

"I love you," Darwin said.

"You're cute." Cammie smiled, and Darwin's jaw tightened. He turned his head to the side.

"I tell you I love you and you make fun of me," he said. "I tell you I don't want you to leave and you ignore my feelings."

"I'm black. Do you know what that means?"

"Probably not."

"It means never knowing whether somebody is taking me seriously," she said. "Are you being nice to me because I'm black? Are you feeling sorry for me? Or do you want me around just so you have some hot black chick to screw?"

"I said I love you."

"Guess how many times I've heard that. Just long enough for some guy to reach down my blouse or pants, then end our relationship because I'm black. Yeah, I heard you. Is there any wonder why I might trust black guys more? At least I can trust them when they say they want a long-term relationship."

He locked onto her eyes. "I want a long-term relationship."

"Damn it, Darwin," said Cammie. "My life is confusing enough already." She slid out of the booth and walked away.

CHAPTER FIFTY-FOUR

1928

George paced. He pushed his hair back. He stared at the floor. The receptionist in the law office brought him a cup of coffee. She gave him a curious stare, as if she were afraid. She fidgeted with her hands.

"Thanks," he said. "Is he just about ready?"

"You didn't have an appointment, Mr. Ruth. He's with another client and will be out just as soon as he's done."

"I don't use lawyers much, at least not for this kind of thing."

A tall man dressed in a three-piece suit walked into the lobby.

"I'm Stanford Briggs. Come back to my office." George followed him down the hallway and into a square office with tall windows on one side. The windows were open and the sounds of the city below were loud: engines humming, horns beeping, a siren in the distance, an occasional whistle from a traffic cop, and the ever-repeating percussion of construction hammers, pile drivers, and jackhammers.

"I need a divorce," George said.

"Why did you come to me?" Briggs asked.

"Bob Meusel had a friend that got divorced, and he used you."

"Have a seat. What's his name?"

"Does it make a difference?"

"You're the baseball Ruth. Right?"

"Yeah, that's me," George said.

"I'm guessing you want to keep this quiet."

"Most of all, I want to get it done in a hurry."

"What's the rush?" Briggs asked.

"I want to get married again."

"Have you talked to your current wife about this?"

"Kind of, a while back," George said.

"And she's agreeable?"

"We're Catholic."

"That can be a problem."

"It ain't fair," George said, "that she can stop me from living my life the way I want."

"We're not talking about fair, Babe. We're talking about religion and law, and they are always behind the times."

"I can't wait."

"Some people choose to live out of wedlock."

"Claire won't do that," George said. He stood up and paced behind his chair.

"Any kids involved?"

"One, my daughter. She was adopted."

"Then maybe you don't care about her," Briggs said.

"I sure do. It's *my* kid, not hers."

"I thought you said she was adopted?"

"It's a long story," George said.

"Does she live here in the city?"

"They live in Boston. Actually, Watertown."

"That's worse," Briggs said. "I thought maybe I could have gone to her attorney and tried to work something out. Does she have an attorney?"

"I doubt it."

"You might be out of luck."

"Isn't there anything I can do?"

"It sounds like you've got three choices," Briggs said. "You can contact her and try to talk her into granting you the divorce or you can wait for the Catholic Church to change or you can wait until she dies."

———

He'd been given the telephone number by a bookie that hung around Yankee Stadium. The bookie went by the name Itchy, and ballplayers had been warned to stay away from him.

"I just want to talk to an old friend," George said.

"How the Yankees going to do against the Red Sox?"

"I can't talk about that, not with you. Don't want to get in trouble."

"Why you want to get ahold of Shoeless Joe?"

"He's an old friend," George said. "Just wonderin' how he's doin'."

"You can get in more trouble talking to him than me."

"I'm not interested in gambling, Itchy. I just want to check up on an old friend."

George dialed the phone from his Ansonia suite. Joe Jackson answered and talked in that slow southern drawl.

"Things is going okay," Joe said. "How 'bout for you, Babe?"

"Don't you read the newspapers?"

"Not too much." George remembered the rumors about Jackson coming from the South, growing up in transition all the time, the son of a sharecropper, and not being able to read.

"I'm doing all right, Joe. Say, I was wonderin' if you ever ran across anybody I could get a hold of that can help me put an end to somebody pesterin' me."

"A bill collector?" Jackson asked.

"Something like that."

"You need to strong-arm him, huh?"

"Or worse."

"There's all kind of guys where I played," Jackson said. "Chicago."

"They got the mob up there. Real mean guys that will do jus' 'bout anything for an extra buck."

"Got telephone numbers for any of 'em?"

———•———

The restaurant was dark and smoky. It was only a couple of miles north of Comiskey Park, where the White Sox played. After the Yankees won that afternoon, George had taken a taxi north on Michigan Avenue to 22nd Street.

He got out, handed the driver a ten-spot, and opened the taxi door. Three men in white long-sleeved shirts and suit pants stood out front. They wore suspenders, shined shoes, and fedoras. Two of them leaned against the brick wall of the Lexington Hotel. The other one walked back and forth in front of the entrance with a cigar in his mouth.

George headed straight for the entrance.

"Who are you?" the man with a cigar asked.

"Babe Ruth," George said. "I got a meeting inside with a fella named Colossimo."

"Babe Ruth, the baseball player?"

"That's right."

"Hey, Tony. Babe Ruth, the baseball player, has a meeting with Louie. Did you know 'bout that?"

"Wait here," one of the other men said. "I'll go check. Hey, are you really Babe Ruth?"

"That's right. Joe Jackson sent me."

"How is he? God, we need him back in Chicago. Never did a thing wrong. Hell of a guy." The man walked inside. George stood outside and looked up and down the street.

A short man in a double-breasted tan suit walked outside. He had a fedora too, but his shoes were two-tone, white and brown.

"How ya doin'? I'm Louie. We talked," he said.

"Babe Ruth." They shook hands.

"Hey, Babe, take a walk with me. You shouldn't go inside. There's lotsa G-men 'round here. We don't want any rumors started so ya get what happened to Joe."

They walked around the corner and inside the restaurant.

"Relax, Babe," Louie said. "Everything will be okay."

"It's got to look like an accident," George said. "You won't gun anybody down, will you?" They sat down at a table in a booth. George looked around to see if anybody was watching.

"Not for you," Louie said. "Everything will be professional. Nobody's goin' to think a thing." He hailed a waitress and ordered drinks, a bourbon on the rocks for himself and a bourbon with Coke for George.

"They serve liquor here?"

"They do for us," Louie said.

"Out in the open? What if a cop walks in?"

"Forget about it. You're in Chicago. We own this town."

George pulled an envelope from his front pocket and slid it across the top of the table. He kept his hand on it.

"I'm scared to death."

"Don't be," Louie said. "Everything will be okay."

"You keep saying that, but I never done anything like this." He lifted his hand, and Louie picked up the envelope. Louie looked to the side and over his shoulder, then opened it and used his thumb to count the bills. "It's all here. How 'bout the tickets?"

George pulled four game tickets from his other pocket.

"Box seats," Louie said. "I'm goin' to take the boss with me." He stuffed the envelope and tickets into his back pocket.

"The boss?"

"Alphonse."

"Maybe you don't need all four," George said.

"The boss will need extras for his bodyguards."

"Do me a favor and don't tell anybody where you got the tickets."

"Sure thing, Babe," Louie said, "and don't be expectin' anything right away."

"What do you mean?"

"I'll wait till long after you leave Chicago, when I know you got an alibi in New York." Louie took a swig of his bourbon. "Want to go up the back and meet the boss? He wants to me you."

"Does he know about this?" George asked.

"Not the details."

"I thought this was just between the two of us."

"The boss needs to get his share. He ain't goin' to tell anybody. Don't worry."

"I know," George said, "everything will be fine."

CHAPTER FIFTY-FIVE

The lines on the wall behind them measured their height. Seven men had walked onto the platform. The second man in the lineup looked like Frank. They faced forward, then turned to the side. Then they turned the other way. Frank had on the same suit he'd worn on the day of the shootings. His hair was the same, thin and combed back. He had that same double chin.

Cammie sat in another room next to Erickson and Lieutenant Wilson. They looked through a one-way window and examined the men in the lineup. Another plainclothes officer, the local detective from Chicago, ran the lineup from inside the adjacent room. Three uniformed cops with revolvers and holsters stood guard.

"Can you have them face the wall?" Cammie asked Wilson. Wilson bent forward and spoke into a microphone wired into the lineup room.

"Have them face the wall," he said. The Chicago officer ordered them to turn around, and the seven men stood with their backs to Cammie.

"That's him," she said. "Number two."

"Are you sure?" Wilson asked.

"Couldn't be more positive. I recognize that little mole on the back of his head, in the bald spot."

"That's Quatrocelli."

"I don't know his last name," she said. "They just called him Frank." The men on the staging area walked out of the room in single file; then the Chicago cop came into the room where Cammie, Erickson, and Wilson were waiting.

"He's got quite a record," the Chicago cop said.

"We'll have to extradite him to KC," said Wilson. "Can we ask him some questions?"

Frank was handcuffed and in an orange jumpsuit the next time Cammie saw him, twenty minutes later. The Chicago cop led him into a stark interrogation room. There was a single metal table and a couple of metal chairs. Overhead fluorescent lighting made the barren room look cold and bleak. Cammie remained with Erickson and looked in from behind another one-way window. The Chicago cop and Wilson questioned Frank in the interview room.

"Did you kill Max Carmichael?" Wilson asked.

"Crawdad did."

"What's Crawdad's real name?"

"Don't have a clue," Frank said. "Max hired him."

"Who killed Crawdad?"

"The girl."

"Cammie Griffin?" Wilson said.

"That's right."

"How did she kill him?"

"Shot him in the head," Frank said.

"Why?"

"Crawdad went nutso and shot Max in the forehead. The girl was scared. I was too."

"Was it self-defense?"

"Damn right," Frank said. "Crawdad was waving his gun in the air and threatened to kill her too."

"Would you testify to that?" Wilson asked.

"Will I get immunity?"

"If you cooperate," Wilson said, "I think we can work something out. At least a reduced charge."

"I ain't gonna save her ass if I don't get anything."

"One more thing," Wilson said. "Who hired you?"

"I was just the driver. Hell, I thought I was going to die too."

"Who hired you to drive?"

"Max."

"Who hired Max?"

"You'd have to ask him," Frank said.

"You know he's dead. You want immunity?"

"I don't know who hired him. He told me the same thing he told the girl that day, that he got his orders from a locker in a bowling alley. I never even got paid all I was s'pose to get."

"You took $10,000 that was supposed to go to the girl."

"Who says?"

"We don't want the girl to have to stand trial. We want you to appear before the grand jury and tell them what you told us, that it was self-defense."

"Will I have to stand trial?"

"There's no crime for being a driver unless you knew what was planned."

"Chauffeur," Frank said. "I didn't know there'd be killin'."

"But if you get difficult and change your story, we might have to inform the grand jury about the $10,000, and that might make you an accomplice to murder in their eyes."

"I'll cooperate," Frank said.

———— ■ ————

Cammie walked south on Broadway. It was dark, but the bright lights turned evening into daylight. Hundreds of people walked up and down the busy sidewalk for the two or three blocks she could see ahead. She put her cell phone to her ear.

"I hate my job," she said.

"Cammie?"

"I never get to perform. Being an extra sucks."

"Come back to KC," Darwin said.

"Erickson wants me to come back for that grand jury. He thinks my testimony will help."

"Most lawyers don't want defendants taking the stand."

"He says it's an investigation, not a trial. He's going to have Frank there too."

"Where are you going to stay?" Darwin asked.

"Can I sleep on your couch? I really don't have the money for a hotel."

"You can sleep anywhere you want at my place."

"It won't be a good idea for me to sleep in your bed."

"I hope you change your mind," he said, "but that's up to you."

"I don't need more confusion in my life right now."

"When you coming?"

"I'm not sure I am," Cammie said. "I'm afraid the media might put a bull's-eye on my back."

"I'll take the days off when you're in town. I'll go everywhere you go."

"Great," she said. "That'll put a bull's-eye on your back too."

"I'm not afraid of that."

"I am. If I knew who wanted to shut me up, I'd send them Ruth's damn letter and tell them they've got nothing to worry about."

"If you were going to the media, you would have done it by now," Darwin said. "They know that."

"I'm convinced there's not just one. I'll never be safe as Cammie Griffin."

"There's a solution to that."

"I'll talk to you later. I'm going underground." She folded her phone, stuck it in her purse, and walked down the steps to the subway station at 50th and Broadway.

———

Darwin walked into Flynn's office and sat down across the desk from him. Flynn looked over the top of his reading glasses with narrowed eyes.

"I'd like a raise," Darwin said.

"So would I," Flynn said, "but the partners only meet once a year to discuss that kind of thing. Now's not the time."

"How have I been doing?"

Flynn sat back in his swivel chair. He had a document on his lap. He gave Darwin a quizzical stare without saying anything.

"I mean, am I doing better? Generating more billing; helping you with your stuff; becoming a respected member of the legal team?"

"What's going on, buddy?"

"I need a raise."

"I can't just give you a raise," Flynn said. "The partners have to vote on it, and they won't even consider it until fall."

"I just brought in a new corporate client, my second one in two months."

"You're doing great, ever since your girlfriend left."

"Have I proven myself?"

"What's the big rush?" Flynn asked.

"I've got an offer from another firm."

"Bullshit."

"You don't have to believe me."

"How much are they willing to pay?"

"I'm not here to hold you up, Bob. I wouldn't do that. It's just that they think I could bring in new clients with me."

"Which firm?" Flynn asked.

"I can't divulge that."

"You're bluffing. You've been watching too much poker on TV."

"I don't want to be a nuisance," said Darwin. He stood up to leave. "But I will have been here for a year next month."

"Sit down," Flynn said.

"Forget I said anything." Darwin started away.

"How much more?"

"Twenty percent more on the base and I won't even consider leaving. In fact, I'd rather stay here."

"Then just stay, and I'll forget we discussed it."

"I can't do that. You know I'm worth it, and I want to be with the firm forever."

"When do you need to know?" Flynn asked.

"They want to know by Monday."

"You better not be bluffing. I'm a good poker player. I can tell when somebody's bluffing. You aren't, are you?"

"Do you know who you're talking about? Darwin Barney. Forget I said anything." Darwin turned away again.

"Will you leave if you don't get a raise?"

"Forget I said anything. I don't want to put you in an awkward situation with the partners."

"You *will*, won't you?"

"But it wouldn't be your fault." Darwin walked out.

"Damn you" Flynn said. He raised his voice. "I've got until Monday, though. Right?"

CHAPTER FIFTY-SIX

1928

The clubhouse erupted in celebration. Illegal champagne sprayed from forty-eight bottles that had been shaken before their corks had been popped open. George held a bottle in each hand like a gunslinger, his thumbs over the openings. He put one down and slapped Waite Hoyt on the back and hugged him with one arm.

"Great game, kid. You're the best."

In all the noise, Hoyt stood silently, tilted his head, and stared at George as he walked away. Meusel approached Hoyt.

"Babe Ruth just told me I'm the best," Hoyt said.

Bob Meusel raised his voice above the cheering and locker room ruckus. "That's quite a compliment." Meusel patted him on the shoulder. "You might be on the best baseball team in the history, and the best player ever just told you *you're* the best."

"He really is the best ever, isn't he?"

Meusel walked over to George, standing by his locker. George had a towel around his neck and used it to wipe champagne from his face.

"That's the last time you'll wear that uniform," Meusel said.

"I've been traded?" George asked with a grin.

"They're putting numbers on our jerseys next year."

"What the hell for?"

"So the fans know who we are," Meusel said.

"They know who we are," George said. "Hell, we're the world champions. I wonder what number I'll be."

"You bat third; you'll be number 3."

"That's a crazy idea. It'll never last."

Meusel sat down on a stool, took off his spiked shoes, and began pulling off his stockings. "Hey Babe, are we still going barnstorming?"

George hesitated. "I got a lot going on this fall. I'm thinking of getting married."

"Congratulations," Meusel said. "When?"

"I'm not sure yet. Think the fellas will mind if I cancel? We'll make quite a bit for winning the Series, and I'd love to take a winter off for a change."

———

Claire answered the telephone at George's new suite in the Brunswick Hotel.

"George, it's for you. A man named Louie."

She handed him the receiver.

"What is it?" George asked the caller. "I told you not to call me here." He walked back and forth, as far as the cord would reach. "What happened to what I gave you?" There was a pause. "I thought nobody else would be involved. How much?" He listened for a while, then hung up. "Let's go, honey."

"Where to?" Claire asked.

"Over to Joe Dugan's place. A bunch of ballplayers and their wives have been invited for dinner."

"Why all of a sudden?"

"I was invited before but forgot," George said.

348

"Give me some time to get ready."

"We'll be late if we don't go now."

"I'd rather not."

"It's important that I be there. The fellas are expecting me." On the way out of the hotel, George stopped at the front desk. "If anybody calls, I'll be at Joe Dugan's home. Here's the number." He handed the man a slip of paper.

Joe Dugan was the third baseman for the Yankees and one of the few players on the team still willing to socialize with George. When they arrived late, Joe answered the door.

"I've been waived," Joe said. "It's turned into a goin'-away party."

"The Yankees let you go?" George asked. "Bullshit. I'll talk to Miller in the morning."

"No need to wait, Babe." Miller Huggins walked up next to George.

"How can you let Joe go? We just won the World Series. Some say we're the best that ever was."

"It wasn't my choice. Ruppert got a deal."

"Don't worry about it, Babe," Joe said. "It can't be changed." Dugan blushed and tried to smile at the same time. "Anyway, the fans have been tough on me this year. If I got a single after Murderer's Row was up, the crowd felt I was breaking up a rally."

George patted him on the shoulder. "You'll always be a Yankee to me, and one of the few friends on the team I ever had."

George and Claire circulated among the twenty special guests Dugan had invited to his apartment on the Upper West Side. He had told George the party was held at his apartment so he could sneak liquor in.

"Hey Babe, a phone call for you," Joe shouted from across the room. George bit his lower lip and walked over to the telephone. He put his drink down, held the receiver to his ear with one hand, and covered his other ear with the empty hand.

"This is Ruth," he said. His expression was serious. He listened. When a grimace appeared on his face, Claire stepped closer. "Okay, I'll catch the next train." He hung up but didn't say anything. He breathed harder and faster.

"What is it?" Claire asked.

"Helen. She died."

"What happened?

"A fire," George said. "She suffocated."

"What about Dorothy?

"I don't know. I gotta get up there."

———◆———

He took the first train out of Grand Central Station. He arrived in Boston early the next morning and was met by Art Crowley. Crowley was the son of the Boston Police Commissioner and an old friend of George's from his days with the Red Sox.

George was unshaven. He was dressed in a suit but wore no tie. His shirt was unbuttoned at the neck and he wore a black overcoat.

"How are you holding up?" Crowley asked.

"I'm a mess. How'd it happen, Art?"

"Nobody knows for sure."

"What about my daughter?"

"I don't know."

"Was she in the fire too?"

"I don't think so," Crowley said. "I mean, no. She wasn't."

"I want to go there."

"To the house? It's practically burnt to the ground."

"I got to find Dorothy."

When they arrived in Watertown, the house was still smoldering. A few firemen stood by the blackened frame of the home. A squad car sat out front with two Boston cops in it. Several neighbors stood on the sidewalk with their arms folded.

One shifted feet as if moving to keep warm. Their breath rose in the brisk dawn air.

A man stood inside the framework of the house. He looked down. He wore an overcoat that hung open. George and Crowley got out of the car and walked up to what was left of the house.

"Kinder?" George said. "What'd you do to my wife?"

The man standing inside the perimeter of the charcoaled house looked up from his trance. He looked at George as if it took awhile for it to register who he was.

"She's dead."

"Why aren't you, you son of a bitch?"

"I was at the fights," Kinder said, "at Boston Gardens."

"Where's my daughter?"

"At school. She's all right."

"What school? Where?"

"Up at Wellesley, the Academy of the Assumption."

"Does she know?"

"About Helen? Not yet."

Crowley turned to one of the firemen. "How'd it happen?" he asked.

"Don't know yet," one of the firemen said.

"Any chance of arson?" Crowley asked.

The fireman shrugged. "Don't know."

———

Two nuns walked ahead of George and Claire. George held his hat in his hand and almost bumped into the nun ahead of him. She turned and glared at him.

"Excuse me, Sister. I'm just anxious to see her."

The nun turned back and kept walking, and without facing him, said, "Why haven't you been here before?"

"I didn't know she was here," George said. "My wife put her here without telling me."

"Where's the other man? I thought he was her father."

Claire spoke up. "George is the real father. That man doesn't even have custody."

George and Claire waited in a lobby. The nuns disappeared. George paced and fidgeted with the driving cap he held.

He looked down a narrow hallway. Dorothy walked toward him. Then, as if she suddenly recognized him, she ran. Her footsteps echoed off the walls and tile floor.

"Daddy." She leaped into his arms. He hugged her and his eyes welled up.

"Did they tell you, honey?" he asked.

"Yes, I know all about it." He put her down. She had tears running down her cheeks. "Who is this?"

"This is going to be your new mommy," George said. "And you're going to live with us from now on."

CHAPTER FIFTY-SEVEN

Cammie walked out of the baggage-claim area pulling a small pink bag on wheels. Her heels clicked against the hard floor and that made Darwin uncomfortable, because the heels made her an inch taller than he. She wore dance leotards and a baggy sweatshirt, and he knew she'd caught him staring at her legs. He blushed.

She bent closer and let him kiss her on the cheek. She wrapped her arm around his shoulder and squeezed, then scanned the crowd.

"I was hoping you'd bring a bigger bag," he said.

"I'm only going to be here a couple of days."

"When do you meet Erickson?"

"Tomorrow morning," she said. "I was thinking I could go to work with you."

"I'm not working there anymore."

Cammie stopped walking. "What happened?" Darwin stopped too.

"I'm working for a different firm now—in Overland Park: Whitehill, Dawson & Smith."

"Why?" She looked worried.

"You got me thinking when I was in New York," Darwin said. "You said, 'go back to Kansas.' I did."

"But you loved your job." They started walking again.

"There are other law firms, and Overland Park is growing. Plus, I'm out of Missouri." Darwin loaded her suitcase behind the seat of his sports car.

"What's wrong with Missouri?" Cammie asked.

"*You* didn't want to be there." They drove west on Interstate 435.

"Why are we going this way?"

"I live in Kansas now too."

"You sold your condo?" she asked.

"I was just renting."

They sped down the highway and pulled into an established neighborhood with small bungalows and tall trees. Darwin drove into a driveway.

He placed an open bottle of California merlot on the table, then two wine glasses. Candles were lit; the lighting had been turned low. The table was set on a white linen tablecloth. A large bowl of Romaine lettuce mixed with tomatoes and carrot shavings sat on a side table.

"You didn't have to do all this," Cammie said. Darwin poured her more wine, then stood up, walked into the kitchen, and came back with two plates, each with a steak, baked potato, and asparagus. "You're treating me like a queen. Do you know something I don't? Like maybe this is my last meal before I go to jail?"

"I phoned Erickson. He thinks everything will be fine."

"I'm worried something might go wrong."

Darwin pulled a small box from his pocket. It was wrapped in gray paper and a maroon bow. He reached across the table and placed it next to her plate. She stared at it. Then at him. She opened it.

"I don't know what to think," she said.

"Your name will be different and we'll live in Kansas."

"I'd have to give up Broadway."

"It sucks anyway," Darwin said. "You can come back here and dance in the Kansas City Ballet and be the star."

Cammie used a linen napkin to dab under her eyes. "You make it hard to go back."

"There's no reason to." Darwin lowered himself from his seat onto one knee next to her. "Will you marry me?"

"What would you parents think?"

"We can ask them; they only live a couple miles away."

"Is this neighborhood all-white?"

"Not anymore," he said. "And when you're ready, we can double or triple the black population."

"Our kids probably won't be that dark."

"Is that a yes?"

"Let's wait and see if I have to serve time."

———

She met Erickson at the offices of Goldberg, McIntosh, Hartwood & Flynn. Darwin had come in with her and waited in the lobby, talking with Jody.

"I miss you," she said.

"I miss this place too."

"Does anybody get you coffee the way I did?"

"Nobody will replace you, Jody."

"Flynn's going bonkers without you," she said, then spoke more quietly. "Now he knows how important you were."

"Talking about me?" Flynn said. He had rounded the corner and reached out to shake Darwin's hand. Darwin stood up and came to meet him.

"I was saying I hope I didn't leave you stranded." They shook hands.

"You got a couple minutes?" Flynn asked. "Come on back."

They sat at his desk. Darwin felt comfortable in the same chair he'd sat in so many times before.

"I was always so uncomfortable sitting here."

"I scared you away," Flynn said. "I knew it."

"Not at all. It was me. I was always afraid I'd do something wrong and disappoint you."

"You never did."

"Thanks, Bob. Are you mad at me?"

"Why would I be? It was my fault you left."

"I asked Cammie to marry me."

"Congratulations." Flynn reached over his desk with an outstretched arm.

"She hasn't said yes yet," Darwin said.

"She will. She's a classy lady. You're lucky."

"I always thought you felt she was, well, you know."

"Black?"

"That too," Darwin said. "But more than that—kind of beneath us."

"I'm probably more of a bigot than I'd like to admit." Flynn shrugged.

"When I saw her flying around on that stage and landing like a butterfly, I knew she was special. And hell, she's a smart lady too."

"Berkeley," Darwin said.

"She doesn't have a law degree, does she? I'm in trouble."

"You? I don't believe it." Darwin grinned.

Flynn turned up the corner of his mouth.

"I need another law firm to represent me. A small conflict-of-interest charge by the opposing attorney in the Warren Trucking case. They're just throwing obstacles in our way. Trying to get me off the case. It's the one you helped me on."

"I thought that would be over by now."

"They still owe Warren over a million bucks, and they say I can't represent them because I was old man Warren's attorney when the company was acquired." Flynn's phone rang, but he ignored it. "I want you to defend me."

"Why me?" Darwin asked.

"You're a good attorney, thorough, smart, and I can trust you."

"Why don't you have somebody in the firm handle it?"

"Can't," Flynn said. "They named me and the law firm as defendants."

"So I'd be representing Goldberg, McIntosh, Hartwood & Flynn?"

"Yep," Flynn said. "I already talked to the partners. They think it's a good idea."

"Won't the judge consider *me* a conflict of interest, since I worked here?"

"He already knows it's just a delay tactic. I'll pass your name by him and see what he thinks."

"I'd love to do it," Darwin said. Then he smiled. "Just as long as it isn't a lechery charge."

"I'd have to confess," Flynn said. "By the way, I miss our breakfast meetings."

"We can still meet."

"You remember the one with the long legs, Peg? The one from the diner? I had a date with her."

"I don't practice that kind of law."

Erickson stuck his head in the door.

"We're leaving now," he said. Cammie stood behind him with her hands folded.

Darwin stood up. "I'm coming with you."

CHAPTER FIFTY-EIGHT

George sat alone in a sterile, gray room. He waited. There were no wall hangings and no clock. It seemed like he'd been there forever. He stood up and circled the lone table, then sat down again. He tapped his fingers on the tabletop. Two men in suits walked in. One slapped a folder on the table. The other one grabbed a chair, turned it around, and sat on it backward.

"Where were you?"

"During the fire? At a party in New York, at Joe Dugan's place. Why?"

"We'll ask the questions," one of the detectives said.

"Why are you doing this? I'm all busted up about this." George bent forward in his chair and buried his head in his hands.

"We understand you had a meeting with your wife last month and with a man named Christy Walsh. "

"So what?"

"Isn't Walsh an attorney?" one of the detectives asked.

"Yeah, but he's also my business manager. Am I being accused of something?"

"We're just trying to find out what happened."

"I want to talk to Art Crowley," George said.

"The commissioner's son?"

"That's right. I want to see him. Right away."

"He's not a lawyer." The detective still standing walked around the table and behind George.

"I still want to see him. He'll tell you," George said. George spun in his chair and looked at the detective behind him. "He was the one that called me in New York. He met me at the train station."

"You know a lot of people, don't you Ruth?" one of the detectives said. "We want to know more about the meeting with Walsh."

"We met and tried to work things out."

"You wanted to make your marriage work?"

"We were trying to work out a divorce settlement," George said.

"We were informed she didn't want a divorce."

"She was living with a guy, Ed Kinder. It was his house she died in," George said. "You guys hate me because I left the Red Sox?"

"I'm not a baseball fan," one detective said. "I don't care who you play for."

"Isn't it obvious? I was in New York. She was at Kinder's place. Did you drag him in here yet?"

"He didn't have anything to gain by having her killed," the detective said.

"Do you know Nora Woodford?" the seated detective asked.

"That's Helen's snot-nosed kid sister. Ain't seen her in years."

"She said she saw you threaten to kill Helen, up in Sudbury, three years ago."

"You got a wife?" George said. "Don't tell me she don't make you want to kill her at times. It doesn't mean you do it. I loved Helen."

"So much that you were living with another woman," a detective said.

"I wanted to live with Helen. She wouldn't let me."

1929

George walked to his car. He was still in his baseball gear. He sat on the running board of his rented car and lifted a bottle of

Coca-Cola to his lips. He wiped sweat from his brow with the back of his hand. The St. Petersburg sun speared down out of the glowing sky.

"Hey, Babe." George looked up but couldn't make out the face of the man blocking the sun. "Remember me?" George tilted his head and held up a hand to shield the sunlight. A black man that looked to be in his midtwenties was gazing down at him. The man had his hands in his pants pockets. He was handsomely dressed in an ivory suit. He was lean and donned a matching fedora that was creased down the center and angled slightly to the side.

"I meet a lot of people," George said.

"LeRoy. LeRoy Griffin. From Kansas City. I gave you a ride to your hotel in Omaha. You knocked up my sister."

George stood up fast.

"How you doin', LeRoy. You're a hell of a ballplayer. I remember that."

"I wished I could play in the big leagues, like you."

"Well, you're a colored kid," George said. "Ain't no coloreds in pro ball."

"What about you?"

"What about me?"

"We was layin' on the grass under a tree, and you told me you thought you might be colored."

"Oh, that," George said. "I was just wonderin' what it would be like to be like you, not getting to play professional ball and all. It's a damn sad state of affairs, isn't it?"

"Yessir, it is. Can I ask you a couple questions? I ain't mad at you, even though I should be, seein' as you knocked up my sister and ain't so much as sent her a card in over three years."

"That's a damn sad state of affairs too," George said. "I need to send her some money to help her out."

"That would be nice. More than that, she'd like to hear from you. You know women, all dreamy-eyed and hopin' maybe you might think of them time and again."

"I should send a letter. I don't even know if I got her address anymore. Maybe you can give it to me, boy."

"LeRoy."

"Yeah, right. LeRoy.

"Babe, I got a favor to ask."

"Go ahead," George said. "But first, let's go get some more soda. Do ya mind?"

"No sir." They walked together to a concession stand.

"Hey, honey, give me another Coca-Cola. You want somethin', LeRoy?"

"I'll take an Orange Crush." The woman behind the counter handed George two bottles of soda pop, and George handed the icy orange one to LeRoy. "Let's take a load off our feet." George motioned to a picnic table under a shady tree.

"I want to play pro ball," LeRoy said. "You know, in the big leagues."

"You're way too dark."

"You think it's ever gonna change so ballplayers my color can play?"

"Not while that damn Judge Landis is in charge. He's a racist."

"He lets you play," LeRoy said.

"He don't know for sure. Plus, I proved myself, and Jake Ruppert, the owner of the Yankees—he'd throw a conniption. And the other owners would too, because I bring lotsa paying fans into their ballparks."

"So they don't care."

"Not as much as Landis," George said. "Maybe when he dies off, another commissioner might let you boys play."

"You can make a difference, Babe. Maybe you can tell 'em youse colored so they'd have to let the rest of us play too."

"Hell no. Landis would just kick me out of the game and take all my records away. I got bills to pay too, just like everybody else."

"Maybe when you quit playing," LeRoy said.

"Maybe."

"How come you ain't barnstormin' no more?"

"I been havin' a hell of a winter, kid. Been too busy. Maybe next year."

"If you do, we'd like to play ya again," LeRoy said.

"I'd like that. The Monarchs, right?"

"You still want that address?"

———

He wore a long black cassock and folded his hands in prayer at his chest. Father William Hughes bowed to the crucifix. When he turned, George stood in front of him, several steps beneath the St. Gregory church altar.

"Sorry to bother, Father. My name is Babe Ruth."

The priest smiled. "I know who you are. What can I do for you?"

George wore a white shirt buttoned high on his neck. His hands were cupped and folded together.

"I need advice. I'm thinking about getting married. Remarried," George said, "but I don't know if I've waited long enough, and I was wondering what you think."

"I read about the tragedy in Boston—your wife."

"Yes, Father. I'm a lonely man and, well, I found a woman that loves me. But I'm afraid I'll lose her if I don't marry her soon."

The priest motioned. "Have a seat." They sat down and Father Hughes rested his arm on the back of the pew.

"My wife, the one that died in the fire, was living with another man."

"I'm sorry."

"She wanted to live in Boston and my job was here in New York. I was away a lot," George said, "and I guess she was lonely."

George bowed his head, then looked up with sad eyes. "Now I got a chance to be with someone that loves me, but it's only been a couple of months."

"I don't see anything wrong with getting married, under the circumstances."

"Will you marry us?"

"I'd be pleased to."

"Tomorrow morning? My business manager thinks I should tell the media I'm getting married so they don't make a big stink about it, but we figured nobody would come if we have the ceremony real early."

"I've got early mass at 6:30," Father Hughes said.

"How 'bout 5:30?"

CHAPTER FIFTY-NINE

The courtroom was silent. The prosecuting attorney paced in front of the jury. The judge rested his elbow on his desk and his chin in his hand. Cammie sat with Darwin in the audience.

"Two men died," the prosecuting attorney said. He was short, wore a navy suit, and held his hands in his pants pockets. "They were known criminals. You've heard testimony that there was a dispute between them. One shot the other. The remaining man waved a gun and threatened Miss Griffin. She shot him. The question remains: was it premeditated?" The prosecutor paced back and forth and rubbed his chin. "We know the gun was unregistered."

The prosecutor paused and walked back and forth in front of the grand jury. He raised his head and stared into the eyes of several of them.

"You've heard considerable testimony, but the fact that the defendant had an unregistered gun is overwhelming. Why else would anyone hide the fact that they were concealing a killing weapon? This wasn't a weapon she used for recreational hunting. This was a pistol she hid in her purse." He raised his hand to his chest and placed it over his heart. "You cannot overlook the fact that she made an effort to obtain a deadly weapon. She went down the street in her neighborhood and sought to buy the gun.

She concealed it. And she held her hand on it, ready to fire, waiting for the victim to turn before she murdered him. That, ladies and gentlemen, is premeditation, and that makes Ms. Griffin guilty of cold-blooded murder."

Erickson took his turn and presented his closing remarks. He stood and approached the jury, then turned and leaned back against the table that had served as his station during the trial. He folded his arms and raised one palm to the side of his face.

"If you indict Ms. Griffin, you will have to do so in the face of convincing testimony that she acted in fear and self-defense. She had just seen the man next to her murdered, shot in the head. The man that shot him was angry, threatening to shoot again, and waving a gun." Erickson started pacing and folded his hands as if in prayer, touching his fingertips to his lips. "Don't forget. Ms. Griffin had been kidnapped by these same men. Less than a month before, her house had been broken into and ransacked. She'd been threatened.

"You've heard testimony from Detectives Wilson and Gilmore that she'd been stalked. A man attempted to murder her backstage where she worked and performed for the Kansas City Ballet." Erickson leaned on a railing separating him from the jury. "Finally, you've heard Frank Quatrocelli, a felon and member of the party that kidnapped Ms. Griffin. He testified that he was frightened for his *own* life because of the rage of an evil, gunslinging killer nicknamed 'Crawdad.' Quatrocelli said Ms. Griffin was frightened, and was justified in her fear. Ladies and gentlemen, Ms. Griffin was a *victim* in this matter."

----•----

Cammie walked out of the courthouse with Erickson on one side and Darwin on the other. Behind her were Wilson and Gilmore. There were no reporters, no photographers. The grand jury proceeding had not been open to the public.

"When will we find out?" Cammie said.

"It might be a week, not any longer," Erickson said. "You'll be all right. Everything went our way. About the most they could do is charge you for carrying an unregistered handgun."

"Any chance they'll indict her?" Darwin asked.

"It would be a total shock. Most likely, Cammie will have this matter behind her." He placed his hand gently on her shoulder. "You don't have to hide out anymore, honey."

"Maybe not for shooting Crawdad, but I'm not sure others won't be trying to shut me up."

"Can I take her with me?" Darwin asked.

"There's no need for her to ride back with me," said Erickson.

"I'll follow you out of the parking lot," Wilson said. "Just to be safe."

———

Cammie stood by the side of his bed and packed her clothes in her pink suitcase. Her head was down.

"You don't have to go back," Darwin said.

"It's best this way." She zipped the side of the bag. "When do we have to be at your parents'?"

"Whenever you're ready," he said.

They drove to his parents' home. His mother had a Sunday afternoon meal waiting. It was just the four of them in the dining room, Cammie, Darwin, and Darwin's parents. The table was set over a white linen tablecloth. A roast sat in the center of the table with broccoli, mashed potatoes, gravy, homemade bread, and a bowl full of Romaine lettuce beside it.

Colleen Barney walked into the dining room with a pitcher of ice water and poured it into four clear glasses, then sat down and broke the silence.

"Darwin tells us you're a Broadway performer now."

"Just an extra," Cammie said.

"She's in *The Color Purple*," said Darwin.

"Wonderful," Mrs. Barney said. "You must be proud."

"I'd prefer to be a regular cast member. It gets boring when I'm not on stage."

"You still get paid, don't you?"

"Yes," Cammie said, "but it's not the same."

"When will you be coming back to KC?"

"I'm not sure I will."

"Then how are you going to marry our son?" Mr. Barney asked.

"Dad," Darwin interrupted.

"Darwin told us he proposed to you."

"Yes, sir. I was surprised," Cammie said.

"We would like you to be part of our family."

Cammie placed her fork on the table. "You would?"

"Obviously, you're intelligent," Mr. Barney said, "and you're talented. Who wouldn't want you for a daughter-in-law?"

"But I'm a black woman."

Colleen Barney's eyes grew larger. She put her fork down too. Darwin's face became red. He glanced at his father, then at his mom. He wiped his chin with his napkin.

"And a damn beautiful one," Mr. Barney said.

"I have to admit, sir, I didn't think you would be too pleased about it," Cammie said.

"I was shocked at first. I admit it. But my son loves you. How could I not?"

Colleen Barney smiled. Darwin bit his lower lip.

"What if we had children? How would you feel about a couple of little black kids running around your house?"

"I'd be proud whatever color they were."

"With my luck, you'd probably get a granddaughter."

"Then I'll watch her dance."

"Cammie," Colleen Barney said, "we want you to know we'd be proud to have you as our daughter-in-law."

"Thank you. I have something for you, Mr. Barney." She lifted her purse from the floor and opened it. She pulled out an old envelope and handed it to him.

"What is it?"

"A letter from Babe Ruth to my great grandmother."

"Why are you giving it to me?"

"I was going to burn it. Then I thought about giving it to the Negro Leagues Baseball Museum, but I decided I want it to be confidential, at least for now. Just promise me you won't give it away."

"Are you sure you want me to have it?" Mr. Barney said.

"Hold onto it. Maybe you can put it in a safety deposit box. Maybe someday it will be worth something and not lead to danger. When times change a bit more."

"Your secret's safe with me, honey."

"Thank you, Mr. Barney."

"I'd rather you call me Dad."

Cammie paused, then a tear slipped down her cheek. Colleen Barney began to tear up too. Darwin placed his hand on Cammie's. She lowered her head and opened her purse again, this time pulling out the small ring box. She took off the lid and handed the ring to Darwin. She held her hand out to him, and he slipped it on her ring finger. They embraced, and Cammie cried some more. Colleen Barney walked around the table and joined the hug.

"Does this mean you're staying in KC?" Mr. Barney asked.

"I better go back long enough to pay my legal fees. That Erickson is expensive."

"No need to do that," Darwin said. "I've already reached a deal. Law firms exchange services. It reduces taxes. I'm defending Flynn in a conflict-of-interest case. We've arranged to swap services."

"What about your name?" Mr. Barney asked.

"I'd be glad to use Barney," Cammie said.

"Great, but that's not what I meant. Darwin told us you've been going by a different name back East."

"Millie Stinson," Cammie said. "I took Millie from Camille."

"I like it," Colleen Barney said. "A new name and a new home in a new state. Kansas rather than Missouri, just a few miles away, and you can both still drive to work. Nobody will ever know. It will be our little secret."

"I love you guys."

"Then there's no need to go to the airport," Mr. Barney said. She walked between Darwin and his mom. They placed their arms around her shoulders, and she put her arms around their waists. They moved toward the front door, and Darwin's dad followed. "What's the hurry then?" he said. "Why don't you stick around?"

"I want to go home," Millie said, "in Kansas."

CHAPTER SIXTY

1948

He spoke with a quiet, raspy voice. He'd lost forty pounds and walked with a cane. He came out of the hospital with his suit coat draped over his shoulders and his arms not through the sleeves, and he lowered himself into a taxi.

"Where to, Mack?" the driver asked.

"Yankee Stadium."

"Goin' to the game?"

George nodded.

The cabbie looked in his rearview mirror. "Are you who I think? Babe Ruth?"

George nodded again.

"I didn't recognize you. You lost a bunch of weight or somethin'."

George coughed a couple times and said simply, "Yeah."

He'd been in for his daily shot of Teropterin, a synthetic version of folic acid. The radiation had worked. He could speak now, but he still had a difficult time swallowing.

Claire waited on the sidewalk in front of Yankee Stadium. The taxi pulled up, and she opened George's door for him. He handed the driver a ten, and Claire reached down and helped him out and up.

"I don't know why you didn't let me go with you," she said. George ignored her. She hung onto his arm, and they moved toward the clubhouse entrance. "I wish you wouldn't let them experiment with you like you're some kind of laboratory rat. Chemical therapy: I never heard of it."

"Chemotherapy," he whispered. "It's new." He wore a somber expression and struggled with each step when a man walked up to him.

"Let me take him from here, ma'am." It was Waite Hoyt. He wore a suit and took George by the arm. Claire stepped back.

"Okay, then," she said. "I'll see you after the game. Bye, George." She stood and watched Waite escort him inside the clubhouse.

"Thank God," George said.

"It's great to see you, Babe. I hear things have been kinda rough lately."

"I feel like hell, kid."

Waite's voice was loud, as if he didn't think George could hear him. "Hang in there, Babe. You've always been my hero. Don't let me down now." Waite took a firmer grip on George's arm as they walked down stairs into the lower level. "I understand they're making a movie about you."

"They don't know nothin' 'bout baseball."

"William Bendix is going to play you. He's a star."

"I could outhit him today." George tried to clear his throat. "He's not an athlete." George pulled up and took a deep breath. "Hey, Waite. Just because I can't talk doesn't mean I can't hear."

George took a good twenty minutes to get his old uniform on. He had to stop several times for breathers. He bent over with his elbows on his knees.

Waite sat across from him on a short stool and pounded his fist into a mitt he'd found on the locker-room bench.

"Feels just like old times, Babe. Those were some great times. How does it feel to have your number retired?"

George lifted his head and had tears in his eyes.

"I miss the old guys: Huggins, Lazzeri, Herb, even Gehrig."

The early June day was rainy and chilly. George waited in the runway beneath the grandstand. He wore his camel-hair coat over his Yankee pinstripes. He had put on his entire uniform: navy liner, number 3 jersey, pants, long stockings, and hat. Announcer Mel Allen's voice echoed through the air as George stood in the shadows. He stepped out from under his overcoat and handed it to Waite and made his way slowly up the dugout steps and onto the field. The crowd roared, and he doffed his cap and waved to them as he hunched over, using a bat for a cane. He made his way to a microphone standing on home plate.

"Ladies and gentlemen," he said, struggling in that croaky, sandpaper voice. "I am proud I hit the first home run here in 1923. I'm proud and happy to be here today, twenty-five years later."

In the locker room, old teammates congratulated him and wished him good luck. A man in a tailored double-breasted suit approached George, put his hand on his shoulder, and shook his hand.

"We've never formally met. I'm Hap Chandler, Commissioner of Baseball."

George's eyes lit up, and for a moment his voice cleared. Chandler had been voted by the owners to replace Kenesaw Mountain Landis after Landis died. The smooth-talking Chandler had grown up in the South and was a former governor and U.S. Senator from Kentucky.

"Thank God," George said. "There's one man I don't miss: Judge Landis."

"I've heard tales about you two."

"Whatever you heard, it was worse."

"Let me know if there's anything I can ever do for you, Babe," Chandler said.

"You already have. You let Jackie Robinson play."

"He won't be the last."

"I got news for you," George said. "He wasn't the first."

"Did you really write that letter? The one LeRoy Griffin showed me?"

George lifted his hand to his throat, coughed, then winked.

———

Boxes of mail filled the room on the eighth floor of Memorial Hospital. Several envelopes were torn open, and handwritten letters were scattered on George's bed and nightstand.

People had visited for days, but now Dorothy had taken charge, even over Claire, and limited the guests to several in the morning and several in the afternoon. She was in her midtwenties with dark hair and dark eyes. She had to approve anyone seeing him.

"Absolutely not," she said when she heard a reporter from the *Times* wanted an interview. "No," she said when a fan sought an autograph on a baseball. "Over my dead body," she said when an ensemble from the St. Patrick's Cathedral Choir wanted to serenade him.

"I'm Loretta," a tall redhead said. She had a pencil-thin waist and padded shoulders. "I've been his girlfriend for most of the past ten years."

"I don't believe that," Dorothy said. "He's married."

"We've been boating, hunting, and fishing. I've even played golf with him. Do you know Claire?" Loretta said. "Well?"

"Wait here." Dorothy walked into George's room and came out thirty seconds later. "Go on inside. He can't wait to see you." Dorothy grinned. "Good for Dad."

A thin black man stood by a water cooler as Dorothy screened visitors. A nurse came by and motioned at the man. "What about him? He's been here all morning."

"No," Dorothy said. The nurse walked over to him and said something and he started away, carrying a small brown paper bag and using a baseball bat as a cane. "Just a minute, sir." She walked several steps after him. "Excuse me, sir."

The man turned, didn't say anything, but looked her squarely in the eyes.

"Where did you get that bat?"

"The Babe, he gave it to me—at Yankee Stadium after they retired his number."

"You were there?" Dorothy asked.

"Yes ma'am. I comed all the way from KC. Wouldn't have missed it for a thing."

"You don't look like you need a cane."

"It's a bat, ma'am," the man said. "I was hopin' the Babe would autograph it."

"Do you know Daddy?" Dorothy asked.

"Yes ma'am. You might say we're related. I played against him once in Omaha and gave him a ride in my car back to his hotel, and my sister Issie was with me, and she goed up to his room."

"That's enough," Dorothy said. "How long have you known him?"

"I met him firs' when I was jus' eight. I was shining shoes outside the old ballpark in Providence. The Babe, he comes down from the Sox to help the Clamdiggers for the las' two weeks of the season. He gave me a quarter when everybody else gave me a dime. The Babe had a heart big as the sky."

"What's in the paper bag?"

"A statue of the Negro saint, Blessed Martin D'Porres. Maybe he can put it by his bedside."

"Why would my daddy want a statue of the Negro saint in his room?"

"Well ma'am, played against him one time in Omaha. We gets to yappin' after the game, and the Babe says he might be part darky like me. I laughed, but the Babe, he wasn't laughin'."

Dorothy raised her hand. "Never mind. Go on in. I'm sure he'll be glad to see you." As the elderly man passed her, she asked, "What's your name?"

"LeRoy Griffin, ma'am, but you can call me 'Choo-choo.' That's what they called me in the Negro Leagues."